OBJECT OF MY ADDICTION

ANDREA SIMONNE

Liebe Publishing

Object of My Addiction

By Andrea Simonne

Copyright © 2019 Andrea Simonne

All rights reserved. Published by Liebe Publishing

First Print Edition, July 2019

ISBN-13: 978-1-945968-02-0

Edited by Hot Tree Editing

www.hotreeediting.com

Cover Design by LBC Graphics

No part of this book may be reproduced in any form or by any means, electronic or mechanical, including photocopying, recording, or by any information storage and retrieval system, without the express written permission of the author.

Publisher's Note: This is a work of fiction. Names, characters, places, and incidents either are the product of the author's imagination or are used fictitiously. Any resemblance to actual persons, living or dead, business establishments, events, or locales is entirely coincidental.

CHAPTER ONE

"MISS FANCY PANTS IS HERE, and, girl, her daddy is *so* hot."

Tori looks up from the computer. "Her daddy?"

"Yes, that little dog's human daddy." To emphasize her point, Peyton picks up a patient folder and fans herself. "I just checked him in at the front desk, and that man is six feet of heaven."

"I've never seen him here before." Miss Fancy Pants, a little white shih tzu who comes in to the animal hospital regularly for checkups and teeth cleaning appointments, is an office favorite. However, she's usually accompanied by her owner, Rachel.

"He's as handsome as Dr. Adrian."

"Really? I find that hard to believe."

"Oh, trust me. He is."

Tori doubts that's true. Dr. Adrian, the new vet who started at the animal hospital two months ago, was exceptionally handsome. Most of the female staff was in love with him. Tall, blond, and with striking blue eyes. Even Tori, who usually goes for guys with dark hair and eyes, thinks he's appealing.

Dr. Adrian Grant is the perfect man.

Tori happens to know he's interested in her too. Right after they met, he gave her a dazzling smile, but then his eyes dropped briefly to her chest. It happened in a flash.

But she knew what it was—a *look*. He was checking her out.

That's when Tori began paying attention to him, and she couldn't help but notice how Dr. Adrian is a great guy. The way he always puts everyone at ease. And with his shiny blond hair and square jaw, he looks just like Prince Charming from a fairy tale.

Then last month something else happened. A patient's owner sent Dr. Adrian flowers as gratitude for a surgery he performed on her dog. Tori was standing by the back door, and just as he was leaving, he stopped in front of her.

"For you," he said with a smile, pulling out a flower from the bouquet.

It was a pink daisy. She loved pink. And she loved daisies. How did he know?

"Thank you," she gushed.

Captured under the spell of his blue gaze, she decided it was time to try something new, something different, something called Dr. Adrian.

So what if he isn't exactly her type? She's been dating her type for years, and where has it gotten her?

Still single at thirty-three.

She's been fantasizing about the happy life they're going to have ever since he gave her that flower. The long walks on the beach together. Picnic lunches in the park. The Christmas cards they'll send to family and friends of them wearing cozy sweaters alongside their dogs. She's always wanted to send out cards like that. She's already knitting dog sweaters, though it's only May.

"Speaking of Dr. Adrian, I heard he volunteers three hours a week at an animal shelter," Peyton says, leaning closer.

"He does? I didn't know that!"

"Don't you do the same thing?"

"I do."

Peyton grins. She's the only one at work who knows about Tori's crush. How Dr. Adrian gave her a *look* along with that flower. "Girl, you two are going to make the cutest couple."

Tori smiles. "I know. We're perfect for each other." She can't wait for those Christmas cards. "I hope we'll be as happy as you and Lamont."

Lamont is Peyton's husband. The two of them are one of those lucky couples who've been happily married for years.

"Oh, honey, you will be. I just know it."

As far as Tori can tell, there's only one thing standing in the way of her and Dr. Adrian's happiness. He's nursing a broken heart. Unfortunately, he doesn't seem interested in a new relationship.

Tori knows this because she overheard him talking to a woman named Renée on his phone one day. It happened in the parking lot outside the animal hospital where Dr. Adrian was sitting in his midnight blue Tesla with the window rolled down. He was obviously upset. She heard him pleading with Renée about their canceled engagement.

She told Peyton about it, and they agreed to keep it to themselves. They figured he wouldn't want his broken heart broadcast to the whole office.

Tori closes out the patient file on the computer and reaches around for her green smock. There's a patch in the left corner with her name embroidered on it.

When the phone rings, Peyton reaches for the receiver. "Oh, I almost forgot. Would you mind prepping room three? Dr. Adrian is squeezing Miss Fancy Pants in before closing tonight."

"Sure, no problem." Tori leaves to go wipe down and set up the room. When she's done, she heads out to the reception area.

Right away she sees who Peyton was talking about. There's a tall, broodingly handsome guy with dark hair and eyes standing next to Miss Fancy Pants's pink purse carrier. He's studying his phone.

She walks over and peeks inside. The little white dog, who's usually a bundle of energy, whines as she halfheartedly wags her tail.

"Hey, sweetie," Tori says softly. "What happened?"

"There appears to be something wrong with her left rear leg," the man standing beside her says in a clipped tone.

She nods. "Hi, I'm Tori. Why don't you come on back, and we'll have Dr. Adrian—I mean, Dr. Grant take a look."

Except the guy doesn't move. He's gone completely motionless and is staring at her for some reason.

"Is everything okay?" she asks. Oddly, he looks sort of familiar.

Finally, he blinks and clears his throat. "Yes, of course."

Reaching down, he picks up the pink carrier and follows her into the examination room. He places the carrier in the middle of the table. Tori unzips it to look inside.

Right away, it's obvious the shih tzu isn't her normal self. Besides being in pain, the dog's long coat, which is usually well-groomed and pulled into a ponytail, looks knotted and is falling in her face.

"I came home for lunch today, and she escaped out the front door chasing a squirrel," the guy tells her. "When I finally caught up, her left rear leg was injured, and she was limping."

"It sounds like it might be a sprain or even a torn ACL. Dr. Grant will diagnose it for sure." She glances at him and notices the way he's still staring at her.

Before she can say another word, the door to the exam room opens and in walks Dr. Adrian Grant.

Tori sighs to herself. He's wearing a blue shirt tucked into his khaki pants. The shirt is one of her favorites because it brings out the color of his eyes.

He introduces himself, then asks a few questions as he examines the little dog. His tone is soothing as he handles the shih tzu with quiet competence.

Tori's worked with a number of vets over the years, and Dr. Adrian is one of the best she's ever seen.

After some discussion, they agree to give Miss Fancy Pants a mild sedative and run some tests. The guy waits in the lobby, studying his phone again. After some X-rays and an anterior draw, they determine it's not a torn ACL.

"Good news," Dr. Adrian says once they're all back in the exam room. "It's only a sprain, which should heal on its own. Try to restrict her movement for the next week, and take her on shorter walks."

Tori gently pets the sleeping dog, who's back in her carrier. She tries to smooth out some of the tangles in her coat.

Dr. Adrian continues to explain how Miss Fancy Pants will need rest and can't be allowed to run or chase anything. "If it's still bothering her after a week, you might want to bring her in for physical therapy."

"Physical therapy?" The guy frowns, glancing down at the dog. "Is that necessary?"

Dr. Adrian describes the benefits and how it can increase mobility, though Tori notices the guy seems put off.

"The thing is, she's not exactly my dog." His voice is deep, and when he speaks, Tori notices his bottom lip is fuller than his top one. His mouth has a sensual look about it.

He glances her way, and their eyes meet. His are a rich dark brown. There's something about him tickling her memory. She figures maybe she's seen him around the animal hospital, but doesn't think that's it.

Dr. Adrian nods. "No problem. Just have Rachel call me if she has any questions." He turns to Tori. "Would you make sure he gets a copy of all the care information? I'll write up a prescription for painkillers."

"Of course." She smiles and watches him leave the room, nearly sighing out loud.

So brave. And always so professional too, though he's suffering from a broken heart. It breaks her own heart at how well he's hiding it. But if this Renée can't see what a wonderful man he is, then she's not good enough for him.

Tori senses the dark-haired guy still watching her and is getting annoyed.

"Are you Rachel's husband?" she asks. She's not usually nosy with their patients' owners but figures maybe this guy needs a reminder that he has a wife.

"No," he says, picking up the dog carrier. "I'm not married."

He follows her out to the reception area. Peyton is manning the front desk, and Tori's glad to see her. She eyes the time on the wall clock. It's already after six, and she's supposed to meet her brother, Road, and his wife, Blair, for dinner tonight. Apparently they have some news. Tori hopes it's that Blair's pregnant.

"Would you mind taking care of this?" she asks Peyton, motioning at the guy who's standing in front of the main desk. "He needs all the care information for a sprain printed up."

"No problem," Peyton says with a grin. "Go find out if you're going to be an auntie."

Tori heads into the back and takes her smock off, then remembers she forgot to mention the painkillers Dr. Adrian prescribed.

When she arrives back out at the desk, Peyton has printed up the information for the little dog. "Can I add your name for the contact information?" she asks him.

"Sure, it's Liam Castillo."

Tori stops in her tracks and stares over at the guy. The one who's noticed her hovering in the doorway.

Liam?

Their eyes meet again, and this time the truth hits her on the head like a cartoon anvil—an ironic image in this case. Her pulse shoots up. Even after all these years, she still remembers what he did to her.

That's why he looks so familiar. That's why she thought she knew him from somewhere. Because she does. He's changed and isn't the same teenager he was in high school. He's all grown up now.

I'll bet he's still the same asshole though.

CHAPTER TWO

TORI CHURCH.

He recognized her right away. It didn't matter that it's been over a decade. He spent half his junior year of high school sitting behind her in history class. She's as pretty now as she was then.

Judging by the look on her face, she finally recognizes him too.

And she still hates me.

It figures.

He had a terrible crush on her in those days. It started the moment they met. There was something about her that pushed all the right buttons for him.

They were friendly in class and occasionally outside of class, since their lockers were near each other. It took him weeks to work up the nerve to ask her to fall homecoming. And when he did, she turned him down.

That would have been the end of it, and they would have remained friendly too, if it wasn't for what happened at the dance.

The incident that changed everything.

"How have you been, Tori?" He keeps his expression neutral. He doesn't need his FBI training to see she's displeased by the sight of him. Any idiot could see that.

"I'm fine, thank you." Her voice has a frosty tone. She doesn't bother asking how he's been. It's clear her politeness doesn't run that far. "I forgot to tell you about the painkillers Dr. Grant prescribed for Miss Fancy Pants." She explains the dosage and how to best administer the pills.

Despite the frost, he still has trouble taking his eyes off her. She doesn't look that different. A little older. A few faint lines on her face. She's filled out and is a little curvier than those days, but that's it.

Except Tori Church is the last woman he wants to see right now.

After everything he's gone through with Rachel, he's had enough female drama to last him a lifetime.

He was surprised Tori didn't recognize him right away. It gave him the opportunity to study her in the exam room. No wedding ring. Still quick with a smile. Judging by how comfortable she seems in this environment, she's worked here a while.

"It's best if I speak to Rachel," she states. "I'm sure she'll be the one administering the painkillers. Can you have her call us?"

Liam glances down at the pink carrier. "Rachel is... unavailable."

"Oh?" Her voice lilts higher. "Is she okay?"

"She's fine." Liam tries not to scowl.

He watches her debate with herself over whether she should ask him nosy questions about his ex-girlfriend.

She purses her lips and apparently decides against it. "Well, if you're unclear about anything, be sure and contact Dr. Grant. We wouldn't want Miss Fancy Pants to be uncomfortable."

She turns and walks off. No goodbye or "nice to see you" after all these years.

Not that he expected it.

He pays the vet bill with a credit card, wondering how he's going to deal with this dog. He doesn't know anything about dogs, especially not one this high maintenance. Miss Fancy Pants belonged to Rachel, and she fussed over the thing incessantly, but now she's his problem.

Along with everything else Rachel left behind.

He gathers the paperwork and medication and heads toward the glass doors in front. Behind him, his radar for trouble goes off when he hears Tori running back to the reception area in distress.

"Oh my God, Peyton. Mable is gone!"

The woman behind the counter turns toward her. "What do you mean, gone?"

"There's no sign of her anywhere!"

Liam's hand pauses on the door. Instead of leaving, he turns and strides back over to where Tori and Peyton are both speaking excitedly.

"What's happened?" he asks on alert.

Tori turns to him, frantic. "Mable is missing! She's been taken."

His brows slam together. "Taken? Someone's missing?"

"Yes! I left her right there in back!"

"How old is she?"

"Twelve."

He sets the dog carrier down and pulls his phone out to contact Lewis, the special agent in charge of his squad. They worked White-Collar Crime, but Lewis can get the wheels in motion to Violent Crime quickly. "Call 911 right now," he tells the seated woman. "Does she have a cell phone? Have you tried calling her?" he asks Tori as he puts the phone to his ear. "When did you last see her?"

"A few hours ago. No, she doesn't have any kind of Bluetooth or GPS, though I've thought about installing it."

He stares at her. "Wait a minute. *Who* is Mable?"

"My minivan."

Lewis answers on the second ring, but Liam tells him to forget it, that he'll explain later. He flashes his gaze over to Tori as he ends the call. "Your minivan?"

"I can't believe this is happening." She chews her bottom lip. "What should I do?"

"Your minivan is named Mable?"

She nods. "I parked her right out back, but now she's gone. Someone stole her."

"Are you sure you didn't park her—" He shakes his head. "—*it* somewhere else?"

"Of course I'm sure!"

Peyton says she has the authorities on the line, and he reaches for the phone. He speaks to the 911 operator, explaining the situation. They ask a few questions, and he gets the answers from Tori.

"The police will be here shortly," he tells them, handing the receiver back. He turns to Tori. "For future reference, you should make it clear you're speaking about a vehicle and not a person."

She looks at him like he's nuts. "Why would you think Mable was a person?"

"Because you told me it was."

"No, I didn't."

"Yes, you did."

"All right, *fine*." She seems embarrassed and shifts the purse on her shoulder. "I guess I could see why you might have thought that."

He's ready to say more, but decides not to embarrass her further. "Does anyone else have the keys to your van?"

"My brother, Road, has a spare key. I've lost mine a couple times, so I gave him my extra."

Unfortunately, he remembers her brother all too well. Road was a senior back then. Right after the incident, her brother threatened to beat the shit out of him. "Maybe Road borrowed your van and forgot to tell you."

Tori rolls her eyes. "That's crazy. Road did *not* borrow Mable."

"It's a possibility. The police will want to check it out."

"They will?" Tori goes quiet. She glances at Peyton, who's watching their exchange with concern. He can tell by Tori's expression the reality of the situation has sunk in. He remembers her family was a rough crowd and inclined to avoid the authorities.

"Do you have the van's license and VIN number?" he asks. "They'll need those too."

"Maybe at home, or my cousin Brody might have it. He's the mechanic who works on her."

He nods. "Your insurance company will also have that information. You should call them."

Tori starts digging through the large tan purse at her side, apparently searching for her phone. He watches as she pulls out various items—a pack of tissues, a bag of dog treats, and two leashes. She places them all on the counter in front of her. She digs around some more and pulls out a hairbrush, a small doggie raincoat, a large planner, and an iPad.

Liam fights back a smile at the amount of stuff piling up in front of her. Tori was always eccentric. He remembers how she used to put streaks of pink and purple in her hair. He liked it though. Always liked how she was different and marched to her own beat.

"Gosh, where's my phone?" she mutters, still rummaging.

When she pulls out a can of tennis balls, he can't help his grin. "Is that like a bottomless Mary Poppins bag?"

She glances up at him, except their eyes catch hold, and there's something about her expression that transports him back in time. Back to the sixteen-year-old kid who thought Tori Church was the prettiest girl he'd ever seen.

A peculiar ache tugs at his chest, and he recognizes it.

She frowns. "Why are you even here?" She goes back to

rummaging through her purse. "This is none of your business. You should just *go*."

He licks his lips, still reeling from the trip back in time, from the longing he used to feel for her.

But then he remembers how she treated him after the incident. She wouldn't accept his apologies, wouldn't talk to him. Instead, she believed all the rumors. Not to mention the threats he had to deal with from her pissed-off older brother.

He knows whatever feelings he might have once had for Tori are best left buried.

"I'm a federal agent," he says. "That's why I'm still here."

This gets her attention, and she tilts her head. Tori's nature was a kind and forgiving one, and he can tell that hasn't changed. It's one of the things he found so appealing about her.

The problem is she was kind and forgiving to everyone except him.

"I think the police have arrived," Peyton says, standing up from behind the desk and motioning outside. "Should I come too?"

Liam turns toward the glass doors and sees a dark blue SUV with Seattle Police on the side pull into the parking lot. Despite Tori telling him to leave, he stays, figuring maybe he can offer some kind of help. "Yes," he says. "They'll want to know if you've seen anything."

He picks up the dog carrier and heads outside with the two women.

The three of them stand in front of the animal hospital and speak with the officers. He flashes his FBI badge, introducing himself. They're confused at why he's here, but he explains how it's just a coincidence, and he was only bringing his dog to the vet.

Both officers take this in, glancing down at the girly pink dog carrier.

He stays by Tori's side as they question her and Peyton. Neither of the women noticed any suspicious activity in the parking lot. Tori calls her insurance company to get the VIN number and report her van stolen. While she does that, Liam asks about other car thefts in the area. Eventually, after getting all the information, the officers tell her they'll put a broadcast out with the plate number and description of the minivan. One of them hands Tori his card and says they'll be in touch.

"Poor Mable," Tori laments after the police leave. "I hope she's okay and they find her soon."

"Me too." Peyton gives her a hug. "I'd better go back inside. I'm closing tonight and still have to clean up."

"Thanks for coming out here with me."

When he and Tori are alone, she turns to him. "Do you think there's any chance they'll find Mable?"

Liam studies her. Strands of silky hair have slipped from her ponytail, and most of her makeup's faded. A pretty flower wilting after a long day. She's obviously dispirited. He sees no reason to make her feel worse.

"Actually, there is a good chance."

"Really?" Her face sparks with hope. "But how? Isn't it like finding a needle in a haystack?"

"Not necessarily. They have automated license plate readers, or ALPRs, and they're all over the place—including police cars. So if whoever stole Mable drives near one, it'll trigger an alarm."

"I didn't know that."

"They scan thousands of license plates every day."

There's some barking and movement from inside the carrier at his side. He'd almost forgotten about the dog.

Tori bends over to peek at Miss Fancy Pants. "Looks like someone's awake," she coos in a soft voice. "I'll bet you're groggy though."

"Would you like me to give you a ride home?" he asks, figuring it's the reasonable and polite thing to do since her car's been stolen.

Apparently, it isn't.

Tori straightens and seems to remember who he is. She turns and glances toward the parking lot. "No, thanks. I'll call Blair to come pick me up."

"Blair Thomas?"

"She's my sister-in-law."

"Really?" Liam's eyes widen. Except for a few of his baseball teammates, he's never really kept in touch with anyone from those days. "Blair is married to your brother?"

"Yes, she is." Tori eyes him. "Why is that so surprising?"

Blair and Tori were best friends in high school, but as he recalls, Blair—a classy redhead—didn't seem the type to be involved with Road. "No reason."

She scowls at him again, and it's obvious the cold shoulder has returned. "You still think you're better than everybody, don't you?"

Liam is taken aback. "No, I don't think that. I've never thought that." Maybe after all these years, they can finally clear things up between them. "Look, I know you hate me, but what happened that night was an accident."

She scoffs. "Yeah, right."

"It was," he insists. "I would have never done that to you on purpose."

Tori's eyes flash with anger. "Look, I heard you laughing, okay? Everybody saw you do it. After all these years, why don't you just tell the truth?"

His muscles tighten with a familiar frustration from long ago. Nothing's changed. She still doesn't believe him. Hell, nobody believed him. "I *am* telling you the truth."

"Whatever." She holds her hand up. "I don't need this, especially not today. I've got enough with Mable stolen." She shifts her purse on her shoulder. "Just leave me alone."

Liam watches her head back toward the entrance to the animal hospital.

He didn't need this today either.

Miss Fancy Pants barks from her carrier again, demanding to be let out. He glances down at the little dog, barking and scratching at the zipper.

It figures. One more female determined to give him a hard time.

CHAPTER THREE

"YOU REALLY SAW Liam from high school today?" Blair's hazel eyes widen with amazement. "After all these years?"

"He stayed the whole time the police were there," Tori says. "I don't know why he bothered. Just butting in where he wasn't wanted." Though if she's honest, she was sort of glad he stayed. It was nerve-racking talking to those cops. At least he knew all the right questions to ask and things to say.

"Remind me. Who is Liam again?" Road pops a tortilla chip in his mouth.

They're eating dinner at a Mexican restaurant. She called Blair from work and explained the situation, and they immediately came and picked her up.

Blair turns to him. "Don't you remember? He asked Tori if she'd go with him to homecoming. She said no, and then at the dance, he poured a milkshake over her head."

"*That* guy?" He nods, chewing slowly. "I do remember him."

Tori remembers him too—especially that night. It was her first high school dance, and she was so excited. She wore a gauzy rainbow-colored skirt and this silky pink blouse, with her hair all fluffy and pulled up in front with butterfly clips. She was only fifteen and wanted to have fun with her friends.

The dance had just started when Liam and his obnoxious jock buddies showed up. They came over to her, and out of the blue, she was covered in an icy liquid. She screamed. It was freezing cold, and at first, she had no idea what it was. As it melted, it was in her hair and on her clothes, ruining her blouse and skirt. She can still taste the chocolate running down her face.

People were laughing, especially the jocks Liam hung out with. She'll never forget how callous they were, cackling and pointing at her like it was the funniest thing in the world. Liam was standing right behind her, and there was no mistaking it.

She heard his laughter right along with the rest of them.

Blair was the one who helped her to the bathroom. Tears mingled with chocolate as they tried to clean up the sticky mess, but it was hopeless. She didn't understand how anyone could be so mean. Tori had to go home and miss the rest of the dance. It was awful.

The chaperones and teachers who were there reported it to the principal. By next week, the whole school was talking about how Liam had poured a milkshake over her head.

"He still claims he didn't do it. That it was an accident," Tori says, fiddling with her glass. "After all this time, he has the nerve to tell me he's innocent."

"Everyone *saw* him do it." Blair shakes her head in disgust. "Even I saw him standing right behind you with that cup. What an asshole."

"I know."

"And all because you didn't want to go to homecoming with him."

Tori picks up her iced water. To think she thought he was cute before that whole thing happened. Hard to believe. "We're both adults now. Why couldn't he tell the truth? Just admit he made a mistake and apologize?"

"It sounds like he hasn't changed at all." Blair takes a bite of her food. "Unbelievable."

"He told me he's a federal agent," Tori says. "Does that mean he's with the FBI?"

Her brother glances up from his plate. "Yeah, it does. His father was one too."

Blair looks at Road. "How do you know that?"

"Because I hassled him after what he did to Tori. Let's just say it came up in conversation."

Tori's eyes widen. "I never knew that. You didn't hurt him, did you?"

"No, though I wanted to. I made it clear he better stay away from you."

She wasn't happy hearing this. She didn't condone violence.

"That's when he told me his father was an FBI agent. I thought it was bullshit at first, but turned out to be true." Road shrugs and takes a swig from his beer.

"Well, hopefully I'll never see him again."

"Hopefully not," Blair agrees.

Their conversation goes back to the business of Mable being stolen, and Tori worries how she'll get around without a car. "What am I going to do? I can't exactly take the bus or an Uber with the animals I pet sit."

"Brody might have something you can borrow at the shop," Road tells her. "Give him a call tomorrow."

"In the meantime, you can borrow my Honda," Blair says. "In fact, you can pick it up tonight."

Road shakes his head. "Who the hell would steal that old Caravan? It makes no sense."

"She's not in bad shape," Tori says defensively. "Mable's got character."

"Yeah, lots of character." He chuckles. "Lots of dog hair too."

Tori sighs and reaches for a corn chip. She's not really hungry and has barely touched her food. She hopes they find her minivan soon, as she needs Mable for her Happy Pet Nanny business. "So what is it you guys wanted to tell me tonight?" She leans forward. "Will there be a new family member soon?"

Blair laughs. "No, it's not that. We're thinking about selling my condo."

Tori's disappointed. "You're moving? That's all? I thought you were going to tell me you're pregnant."

Blair glances at Road, and a look passes between the two of them. Her hopes shoot up. "I saw that. *Are* you guys pregnant?"

"No." Blair grins. "But we've decided to let nature take its course."

"Really?" She rubs her hands together with glee. "That's great. I can't wait to be an auntie."

Blair and her brother are still smiling at each other when Road leans over and kisses his wife on the lips. "Babe," he whispers, then kisses her again.

Tori rolls her eyes. "Geez, get a room already." She reaches for another chip and dips it in salsa. "In fact, get a room and get busy, because I want a little niece or nephew."

Blair smiles at her from across the table, the happiness there clear and bright. They've known each other for a long time and were like sisters even before she married Road.

"So is that why you've decided to move?" Tori asks. "In case nature takes its course?"

"We need a place that's both of ours." Road leans back in his seat.

"Plus, it's too small," Blair adds.

They talk about the kind of house they're looking for and which areas in Seattle they plan to check out.

As Tori watches them discuss the merits of different neighborhoods, her thoughts drift back to earlier, back to seeing Liam after all this time. She pictures Rachel, Miss Fancy Pants's owner. A long haired brunette with big brown eyes.

Little did she know Rachel was in a relationship with Liam of all people. Were they dating? Did they live together? She wonders what happened to her and why she's not in the picture anymore, though it's not that hard to figure out.

She probably dumped him because he's an awful person.

IT'S SATURDAY AFTERNOON. Liam's sitting on the couch in his house going over one of his active cases, a guy named Walter Yates who's running a Ponzi scheme while claiming to manage a hedge fund.

From what Liam can tell, Walter pays high dividends, but nothing so impressive as to draw attention. The investors are told up front that they're only allowed to withdraw a small percentage of their money or they'll be charged a hefty administrative fee, which discourages redemptions.

Smart. The whole setup is smart. And from what he can tell, Walter's been running it for at least five years.

In fact, if he hadn't gotten greedy and tried to bring in a wealthy Bolivian investor, the FBI might have never been tipped off. Unfortunately for Walter, the Bolivian got suspicious when it took two months to pull his money out. That's when he contacted the feds.

Liam is running point on this one, and so far things are on track. He contacted Walter recently, claiming to be a relative of one of his current investors. They set up a meeting for next week.

"Knock, knock," his older sister, Elena, calls out as she opens the door in front. "Can we come in?"

"Sure." He closes his laptop and puts it on the coffee table. Good thing too, because a moment later his two nephews—seven-year-old Marcus and five-year-old Sam—run inside and pile on top of him.

"Can we play baseball in the backyard like last time, Uncle Liam?"

"Do you have any pop?"

"I want ice cream for dinner! No, wait, McDonald's!"

Liam laughs, pretending to fight them off. "You two monkeys have overpowered me. If you want ice cream, go get it from the freezer."

"Boys, get off your uncle. And you don't get ice cream until after dinner." His sister's tone leaves no room for argument. "If you're hungry, I'll make you a sandwich."

"A sandwich?" Sam laments. "But Uncle Liam lets us have dessert *first*."

"You weren't supposed to tell her that!" Marcus turns to his brother in exasperation.

Elena gives Liam a look. "Do you really let them eat dessert first?"

"Of course not," he says, using his best poker face. He glances at his nephews, who are giggling like a couple of imps.

She rolls her eyes. "It's probably best if I don't know the truth."

"Probably. Hey, I bought some new water blasters recently," he tells them. "Why don't you guys go in the backyard and check them out."

"Cool!"

Both boys dash over to the sliding glass door and run outside.

Elena plops herself on the couch. "Those two have more energy than the sun."

He chuckles. "You're right about that." He looks over at his sister. She was widowed three years ago, and he knows it's been tough on her. He tries to help with his nephews as often as he can.

"You're so good with them. Amazing, really."

He shrugs. "They're great kids."

She goes quiet, considering him.

"Do you want anything to drink?" He gathers the paperwork on his coffee table together. He's been working a lot of extra hours lately and is glad Elena stopped by with his nephews. He could use a break. "I made a fresh pitcher of iced tea this morning."

"You know, I blame myself for Rachel leaving you."

He stops and glances over at her. "She ran off to Argentina with her podiatrist. How are you to blame?"

"Because I'm the one who introduced them in the first place. I never should have recommended him. He has too much sex appeal."

"Forget it." He snorts and goes back to what he was doing. "Rachel was always impulsive. If it wasn't him, it would have been someone else."

"No, you're not a woman. Dr. Schoen is like a Nordic god. Tall and blond, and you should have seen his ass." She shakes her head. "It's like it was carved from marble."

"Do I really need to hear this?"

"I'm just giving you the facts."

"I don't want the facts," he mutters. "Besides, I met the marble-assed god and wasn't impressed." He tucks his laptop and papers back into his computer case.

"You did?" Her eyes widen. "When did you meet him?"

"I took Rachel in for an appointment when her Jetta was in the shop." He remembers how the doctor's waiting room was covered with pictures of him skydiving, zip-lining, and driving race cars. Obviously an adrenaline junkie. Probably a narcissist too.

Rachel used to tell Liam he was boring, but she loved him anyway. She always said it like a joke, but he could tell part of her meant it. "It's lucky you're so handsome," she used to say, teasing him. "At least *that* will never bore me."

It turns out it did.

"I want more," she told him the day she left. "I'm sorry, Liam, but this isn't enough for me, and it never will be."

All that skydiving and race car driving is what must have made Dr. Adrenaline Junkie so appealing. Apparently living with an FBI agent wasn't as exciting as Rachel imagined it would be.

As he's thinking about all this, Miss Fancy Pants comes limping into the living room, headed straight for his sister. The dog only gives him a dismissive glance.

"What happened to her?" Elena asks with concern. "Why is she limping?"

He tells her about the sprained leg. "I'm not really equipped to deal with this. I mean, what do I know about dogs?"

The furball manages to jump onto the couch, sitting next to his sister. "I don't think she should be jumping like that. Not with an injured leg."

Liam shakes his head. "I don't know how to stop her. The damn thing is a daredevil."

"Poor little daredevil." Elena scratches Miss Fancy Pants behind the ears. "She probably misses Rachel. I can't believe the way she abandoned her."

The dog lets out a huff of pleasure as Liam's sister continues to scratch gently.

"She told me she plans to send for her once she's settled in Buenos Aires."

Elena rolls her eyes. "Give me a break. I mean, who drops everything and runs off to South America like that?"

It was hard to believe it, but when they first met, he thought Rachel's impulsiveness was a good thing. He knew he could be stodgy at times, too old-fashioned. He thought she might balance him out. The yin to his yang. Instead, they clashed constantly. If he was honest, he'd grown tired of her constant need for attention. Her impulsive ways seemed more like selfishness than anything else.

"Maybe I should take Miss Fancy Pants home with me," Elena says as the dog rubs her head against her leg. "At least until Rachel sends for her, if she ever does."

Liam's tempted by the offer. It would be a relief to get rid of this dog. But then his gaze goes to the backyard, to where the kids are running around yelling and squirting each other with blasters. Miss Fancy Pants avoided his rambunctious nephews whenever they stayed here, and he suspects it's because they made her nervous.

"Let me think about it," he says, not entirely willing to close that door.

"You need to get her groomed too. Her coat is getting really tangled." Elena picks through the mass of long hair. "Do you have a brush? I could try combing some of these knots out."

He gets up and goes into the laundry room where Rachel kept all the dog's supplies. There was a small changing table in the corner with grooming items on it. She used to brush the dog's long coat every night. He grabs a hairbrush.

Miss Fancy Pants had been one of Rachel's many impulses. He came home from work about six months ago, and there was this prissy dog sitting on the couch. No prior discussion about it. No asking if he even wanted a dog.

After handing his sister the hairbrush, he picks up his empty glass from the table. "You sure you don't want any iced tea?"

"Okay, I'll take a glass." Miss Fancy Pants lies on her side and seems content as Elena brushes through her coat.

He reflects back to the vet visit as he heads into the kitchen. He's been thinking about it a lot. "You'll never believe who I saw at the animal hospital."

"Someone we know?" Elena's head is bent down as she keeps brushing.

"Yeah, from high school. Tori Church."

"You're kidding?" His sister makes a face and glances over at him. "The one who accused you of dumping a milkshake on her?"

He adds some lemon to each glass of ice before pouring in the tea. "That's the one." His sister, who was a senior at the time, was one of the few people besides his parents who believed him when he said it was an accident. They knew him better than that. Even his friends seemed to think he did it on purpose. Everybody treated him like he was an asshole the rest of the school year. "She's still holding a grudge too."

Elena shakes her head. "It figures. That whole Church family was nothing but a bunch of hoodlums."

He brings both glasses of tea out to the living room, setting his sister's on the coffee table before wandering over to the back door to check on his nephews.

"I remember her brother was one of the star football players," Elena says, gently brushing around the dog's face. Miss Fancy Pants closes her eyes and seems content. "His whole family would be at the games drunk and loud. People could barely hear us doing our cheers over the racket they made."

He takes a sip from his iced tea, still watching the boys out back. "Her brother threatened to kick my ass."

His sister glances over to him. "He did? You never told me that. What happened?"

He shrugs. "Nothing much. He shoved me around. Made a lot of threats and told me to stay away from Tori."

"You should have reported him to the principal. It was bad enough you were in trouble for something you didn't do." Elena goes back to brushing the dog. "Should've gotten that jerk thrown out of school."

Reflecting back on it, it never occurred to him to report Road. Part of it was he felt bad about what happened with Tori, and the other part was he doubted it would make any difference.

He'd been intimidated by Road. Even though he'd played baseball, he was only a skinny kid back then. Road was bigger and more seasoned. Worried he'd get his ass kicked, Liam warned him who his father was. That made him back down, though he glared at Liam with menace the rest of the school year.

It had been a relief when Liam's family moved to Portland the following summer. The bureau promoted his father to ASAC—Assistant Special Agent in Charge of the Portland office. It turned out, Liam's new high school had a great baseball team that needed a catcher.

He tried to forget about the whole incident.

Liam watches his nephews go over to refill their blasters at the faucet outside. Both boys are soaking wet. He has a flash of how

Tori looked when that milkshake flew out of his hand and drenched her.

After moving to Portland, he tried to forget all about what happened.

He tried to forget all about her too.

But he never did.

CHAPTER FOUR

LIAM'S WORK hours get even crazier, so he's leaving early every morning and coming home after dark. He picks up extra cases, volunteering for things he normally wouldn't.

He figures there isn't much reason to go home.

When Rachel left, she only took a suitcase, but unfortunately half the furniture was hers. A week after she ran off to Buenos Aires, her two sisters came and packed up the rest of her things, including her clothes, the dining room table, bookcases, and all her other odds and ends.

Her sisters were apologetic and kept telling him they thought Rachel was making a huge mistake.

"It's a good thing you guys weren't married," they said. "At least you won't have to deal with lawyers."

A familiar refrain from everyone—as if that should ease the humiliation of being dumped.

He and Rachel used to talk about getting married someday, but it was only offhandedly. After two years of living together, it never occurred to him to propose.

"I think I always knew we'd break up," he says to Matt, a friend on his squad. They're having a beer at Jake's, a local sports bar they sometimes go to after work. "It never felt completely right with her, even before things went south."

Matt picks up his bottle of beer. "You have to follow your gut. When I met Amy, I knew on our first date she was the one I wanted to spend my life with."

Liam nods. Ironically, in his own life, he's surrounded by happy couples. Most of the guys on his squad are married. His parents have been together over four decades. His grandparents too.

He always thought he'd be the same. He's never been a player and didn't see the appeal of dating a lot of women when all he wanted was one good one.

Yet here he was in his mid-thirties and still single.

Some of the guys told him he was lucky, that he should have some fun and enjoy himself. Plenty of women thought the G-man thing was hot.

"Listen." Matt leans forward with an embarrassed smile. "Amy has a friend from work she wants you to meet."

Liam's brows shoot up. "You want to set me up with someone?"

"It's Amy's idea. Her friend Shelby is single. You might like her."

"What does she look like?"

"She's not bad."

"Not bad?"

"I mean, she's cute. Brunette with green eyes. A good body."

"What's she like otherwise?"

Matt thinks about it. "She's nice, actually. Divorced for a few years. Athletic. She runs marathons."

Liam takes a swig from his beer and considers this. He enjoys staying fit. It harkens back to his days playing ball. He runs every weekend, lifts weights when he comes home most nights. Rachel was never into it, not that he cared, but it might be nice to date someone athletic for a change. Maybe they'd have more in common. "That doesn't sound bad. I like to stay in shape."

"Should I have Amy set something up, then?"

He doesn't reply right away, only thumbs the neck of his beer bottle. He doesn't know why he's hesitating. For some reason, he's still thinking about Tori. He's even considered calling her since he knows where she works. It riles him how after all these years, she still hates his guts for something he didn't do.

He keeps wondering if they ever found her minivan, Mable.

Not that he should care.

Who treats their car like it's a person?

She must have known the way her brother came after him in high school.

He needs to forget he ever saw her again.

Liam frowns to himself. This is his problem in a nutshell. The reason why he's still single.

He's attracted to the crazy ones.

"Sure, tell her to set it up." He lets go of the beer bottle. "Shelby sounds great."

It's been a month since Rachel left, and it's time to stop licking his wounds every night. To take some kind of action and move on.

Though he wasn't exactly licking those wounds alone, since he still had her dog to contend with.

In fact, that furball was turning into a real problem.

Every night he came home from work to discover some new mess she created. It was like living with a tiny delinquent. She destroyed everything she got her paws on, shredding magazines, books, and toilet paper, knocking over the garbage can and tearing into the trash. For a dog with an injured leg, she managed quite a bit of destruction.

He figured she was bored being alone, so he went online and found a forum for dog owners. He leaves the radio on for her every morning. He bought a variety of dog toys for her to play with during the day. None of it seems to make any difference.

"Great," Matt says with a grin. "Amy will be thrilled that she gets to play matchmaker. And who knows? Maybe you and Shelby will hit it off."

By the time Liam gets home, it's dark outside. He left a couple lights on for the dog this morning. He wonders what kind of trouble she's gotten herself into today, hoping it's nothing too bad. When he walks in the door, the radio is still on.

Nothing prepares him for the sight of his house though.

For a surreal moment, he thinks it's covered in snow. There are piles of white fluff everywhere. Finally, he realizes it's the stuffing material from inside his couch which has been chewed straight through.

"Dammit, dog! Where are you?" He strides through the house, kicking stuffing material out of the way.

He finds her sitting in bed. On Rachel's side, naturally.

"What the hell are you doing?" he asks, furious. "You think I like coming home to find my furniture destroyed? Do you know how much a new couch will cost me?"

She glances up at him and gives a small grunt, as if to say *whatever*.

"At least have the decency to look guilty."

She doesn't though. Instead, she licks her mouth. And then, he can't believe it, the dog yawns. She actually yawns. Afterward, she gets up and goes over to the large basket at the end of the bed, steps gingerly onto it, and then hops gracefully to the floor.

She walks with a limp right past him.

A furball of destruction.

"Jesus." He snorts. "Tell me how you really feel."

Except he's had enough. That's it. This dog isn't running his life anymore. He digs into his pocket for his phone and calls his sister. She answers on the second ring. "Listen, is that offer to take Miss Fancy Pants still open?"

"Of course. Is everything okay?"

He shakes his head. "This dog hates me."

"I doubt that. Why would she hate you?"

"She blames me for Rachel leaving."

"That's not true. I'm sure she only misses her."

"Yeah," he mutters to himself. "That makes one of us."

THE NEXT NIGHT, Liam comes home to a dog-free house.

Peaceful and serene. No trash to clean off the kitchen floor. No shredded magazines or books to contend with. No destruction at all.

He dropped Miss Fancy Pants and all her paraphernalia off at Elena's this morning. The dog didn't look thrilled. In fact, she seemed surprised. But he knew she'd figure it out soon enough.

He felt a small twinge of guilt leaving her there, then dismissed it. She brought it on herself. There's no reason to feel guilty.

At least she won't be alone all day. Elena works from home as a technical writer, so there's usually someone around.

Liam pours himself a glass of iced tea and brings the Thai food he picked up on the way home into the living room. It's time to relax.

He sits on his lumpy couch. Last night he tried to shove the stuffing back into the cushions, but it was hopeless. Flipping channels, he brings up his favorite ESPN station. They're showing NCAA Division I highlights, and he watches them as he eats dinner. He's looking forward to the College World Series next month.

Eventually he lies back and puts his feet up. The lumps in the couch feel like he's lying on a sack of potatoes. "That damn dog," he mutters. "This is ridiculous."

Since Rachel left, he's been sleeping out here most nights. He should probably move back into the bedroom.

Despite the discomfort, he closes his eyes and drifts off.

Until his phone rings.

Startled, he grabs it from the coffee table, wondering if it's work. Even though his squad is White-Collar, problems can arise at any hour.

He sees his sister's name on the screen and notices the time. It's well after midnight. "Elena? Is everything okay?"

There's a high-pitched sound in the background and then his sister's voice. "Not exactly. We have a problem."

Liam sits up all the way now, more alert. "What is it? And what's that noise?"

"It's Miss Fancy Pants. She's okay, but she won't stop howling."

He can hear the dog. She almost sounds like a wolf. "Why is she doing that?"

"I don't think she wants to stay here. I'm sorry, but you're going to have to come get her."

Liam wipes a hand over his face. *Dammit.* He sighs. "Yeah, all right. Give me a minute, and I'll be there."

By the time he pulls up in the driveway to his sister's house, he's muttered every curse word under the sun.

As soon as he gets out of his truck, he hears the dog through the front door. Glancing around the nice suburban neighborhood, he's surprised no one's called the police.

Elena swings the door open before he can even knock. "Oh, thank God you're here! I've got all her stuff packed and ready to go."

When Miss Fancy Pants sees him, her howling abruptly stops, like hitting the mute button. She's silent, staring up at him. Her long white coat appears neatly combed and is pulled up with a hair band on each side of her face.

He unzips the pink carrier, but the dog won't budge. Elena watches as Liam tries to coax her inside.

"I don't think she wants to go in that thing," his sister says, stating the obvious.

"Come on, dog." Liam brings the case closer, getting annoyed. When he tries to pull her inside, she growls. "For the love of...."

"Maybe put her on a leash. She can still ride in the car like that."

"Fine. Give me the leash."

She hands it to him, and he clips it to the dog's collar.

"I'm sorry it didn't work out. I was really hoping she'd like it here."

Liam nods. "Me too. Thanks for trying."

He winds up helping Miss Fancy Pants into the passenger side of his truck. The dog sits on the seat demurely, though once they start moving, she shifts to her hind legs with her paws on the edge of the window.

He grips the steering wheel. "You've become a real pain in the ass, you know that?"

Her ears twitch toward him, but she seems more interested in the scenery outside.

"You couldn't handle it there for one day? Not even twenty-four hours? You might have liked it."

She pats the glass.

"You should have given it a chance," he mutters, then huffs in frustration. He runs a hand through his short hair. "Listen to me, talking to you like you understand what I'm saying."

The problem is he didn't grow up with a dog and knows nothing about them. He's never even considered getting one. If he had though, it wouldn't be a dog like this. No way. He'd get a big masculine dog. A black lab or a German shepherd.

Not this fussy little thing with pigtails.

Miss Fancy Pants continues to paw at the window. She yips softly a couple times.

"I should take you to animal control and be done with it," he tells her. "It's not like you're *my* dog."

He knows he could never do it though. It isn't in him to be unkind to an animal. For better or worse, he's stuck with this furball until Rachel sends for her.

If she ever sends for her.

Miss Fancy Pants barks once at the glass, then looks at him like he's an idiot.

"Fine." He sighs. "I get it." He hits the switch that lowers the passenger side window.

The dog immediately sticks her face out to catch the breeze. He watches for a second as her tongue lolls out and her eyes close. It's almost like she's smiling.

He didn't know dogs could smile.

"Well, how about that," he says. "At least one of us is happy."

"WHAT ABOUT A DOG SITTER?" his sister suggests on the phone the next day. "You could find someone to come by and walk Miss Fancy Pants while you're at work. Maybe she wouldn't be so destructive."

"Where am I going to find someone willing to do that?"

"There must be agencies that hire out or something."

Liam rolls his eyes. How had this gotten so complicated?

"I don't see how you have much choice. Even if you gave her to someone else, I think she'd start howling again."

He knew his sister was right.

"Plus, I feel sorry for her," Elena continues. "It must be hard being ditched like that."

Miss Fancy Pants isn't the only one Rachel ditched, but he doesn't say that aloud. "I'll call around and see what I can find."

They hang up as he pulls into the FBI's field office in North Seattle. He has a meeting with a few of his squad members to go over a couple of the cases they've been working on. Walter Yates has risen to the top of Liam's list, and he has an appointment to meet with the man downtown.

The squad meeting is over in less than an hour, and they decide Matt will come with him to Yates's, staying behind as backup. Neither of them expects any trouble, but they're still cautious. As far as Yates knows, Liam is a program manager at Microsoft whose uncle recommended the fund.

They park in a garage near Yates's Seattle office building. When Liam first joined the FBI years ago, he was placed with a Violent Crime unit in Virginia. Ironically, since transferring to Seattle and joining White-Collar Crime, he's done more undercover work than he ever did working VCMO—Violent Crime/Major Offenders.

Liam rides the elevator to the twelfth floor. The snug weight of his Glock rests in the hidden holster at his waist. He's wearing a loose shirt and a lightweight jacket to hide the slight bulge. Luckily, he doesn't anticipate having to use it.

When the doors open, he's let out into a spacious office with an attractive young woman at the reception desk. There are a couple guys there too, tall, fit, and dressed in black. Obviously security.

He has to wonder why a simple hedge fund would need this kind of muscle hanging around.

"Hello. You must be Mr. Sanchez," Yates says, coming out from his office. He smiles and puts his hand out.

Liam smiles in return, recognizing him from his photo. "You can call me Pete."

"And please call me Walter."

They shake hands, and Liam sizes the man up. He already knows Walter is fifty-five years old. He's a big guy, overweight with a head of thick gray hair. He comes across as easygoing and friendly, but from the evidence Liam's seen, Walter is, in fact, cold and calculating, robbing people of their life savings with a smile on his face.

Liam can't wait to take him down.

"How can I help you?" Yates continues in his congenial way. "I understand you're looking for a place to invest some money you inherited."

"That's right."

Liam follows Walter into a spacious and well-kept office. This was the primary address shown on the hedge fund's paperwork, though after a little digging, there were a couple of warehouses also listed.

In fact, the deeper Liam's been digging on this case, the more he's convinced there's more to Walter's operation than meets the eye. He suspects running a Ponzi scheme may only be the tip of the iceberg. However, Yates seems smart and careful.

"Nice office," Liam says. "Have you been here long?"

"About ten years."

Liam knows he's only been here three. "And this is your only office?"

The man's washed-out blue eyes study him. "Yes, it is. We like to keep the fund small and selective. More personal attention that way." He shifts back to his easygoing veneer. "Were you expecting something larger?"

"Not at all." Liam shrugs and acts casual. Working undercover is tricky. You want to push your subject, but not too hard. "I prefer parking my money with people I've met and feel I can trust."

The man smiles and motions for him to have a seat. "I feel the same way. We like to think of our clients as family."

There's a picture on his desk of a young woman. "Is that your daughter?"

"Yes, she's headed off to college soon. Plans to study finance just like her old man." He chuckles.

"Good for her."

Except Walter doesn't have a daughter. From the intel they've gathered, he has a wife and son. The son lives on the East Coast, and the two of them appear to be estranged. It's obviously a stock photo which means Yates guards his private life zealously, and lying is second nature to the man.

Of course, Liam's been trained to spot a liar.

It's what made all of Rachel's sneaking around on him so ridiculous. Did she really think she could fool him? That he wouldn't notice all of her clumsy attempts at deception?

The way she told him she was staying late at work when he could hear sounds of a restaurant behind her. The times she snuck out of bed to go in the backyard and talk on her phone. After living together so long, you think she'd have noticed he was a light sleeper. To make matters worse, he could hear her through the open window.

Then there was the way she tried to hide the texting she did at all hours. She didn't seem to realize he could see the light from her screen beneath the bathroom door at midnight. When he pointed it out once, she babbled on about how she couldn't sleep and was working.

Rachel was such a sloppy liar that he was embarrassed for her.

Embarrassed for himself too.

The dieting and new clothes. The constant subtle criticisms toward him. When he asked her why she joined a gym halfway across town, she claimed it was easier to drive there, though it obviously wasn't.

They'd stopped having sex months ago. He'd lost all desire for her.

As soon as the first lies started, when the first suspicions crept in. He traced it back to those appointments with the podiatrist, the adrenaline-fueled Dr. Schoen.

Liam's not sure why he didn't confront her. Hell, he could have gotten the truth out of her in a matter of minutes.

"And your cousin is Rick Sanchez?" Walter asks. His light gray shirt is too tight around his waist.

"No, I'm his nephew."

"Ah." He nods and reaches for some paperwork. "That's right. I understand Rick and his wife, Pam, are traveling to the Bahamas soon. It sounds like quite a trip."

"He hasn't mentioned anything to me. And my aunt's name is Gwen."

Walter appears momentarily confused, though Liam knows it's an act. "Yes, excuse me. I'm thinking of another client."

He already knows Walter called Rick to check out his story. It only confirms Yates is careful.

"The minimum deposit for any of the funds is one hundred thousand," Walter says in a fatherly tone. He rattles off some information about redemptions and the various fees involved.

Liam interrupts him. "I can have the money wired to you next week from California. It's from an inheritance. I'm just waiting for the funds to clear."

He goes still and appears concerned. "I thought you were giving me a check today, and that was the purpose of this meeting."

"I was planning to, but there's been a small snag." Liam plays it cool and relaxes in the chair, though he's anything but relaxed. "It's resolved now. I figured it would be good to meet in person anyway."

"Sure." He nods cautiously.

"In fact, I'm planning to invest a little more than I initially told you." Liam leans forward and pretends to act chagrined. "My uncle told me how well he's done with you, and I realize now I was being overly cautious."

Walter's brows rise with interest. "How much more?"

"A few hundred thousand."

Yates seems to consider this, and Liam sees that greed is winning out. It also means Walter isn't always careful. Greed is a powerful motivator for many people, and it makes them sloppy.

"All right, then," Walter says. "Let's get started opening an account for you, and you can send the money once you've got it." He appears to relax and goes into his sales pitch. "I'd hate for you to miss out. A couple of these funds are bringing in double-digit returns right now."

"Sounds great." Liam smiles to himself at the lie. He's already contacted the SEC and a prosecutor with the U.S. Attorney's Office. The wheels to take Walter Yates down have been fully set in motion.

CHAPTER FIVE

TORI'S new favorite coffee drink is a vanilla almond milk latte with cinnamon on top.

That's what Dr. Adrian likes.

"These are good," she says to Peyton, taking a sip. It's a warm day, and normally she'd have ordered something cold, but drinking the same thing as Dr. Adrian makes her feel close to him.

Peyton sucks on her Frappuccino's straw. They make coffee runs regularly for everyone at the animal hospital. In fact, today something thrilling happened. When Tori handed him his coffee cup, the tips of Dr. Adrian's fingers brushed against hers.

She's noticed he does that a lot. Lightly touching her shoulder or arm, or her fingers in this case.

"Thank you, Tori," he'd said with a smile in his blue eyes.

His eyelashes have a natural curl to them and are tipped blond at the ends.

She constantly notices things like that about him.

"I heard Dr. Adrian mention he might go to the Arts Festival at Seattle Center in a couple weeks," Tori tells Peyton in a low voice. They're both behind the counter at the front desk. It's lunch, so the office is closed. "Do you think I should ask him if he'd like to go with me? Is that being too forward?"

Peyton seems to consider this. "You could hint around and see what he says."

"I wish he wasn't still getting over Renée." Tori sighs. "Maybe I should give him more time."

She thinks back to how Dr. Adrian's fingers touched hers and figures he'll make his move eventually.

"Oh, I almost forgot," Peyton says, swishing her Frappuccino around to keep it from separating. "Someone called this morning looking for a dog sitter."

Tori perks up. "Really? That's great. Did you give them my number?"

"I did." She smiles. "And you'll never believe who it was. Remember that hot FBI guy who came in with Miss Fancy Pants last week?"

Tori's mouth opens with repulsion. "*Liam?*"

"I gave him your number and told him all about the Happy Pet Nanny."

She groans. "Are you kidding me?"

"He needs a dog sitter." She leans closer. "And guess what? I don't think he's with Rachel anymore either. I think they broke up."

"There's no way I'm working for him. Not in a million years."

"Why not? He seemed like a nice guy. Remember how he stayed and helped with the police?"

"That's because you don't know the whole story. We have history." Tori relays a brief version of what happened with the milkshake incident.

To her surprise, Peyton only shrugs. "Honey, that was high school. People change. You can't hold that against him all these years later."

Normally Tori would be the first to agree with that. She's always willing to give someone a second chance, or even a third one. But not Liam. Not after what he did to her. The way he ruined her first dance. The way he and his friends laughed and pointed at her. That humiliation is burned in her brain forever.

"Forget it." She snorts. "And he *better* not call me."

LIAM STARES AT THE NUMBER. The last one on his list. He's hired two dog sitters this week, except Miss Fancy Pants wanted nothing to do with either of them. She growled and barked at them both, refused to go for a walk, and even tried to bite the second one.

The poor woman ran out of here like there was a devil on her heels.

He's been forced to come home for lunch every day and take the damn dog out himself. If he doesn't do it, she pees all over the house. Her latest form of rebellion. He still hasn't replaced the couch she destroyed, figuring there's no point buying a new one since she'll only destroy that too.

It's like he's being held prisoner in his own home by a fluffy white demon.

There isn't any reason to believe things will be different with Tori, except Miss Fancy Pants knows her from the vet.

Though he doubts Tori will agree to it.

She hates me.

But then he remembers the piss puddle he stepped in last night.

There was another one in his shoes this morning. Perfectly good shoes he'll have to throw away now.

So what if she hates me?

I'm desperate.

He takes a seat on his torn and lumpy sofa and calls the number he got from the vet's office. It starts to ring, and his throat dries up. Talking to Tori makes him feel like a nervous teenager.

Except she doesn't answer. The line goes directly to voicemail, where she thanks him for calling Happy Pet Nanny. He listens as she tells him to leave his name and number and ends the message with "Have a purrrfect day!"

"Hi, Tori, this is Liam Castillo." His voice is scratchy. He swallows. "I'm, uh, looking for a dog sitter. I know we've had our differences in the past, but maybe we can put that behind us. Basically, I need someone to take Miss Fancy Pants for a walk every day. I'm willing to—"

Beeeeep.

The voicemail cuts him off. Dammit. He didn't even have a chance to leave his number.

"Hi, this is Liam again. I'm sure you're thrilled to hear my voice a second time. It's just that... this dog has been a real handful to deal with. She's destroying my house. She urinates everywhere. Though you probably think I deserve that after what—"

Beeeeep.

"Yes, I'm calling a third time. I know you hate my guts. It turns out I'm desperate, and I hope you'll take pity on me." Liam pauses. *Did I really just say that?* "Please call me back." He leaves his cell number and hangs up.

He puts the phone on the coffee table and stares at it. "I sounded like an idiot. A *pitiful* idiot."

He leans forward, scrubbing his face with frustration.

There's movement to his right. Miss Fancy Pants comes over and hops on the couch. He notices, despite her sprained leg, she seems to get around just fine.

She's been joining him out here the past few evenings, sitting on the opposite end of the sofa, watching ESPN with him until they both fall asleep.

He sighs and looks over at her. "You've got to stop pissing everywhere. I can't take it anymore."

The dog's dark eyes gaze at him. For the first time, he realizes Elena is right. She seems sad. He puts his hand out, and to his surprise Miss Fancy Pants moves closer.

Her fur is soft as he pets her, more like hair. "Rachel left because of me, not you. I hope you understand that. Though in the end, she left us both, didn't she?"

Miss Fancy Pants seems to take in his words. He wonders if she senses what he's saying. It occurs to him this dog really misses Rachel, misses her more than he does.

He pets her a little longer, then finally gets up to make dinner. After heating up a piece of salmon along with a side of mixed vegetables, he pours Miss Fancy Pants some dry dog food in her bowl, which she ignores.

Once he's seated on his lumpy sofa again, he puts his feet up on the coffee table and flips through channels. He keeps glancing over at the dog, wondering why she's not eating her food.

He stares at his plate of salmon. Finally he figures what the heck. He cuts off a chunk for her and places it on the couch between them. Dogs are related to bears, right? Salmon should be okay.

Miss Fancy Pants gets up and sniffs at the fish. Liam watches as she gently picks it up with her teeth and brings it over to her corner of the sofa. She settles back down with the salmon between her paws, licking and taking delicate bites.

Satisfied, he leans back and grabs his fork again. The two of them eat their salmon as they watch a game replay from the NCAA Division I with a couple of his favorite teams.

He's so tired that he falls asleep halfway through the third inning. He jumps, startled, when his phone buzzes on the coffee table. The plate on his lap clatters to the floor.

"Shit." Liam grabs the buzzing phone. The number is a local one from Seattle, but he doesn't recognize it. "Castillo."

There's silence on the other end of the line. But then he detects music in the background.

"I can*not* believe I'm calling you back," a feminine voice says.

"Who is this?"

"Three messages in one day. That's practically stalking. You know that, don't you?" The voice has a familiar lilt to it.

He blinks. "Tori?"

"Yes." She sighs. "I'm only calling you because I'm worried about Miss Fancy Pants. That's it."

Liam glances over at the dog, who's also awake now.

"Thank you," he says. "I appreciate it."

"You don't deserve my help, but *she* does. So tell me, what exactly is going on with her?"

He licks his lips and explains all of Miss Fancy Pants's recent behavioral issues. The destruction and how she's been urinating all over the house, including inside his shoes.

"She peed in your shoes? That's a lot of anger. She's really upset."

"Tell me about it. I put them on without even noticing they were full of piss."

"Yuck." He can hear her laughing.

"You don't have to sound so gleeful about it."

She laughs some more. "Sorry."

She doesn't sound sorry.

"Has something happened recently? Where's Rachel in all this?"

Liam rubs his jaw. Tori Church is the last person on Earth he wants to tell the sad story of his love life to, but it appears he has no choice. "She left me."

"Left you?"

"That's right. She ran off to Buenos Aires with her foot doctor."

"Brazil?"

"Argentina."

"I see. So she was your girlfriend?"

"Yes, we lived together for two years."

"Wow." Tori sounds angry. "I had no idea Rachel was such a *monster*."

Liam is surprised by the venom in her tone. He figured she'd be happy to hear about his recent misery. He reaches down to pick up the plate and fork from the floor. "To be honest, I saw it coming."

"That she would do something so horrible?"

"It wasn't pleasant," he admits. "Things were over between us for a while though."

"Running off and abandoning her *dog*!"

Miss Fancy Pants perks her head up at the word dog.

He rolls his eyes. He should have known her sympathy wasn't for him.

"It's no wonder Miss Fancy Pants is upset," Tori continues. "She's taking her anger out on you because Rachel isn't there."

He glances over at the little dog, who's watching him on the phone with interest. "I think she blames me for Rachel leaving."

Tori seems to consider this. "It's certainly possible. One thing's for sure, that poor dog is dealing with an emotional wound."

"She's destroying my house. Do you think you can help me?"

The line goes silent, and he holds his breath. He can sense her thinking it over.

"Let me make something perfectly clear up front. I'm doing this to help Miss Fancy Pants, not *you*."

"I understand."

"She's such a sweetie and doesn't deserve what's happened to her." Her voice softens. "It may take some time for her to learn to trust anyone again."

Miss Fancy Pants has moved into a sitting position, still watching the conversation.

"How soon can you start?" he asks. He doesn't want to sound too eager, but he's desperate to get some control over his life.

"Let me grab my planner."

The line goes silent, except he can hear her exerting herself, like she's reaching for something. It's weird, but the sound of her breath is stirring him up inside.

He listens, even closes his eyes, as he tries to imagine exactly what she looks like. It's late, so she's probably wearing what she sleeps in. A nightgown? Something short and low-cut? He doubts that's the case, but this is his fantasy. In reality, she's probably wearing baggy pajama bottoms and a T-shirt. Though, come to think of it, he'd find that just as sexy on her.

"Okay, got it." She sighs, and there's a sound of pages rustling.

He licks his bottom lip, still listening, still imagining her.

"Hmm, let's see," she murmurs. Her voice is feminine and soft. "When do you need me?"

His eyes are still closed. *Right now.*

"Could you come over tomorrow?" he asks, his voice rough to his own ears.

"What time?"

"Noon."

"You're in luck. I had a cancellation and can squeeze you in at twelve fifteen. Will that work?"

"Sounds good."

"I'm going to add you to my book," she says in an official tone. "We can discuss my payment and any future arrangements when I see you. Text me your address at this number, okay?"

They hang up. Miss Fancy Pants is still sitting there watching him. "Don't look at me like that. I'm doing this for you. She can help."

Though it feels like he's doing it for himself. Between Rachel leaving and him working extra hours, he's been too wrung out to even think about sex. Apparently his body hasn't forgotten though.

Despite her hostility, he remembers how attracted he was to Tori in high school.

Of course, that was before the milkshake happened, before she and her brother made his life hell.

That's the part he needs to remember.

MABLE HASN'T BEEN FOUND YET, so Tori's still driving Blair's Honda as she pulls up to the address Liam texted her last night. It's one of those newer Seattle neighborhoods where the homes all have a cookie-cutter look to them. There are two vehicles already parked in his driveway, so she parks on the street.

As she heads up the walkway with her purse, she notices how all the lawns are the same color green and trimmed to the same length. The sidewalks have been swept clean. She rings the bell to his house, and a few moments later, the door opens.

She's startled by the sight of Liam. He's bigger than she remembers from last week. More handsome too.

"Hello, Tori." His dark eyes stay on her face.

She shifts the purse on her shoulder and nods. "Hello."

The two of them study each other in silence.

"Come on in." He waves her inside.

She follows him into the main living area, which smells like a mixture of dog piss and cleaning detergent.

She should be taking in her surroundings like she normally does on her first visit as a pet sitter, but she can't stop staring at Liam. He's wearing gray slacks with a white dress shirt and a dark blue tie. As she follows him, she tries not to notice the broad set of his shoulders or the way the back of his neck looks sexy.

Her eyes drop lower to the shoulder holster at his side and widen. "Is that a gun?"

Liam turns. "Yes, it is. As I mentioned last time we saw each other, I'm a special agent with the FBI."

"I do remember."

His expression changes to concern. "Does the gun bother you? I can take it off. I just got home a few minutes ago."

"No, it's okay. It doesn't bother me."

"You're sure?"

She nods and takes a deep breath. Liam is having a peculiar effect on her. "So, where's Miss Fancy Pants? I don't see her."

"Probably in the bedroom. You're the third dog sitter, and she hasn't exactly been friendly with any of them."

"The third one?"

"Yep. Let me get her. I'll be right back."

Tori tries to tell him he doesn't have to, but he's already walked off, so instead she checks out his house. The place seems disjointed, like it's missing stuff. The pictures are spaced oddly on the walls, and there's a large gap next to the couch where there was clearly a chair before.

"Oh my God, what happened to your couch?" she asks when he comes back into the living room.

Liam glances at it. "Miss Fancy Pants happened."

"She did *that*?" Tori walks over to the dark brown sofa and touches the once-smooth fabric. The cushions have been chewed up. It's obvious the stuffing was dug out and that someone tried to shove it all back in again. "Poor little dog."

"Poor little *dog*?" He sounds appalled. "Are you joking? She destroyed my couch. I need to buy a new one, except I can't, because she'll destroy that one too."

"She was only trying to get your attention."

"Well, she succeeded."

Tori frowns. "You're going to have to be more patient than that. Think of what she's been through."

Liam is staring at her like he can't believe his ears. It figures. He opens his mouth to say more, but a soft yip comes from behind him.

Tori's thrilled to discover Miss Fancy Pants sitting on the edge of the rug watching her. She ignores Liam and smiles at the little dog. "Well, look who we have here."

"There she is." He nods with affirmation. "Let me grab the leash so you can take her out for a walk."

Tori gawks at him. "Are you crazy? I'm not taking her for a walk." She sits down on the chewed-up couch, laying her purse on the floor beside it. "She has to come to me on her own. That's the way this works."

"You're not taking her out?" His mouth hangs open like he thinks she's the crazy one.

"Only if she wants to."

He puts his hands on his hips and stares down at Miss Fancy Pants. "Well, what's it going to be?"

Tori rolls her eyes. "Do you seriously know nothing about dogs?"

"I've never had one before." He sounds defensive.

"Yes, that's obvious." She motions to the couch. "Have a seat. We need to let her get used to me being here."

Liam glances at Miss Fancy Pants but does as Tori asks, coming over and taking a seat on the opposite end. She notices he's not wearing his gun anymore and figures he must have taken it off in the bedroom.

Tori shifts on the sofa, tugging on her T-shirt so it doesn't emphasize her stomach fat. She's wearing jeans and her pink Heart shirt—one of her favorite bands—but it's a little tight. She wishes she'd worn something more flattering.

Not that she cares what Liam thinks. *I mean, he's no Dr. Adrian.*

A long moment of silence passes.

"What now?" he asks.

"Nothing. We just wait. Give Miss Fancy Pants a chance to decide how she feels about my presence here. She needs to see that I'm not a threat."

"And how long will that take?"

"I don't know."

He stares at her. "Seriously? That's it?"

"Yes, that's it. She's a dog, and dogs are very sensitive to their environment."

"But I need you to take her for a walk so she doesn't start pissing all over the house again. I have to get back to work."

Tori shakes her head. "Wow, are you always this impatient?"

"No." He seems surprised. "Actually, I'm a very patient person."

"You must be kidding. It doesn't show."

Liam studies her with those dark eyes. "That's because you don't know me very well."

"I know plenty," she mutters, turning her head away.

"No, you don't. All those years ago, you only believed what you wanted. And now you're doing it again."

"Excuse me?" She turns back to him. "I know what happened that night. You ruined my first big dance, embarrassed me in front of everyone. And then you and your idiot friends laughed."

"I never laughed."

"I heard you, okay? So stop denying the truth. And let's not forget, you poured a milkshake over my head."

"That was an accident, for which I apologized profusely. Hell, I still feel bad about it."

"Oh, please." She scoffs. "That was no accident. You only apologized because everybody was watching."

"No, I didn't. And you're not exactly innocent here. You obviously had no problem with your brother trying to beat me up afterward."

Tori is outraged. "I had no idea Road went after you! In fact, I just learned about it myself."

"Yeah, sure." He gazes at her with obvious skepticism. "Now who's the one denying the truth?"

"I *am* telling the truth!"

"And so am I." Liam's expression is guarded, but she senses the frustration churning beneath the surface. "I've only ever told you the truth," he says in a low voice. "I'm not a liar."

She looks away, irritated. He sounds sincere, but she knows what happened that night. Her memory is crystal clear. "Let's not talk about this anymore, okay? I'm here to help Miss Fancy Pants, not relive our horrible past, of which you are one hundred percent to blame."

He doesn't respond.

"I should have known coming here would be a mistake." She

shakes her head. "I want to help your dog, but I can't if all we're going to do is argue. Bad vibes are the last thing we need right now."

Still no response. She eyes the front door area and contemplates leaving.

He takes a deep breath. "You're right. Let's not talk about it anymore."

There's a bleak expression on his face. She thought he'd be angry, but instead he looks tired.

She doesn't know why, but a teeny part of her softens. "Treat me like I'm a guest in your home. We want Miss Fancy Pants to see me as someone who's welcome here. Do you think you can do that?"

"Fine."

Tori discreetly glances at Miss Fancy Pants, who's still sitting at the edge of the rug watching the two of them with interest. She's glad to see the little dog is curious.

"Can I get you anything to drink?" Liam asks, his voice gruff.

"Hmm, that sounds nice." Tori crosses her legs and puts a hand on her knee as she plays the part of houseguest. "What do you have?"

"Iced tea, water, or milk."

She considers her options. "I'll have a glass of ice water, please."

Liam gets up and goes into the kitchen while Tori leans back on the couch, trying to get comfortable. It isn't easy as the lumps in the cushions force her to sit at an odd angle.

He's gone long enough that it gives her a chance to study his house some more. It could use a good cleaning. There are dust bunnies in the corner and a bunch of mail stacked haphazardly on the coffee table. The whole place has a neglected air about it.

When he returns with her water, she thanks him and notices he's poured himself a glass of iced tea.

The two of them sip their drinks in silence.

"So, is this what you always do as a dog sitter?" he asks. "Literally sit around?"

Tori glances at him to see if he's making fun of her, but it seems like a genuine question.

She shrugs. "Sometimes. It depends on the situation. Some dogs take to me right away, but others need coaxing. Miss Fancy Pants needs to feel like she's in control because of what happened with Rachel."

Tori sets her water on the coffee table. It upset her when she heard what happened to this dog. She always thought Rachel seemed like a nice person. Appearances certainly are deceiving.

"And your other clients are fine with all this sitting around?" he asks.

"Didn't you go on my website?"

"No."

"Well, if you'd bothered to check, you'd see all the testimonials from people raving about my pet sitting services."

"Is that so?" Liam leans back, considering her.

"Yes, and you'll also find plenty of tips and pointers for how to take care of your dog's or cat's health, both emotional and physical."

As he takes another drink from his iced tea, Tori notices movement from the corner of her eye. Miss Fancy Pants is walking closer.

To her utter delight, the little dog comes right up to her leg and sniffs it.

"Hi there, sweetie," she says softly. She gently puts her hand out, and the dog sniffs that too. She wags her tail, so Tori pets her. "You know who I am, right?"

In answer, the dog jumps up on the couch and sits beside her.

"Great. Finally," Liam says with relief. He leans forward and puts his glass down. "Now you can take her out."

"No, that won't be happening today." Tori continues to pet the dog.

"What do you mean?"

She glances at her watch. Most people use their phones, but she likes to wear a watch when she's working. "My time here is nearly up."

He opens his mouth. "You can't be serious."

"Yes, I am. I have to leave."

"Leave? But who's taking this dog for a walk?"

"You are."

He stares at her, speechless.

"You really need to get her coat trimmed too," she goes on. "If you can't brush it every day, then have it cut short. I can recommend an excellent groomer."

Miss Fancy Pants rubs her head against Tori's hand as she strokes the dog's soft ears.

Liam watches them in what appears to be stunned silence.

"Would you like to schedule my services again? If so, I'll bill you later. If not, you can pay me with cash or check today." She'd already texted him her hourly rate after he gave her his address.

"Are you kidding?" He lets out an ironic laugh. "As far as I can tell, the only thing I'm paying you for is to come over here, sit on my couch, and insult me."

She shrugs. "See it however you like." A part of her hopes he says no. *I mean, do I really want to deal with him again?*

But then there's Miss Fancy Pants to think of. This dog needs her help, and it's obvious Liam is making a mess of things. Big surprise there.

"You definitely need my help," she tells him.

"Oh, really?"

She nods. "You do. You're making a mess of things."

He's silent after that. Finally, he sighs. "Can you come again tomorrow?"

CHAPTER SIX

"HMM, I DON'T KNOW," Tori says thoughtfully. "Let me check my planner."

Liam watches as she reaches down and digs around in that giant purse of hers. Eventually she pulls out a decorative spiral-bound notebook and places it on her lap. He recognizes it from that day at the vet's office.

Miss Fancy Pants sniffs the corner.

"Let's see," Tori murmurs, opening it up. It's some kind of scheduler, but he's never seen anything like it. Every page is covered with bright stickers. "Today's Wednesday. I'm busy tomorrow, but I could come over at noon on Friday. Will that work?"

"Okay," he agrees readily. He can't believe he's willing to pay for this, and what's worse is he suspects he's only doing it so he can see her again.

The pen in her hand is pink, and he watches as she writes "Miss Fancy Pants" in her book with round cursive letters. She doesn't write his name at all. She's wearing glittery pink nail polish that matches her T-shirt, which has butterflies on it and the logo for the eighties band Heart.

Despite her insults, he's spent the past hour drowning in her sex appeal.

She's kooky like she was in high school—kookier even—and it's working for him in a big way.

Except he knows from experience that Tori Church is trouble.

In fact, he's certain this dog sitting is a bad idea.

"Do you think you'll walk her when you come Friday?" he asks.

Both Tori and Miss Fancy Pants look at him like they're already a unit. "I don't know. Does that matter?"

He gazes at her pretty face. At her blue eyes. He tries to fight this attraction.

"I guess not," he mutters.

So I'm paying a dog sitter who's not even going to walk the dog?

"I might in the future," she tells him in a considering tone. "Let's see how Miss Fancy Pants feels about it, okay? We want her to be comfortable with me."

He only nods. As far as he can tell, the dog seems plenty comfortable already.

Tori puts the notebook back in her purse and pets Miss Fancy Pants one last time before getting up from the couch. "I need to go now. I have more work this afternoon."

Both Liam and the dog follow her to the front door.

"Let me walk you to your car," he says.

She shifts the purse on her shoulder. Her honey-blonde hair is pulled back in a ponytail like last time. "You don't have to." But then she stops and gazes down with a smile. "Actually, how about you *both* walk me to my car?"

He glances down at the furball, who seems to be loving this idea.

"I suppose." He only began walking the dog recently, after she started pissing everywhere. He couldn't figure out why she didn't use the dog door and do her business in the backyard like she used to.

He reaches past Tori to get the leash from where Rachel always kept it on a hook. His face is only inches from her hair, and he inhales the scent of tangerines.

Luscious and sweet.

He doesn't know if it's her perfume or shampoo, but she smells like a summer day. Except that smell is having a strong effect on his body. His muscles tighten all over. A flood of desire erupts in him, and with horror, he realizes he's getting aroused.

By tangerines?

He hasn't had to deal with awkward boners since high school, yet here he is, hard as a baseball bat.

He grabs the leash and crouches down to put it on the dog, trying to get away from Tori. He goes over statistics from his favorite players and teams, straining to remember unusual stats, anything to divert his blood flow.

"Are you having trouble with the leash?" she asks. She bends over to assist him, which is the last thing he wants.

"No." His voice comes out louder and rougher than he intends. "I've got it."

"Fine. Whatever." She straightens up.

Eventually he attaches it to the dog's collar and stands, holding his arm in front of his crotch area. Luckily, Tori isn't looking downward. "You go ahead," he tells her. "We'll follow you outside."

She shrugs and opens the door. Miss Fancy Pants trots after her with Liam bringing up the rear holding the leash.

As they walk along the sidewalk, he tries not to notice Tori's ass and the way it's filling out her jeans. There's a sexy sway to her hips that he remembers from the good old days. He used to have dreams about it, dreams where he woke up sweaty and distressed. A teenager in the throes of his first real crush.

He takes a deep breath and forces himself to look out at his tidy neighborhood. Upward at the cloudless blue sky.

Anywhere but at Tori's tantalizing hips and ass.

As she leads them farther along the sidewalk, he manages to gain some control over himself.

By the time they walk up to a silver four-door Honda, he's mostly feeling like his normal self, though he doubts he'll ever feel normal around Tori.

"This is me," she says. "Blair loaned me her car."

He blinks a few times, and it dawns on him that he forgot to ask about her stolen vehicle. He's been too distracted by her charms. "They haven't found your minivan yet?"

Tori sighs, digging through her purse. "No, Mable is still missing. It's very upsetting."

"Have you spoken to the police?"

"I called last week, but they said they'd let me know if they find her."

He nods and makes a mental note to contact the detectives working her case himself.

Tori pulls out her keys, then bends over to pet Miss Fancy Pants again. "And I'll see *you* on Friday," she says in a cooing voice.

Liam stands there stiffly. "So you're headed back to the animal hospital now?"

"Not today. I have my own web design business. I'm working for one of my clients this afternoon. I also have to cook a batch of dog snacks for Happy Pet Nanny."

His brows rise. "You have another business besides the dog sitting?"

"Yes, I create and maintain websites."

He takes this in and has to admit he's surprised. He didn't picture her being so industrious. "And what about the animal hospital?"

She opens the passenger side of the car and tosses her large purse inside. "Oh, I only work there part-time."

"How many jobs do you have?"

She pauses. "Four."

"You have four jobs?" He's starting to understand why she relies on that scheduling book so much.

"The fourth one is my brother. He put me on his payroll for the health insurance. He offers his employees great benefits."

She works for Road? He can't imagine what that guy does for a living and is afraid to ask.

"Well, I'd better get going."

He has more questions, but she's already getting into her car. Before he knows it, she's started the engine and is pulling away from the curb, waving goodbye to Miss Fancy Pants. She ignores him completely.

He and the dog remain on the sidewalk until Tori's car turns left and disappears out of his neighborhood.

Miss Fancy Pants makes a sighing noise.

"I know," he murmurs. "For once we're in agreement."

They trod back to the house together, making a pit stop so Miss Fancy Pants can relieve her bladder. He checks his phone. There's a text from one of his squad members about a case they've been working on together, a bank manager who's embezzling funds from his own bank. He also has a meeting with a prosecutor from the U.S. Attorney's Office about Yates this afternoon.

As he's entering the front door, his phone rings. A Seattle number he doesn't recognize shows on the caller ID. "Castillo."

"Is this Liam?" It's a female's voice.

"Yes it is."

"Hi, this is Shelby. Amy gave me your number. I hope it's okay I'm calling."

For some reason, he was hoping it was Tori. "Who is this?"

"I'm a friend of Amy's."

He thinks back and remembers the blind date Matt's wife wanted to set him up on. Amy texted him Shelby's number last week, but he'd been so busy with work and dealing with this dog, he'd forgotten all about it.

"Yes, of course." He unclasps the leash and hangs it by the door again. "I meant to get in touch with you. I'm glad you called."

"Oh, good." She sounds relieved. "I didn't want to seem too forward, but then I thought what the heck." She laughs self-consciously, and he decides she sounds nice.

They talk as he goes into the kitchen. He fills a tortilla with chili and vegetables from last night, then heats it in the toaster oven. Shelby explains how she works with Amy in the accounting department for an insurance company, and that she started running marathons after her divorce to keep busy.

"I was thinking," she says. "Instead of the usual blind date of coffee or dinner, how about we go for a run together? Amy told me you used to be a professional athlete and that you still stay in shape."

Liam takes a bite of his tortilla wrap and considers this. He runs regularly and figures Shelby's right—it would be an easy first date. "Sure, that sounds great."

They make plans to meet after work tonight at one of the local trails.

After they hang up, he goes into the bedroom. In truth, he wasn't that enthusiastic about a blind date, but he's glad now she called. He needs to get out more, to stop sitting home every night.

He reaches for his gun and holster, which are still on the nightstand, and slips them over his shoulders.

Rachel's been gone over a month, and he hasn't heard a single word from her, not even to check on her dog. He knows she arrived safely in Buenos Aires because her sisters told him. The impression he got from them was how happy Rachel and Dr. Adrenaline Junkie were together, the two of them BASE jumping and zip-lining to their hearts' content.

While Rachel may have thought he was boring and that catching bad guys who wore business suits was dull, he knew the truth.

Catching criminals who embezzled millions or scammed people out of their life savings was plenty satisfying, and all the excitement he wanted in life.

But then Tori flickers through his mind. The way she looked sitting on his couch. That sexy sway when she walked outside.

He closes his eyes and pushes thoughts of her away.

Maybe not all the excitement.

"GOSH, YOU'RE IN GREAT SHAPE," Shelby says when they stop for a breather at a coffee place near the Burke-Gilman Trail.

Liam cracks open a bottle of water. "So are you."

"Thank you." She smiles. "I never thought I could be this athletic. I had to keep busy after my divorce though."

"How long were you married?"

"Eight years. One day he wakes up and tells me he isn't in love with me anymore. Can you believe that?"

Liam takes a drink from his water and then shakes his head. "I'm sorry. That's rough."

"It was at first." She shrugs and opens her own bottle. "But now I think it's the best thing that could have happened to me."

He nods. "I went through something similar recently."

"Yes, Amy told me you ended a relationship not long ago."

"Not a marriage, but we lived together for two years." He glances around the area. There are other people out, some of them jogging, a few on bikes. He and Shelby have been running a part of the trail that goes near the water. The sky is blue while the sun shines a citrus yellow.

The color makes him think of Tori. Unfortunately, she's been sneaking into his thoughts all afternoon.

"I'm sorry," Shelby says. "I know how hard it is when a relationship ends, especially after you've put so much time and effort into it."

She talks about her marriage and divorce, how it took her a long time to start dating again.

Liam tries to listen, but his mind keeps going back to earlier. To how Tori smelled like tangerines, and how he got turned on by it. It was odd.

It must have been pheromones affecting him so strongly.

"In the end, sometimes two people aren't meant to be together," Shelby says. "Don't you agree?"

"Yes," he says definitively, putting the cap back on his water bottle. "I agree 100 percent."

Like him and Tori Church. Not meant to be. Ever.

Shelby smiles, and Liam realizes he needs to focus more on his date. The fact is, she seems great in every way. Attractive, with brown hair and green eyes. An athletic body.

Most important of all, he can tell she's not odd or kooky. No craziness at all.

"Amy told me you played baseball in college and then went on to the majors," Shelby says. "I should warn you, I'm a huge baseball fan."

"Are you?"

"I am. In fact, I have a little confession to make." Her expression turns sheepish. "When Amy told me your name and that you played pro ball, I sort of looked you up online."

"What did you find?"

"Well, you went to Portland and played college ball. After that you played in the minors but didn't finish the season because you were picked up by San Diego. You were their catcher for three years, until you were forced to quit." She meets his eyes. "I'm sorry about your knees."

Liam nods. He's gotten used to the apologies from people over the years.

"That had to be rough. You had a .330 batting average and the fewest errors of any catcher your third season. You were in your prime." Her expression turns sympathetic. "I can't even imagine how difficult it was to walk away."

He shrugs. He's had this conversation a lot too. "If I hadn't walked away, I wouldn't have been able to join the bureau." He consulted a few doctors back then, and they all told him the same thing: he could get a few more seasons out of his knees and risk damaging them permanently, or he could stop playing altogether. He didn't want to risk permanent damage, and more importantly, he didn't want to risk not joining the FBI. "Being a federal agent is what I've always wanted to do."

"But it must have been terrible to give up a professional baseball career."

"I know how lucky I was to have had that experience, but in the end, this is where I want to be."

She nods but is still wearing a look of sympathy. "Good for you, then."

He tries not to get irritated. While it was a rush playing ball, he loves being an agent. Catching criminals is far more satisfying than catching baseballs.

She leans toward him. "Amy sometimes tells me about Matt's work, and it sounds exciting."

He knows he should be feeling some kind of chemistry right now. It's obvious Shelby is a nice, normal woman. The kind he should be involved with. The kind a man builds a life with.

While he might not feel a spark right now, he figures he needs to give it more time. He decides right then to make a real effort with her.

He leans closer. "This has been fun. Would you like to do it again?"

LATER THAT EVENING, once he's back home settled on his end of the lumpy sofa, he reflects on his date.

"I think you'd like her," he tells the furball, before biting into a piece of roasted chicken he picked up from a takeout place on the way home. "Shelby is exactly the kind of woman you and I both need in our lives."

The dog seems to eye him with skepticism as she holds the drumstick he gave her between her front paws.

"Trust me. She's nice and stable. No chance she's running off to South America."

Miss Fancy Pants chews on the bone from her chicken leg.

He put out dry dog food when he got home, but as usual she wanted nothing to do with it.

"I hate to break it to you," he says, "but Rachel isn't worth mooning over. She's selfish and always has been."

Leaning back on the couch, he wonders if he should have kissed Shelby after their run. Was she expecting that? It hadn't even occurred to him.

When he and Rachel had their first date, it was dinner and a movie. They made it halfway through the film before she insisted he take her home. At first he thought he'd done something wrong, but to his surprise, she pulled him into her apartment, led him straight to her bedroom, and proceeded to jump his bones all night.

Impulsive as always. Not that he complained at the time. They had good chemistry back in those days. Back when he was still flavor of the month.

It wasn't long afterward that she moved in. Later on he found out she'd had a boyfriend when they met, whom she dumped for Liam. He wasn't happy to learn that. In fact, they had a big fight about it.

As he's reminiscing over all this, Miss Fancy Pants stands up and coughs.

Liam turns toward her. "Hey, what's up? You okay?"

The dog coughs again, then again, wheezing between coughs.

Quickly, he shoves his plate aside and moves next to her.

She coughs some more.

He starts to panic. If she were a person, he'd give her the Heimlich, but he doesn't know what to do in this case. "That's right," he encourages her. "Go ahead and get it out."

She coughs and paws her face.

Just as he's ready to grab her and shake her upside down, she coughs loudly and finally seems to clear the blockage, bringing up the entire contents of her stomach with it.

"Good girl." He pats her on the back with relief. She licks her mouth a few times and looks over at him. "Damn, Fancy, you scared the hell out of me. Everything okay now?"

The dog yawns and licks her mouth once more, but thankfully, as far as he can tell, she seems fine.

He pets her, then removes the partially chewed-up bone along with the rest of the chicken meat and throws it in the trash.

As he gets cleaning supplies from the kitchen, he goes over what happened and, with frustration, realizes he doesn't know enough about dogs.

He finds Tori's number and, when her voicemail picks up, leaves a short but detailed message. She works at a vet's office, so she must know how to handle this kind of thing.

Just as he's done cleaning up the dog vomit, including wiping Fancy's face with a wet cloth, his phone rings.

"Are you crazy?" a familiar female voice rants. "You can't give a dog cooked bones! They'll splinter. Don't you know anything?"

"I thought bones were good for dogs."

"Not cooked. They have to be raw, and not just any old bone either." Tori seems to be trying to calm herself. "How is Miss Fancy Pants doing now? Is she okay?"

Liam glances over at the dog. She's perched on the edge of the couch like she's the Queen of Sheba, watching him. He's still sitting on the floor with all the cleaning supplies. He reaches up to pet her again, deciding not to tell Tori how panicked he'd gotten. "She seems fine now."

"Good. You have to careful with the kind of human food you feed her. There's a lot of stuff dogs can't eat."

"Really? I figured they could eat anything. I mean, wild dogs are scavengers."

He can almost hear Tori rolling her eyes. "Domesticated dogs are *not* wild dogs. Have you gone on my website yet?"

"No."

He hears another eye roll in progress. "Please go on my website and educate yourself. And please don't feed her anything until you're sure it's safe. I have a list on there you can check."

"She doesn't seem to like the dry dog food. She'll eat it in the mornings but not at night."

"Well, then get her some wet food for dinner. Dogs are like people in that some don't mind eating the same thing all the time while others prefer variety."

He takes this in. The furball is studying him, and he suspects she knows he's speaking to Tori about her.

"How do you handle it if a dog chokes?" he asks. "Is there a version of the Heimlich maneuver?"

"Yes, there is. If you'd like, I'll teach it to you."

"That would be great, thanks." Normally he could handle himself in any emergency, and he doesn't want a repeat of what just happened.

There's some kind of loud noise in the background, like a guy's voice yelling. Tori sighs. "I'd better go."

"Is everything okay?"

"It's fine."

There's more yelling, this time a woman, and Liam grows concerned. "Who is that?"

"My mom. Like I said, I have to go. I'll see you Friday at noon."

"Hey, wait a minute." He wants to find out more, but the phone is silent. Tori's already hung up. He's tempted to call her back but knows she'll only tell him to mind his own business.

He glances over at the dog. "All right, let's go look at that website."

CHAPTER SEVEN

"EVERYTHING OKAY, HONEY?" Peyton asks. "You look kind of tired."

"Just a long night." Tori doesn't want to go into any details. It's been two nights in a row with her mom, who's been on a real bender lately. Peyton doesn't know anything about it—most people don't—and she has no plans to tell her.

"Girl, you work too much. I don't know how you do it, or why either. When's the last time you had a vacation?"

She slips her smock on while thinking it over. "I can't remember."

Peyton shakes her head. "That's not healthy. You need to take some time off. Go do something fun."

"I suppose." She thinks about all her various jobs, all the people who rely on her. Then she thinks about her mother, who's basically another job. She could have called Road to come help, but she didn't want to bother him and Blair.

"Lamont and I are headed up to Truth Harbor next weekend. We're staying at a cabin on Treasure Lake. Did I tell you about that?" Peyton sips her iced coffee. "My cousin Tara owns it and is letting us borrow it for a few days."

Tori imagines herself staying at some lakeside cabin, lazing around in a bikini after a swim. It sounds like heaven.

"It's our seven-year wedding anniversary."

"Congratulations," Tori says. "That's wonderful."

Peyton smiles and shakes her head as if she's amazed herself. "It is wonderful. I can't believe I found myself such a good man. I had to kiss a lot of toads to get here though."

"You deserve it."

"And so do you, honey. Eventually things will happen for you and Dr. Adrian."

"Actually, I'm going to ask him to the Seattle Arts Festival today," Tori announces to her friend.

She decided it on the drive over here this morning. After *the look* when they first met, she figures he's obviously attracted to her. And then there's the way he touches her lightly all the time. Maybe he's gun-shy after breaking up with his fiancée. Something about seeing Liam the other day made her realize it was high time this relationship moved forward.

Her friend nods with approval. "Good for you. I say go for it."

"Hopefully, he says yes."

"Say, listen." Peyton leans closer. "I wanted to run over to Target before lunch. Do you think you can cover the desk for me?"

"Sure, but only until eleven thirty. I have a dog sitting job at noon." Tori brings up the day's schedule on the computer, hoping to see an obvious break where she can corner Dr. Adrian. Unfortunately, they're busy all morning.

"Is it with that FBI guy you went to high school with?"

"Yeah, it's him," she mutters.

Peyton raises an eyebrow. "Well, I'll be."

"Don't look at me like that. I'm only doing it to help Miss Fancy Pants."

"I know, but you have to admit he's hot."

Tori snorts. But then she thinks about how strange it was seeing Liam the other day. How unsettling.

It isn't until their ten o'clock appointment calls to say they're running late that she finally sees her opportunity. Dr. Adrian is sitting alone in the break room eating a tofu breakfast burrito, studying his phone.

To her astonishment, she recently found out he's a vegan just like she is. One more way they're perfect for each other.

She goes over to the fridge and pretends to look inside for something before glancing over her shoulder. "I eat those too," she says, closing the fridge door. She walks over and joins him at the table. "I'm not sure if you know this, but I'm also a vegan."

"You are?" He looks up from his phone. "I didn't know that."

"I've been one for a few years now."

"So have I."

Their eyes meet, and he grins. "I've noticed you and I have a lot in common."

She laughs flirtatiously. "I've noticed the same thing."

"Have you tried that new vegetarian restaurant on Roosevelt?"

"Not yet, but I plan to."

There's a smile in those blue eyes. "Maybe we should check it out together sometime."

A thrill rushes through her. She knew it was a good idea cornering him today. "That sounds great."

They talk more about various restaurants in the city they've both tried. He doesn't ask her out specifically, but he seems to be laying the groundwork.

He takes another bite of his burrito and glances at his phone, chuckling over something.

"What is it?" she asks.

"It's these cat videos. I watch them to relax sometimes."

"Me too. I love cat videos!"

He waves her toward him. "Well, scoot closer. You have to see this one."

Reaching over, he helps pull her chair right next to his, then holds his phone out. It's one of those videos where the cat knocks items off a counter one at a time. In this case, the cat is a fluffy gray Persian.

They watch as she knocks off a hairbrush, then a small bottle of shampoo, then a box of facial tissue. The next item in line is a ladybug toy.

The cat seems startled by its bright red color. She stares at it for a long moment. Her tail twitches, twitches again, and then her paw comes out and the ladybug goes flying.

Tori and Adrian laugh.

"I swear, cats have the best comedic timing."

"They do," she says in agreement.

The two of them watch a few more videos, laughing together. Tori has a warm feeling inside. Her eyes roam discreetly over Dr. Adrian's handsome profile. His eyebrows are the same blond shade as his hair. A smattering of freckles runs across his cheeks and nose. It occurs to her that they have similar coloring. This gives her pause. She hopes they don't look like brother and sister on their cozy sweater Christmas cards.

But then decides that's silly.

While she may not be attracted to Dr. Adrian physically, she definitely likes his personality. She can tell he's a good guy and figures the physical part will come with time. It's all a part of trying something new.

"Do you like art?" she asks him.

"Art?" Those blond brows move up slightly. He's staring at his screen and chuckling at another video. "I suppose I do."

She takes a deep breath. There's a lot riding on this next question. For all she knows, Dr. Adrian is her special someone. "Are you going to the Seattle Arts Festival this weekend? Because I was thinking of going."

He glances at her.

"I was hoping we could go together," she clarifies.

"That would be great. My sister and I are planning to go." He studies her. "Would you like to come with us?"

She sucks in her breath. "I'd *love* to."

He nods. "This is perfect timing. I've been thinking how I'd like to get to know you better, Tori."

"Really? Me too."

They grin at each other.

A thrill rushes through her. It's finally happening. Dr. Adrian has finally asked her out. So what if she had to prod him a little? At least he's not pushy like so many other guys.

This is exciting. She can't wait to ride in that midnight blue Tesla.

He's gone back to his phone. Meanwhile, she's thinking about their date. It's a good sign that he wants her to meet his sister. Most men don't want a woman to meet family members unless they really like her.

She studies his face as he studies the screen. That square jaw and those perfect blond-tipped lashes. Dr. Adrian really does look like Prince Charming.

"So, what day are we going?" she asks.

"I'm not sure." He tilts his head. "Let me talk to Gina. I think it was Sunday. How does that sound?"

"Perfect. I'm really looking forward to it."

"So am I. Let me get your number." He shuts down the cat videos, and Tori rattles off her phone number. "I'll text you when I find out the time."

"Sounds great."

After he leaves the room, Tori hugs herself, elated. *See, that wasn't so hard?* She should have cornered him sooner. Heck, who knows where they'd be now.

Heading back out to the front desk, she can't wait to tell Peyton. She has to text Blair too. Blair hasn't met Dr. Adrian, but Tori's told her all about him.

She has a feeling it won't be long before she's introducing him to everyone as her new veterinarian boyfriend.

PEYTON'S REACTION to her date is pure enthusiasm. "Girl, that's wonderful!"

"I know! Isn't it?"

"Everyone's going to be so jealous," she says, referring to some of their coworkers who have crushes on Dr. Adrian. "They won't believe it."

She texts Blair next and hears back immediately.

Dr. Adrian sounds like the perfect man for you. I can't wait to meet him!

Tori smiles and is still smiling when she heads over to her pet sitting appointment with Miss Fancy Pants. She's in such a great mood as she rings the doorbell to Liam's house that nothing can ruin her happiness. Nothing. It's too magical.

But then Liam Castillo opens his front door.

Like last time, his size and appearance are unexpected. He's even more handsome than before. *Does he get better looking every day?* He's wearing gray slacks and a white dress shirt, but his tie is forest green today. The color brings out the brown in his eyes.

She's always liked men with dark hair and eyes, liked how they were so different from her own light coloring.

Blue eyes are nice too, she reminds herself. *Dr. Adrian's eyes are a dreamy blue.*

The shirt hugs Liam's broad shoulders, and she follows it down to where it's tucked in at his waist, which is narrow and solid.

He smiles at her with that sensual mouth. A flash of white teeth.

Except she doesn't like it. Not one bit.

Annoyed, she glares at him. Her day's happiness is now hovering on the edge of ruin. "Is that how you always dress?" she complains, stepping inside the foyer. "I thought FBI guys wore nothing but cheap black suits."

He chuckles, and to her further annoyance, the sound is a low rumble that sends tingles through her.

"It depends on what case I'm working. I deal with a lot of financial institutions, so I typically dress the part."

She notices how he took his gun off already. The gun didn't bother her, but she appreciated his concern. Oddly, despite their infamous past, there's something about Liam that makes her feel safe. "Is that what you were doing today?"

"No, I was in court this morning. I had to testify against a guy who embezzled from the healthcare company he used to work for."

"You're the one who arrested him?"

Liam nods. "I was lead on the case. I worked undercover for three months to catch him."

Tori's eyes widen. "That sounds dangerous. How much did he steal?"

"Five million and change."

"Are you allowed to tell me those details?"

He shrugs. "The FBI isn't the CIA. I can usually discuss cases after they're adjudicated—been through the court process."

"Really? I didn't know that."

There's a flash of white again. "Now you do."

She follows him into the living room, trying not to watch him walk. His walk is confident. Sexy. Dr. Adrian has a nice walk too. Or at least she thinks he does. To be honest, she's never noticed it, but she's sure it's as perfect as he is.

"How is Miss Fancy Pants after the other night?" she asks,

concerned. "Is she still okay? I hope there's been no more choking incidents."

"She's back to her normal self."

"Good. Did you go on my website for the list of foods that are safe and ones to avoid?"

"Yes, I saw it."

Tori sighs with relief.

"Have a seat." He motions to the same lumpy couch she sat on a couple days ago. "Can I get you anything?"

"Ice water would be nice."

He heads off to the kitchen, and Tori takes a seat on the couch, placing her purse on the floor again. She looks around for Miss Fancy Pants but doesn't see her.

Liam returns with two glasses. They sit on opposite ends of the sofa, same as last time, except now she's too aware of his proximity.

Her eyes keep roaming over him. She can't seem to stop herself.

It's his whole masculine vibe. It occurs to her that the male energy he puts out isn't quite like Dr. Adrian's. It's different. And the way Liam keeps watching her with those dark eyes isn't like Dr. Adrian either. That's different too.

Very different.

Her stomach dips. Butterflies start fluttering.

But then she's angry with herself. Why is she comparing the two men? That's like comparing a sweet angel to Beelzebub.

"Are you all right?" he asks, studying her with concern.

"Of course." She puts her drink on the table and accidentally sloshes some over the edge. There's a napkin nearby and she uses it to mop up the water. "I'm having a great day. *Just* peachy."

"I'm glad to hear it."

She leans back and crosses her legs. She's wearing jeans and a flowered pink top that's one of her most flattering. It's loose enough to hide any sins but tight enough to show some curves.

Liam's eyes flicker down her body. She smiles to herself. Not that she wore this top for him. Please. That would be ridiculous. In fact, she likes the way he's checking her out, because it reminds her of Dr. Adrian on the first day they met.

"Was everything okay that night after we talked on the phone?" he asks.

"What do you mean?"

"With your mom."

Tori stiffens. She can't believe he has the nerve to bring that up. But then he probably thinks an FBI badge gives him permission to be nosy. "That's not something I care to discuss with you."

He leans a little closer. "Listen, I called the police about your missing vehicle yesterday."

"You did?" This gets her attention. "What did you find out?"

"They haven't found your van, but there's been a string of missing minivans lately. They suspect they're being used to smuggle stolen goods."

Tori clutches her chest. "Poor Mable. That's terrible."

"I'll let you know if I hear anything more. I'm really sorry."

With distress, she reaches for her water again. What kind of person steals a minivan and abuses it like that? She hears a flapping noise, and when she turns, discovers Miss Fancy Pants barking and galloping around the corner toward her.

"There you are," Tori says with a laugh. She puts her glass down and pets the little dog, whose tail is wagging enthusiastically. "I'm so glad you're here, sweetie. You're just in time to cheer me up."

"She was outside doing her business," Liam tells her. "She's been using the back door again."

"Is that so?" Tori scratches behind the dog's ears. "What a good girl."

"Yes, I'm happy to report there hasn't been a single piss puddle since you were here Wednesday."

"That's great news."

He nods and sips his iced tea. "I'm hoping we've reached a turning point."

Miss Fancy Pants jumps up and sits beside her on the couch.

"You really should get her coat trimmed," she tells him, petting the dog. "It's too overgrown. I'm sure it's bothering her."

"You're right. I'll take care of it."

His gaze lingers on her again, and there's something about it that makes her feel self-conscious. She continues petting the dog, who's settled in and relaxed.

Tori wishes she could relax. Every time she meets Liam's eyes, her stomach flutters.

She needs to remember what he did to her, and all the reasons she dislikes him.

"So, do you have any plans this weekend?" she asks, figuring it's time to let him know there's a man in her life, and that he needs to stop looking at her like she's a dish of ice cream. Though he reminds her of the chocolate sauce. It's those brown eyes and that sensual mouth. All his male sexual energy. It's too much. It's confusing her.

He glances away. "I do, actually."

"You do?"

He nods. "How about you?"

Tori is surprised. "Who do you have plans with?" She figures he'll tell her it's his family or one of the guys from work.

"A blind date I was set up on."

"You were set up on a blind date?" She takes this in. Blind dates are notoriously bad, and for some reason she's relieved. "Good luck with that."

"We've already met." He tells her how they went for a run together recently and how he's taking her to a baseball game tomorrow. "Her name's Shelby. She seems nice."

"Is that so?" Tori tries to regroup and flicks her hair back. She added extra gold highlights recently. It figures this Shelby would be athletic and into sports. Not that she cares. "Well, I have plans this weekend too. I'm headed to the Seattle Arts Festival with the man in my life."

Liam studies her, his expression unreadable. "I didn't know you were involved with someone."

"I am. We've just started seeing each other." She nods to herself. It's not exactly a lie, more like a version of the truth. "I've had a crush on him for a while."

He grows quiet.

She smooths out an imaginary wrinkle on her pants. "You've met him, actually."

"I have?"

"It's Dr. Adrian."

"Who?"

"You know. Dr. Grant." She lets that sink in. *Yes, that's right. I'm dating a doctor. A wonderful veterinarian.* "Adrian is his first name," she informs him.

Except Liam still seems confused.

She sighs with irritation. "From the animal hospital. Remember? He's the vet who saw Miss Fancy Pants when you brought her in."

"I know who you're talking about. I just don't believe it."

"What's not to believe? I just told you we're involved."

"No, you're not."

"Yes, we are."

He grins.

"What's so funny?"

"Nothing. Except he's gay."

"*What?*" Tori's taken aback. "No, he isn't. That's absurd."

Liam chuckles and seems to relax. "I'm sure he's a good guy, and a great vet, but there's no way you two are involved."

"You don't know what you're talking about. He's not gay. That's silly."

He gives her a long, considering look. "Have you slept with him?"

She gawks. "That's none of your business! I can't believe you have the nerve to even ask me that." And that's when it comes to her. "I know what this is. You're doing it again. I can't believe it."

"Doing what?"

"You're trying to ruin my happiness just like you did in high school."

Liam appears stunned. He sits up straight and focuses on her with intensity. "Listen to me, Tori. That's *not* true. It wasn't then, and it isn't now."

"Oh, really? Then why would you make up something like that about Dr. Adrian?" She pets Miss Fancy Pants, who's following their exchange with interest. If it wasn't for this dog, she'd leave right now.

He grows quiet and seems at a loss for words. He leans back again. "All right, fine. Tell me more about Dr. Adrian. How long have you two been seeing each other?"

She wonders if she should even answer. "It's our first date on Saturday," she admits.

"And how did this date come about?"

"What do you mean?"

"Did he ask you out or what?"

"Yes, he asked me out. He asked me to the Arts Festival. It happened in the break room at work."

"And it's just you and him going together? No one else?"

She stares at him. "What is this, an FBI interrogation? Am I under arrest?" She turns her head away. "I don't have to answer your questions."

"Don't be silly. I'm not interrogating you."

"It sure feels like it. I don't know why you even care."

Liam runs a hand through his short hair and seems frustrated. "Just tell me who's going on the date with you besides him. Is it someone else from the vet's office?"

She sniffs. "If you must know, it's his sister."

There's the hint of a smile on his face, but he doesn't say anything more, just picks up his glass of iced tea.

Tori glances at her watch with irritation. "Our time is nearly over. I sure hope you got your money's worth today."

"Come on. Don't be like that. I just don't want to see you get hurt."

"Oh, that's rich coming from *you*, of all people."

"You should be with a man who'll appreciate you."

She pets the dog again and gets up. "I'm leaving now. Next time we schedule this, let's do it so I have some alone time with Miss Fancy Pants. I believe she's ready for that."

Liam nods. "At least let me walk you to your car."

"That won't be necessary."

To her annoyance, he walks her out anyway. She goes ahead of him, but not too far because she doesn't want Miss Fancy Pants to feel ignored.

Before leaving, she bends down and tells the dog she's looking forward to seeing her again. Miss Fancy Pants wags her tail.

She pointedly ignores Liam, though she can feel those brown eyes on her. He's got a lot of nerve acting like he cares about her. She can't believe he'd stoop so low as to make up stuff about Dr. Adrian.

It isn't until she's in the car driving away that she realizes she forgot to teach him the Heimlich maneuver. She'll have to show him next time. A part of her wishes she didn't have to see him again. She doesn't like this weird attraction she seems to have for him. But Miss Fancy Pants needs her help.

"It's okay," she tells herself. "Everything will be fine once Dr. Adrian and I fall in love with each other."

CHAPTER EIGHT

"I CAN'T BELIEVE IT." His sister, Elena, sounds incredulous over the phone. "You hired Tori Church as your dog sitter? Of all people, you couldn't find someone better than that?"

"Fancy likes her." Liam glances down at the little shih tzu, who's playing with a new dog toy he got her recently.

"I hope you haven't left that woman alone in your house."

"Stop it, Elena."

"You know what that whole Church family is like. Nothing but trouble. Don't tell me you've forgotten what happened in high school?"

He takes a drink from his coffee. It's Saturday morning, and he's been up since six. He worked out at the gym, then went to the gun range. He has to pass quarterly proficiency tests for work and goes regularly.

"I haven't forgotten anything," he says. "You're not the one dealing with dog piss everywhere. Fancy hasn't peed inside the house even once since Tori started coming here."

Elena snorts. "It's probably a coincidence."

"I doubt it. She seems very knowledgeable about animals."

"So what?" But then she goes quiet. "Please tell me she isn't taking advantage of you in your current state."

"What do you mean?"

"Of being heartbroken."

"I'm not heartbroken."

"I don't trust her. She's weird. Is she still single? I'll bet she's putting the moves on you."

Liam laughs. He only wishes Tori would put some moves on him. "You have no idea what you're talking about. She wants nothing to do with me. Besides, I'm sort of seeing someone."

"You are?"

He tells her all about the blind date, how he's taking her to a baseball game that afternoon.

"You don't think it's too soon after Rachel?"

"She's been gone almost two months."

"That's not very long. You don't want to rush into some kind of rebound situation."

Liam shakes his head. He never told his sister he knew Rachel was cheating, how he was relieved when she finally left. "I'm fine. Believe me, I'm ready to meet someone, or at least have some fun. This is only a second date."

"I have to admit, you work a lot. You're just like Dad. All the men in our family are workaholics."

"The job demands it at times."

"I suppose it's a good thing you're moving on," she muses. He can hear the wheels in her head turning. "Whatever you do, don't get involved with Tori Church."

Liam looks up at the ceiling in amazement. "I told you I'm seeing a woman named Shelby."

"I know, but didn't you ask Tori to homecoming? Isn't that how the whole mess started?"

"It was a mistake."

"Exactly. I don't want to see you make the same mistake twice."

When they finally hang up, he's relieved to get her off the phone. Sometimes Elena takes her big sister act too far.

He sits and reads through his text messages. There are a couple from work, but nothing that requires his immediate attention. He requested a surveillance team be placed on Walter Yates, and it was approved yesterday.

He opens the text Tori sent him last night. It's the phone number of a good dog groomer. He was surprised when he saw it. She was obviously angry when she left, but apparently her anger wasn't getting in the way of her assistance with Miss Fancy Pants.

He lingers over the message. She uses a lot of exclamation marks and emojis. He likes it. It would never occur to him to send such a colorful text.

But then he closes the message and sighs to himself. Elena is right. The last thing he wants to do is make the same mistake twice.

THE PLAN IS for Shelby to come over before the game. Liam offered to pick her up, but since she was having coffee with a friend in north Seattle, she told him she'd meet him at his place. She texted once she was on her way over, and he noticed there were no exclamation marks or emojis. Nothing colorful at all.

"Hi." She smiles when he opens the door. "What a nice neighborhood. I really like it."

"Thank you."

His neighborhood is clean and well-kept. Most of his neighbors are professionals like him—not that he knows any of them. They occasionally wave at each other in passing, but it's usually so quiet outside, you can hear a pin drop.

Sometimes he wonders if he made a mistake moving someplace so bland and lifeless. There are no kids or old people. Each house on his street looks the same as the next one.

"Come on in," he says, motioning Shelby inside. "I'd give you a tour, but there isn't much to see right now."

She smiles. "You don't have to impress me. Don't you know that I'm already impressed?"

"You are?" He glances over his shoulder at her.

"An FBI agent who used to play baseball?" She sighs theatrically. "That's too much for a girl to resist."

Liam laughs, his face growing warm at the compliment. "I'm not sure how to respond."

"And now you're taking me to a game. Do you know my ex-husband never once agreed to come to a baseball game with me?"

"I'm sorry to hear that."

She waves it away. "It's all water under the bridge." Her eyes widen as they enter the living room. "What happened to your couch?"

He glances over at the fiasco. "It's a long story."

"It looks like it was mauled by wolves."

"You're not far off."

There's a barking sound from the hall, and Shelby turns toward it. "I didn't know you had a dog."

"Yes, I do sort of have a dog."

"Sort of?"

Miss Fancy Pants appears at the end of the hallway. She trots out, then stops when she sees Shelby.

"What a cutie." Shelby smiles and moves toward the little dog. "Is she friendly?" When Shelby tries to move closer, she's greeted by a low rumbling. "She's growling at me."

Liam walks over. "Fancy, that's enough. Behave."

The dog stops growling but doesn't seem pleased either. Her dark eyes remain on Shelby.

"I guess she's not friendly." Shelby seems baffled. "Most dogs like me."

"Trust me, it's not you. It's her." He explains how Miss Fancy Pants was Rachel's dog and how she left Fancy behind when she ran off to Buenos Aires.

"Why didn't she take the dog with her?"

"I don't know." He figures Dr. Adrenaline Junkie didn't want a dog cramping his style. "Rachel claims she's going to send for her."

Shelby shakes her head. "Dogs are a big responsibility. A lot of work too. That's the reason I never got one."

He nods. It's the same reason he never got one.

They both look down at Miss Fancy Pants, who appears to eye them with disdain.

Liam can't help smiling. The furball doesn't put up with much.

They head out to his truck, and he watches Shelby walk in front of him. He can't resist checking her out. Her dark hair is pulled back in a ponytail. She's wearing a team jersey with khaki shorts, and her long legs are tan and shapely.

She's an attractive woman. And they seem to have a lot in common. He should be all in, except he can't stop picturing Tori's hips sway. The way her ass looked in those jeans she wore yesterday. The way she shines so bright it warms everyone around her, including him.

On the way to the game, they talk about some of their all-time favorite players. Shelby impresses him with her knowledge of baseball. She's easygoing and fun to be around.

When they get to the stadium, he leads her to their seats on the third baseline.

"Wow, these are great." She looks at out the field. "Maybe we'll catch a foul ball."

He grins. "It's been known to happen."

The floor is sticky as usual, and the crowded stadium smells like a combination of popcorn, beer, and hot dogs. If he could bottle that scent and use it as air freshener, he would.

Once the game starts, Liam's having a good time. They're both eating a couple of dogs, commenting to each other about plays. He watches as Shelby licks mustard off her fingers.

"Come on," she shouts during the sixth inning when the umpire calls a strike on an inside pitch.

He has to admit he's never been with a woman like this. They seem perfectly matched. Most girlfriends he'd ever taken to a baseball game were bored and wanted to leave by the fifth inning.

After Seattle wins and Shelby is done cheering with excitement, he tells her he has a surprise.

"What kind of surprise?"

"How would you like to meet Nelson Coby?"

Her jaw drops. "Are you kidding? I'd love to. Do you know him?"

"He's a friend of mine. We played ball together in college."

Shelby seems dazzled. "I didn't know that!"

Nelson was the starting pitcher for the Seattle team tonight. They only played together for a year in Portland, but they'd hit it off and remained friends.

"So where are we headed?" she asks once they're in his truck.

"The Paradise. It's a bar downtown where a lot of the players go after a game. I told Nelson we'd meet him there."

She nods. "I think I've heard of it. This is so exciting! I can't believe I'm going to meet him."

Liam chuckles. "He's a good guy. You'll like him."

They drive over to Pioneer Square. He finds street parking, and the two of them walk up toward the bar. It's after ten on a Saturday night. The area is filled with people out club hopping, and live rock music drifts out from some of the venues.

The Paradise is a two-story hole-in-the-wall, but when they arrive, people are lined up outside the door.

"What do we do?" Shelby asks. "How will we get in?"

"It's all right. Follow me."

He leads her to the front of the line and tells the bouncer he's on the list for the second floor. The guy asks for his name and then scans his meaty finger down an iPad. Finally he nods. "Can I see some ID?"

Liam shows him his driver's license.

The bouncer opens the chain blocking the way upstairs. "Go right ahead, Mr. Castillo."

Meanwhile, Shelby is taking it all in, looking around with excitement. "So the team has the second floor to themselves?" she asks as they climb the stairs.

"Yeah, typically. It's easier for the players to relax after a game when they don't have to worry about fans."

Once upstairs, he sees the familiar long bar. Tables and chairs are filled, along with the pool tables in back. He's been here a number of times, and it's always crowded. They make their way deeper into the room. Since the team won tonight, spirits are high and everyone's enjoying themselves. A Luke Bryan song plays on the jukebox.

He looks around for Nelson and finds him sitting at a table talking with a few people.

"Liam," Nelson says when they walk over. He stands and they give each other a quick hug. "Man, it's good to see you."

"You too. It's been a while."

"It has. Have a seat." He gestures to the table, and the people who were there moments ago leave.

A server comes by, and Nelson orders beer and nachos for everyone. Once she leaves, his gaze slides over to Shelby. "And who do we have here?"

"This is a friend of mine." Liam introduces them.

Shelby's eyes are shining bright. "Hi, Mr. Coby," she gushes, putting her hand out. "It's great to meet you. You're one of my favorite pitchers."

Nelson chuckles and shakes her hand. "That's nice to hear. You can call me Nelson."

"Great game," she says. "Your fastball was really on tonight."

"Yeah, thanks. It felt good."

Shelby leans toward him, her expression coy. "I hope this is okay, but do you think I could ask a small favor?"

"And what might that be?"

"Could I get a selfie with the two of us?"

Liam nearly interjects. The second floor at The Paradise is a place for the players to relax and not be "on" for their fans. He thought he'd explained it, but maybe not well enough.

Luckily Nelson doesn't seem bothered in the least. "Sure," he says. "No problem."

They scoot their chairs closer, and Shelby gets her phone out. She has a thrilled expression on her face as she takes a couple photos.

"Could I get a kiss on the cheek too?" she asks with a coy smile.

Nelson's brows go up, and he flashes Liam a questioning look.

He shrugs that it's fine.

"Lean closer," Nelson tells her, then kisses her right cheek as Shelby giggles and takes more photos.

"Thank you so much," she says afterward as they pull apart. She studies her phone with a wide grin. "No one at work is going to believe me when I show them these."

"How do they look?" Nelson asks. "Can I see?"

Shelby holds up her phone as the server brings their pitcher of beer along with three glasses.

"Very nice," Nelson says in a satisfied tone. Liam remembers that tone from when he caught for him in college. As an athlete, his friend was an artist, but he had an ego too. Being Nelson's catcher required kicking his ass occasionally. "How about you send me one of those," Nelson tells Shelby. "I'll put it on my fan page."

She gives him a flirtatious smile. "I don't have your number."

Nelson takes the phone from her hand. "You don't mind, do you, Liam?"

He shrugs. "Not at all." Another server brings a large plate of nachos, and he helps himself to the food.

Shelby looks like she's died and gone to heaven, and he can't help chuckling. Nelson was always great with his fans—especially the female ones.

After they get the selfie situation sorted out, the three of them talk some more about the game. Shelby gushes over how many strikeouts he had. "Twelve tonight. That's incredible. You were so hot."

"Sure, but this guy here is the *real* badass," Nelson says, shifting gears and pointing at Liam. "Catching criminals and putting them behind bars. That's no joke."

"I know." Shelby nods. She smiles at Liam, but her gaze fixates mostly on Nelson. "It's super impressive."

Liam pours himself some beer. He should probably be insulted that he's taking a back seat on his own date, but he's not. Shelby seems happy, and it's obvious, for her, meeting the starting pitcher is like meeting a rock star.

There's a buzz in his pocket, and he reaches for his phone. His first thought is it's someone from his squad contacting him about the surveillance on Yates, so he's surprised to see Tori's name.

His forehead creases with concern. It's late, and she'd never call him socially, so something must be wrong. "Tori?"

She's babbling in his ear and sounds upset.

"Are you okay?" Unfortunately, he can't hear a word she's saying. He covers his left ear, but the bar is too loud. "Hang on a second."

He turns toward Nelson and a giggling Shelby, who have discovered a mutual love of paintball. "Sorry, I need to take this," he tells them, getting up from his chair. "I'll be back."

They nod as he walks off to try to find a quiet corner. The whole place is noisy. Finally he locks himself in the bathroom.

"Okay, talk to me. Are you all right?"

"You're still on your date, aren't you? I don't know why I'm calling you." She babbles more about how she didn't know what else to do and then makes a sound like a hiccup.

"Tell me what's going on."

Her breath shakes as she quietly says, "They found Mable."

It takes him a moment to remember who that is. "Your minivan?"

"Yes, of course! Who else? The police just called me."

Liam nods. "Tell me exactly what they said."

"They said...." Her voice quivers. "They found her abandoned out near the docks in Seattle. And that she's been... damaged."

"Where is she now?" Liam almost corrects himself to say "it" but decides not to.

"At the police impound lot. They had to tow her there. They said she was undrivable."

Her breath shakes again, and it sounds like she's crying. He's never liked to hear a woman cry, but coming from Tori, it's terrible. "What can I do to help? Tell me."

"Can you take me there? The police said the lot is open twenty-four hours." She sniffs and then hiccups again. "I know it's a lot to ask, and you obviously dislike me, but I don't have a car."

"Where are you now?"

"At home."

"I'm in Pioneer Square. Text me your address."

"But what about your date?" She sounds upset. "I shouldn't have called you. I don't know what I was thinking."

"The date's almost over." Not exactly a lie, but not exactly the truth either. He can't say no to her though. "I'll take you there tonight."

"Really?"

"I'll pick you up, and we'll go to the impound lot together. Okay?"

"Okay." Her voice softens. "Thanks."

After they hang up, he exits the bathroom, then stops and looks over to where Shelby and Nelson are sitting. She's laughing at something he said. It occurs to him that this is kind of an awkward situation.

"Sorry about that," he says, arriving back at the table. "Something's come up." He turns to Shelby. "It looks like we have to leave."

Her expression changes, and he can see she's disappointed. "Already? That's a shame. We're having such a good time."

He doesn't know what else to say. He feels bad, but there's nothing to be done about it.

"If she wants to stay longer, I can take her home," Nelson interjects.

Liam's brows rise. "You don't mind?"

"Not at all." He turns to Shelby. "If that's all right with you."

Her face lights up, and it's obvious she doesn't mind one bit. "That would be great."

"Her car's at my house," Liam points out.

"Oh, that's right," she says. "I forgot about that."

Nelson shrugs. "Then I'll drive her to your house. It's no problem."

Liam's a little surprised that his friend is so accommodating, but the two of them seem to be enjoying themselves. At least he won't have to feel guilty about ending his date early. "Okay," he says. "I appreciate it."

"No worries," she says with a smile. "I understand. When duty calls, you have to answer."

Obviously they think he's been called away for work. Liam sees no reason to enlighten them. "Thanks. I'll text you both later."

IT TURNS out Tori doesn't live that far from where he does, though her neighborhood couldn't be more different. All the homes are small and older, many of them in need of repair. Tori's home is small and older too, but it appears well cared for. The lawn is mowed. Flowers out front. Various clay pots with more plants and flowers by the front door.

As soon as he rings the bell, he hears what sounds like a madhouse of dogs inside. When she opens the door, the sound only increases. "Quiet now," Tori says to them, and surprisingly, the dogs obey.

Right away, he's glad he came. Her face tells him everything he needs to know. Tori's usual brightness has gone dim. Her eyes are red, her cheeks pink. It's like a foul ball to the gut seeing her this way.

"Hi," she says. "Come on in."

He walks past the threshold and three dogs swarm around him, sniffing at his clothes and fingers, clamoring against each other, tails wagging.

"These are my boys," Tori says, then gives their names like an introduction, though he can't hear any of it. He's still trying to get over the fact that she has three dogs when he can barely manage one.

She watches, seeming bemused, as he tries to figure out how to deal with them. "You can pet them. They're very friendly."

"I see that. I just don't know where to start."

"Okay, boys, that's enough." She pulls the dogs back. "Let's not overwhelm Liam."

His eyes go to her face, and an odd sense of elation rushes through him. It's hearing his name. He's never heard her say it in a context that wasn't angry.

The dogs all move off as she herds them away like cattle.

"You can have a seat," she says over her shoulder. "I need to put out some snacks for them before we leave."

He glances around her house. There's a worn-out looking couch with a lamp on each end. A couple of chairs. Shelves against the wall packed with books and picture frames. A television off to one side.

The room smells like apples, not tangerines. It's all clean and tidy.

He goes over to the couch, where a blond tabby cat eyes him warily.

"Hello," he says.

Unlike the dogs, the cat just stares at him.

He sits and discovers the couch is surprisingly comfortable. Tori's in the kitchen speaking in a lilting voice to her dogs. He can hear her telling them all to be patient. Fashion magazines are spread out on her coffee table, along with a few bottles of nail polish, most of them various shades of pink and red. There are knitting needles and green yarn. She appears to be knitting a small sweater.

He takes it all in with a rush of excitement. He wants to grin from ear to ear. *I'm in Tori Church's house.* The sixteen-year-old kid inside of him is thrilled.

The cat gets up and moves closer to him for an inspection. He puts his hand out to be sniffed.

"I see you've met Lita," Tori says, coming back into the room. She glances around. "My other cat, Joan, should be here somewhere too."

"You have *another* cat?" he asks, amazed, petting the one beside him. "And three dogs?"

"You should see your face right now."

He looks up at her. "Why?"

She only shakes her head. "I think Lita likes you. She's not normally that friendly with strangers."

He glances down at the cat who's draped herself across his thighs like she's claiming ownership.

Tori watches the two of them, then sighs. There's a bleak sound to it.

It gets his attention. "Are you all right?"

"No." She shakes her head. "I'm dreading this, but we should get it over with."

Liam gently pushes the cat off his lap. Tori grabs her large purse and follows him out to his truck. He's been to the police impound lot for work a few times and knows the way.

She doesn't say much on the drive there, and he's not sure what to say either. He knows some people are emotionally attached to their cars, and clearly Tori is one of them.

"Was the detective who called you today the same one we met when your vehicle was stolen?"

"I think so."

"Can you remember anything else he said? Did he say whether they have a suspect?"

She shakes her head. "I can't remember. I don't think so."

He figures he'll call the detective himself. "At least they found her," he offers.

"That's true."

But then she goes quiet again. Liam wishes he knew the right words to make her feel better. He knows from experience how sometimes there are no right words, that it's just good not being alone.

He glances over again. If things were different between them, he'd reach for her hand. He's tempted to do it anyway but worries it might be misconstrued.

Or it might be construed exactly right.

To be honest, he's not sure which is worse.

CHAPTER NINE

TORI DOESN'T KNOW what crazy person inside her decided to call Liam. She must have lost her mind. When that detective told her about Mable, she burst out crying. Right afterward, she searched for his number on her phone.

She glances over. His hands are firm on the steering wheel. Apparently he already knows the way to the impound lot.

Calling him was the right thing. She knew it the moment she saw him standing on her front porch. Despite everything, her instincts tell her he's the kind of man you want around if there's trouble.

And then there was his expression when he petted Lita. Something about it reminded her of the kid he was in high school, but not in a bad way. Before he ruined that night for her, back when she still thought he was cute.

Eventually he pulls into a parking space in front of a chain-link fence. "We're here," he says, turning the engine off. There are bright street lights, and she can see the lot in front of them is filled with cars. His voice is low when he asks, "Are you ready to go inside?"

"Thanks for bringing me."

"It's okay."

"And for not acting like I'm a freak. Even though you probably think I am."

"I don't think that."

She glances out the window. "I know most people aren't like me. They don't give their car a name and treat it like it's a member of the family."

"Some do."

"I'll bet you don't."

He smiles at little. "No, but sometimes I wish I was that sort of person."

"Really?"

He nods. He looks like he wants to say more but doesn't.

They regard each other in the truck's quiet, his scent tickling her nostrils. Clean and male.

"We should go inside," she whispers, though she doesn't move.

He doesn't move either.

Their eyes meet. They might not like each other, but she senses the pull of him. There's something in the air between them, something primal. It's giving her a funny feeling inside.

Finally, she turns and reaches for the door handle. It doesn't open until Liam clicks a button, unlocking it.

Once outside in the night air, she takes a cleansing breath. *I'm just emotional right now, that's all.*

They head over to the police building, which is small and well-lit.

She follows Liam, who thankfully seems to know where to go and what to do.

Once they're inside, he assumes control and speaks with the officer at the front desk as she hangs back. She was raised to distrust cops, and it makes her awkward around them.

Tori shows her ID and has to fill out some paperwork. The officer tells them her minivan might have been used in a crime. She can see Mable, but isn't allowed to retrieve any personal belongings, and they won't be releasing the vehicle to her yet.

She nods, a sense of disbelief settling over her. A part of her still doesn't understand how this could have happened.

Meanwhile, Liam is asking more questions about the crime. Things she never would have thought of. Smart things. Questions about how they found Mable and whether there were any location hits on something called ALPRs, which she now remembers him explaining. He confirms the name of the detective in charge of the case and obviously plans to call him.

She watches his handsome profile as he speaks. Whoever thought she'd be glad to have Liam by her side?

Finally, the officer leads them out to the impound yard.

She's nervous. She knows Mable is just a minivan, but that's not how it feels. It feels more like Mable is a helpful friend, always taking her where she needs to go. She's been a part of Tori's life for the past eight years.

"Here we are," the officer says.

But Tori has already stopped walking. She spotted her van ten feet away. That light metallic blue color, her familiar stickers on the back—"Animals on board" and "Happy Pet Nanny."

It's Mable.

The two men watch as she moves closer, walking around the outside in disbelief. The front end is bashed up, and there are dents all over the side. The panel door is wide open, and when Tori sees the interior, she sucks her breath in with horror.

It's a blackened hole.

Someone torched the inside of Mable.

She bursts into tears. She can't help it. Just stands there with her face in her hands sobbing.

Liam is beside her, hugging her shoulder. "It's going to be okay. We'll fix it."

"No, we won't." She sobs some more. "This is too much. Just look at her."

She's surrounded as he pulls her in close. If she wasn't so upset, she'd probably notice how good his muscular body felt against hers, how his smell is even better with her nose pressed into his shoulder.

She tries to gain some control over herself. "There's nothing more to be done," she chokes out. Pulling away, she walks closer to her minivan and lays her hand on Mable's metal exterior. "Goodbye," she whispers.

Liam is quiet behind her.

When she turns around, her big purse hits his arm as she tries to find a tissue. "We can go now."

The three of them head back to the police building. It isn't until they're inside that she realizes Liam was holding her hand. She only notices it when he lets go and she loses his warmth.

The officer says they'll call and let her know when she can retrieve her van. He mentions a couple of local towing companies, but Tori doesn't pay any attention.

It's a relief when they're finally back in his truck.

"Please just drive," she says. "Get me out of here."

He starts the engine, and soon they're headed away from that horrible place. Away from poor Mable. Her eyes sting with more tears as she hiccups.

Neither of them speaks. The only sound comes from the road noise and her hiccuping.

"I think if you hold your breath and count to ten, they'll go away," he says. "That's what I've always heard."

"Peanut butter," she croaks.

"What?" He glances at her.

She wipes her wet cheek with her palm. "A spoonful of peanut butter is the best hiccup cure."

"Really? I didn't know that."

"I always get them when I cry, so I've tried every—" She hiccups again. "—thing. When we were kids, Road used to jump out of the closet in my room trying to scare them out of me."

"Did it work?"

"No." She smiles, remembering the way her brother used to fly out, yelling, "Boo!"

Liam chuckles. "I used to do that to Elena, though it wasn't to cure her hiccups. It was mostly for fun."

Tori tries to imagine Liam jumping out of a closet. "What did she do?"

"Scream and chase after me. I was too fast for her though. Our whole family did it."

She looks over at him. "Did what?"

"Jumped out of closets or any hiding place."

"You're kidding me."

"I'm not. We enjoy startling each other."

"Seriously?" She smiles. "And I thought I was weird. I guess you're even weirder."

He chuckles. "I've never thought of it as weird, but I suppose it sort of is. Your family didn't do that?"

"No." Tori thinks back to how she grew up. Her mom and her loser boyfriends were always throwing parties of one kind or another. It could be a rough crowd with everybody drinking. If you jumped out of a closet, you'd probably get yourself shot. But then she remembers something else. "Isn't your dad in the FBI too?"

"Yes, he is. So was my grandfather."

"Really? Three generations?"

He nods. "In fact, my grandfather was one of the first Latino agents."

"Wow, so all these law enforcement guys packing a gun raised you. How did that work with all of you jumping out of hiding places?"

Liam laughs out loud, his white teeth flashing at her. "Happily, it was okay. It's not like we don't know each other. Also, none of us wear a sidearm at home."

And it's not like you're all drunks either. "Liam isn't a Hispanic name," she points out.

"No, my mom's family is Irish."

"And Elena's your only sibling?"

"Yes, she's a year older than me. You remember her from high school, don't you?"

Unfortunately, she does. Elena was a cheerleader, and after the milkshake thing happened, she made it a point to bad-mouth Tori every chance she got.

Liam takes the turn onto her street. Her house sits on a cul-de-sac. She's glad to see her little home again, glad to be back with her animals. Except her heart aches. If only Mable were here too.

He pulls into her driveway to let her out. Tori's still sad, but the conversation with him was a good distraction. Which must be why she says the next thing that comes out of her mouth. It must be the gratitude talking.

"Would you like to come inside?"

He seems surprised by the invitation, though she can tell he's trying to hide it. "Sure, I'd like that."

"Just for a quick lemonade," she clarifies. "Or maybe a beer. I think there's still some in the fridge."

"Sounds good."

"It's only as a thank-you for helping me. Nothing more."

His lips twitch.

"And you can't stay long. I have my date with Dr. Adrian tomorrow."

His lips do a gymnastics floor routine.

They get out of the truck. As soon as she enters the front door, her dogs scramble to come greet her.

"Hi, boys," she coos at them, petting each one. "You guys didn't have to get up for me."

Liam is right behind her, and this time he reaches down to pet them too. Tori smiles, watching him from the corner of her eye.

"Let me see what I have in the fridge," she says. The dogs all follow her into the kitchen, hoping for a second treat. Liam follows too. The only thing he's getting from her is a refreshing beverage.

"How long have you lived here?" he asks, leaning against the counter. The dogs have gathered around him with curiosity.

"About twelve years. I inherited the house from my uncle Lance." She opens the refrigerator. "There's beer, lemonade, almond milk, or water. I have vodka in the freezer too."

"I'll take a glass of lemonade."

She glances over at him. "You can have a beer if you want. I don't mind."

He shakes his head. "It's late, and I'm driving."

She pours them each a glass of lemonade. The beer is for visitors. She rarely drinks the stuff. Something stronger sounds tempting, especially after seeing Mable, but she wants to keep her wits about her when she's with Liam. He has a way of confusing her.

She hands him his glass, and they both head back into the living room. He takes a seat on the sofa, and she sits in one of the opposite chairs.

"Your hiccups are gone," he points out.

"They are. Sometimes they go away on their own."

He sips his lemonade. "This is good. Did you make it?"

"I did. I usually make it during the summer months."

"I taste spearmint."

"Yes, I grow it in my backyard. I like to add different flavors each time."

He takes another drink from the glass, then licks his bottom lip. It's plump and fuller than his top one. A peculiar desire to bite it comes over her.

She turns her head in a wash of guilt. *What's wrong with me?* It's like she's cheating on Dr. Adrian, and they haven't even started dating yet. She tries to remember what *his* bottom lip looks like.

"What are you thinking about?" he asks.

"What?"

"You look deep in thought. Is it about Mable?" He tells her how he's sorry the police didn't find her van sooner, how he could help her look for a new vehicle.

She nods, distracted by that sensual mouth. By his dark eyes and that black hair. She wishes he were ugly. Why did he have to be this hot? Her gaze drifts lower, remembering how it felt when he hugged her earlier, his body hard and solid.

"I'd be happy to help," he continues.

Thank God she didn't have anything stronger to drink. She tries to remember all the reasons she dislikes him. What he did to her at homecoming. The things he said to her at his house yesterday. She tries to think about Dr. Adrian too but can barely remember what his face looks like.

But then finally she *does* remember something. She leans forward and puts her glass on the table. "How was your date tonight?"

Liam's brows shoot up. He seems surprised at the change in subject. "It was good."

"What did you guys do again? You went to a baseball game?"

He tells her about the game and how they met a friend of his afterward. Some guy who's a pitcher for the Seattle team. "Are you into baseball?" he asks.

"No, I'm not into sports."

He doesn't seem surprised.

"My brother is though, and so is my cousin Brody. They're both huge baseball fans."

"Road is into baseball?"

"I like the uniforms." She ponders it. "They're pretty cute, actually. Does that count?"

Liam stares at her and doesn't seem to know what to say.

She leans forward in her chair. "So, I want to hear more about your date. Are you going to see her again?"

"Maybe." He seems to think it over. "She's nice, and we seem well matched."

A dark emotion twists in her. "Well matched how?"

He shrugs. "We like all the same things."

"Did you and Rachel like all the same things too?" She knows she's being overly nosy but suddenly finds herself intensely curious about these women.

He stares into his drink. "Let's not talk about that."

She's planning to continue her nosy questions anyway but hears Bon Jovi's "Livin' on a Prayer" coming from inside her purse. "That's my phone. I better get it."

She gets up and goes to where she left her purse by the front door. It takes her a moment to dig it out. There's a pocket inside, but she always forgets to use it.

The ringtone is halfway through the song's chorus, so she knows it'll go to voicemail soon.

But then she sees who's calling. "Oh, no. Not again."

"What's wrong?" Liam asks from the couch. He puts his glass down. "Who is it?"

Tori only shakes her head. This is the last thing she needs right now.

LIAM WATCHES as Tori answers the phone, her voice changing to one of false cheerfulness.

"Hi! What can I do for you, Donna?" Tori pastes a fake smile on her face. "I'm so sorry. I know you have to be up early in the morning." She pauses. "I understand. I'll head over right now." She nods and listens. "Thank you. I appreciate you not calling them too."

Tori puts her phone back inside her purse. "Shit."

"What's wrong?" From what he's observed, she rarely uses swear words.

"Nothing."

Her body language says otherwise. Where moments ago she had some of her usual bright energy, it's now gone dim.

"I have to go deal with this," she mutters. She looks directly at him. "You have to leave now."

"Okay." Though he doesn't move. "Can you tell me what's happening?"

She shakes her head and looks to the side. "It's my mom."

He's confused. "That was your mom?"

"No, that was her neighbor." There's a hard edge to her voice. "She called to tell me my mom is in her front yard making a spectacle of herself again."

"What does that mean?"

"She's drunk."

"I see."

Their eyes meet, and there's honesty in hers. He can see she's carrying a burden, a heavy one.

But then it all changes as a mask slides into place. "Listen, thanks for everything tonight." There's a false lilt to her voice. "I really appreciate it."

"Let me take you to your mom's. I can help."

"Oh, that's not necessary." She tucks her hair behind her ear and gives him a fake smile, one that's almost convincing. He suspects she's had years to perfect it. "It's really no big deal. She'll just sleep it off. Actually, it's nice that Donna calls me."

He watches her. This act probably fools most people, except he's not most people.

"Sorry to cut the evening short like this. I'll text you about pet sitting next week."

He stands. Obviously she's trying to get rid of him. "Let me at least drive you over to your mom's."

"No, thanks. I've got this under control." She's already at the front door, opening it for him. "Believe me, I deal with it all the time. It's really nothing."

"How will you get there without a car?"

"What?" This seems to give her pause. She looks out to her driveway like she expects a car to materialize. "Wow, I forgot."

"Come on," he says. "I'll give you a ride."

She appears to be thinking it over. He's practically holding his breath.

"All right, fine. You can drive me, but that's it."

He waits by the door for her as she puts the glasses in the kitchen and checks on her dogs one last time. He scrolls through the messages on his phone. It's not quite midnight. There are only two new texts—one from his sister asking how his date went, and one from Matt asking the same question. Apparently Shelby texted Amy while they were at the game and told her how much she liked him.

That should make him feel like a million bucks, but it doesn't. Instead, he feels guilty.

Tori comes out from the kitchen and walks toward him. Despite his guilt, he can't pull his eyes away. The jeans hug her hips while her sparkly T-shirt shows off every curve. Her blonde hair isn't pulled into its usual ponytail but flows down her shoulders and back.

If a person could personify sunshine, Tori Church is the closest thing to it he's ever seen.

There's a sweetness about her, and of course, she's sexy as hell too. He watches as she grabs that huge Mary Poppins bag of hers, then looks at him.

"What?"

He shakes his head. "Nothing. Are you ready to go?"

She calls a goodbye to her animals and they head out. Her neighborhood is surprisingly lively at this hour. He hears someone's music through a window, and there are people sitting on their front porch talking. She waves hello to one of her neighbors.

Once they're seated, he smells tangerines and wonders how long her scent will linger in his truck.

Hopefully a long time.

"Take a left turn out of my neighborhood," she tells him.

He follows her directions as they drive and tries to get her talking some more, but she's not having any of it. A quiet resolve seems to have settled over her.

Eventually they pass a trailer park, and Tori has him take the next right. It's a neighborhood a lot like hers with mostly small older homes, many of them in need of repair.

"It's that rambler there on the end of the street," she tells him as he drives slower.

He sees the house she's talking about. He can't tell the exact color, but it's some light shade with a single car garage. There are two vehicles parked in the driveway, and one more in front.

"It figures," Tori mutters.

"What?"

"Wayne's here."

He pulls his truck across the street since there's no other parking. There's a graveled area to the right, but he's not sure if that's the neighbor's. "Who's Wayne?"

"My mom's boyfriend." She stares out the window at the cars in the driveway. "That's his yellow Charger over there."

"What's wrong with him?"

She snorts. "Everything."

Liam studies the house and sees the car Tori's talking about. "I'm coming inside with you."

"No." She shakes her head. "I told you that's not necessary. I've dealt with this plenty."

He studies her face. Her skin is pale in the darkened cab, almost fragile, amplifying a shadow beneath her eyes. Despite her appearance, he suspects Tori is a lot tougher than she looks.

There's yelling outside and they both turn toward it.

A woman with bleached blonde hair is by the front door dressed in a tight leopard-print nightgown. She's holding something in her hand, swaying on her feet as she walks outside. She yells again, but Liam doesn't understand her.

"I have to go," Tori says, pushing on the truck door. "Can you open this thing?"

"I'm coming with you."

"*No.* I just told you."

"There's no reason for you to deal with this alone."

There's more yelling. This time it's a man's voice. Liam turns and sees some guy in his forties. He's tall and skinny, wearing jeans and a white T-shirt. Both his arms are covered in tattoos.

Tori watches the guy with irritation.

"Is that Wayne?"

She nods.

"I don't care what you say." He unsnaps the lock on his seat belt. "I'm coming."

"Fine." She huffs. "Whatever."

They get out of the truck and cross the street together. Liam glances around the neighborhood but doesn't see anyone else. He wonders which house belongs to Donna.

As they walk up the driveway, the guy yells again, "Goddammit, woman, I said get back in the house."

"Go fuck yourself, Wayne!"

Liam watches the two of them squabble. They're making quite a racket. It's a wonder none of the other neighbors have called the police, but then this is obviously a regular thing.

He doesn't have much experience with domestic disturbance since that's not FBI territory. Though he worked Violent Crime four years before transferring to White-Collar, so he's seen some crazy stuff. He scans the front of the house and wonders if anyone else is inside. He doubts he'll need it, but he's still glad for the snug weight of his sidearm.

It isn't until he and Tori are up on the lawn that Wayne suddenly notices them. "Tori?" he calls out. "That you?"

"Yes, Wayne, it's me."

"Who do you have there with you?"

They continue to walk closer. Liam keeps his eyes on Wayne, assessing the man. He's about six feet tall and wiry. He doesn't appear to be armed, though Liam would bet money the guy has done time somewhere.

"This is my friend Liam," she says.

Her mom turns around now, stumbling to maintain her balance. "Tori?" Despite wearing a nightgown, she's also in extremely high-heeled sandals. She's holding a tumbler of what looks like whiskey in her hand. "What's my baby girl doing here?"

"Visiting you."

"Isn't that... sweet." Her mom smiles, and it's obvious she's drunk. Liam tries not to look at her middle-aged body, which shows clearly through the nightgown's thin material. Her breasts are almost falling out. "And you brought a friend?" She smiles at him too, but then as he moves closer, her smile fades. Instead, her eyes grow wide as saucers. "Are you kidding me?"

"What is it?" Tori asks.

For a second, he wonders if her mom recognizes him from years ago. He certainly recognizes her. After the milkshake incident, the principal called their parents into the school to have a meeting. He'll never forget the way Tori's mom came strolling in there with a short miniskirt and high heels, her blonde hair piled on top of her head like a cross between a movie star and a stripper. She didn't look like anybody's mother he'd ever seen.

"You brought a fucking cop to my house?" her mom shrieks. "Have you lost your mind?"

Wayne's body stiffens, and his eyes flash over to Liam. "Calm down now, Lori. We don't know who that is."

"Liam's not a cop," Tori says.

But her mother shakes her head. She points at him, yelling, "You think I don't know a cop when I see one?"

"He's not a cop," Tori repeats. "Trust me."

"Then what the hell is he?"

Tori glances at Liam, and he thinks he detects the hint of a smile on her lips. "He's an FBI agent."

Lori's eyes pop out of her head. "That's even worse!"

Wayne's mouth drops open. His eyes pop out too. They're both gaping at Liam like he's going to arrest them any second.

"What the hell?" Wayne seems to have gone on high alert. His long arms flop around. "This makes no goddamn sense. You really a fed?"

Liam nods. "I am."

Lori and Wayne continue to gape. Wayne looks scared, while Lori looks like she's ready to grab a garden rake and chase him off her property. If this whole thing weren't so pitiful, it would be amusing.

"Mom, he's just a friend of mine," Tori tries to calm her down. "That's all."

"Since when do you have friends who are... in the FBI?"

"It's no big deal. He gave me a ride," she explains. "Someone stole Mable, remember?"

This seems to get Lori's attention off of him. Her expression changes. "Of course I remember, baby girl." She rubs her cheek, words slurring. "What a terrible thing."

"Let's go back inside the house." Tori's voice is measured. She reaches down and takes her mom's glass. "Here, I'll refresh that for you."

Her mom glares at Liam with comical suspicion but follows her daughter's lead. "It's a tragedy what happened to Mable. A real tragedy."

The four of them head inside with Liam walking in last.

He wonders how many years Tori's been dealing with this. It saddens him to even think about it.

CHAPTER TEN

TORI TAKES the glass of whiskey into the bathroom and pours it down the drain. She grabs a towel to wipe the puke off her sneakers.

At least after throwing up, her mom agreed to go to bed. Tori encouraged her to lie on her side, then tucked some pillows behind her back. Some nights were worse than others. Tonight her mom was mostly agreeable, though she was still muttering about Tori bringing the law here.

She heads out into the living room to find Wayne looking wide-eyed and nervous, sitting in the corner of the same faded couch she grew up with. Liam is there too, leaning against the wall with his arms crossed.

He looks narrow-eyed and formidable.

"Do you think you could at least stop her from drinking so much?" Tori says to Wayne with frustration. "What's gotten into her lately, anyway?"

He shrugs. "You know your mom. She does what she wants. I've been trying to help her." His voice sounds earnest, but Tori knows he's not helping at all. He reaches for the beer bottle on the side table and takes a swig as if he's made some kind of point.

There's something about him that worries her more than her mom's other boyfriends. She suspects he's not quite the harmless loser he pretends to be.

"This is the third time in a week she's been drunk like that."

Wayne shrugs. "I don't know why you're making such a fuss. Your mom likes to have a few drinks and relax. So what? That's not a crime." His eyes skitter over to Liam. Wayne seems on edge. It doesn't help that Liam's glaring at him like he wishes it *were* a crime.

"Donna called me again," Tori says. "One of these nights, she's going to call the police instead."

"That nosy bitch." Wayne sits up straight, clearly agitated, and reaches for his cigarettes. "She needs to mind her own damn business."

"Not when you guys are out there at midnight screaming at each other. You're lucky nobody else called them."

He takes one from the pack and lights it. "Hell, why are you blaming me? You saw it with your own eyes. I was trying to get Lori to come back inside."

"How about you stop her from drinking so much in the first place? Ever think of that?" It infuriates Tori. What does her mom see in this guy? For starters, he's too young. He's only in his early forties, while her mom is fifty-seven—though she lies and tells everyone she's younger.

Tori glances around the dingy house she grew up in and is embarrassed that Liam's here. It hasn't aged well. Not that it was ever much to look at. They've painted the walls a couple times, but most of the furniture is the same stuff from years ago. He probably already knew she grew up like this, but imagining it is one thing, whereas seeing it is another.

Her eyes land on a black lacquer box on the coffee table that wasn't there last time she was here. The top is inlaid with mother-of-pearl.

"What's that?" she asks, moving over to pick up the box. She opens it. It's empty except for a few pieces of lint.

Wayne smiles with pride. "I gave it to your mom for her birthday."

Tori has to admit she's surprised. It's classy and tasteful. She can't imagine Wayne picking out a gift like this. He seems more the type to buy margarita mix and stick a bow on it.

"Where did you get it?" she asks. The box looks expensive.

"I saw it at a pawnshop."

She closes the lid and puts it back on the table. "It's nice."

"Your mom deserves nice things, and I'm just the man to give them to her." He takes a drag from his cigarette. "I want to take care of her."

Over the years, Tori's heard a lot of men say they want to take care of her mom. Not one of them was ever telling the truth.

"Just stop her from drinking so much. That's the best thing you can do."

Wayne glances at Liam. "It's getting late. You and your, uh, FBI friend here probably want to get going."

Tori smiles to herself. She's enjoying how much Liam's freaking Wayne out. She sits on the couch arm. "Listen, I don't want to get another phone call at midnight, understand? And don't give Donna a hard time either. Be glad she hasn't called the cops on you two."

At that moment Liam sucks in his breath. He refolds his arms in front of his chest in a way that says he'd love to get the police involved.

Wayne shifts uncomfortably. He clears his throat, though it sounds more like a squeak.

Tori has to bite her cheek to keep from laughing. This is fun. Having Liam here is like having her own personal guard dog. She doesn't like upsetting her mom, but watching Wayne squirm is better than a carnival ride.

"I'll be checking in on my mom tomorrow night, and she better be sober," Tori says in a stern voice. She already knows that's an impossibility, but can't resist messing with Wayne.

He nods with enthusiasm, obviously willing to agree to anything at this point. "I'll make sure she doesn't touch a drop."

Tori glances over at the kitchen and is tempted to empty out all the liquor in the house, but it won't make any difference. Her mom will just buy more. She'll buy alcohol before food if it comes down to it, and Tori doesn't want that.

"I guess we'll go now," she says to Liam.

"Good idea." Wayne stubs his cigarette out and seems eager for them to leave. "I'll keep an eye on your mom, don't you worry."

She picks her purse up from where she put it on the chair. Right before they step outside the door, Liam stops. Tori looks at him questioningly. He doesn't say anything, just gives Wayne a long stony glare.

From over on the couch, Wayne's eyes widen. He blinks a few times and seems terrified.

By the time they're back in the truck, Tori is giggling out of control. She can't help herself. "That was incredible. You were amazing!"

"I couldn't resist."

"I thought he was going to cry," she says, still laughing.

He smiles, but she can tell there's something behind it.

"What is it?"

He shakes his head. "Your mom needs help. And that Wayne guy isn't the answer."

"You think I don't know that? She's needed help for a long time but refuses to get any."

He starts the engine. "I'm almost certain that guy has done time. What's his last name?"

"I don't know. Johnson or Jackson maybe?" Tori sighs with frustration. "My mom's boyfriends are all cut from the same cloth."

They head back toward her house with Liam following the route that brought them there. She can't stop reliving the last hour in her mind. That scared look on Wayne's face fills her with glee.

"I thought he was going to pee his pants when I told them you were in the FBI."

Liam chuckles. "I thought your mom was going to chase me off with a garden rake."

"You're lucky she didn't."

He raises a brow and glances at her. "So you were raised to distrust the law, huh?"

"What makes you say that?"

"I saw how you acted with the officer at the impound lot earlier." He seems to remember something. "And with the detectives we spoke with after Mable was stolen. You seemed uncomfortable."

"It's not that I distrust them, but I was raised that we take care of our own problems. We don't get the law involved." Something occurs to her. "I'll bet you were raised the exact opposite, huh?"

"Basically." He glances at her again. "But then my family is different from yours."

She can only imagine how different.

Despite the fun of messing with Wayne, she cringes at what Liam saw tonight. The darker parts of her life. Except for Blair, who'd been Tori's best friend long before she married Road, no one outside of her family knows what her mom is really like. In truth, even Blair and Road don't have the full picture, because she rarely calls them to help. She doesn't want to bring all those troubles into their happy marriage. She and Road have a younger sister, but Kiki—or Kathy, as she goes by now—is married and lives out of state. She wants nothing to do with their mom.

So Tori deals with it alone. Like always.

It isn't long before they're pulling up to her driveway. It's well past midnight. She thinks about her date with Dr. Adrian tomorrow. He hasn't texted her yet about what time they're going to the Arts Festival. She hopes he hasn't lost her number, or there hasn't been some kind of emergency.

Liam turns his engine off.

"It's too late to invite you inside," she says quickly.

"I know. I'm just walking you to your door."

They both get out of the truck. It's quiet out. Even the neighbors who usually party on Saturday have turned their music off.

Once they reach her porch, she turns and faces him. "Well, here we are. I appreciate everything you did for me tonight."

"I was glad to help." The corner of his mouth turns up. "Even if I was only there to muscle Wayne."

At the mention of muscles, her eyes travel to his shoulders and chest, which are, let's face it, pleasingly muscled. She imagines running her hands over them and quickly pushes the thought away before it leads to other thoughts.

Liam looks like he wants to say more, but there's a buzzing noise in his front pocket. He reaches inside for his phone. "Sorry, but I need to check this. I'm running a surveillance on someone."

"Really?" She leans forward, curious.

He stares at the text message. "Never mind. It's nothing."

But she saw the screen, and it wasn't nothing. It was a message from someone named Shelby. "That's from your date tonight, isn't it?"

He nods and puts his phone away.

"What does she want?"

"She wanted to tell me she had a great time and to call her."

"Are you going to?"

"I don't know. Is there a reason I shouldn't?"

Her breath catches at the way he's looking at her. Her eyes slide to his shoulders and chest again. Without warning, desire blazes through her like a wildfire. She tries to stamp it out. "If you like her," she says softly, "then you should call her."

"Can I ask you something?"

"Okay." Though she's nervous about what he's going to ask. She's not sure how strong she is at the moment and prays he doesn't want to come inside. He's standing close enough that his scent is messing with her head. She tries desperately to think of Dr. Adrian's scent, but unfortunately he smells like the antiseptic soap they use at the animal hospital.

"Why did you say no all those years ago?"

"What do you mean?"

"In high school, when I asked you to homecoming. Why did you say no?"

She blinks. It's not the question she was expecting. "I'm not sure." She licks her lips and thinks back to that time, to Liam, who seemed to come from a different planet than her.

"You didn't like me?" he asks.

"No."

"I see." He nods, though he seems disappointed.

"I mean, no, it's *not* that I didn't like you," she says hastily. She tries to put it into words. "I thought you were cute, but I was only fifteen. I'd never been asked out before, at least not from someone like you. I guess I panicked."

"Someone like me?"

"So... normal."

He takes in her words. "You thought I was cute?"

She nods.

There's a hint of a smile around his mouth. "You were attracted to me?"

Her heart beats faster. "You could say that."

His eyes drop to her mouth.

"Come here," he says pulling her in close.

Her breath trembles. Patches of wildfire have blazed up in her again. She's trying to stomp them out, but there are too many. They seem to be multiplying and having baby wildfires.

"What you said earlier about me is wrong," he whispers. "I *do* like you."

"You do?" She stares at that sensual mouth, remembers how she wanted to bite his bottom lip. "I thought you didn't."

"I've always liked you." And before she knows it, that sensual mouth is on hers.

His kiss isn't rough like she expects but gentle. She's lulled by it. Lulled by his hard body pressed against hers, by his clean male scent. It's so good.

Without realizing it, she slides her arms around his neck. The kiss grows deeper, their mouths tangling together. A delicious heat slides through her belly with the promise of more pleasure to come. That wildfire spreads everywhere, burning her up, and she lets it.

To hell with everything. To hell with the past. To hell with the future.

To hell with Dr. Adrian.

She gasps and pushes Liam away.

"God, Tori," he breathes. "I think you're amazing."

She tries to get her bearings, to ground herself, to stamp out that fire. "You're tricking me. That's what this is. A big trick."

His mouth gapes for a second. "What?"

"You want to confuse me."

He's the one who looks confused. "What do you mean?"

"You're trying to ruin everything for me and Dr. Adrian."

His eyes meet hers, and there's sympathy in his gaze. "Tori, there *is* no you and Dr. Adrian."

"Yes, there is. And you're trying to mess it up. Don't deny it!" She steps away from him. A part of her misses his warmth, how good he feels, but she ignores it. "I have to go inside now. I'm not doing this, whatever *this* is."

Liam doesn't say anything, only studies her.

"Stop looking at me like that."

"Like what?"

"All sexy and stuff."

He chuckles and stares up at the sky. "I don't believe this."

"I'm going into the house. I have to think about my future, and you should do the same."

"The only thing I want to think about is you."

She shakes her head. "What about Shelby? You just had a date with someone you like, someone you have lots of things in common with. You and I have nothing in common."

"I don't care. I like how you're different from me." He lets his breath out. "I left my date with Shelby for you," he confesses.

Her eyes widen. "You did what?"

"When you called me, I ended my date to be here for you."

A myriad of emotions twists inside her. She can't decide if she's bothered or secretly pleased. "Are you crazy? What a terrible thing to do."

"You needed my help." He says it matter-of-factly, as if there were no other choice.

She lets out a shaky breath. "You should go. It's obvious we're both confusing each other. It's not right."

"I'm not confused."

"Yes, you are."

"I'm not."

"You are. But you just don't know it!"

His mouth twitches, but then his expression turns serious. And the way he's looking at her. *God*. Those dark liquid eyes. "Trust me, I know exactly what I want."

She hesitates, but then stands up straighter with determination. "I'm saving us both," she says. "From each other." She almost puts her hand out but decides she better not touch him. Instead, she digs around for her keys, ignoring those devil eyes.

He doesn't stop her. She senses he's trying to come up with the right thing to say, except there is no right thing. When she finds her keys, she unlocks the door. "Good night. Thanks again for everything."

She hears him sigh and say her name before she closes it.

She's not going to keep making the same mistake over and over again, falling for the wrong guy every time. She's done with that.

This time she's falling for the right one.

THE NEXT MORNING, Tori wakes to the sound of her alarm going off. She's already hit snooze four times and needs to get up. She has her date today, after all.

Grabbing her phone off the nightstand, she checks her messages. Nothing from Dr. Adrian, though there's a text from Liam.

I can't stop thinking about you.

Her thumb hovers over the screen. Should she respond? She's been thinking about him too, though she doesn't want to. In fact, she had a hard time falling asleep reliving that kiss.

Tori starts typing.

You should stop. This isn't going to happen.

She decides to pretend that kiss was nothing, wildfire or not.

Getting up, she feeds her animals and then takes a shower. By the time she's in her living room combing her wet hair and listening to Europe's "The Final Countdown," she's almost put that kiss out of her mind. Almost.

Except Liam was so nice to her last night. And he didn't seem to judge her after everything he saw with her mom and Wayne. A lot of guys would.

It doesn't matter though. They'd be terrible for each other. Just look at their history. It would be another dead-end relationship, and she's had enough of those.

She stares at her phone again with frustration. "Dammit, where are you, Dr. Adrian?"

It isn't like him to be forgetful. He's usually very thoughtful and kind. She smiles to herself, remembering how she once got him the wrong coffee drink, and he was so great about it, said it was no problem, that he'd drink it anyway.

Her phone plays Bon Jovi beside her on the couch and she snatches it up, her heart racing.

Only it isn't him. It's Blair.

"I'm waiting to hear from Dr. Adrian," Tori blurts out. "He might text or he might call, so I can't stay on the line long." She knows her phone has call waiting, but she uses it so rarely that half the time she gets flustered and hangs up on everybody.

"Your mom just called us," Blair says. "She was in hysterics, claiming you brought an FBI agent to the house last night to intimidate them."

"What? That's ridiculous."

"I know. That's what Nathan told her." Her brother's real name is Nathan, though no one in her family calls him that except Blair.

Tori rolls her eyes. "The only person I cared about intimidating was Wayne."

"He told her you don't even know anybody in the FBI, and that she needs to cut back on the—wait a minute, what did you say?" Blair sounds confused.

"Wayne's the only one Liam acted intimidating toward. My mom was already asleep by then."

"Liam?"

Tori looks at her wristwatch. It's already eleven o'clock. If she doesn't hear from Dr. Adrian by eleven fifteen, she'll contact him herself. She has his number in her phone. If he asks why, she'll say she put it there for after-hours emergencies with the animal hospital. Very reasonable.

"Are you talking about Liam from high school?" Blair sounds shocked.

"He sort of helped me last night."

"Since when is that asshole helping you with anything?"

She shifts on the couch and realizes she hasn't told Blair about pet sitting for him. "He's one of my Happy Pet Nanny clients." Tori tells her how Liam hired her to help with his dog, or the dog his ex-girlfriend left him with.

"You're seriously working for that guy? This is unbelievable. You can't find better clients than that?"

She tries to explain about Miss Fancy Pants, how she was abandoned and needs help, but Blair doesn't seem to hear any of it.

"Please tell me you're not getting involved with him," Blair says. "Not after what he did to you. I know it was high school, but people don't change that much."

"He was helping me, that's all. I haven't even told you what happened yet. They found Mable."

Blair shrieks. "You're kidding!"

Tori explains about the impound lot last night, the way someone torched the inside of her minivan.

"Poor Mable," Blair says. "I'm so sorry. Are you having her towed to Brody's garage?"

"No, not yet." She tells Blair about the police keeping Mable as part of an investigation.

"That's crazy. Seriously?"

The phone suddenly buzzes in Tori's hand. "Oh my God, I think I'm getting a text. It must be Dr. Adrian. I have to go!"

Blair shouts at her to call her back before they hang up.

Tori's heart pounds as she opens her messages and right away sees there's a new one. It's from Dr. Adrian. Finally.

Hi, Tori, I'm really sorry for the late message. We're headed to the Arts Festival at noon. Do you want to meet us there?

Relief washes through her. She knew he wouldn't let her down.

I'm so glad to hear from you! I don't have a car right now. My minivan was stolen. Could I get a ride? She adds three car emojis and two smiley faces.

Tori's surprised he doesn't remember what happened with Mable. She thought the whole office knew someone stole her van.

No problem. Send me your address.

She texts him back, excitement racing through her, then rushes to the bathroom to finish getting ready. After blow-drying her hair and putting makeup on, she stands in front of her closet for five minutes trying to decide what to wear.

It's sunny out, so she chooses cropped jeans, jeweled pink flip-flops, and a gauzy top that you can faintly see her purple bra through. She wishes she knew what a veterinarian's girlfriend was expected to wear.

At five minutes after twelve, Dr. Adrian texts that he's in the driveway, which is a disappointment. Tori had hoped to introduce him to her dogs. When she looks out the front window and sees a dark green Jeep, she's disappointed again. *Where's his midnight blue Tesla?*

Walking toward the car, she sees a woman behind the wheel, while Dr. Adrian's in the passenger seat. Tori waves, and he waves in return. It's obvious that Tori is expected to sit in the back.

The interior has a strong new car smell, a scent so many people love but she personally hates. There's some kind of soft jazz playing on the radio. She hates soft jazz too.

"This is my sister, Gina," Dr. Adrian says, introducing them.

"Hi," Tori says with a smile. "It's great to meet you."

"Same here." Gina's eyes touch hers in the rearview mirror. She has darker hair than her brother, and her eyes aren't as striking a shade of blue.

"Thanks for picking me up."

Gina murmurs an affirmation.

They pull out of the driveway and head toward Seattle Center. As they drive, Tori tries hard to join in the conversation, except Gina and Dr. Adrian discuss people and events she knows nothing about. There's mention of some dinner party they went to recently.

"I'd like to have that recipe," Gina says to her brother. "Could you ask Ned for me? Those vegan appetizers were so good."

Tori leans forward. "I'm a vegan too. I'm not sure if you remember that about me."

Dr. Adrian glances back at her with a grin. "Of course I remember. It's great we have something like that in common."

Gina interrupts. "When do you think you'll see Ned? I'd like to serve them for brunch next Sunday."

"I'll see him at tennis soon."

Tori leans forward again. "I didn't know you played tennis, Doc— I mean, Adrian."

"I do." He turns to look at her again. "Do you play?"

"No, but I've always wanted to learn." She gives him a flirty smile. "Do you know anyone who can teach me?"

He seems to be giving it some thought. "I think my tennis club has some excellent teachers. Let me pick up a flyer for you next time I'm there."

"Um, sure." She studies the back of his clueless blond head as he turns toward the front again.

His sister is already talking about some other friend of theirs.

Tori leans back in the seat with frustration. It's bad enough that she doesn't get to ride in the Tesla, but the new car smell is giving her a headache, while the radio seems to be playing the same horrible jazz song over and over. She almost wishes she'd brought earplugs.

This is turning into the longest car ride of her life.

CHAPTER ELEVEN

ONCE THEY ARRIVE at the Arts Festival, things only get worse. Dr. Adrian is nice, but his sister doesn't make much effort to include Tori in their conversations. She works in corporate finance, and when Tori jokes how she's bad at math, Gina looks concerned.

"Maybe you should get a tutor. Math is very important."

"I'm a little old for a math tutor," Tori says with a laugh. "If I haven't learned it by now, I probably don't need it."

"You're never too old to learn math." She turns to her brother. "What do you think, Adrian?"

"Of course, you're never too old. I still find multivariable calculus fascinating."

"Me too," his sister says with a grin.

They begin a detailed discussion about repeated integration and a hypervolume greater than three dimensions.

Tori listens nervously. It all sounds like gibberish. She hopes she's not going to have to learn multivariable calculus to date Dr. Adrian.

After walking around and viewing a lot of the art, the three of them have a seat near the big fountain at Seattle Center to eat lunch. Tori makes a point of sitting close to him.

"This is fun," Gina says, balancing her sandwich box on her knees. "Sort of like a picnic."

"It is," he agrees.

His sister swallows a bite of food. "I have to admit the art here is a little far out for my tastes. I don't really understand most of it."

"I'm not sure I do either." He turns to Tori. "What do you think of it?"

"I like the art. I don't think it's too far out." They both listen as she explains her point of view. "Some of it really makes you think. Or it makes you smile. My sister-in-law's mom is an artist. She's the one who did all those cactus paintings we saw in the second building."

"Cactus paintings?" Gina asks with confusion. "I don't remember those."

"Yes, they look sort of look like, um... something else." To be honest, they look just like penises, but Tori isn't saying that aloud.

Gina seems perplexed, but Dr. Adrian's eyes light up. "I *do* remember those cacti. You're right. They were fantastic."

"They're kind of humorous," Tori explains to Gina, who still looks lost.

After lunch, they walk around some more. There's a colorful series of cat cartoons that Tori adores so much she takes a photo of the artist's name for her friend Fiona, who's a marketing expert and is always looking for new talent.

For some reason, she wonders what Liam would think of the festival. She's not sure why, but she thinks he'd enjoy it.

Meanwhile, Gina and Dr. Adrian have started a discussion about some political book they read recently that Tori's never heard of. She feels like a third wheel. What's more is she keeps comparing him to Liam, which is the last thing she should be doing.

She stares at Dr. Adrian's lips. They're perfectly nice lips, but she can't help thinking they're not as sensual as Liam's.

She tries to imagine kissing Dr. Adrian. She pictures the two of them in a heated embrace, but as much as she tries to stir up some passion, there's no wildfire.

What's worse is she's doubting everything. Did Dr. Adrian only invite her here as a friend? Is it possible Liam's right and he's gay?

But what about the pink daisy and the *look*? There was no mistaking that look.

She's getting depressed. Here, when she finally thought she'd found a decent guy, it's all going down the drain.

But then something amazing happens.

At one of the exhibits, she sits on a bench to rest while Gina and Dr. Adrian have walked ahead. She leans back and closes her eyes and lets herself doze.

There's movement beside her, but she doesn't pay attention to it at first, not until there's a hand on her knee.

Her eyes fly open. It's Dr. Adrian's hand. He's sitting beside her. His handsome face is directly in front of hers—that strong jaw and those perfect lashes. Does he use an eyelash curler? No, that would be weird.

He squeezes her knee and smiles. "You okay, Tori?"

Her mouth opens. "I'm fine."

"You sure?" He removes his hand but remains near her.

"I didn't get much sleep last night."

"I'm sorry to hear that. I'm also sorry you and I haven't had a chance to talk much today. We'll have to do something just the two of us next time, okay?"

"Okay." She gulps.

Gina calls her brother over to see something, and he gives her an apologetic smile before getting up.

She tries to digest what just happened.

Was Dr. Adrian sitting close to me? Did he touch my knee and tell me he wants to spend time alone together?

Yes, he did.

Maybe there's no wildfire, but so what? All wildfires do in the end is burn out.

When they finally leave the festival, she's feeling optimistic. Even the car ride home isn't so bad this time. There's still the chemical smell, and that jazz saxophone is like an ice pick in her ear, but she's able to tolerate it.

"Here you go," Gina says, pulling into her driveway. "I hope you had an enjoyable time."

"Thank you for bringing me," Tori says politely. She turns to Dr. Adrian. "Would you mind coming inside for a moment?"

His brows go up. "You want me to come inside your house?"

She smiles sweetly. "I'd like you to meet my dogs."

He pauses, seeming to consider it.

Gina huffs with obvious impatience. "No offense, but we have to get going."

"It will only take a second to meet them," she says quickly. "That way when I bring them into the animal hospital, they'll already know your scent."

Dr. Adrian nods with approval. "Sure, I could meet them. I'd like that."

"Great." She reaches for the door handle.

Despite more protests from Gina, Dr. Adrian gets out of the car and follows Tori up the front walk. He waits patiently as she hunts for the key.

"Thanks for doing this."

"It's no problem at all. And I'm sorry this whole day has been kind of a bust. I'm new to Seattle, and Gina tends to be protective over me."

Tori reflects on his broken heart from Renée. "Don't worry, I totally understand."

Her dogs greet them as she opens her door. "Eddie's the golden retriever. Duff's the pug mix, and that little Chihuahua is Tommy Lee." She points to each one as they gather around with their tails wagging.

"Hey there, boys." Dr. Adrian bends down on one knee, petting all the dogs and examining them. "It looks like you have a healthy group here."

"Thank you. I try to take good care of them." She tells him how all three dogs were strays she adopted from the animal shelter she volunteers at.

"My dogs are both from shelters too," he says, glancing up at her. "It's great that you give your time like that. In fact, I do the same thing."

Obviously she already knows that about him. Just one more way he's perfect.

He stands up from petting her dogs, who all adore him. She's not surprised.

"I guess I'd better get going," he says. He smiles at her and seems to hesitate for a moment.

Tori wonders if he wants to kiss her but is too shy.

To help him out, she steps closer and gives him a hug. "I had a nice time today." He's tall and wiry in her arms. She's never been this close to Dr. Adrian and notices he's wearing some kind of subtle men's cologne. It smells good. She usually prefers men not wear cologne, but on him she likes it.

"Me too. Let's do this again soon."

When they draw apart, she turns her face up, hoping he'll take the hint and kiss her.

He's looking down at her, and that's when Tori decides the heck with it. He's obviously gun-shy. She puts her hands up to his layered hair. It's silky beneath her fingers.

Holding his head still, she kisses him straight on the mouth.

To her surprise, Dr. Adrian makes an odd startled noise in his throat.

When she pulls away, he's wearing a stunned expression.

A car horn blares outside. Gina in her Jeep.

"I just wanted to let you know how I feel," she says in a rush. "I hope that's okay."

He blinks a few times. "Tori, I... I think you're great."

She smiles. "I think you're great too." She senses he's bothered and wonders if it was a mistake kissing him. "I know you're still dealing with your heartbreak from Renée. I'm not trying to push you or anything."

His eyes widen. "You know about Renée?"

"I do. And I just want you to know when you're ready, I'll be here."

A car horn blares outside again, longer this time.

Dr. Adrian glances toward the sound and then licks his lips. It seems like he wants to say more, but then he shakes his head. He reaches for her hand, squeezing it. "Let's talk about this later, okay?"

She squeezes his hand in return. "Okay."

LIAM LEARNS Walter Yates isn't his real name. Yates is an alias, and it turns out the guy's real name is Rizzo. They've already got him on charges of mail fraud, wire fraud, and money laundering. Unfortunately, the wheels of justice are slow, especially on the weekend, and they're still waiting for an arrest warrant.

"I don't care if he gets on an airplane tonight," he says to Matt as they watch Rizzo's house from inside his bureau car. "I'm following him." The more they investigate Rizzo, the more criminal activity they're discovering. It's gone well beyond the Ponzi scheme. The guy has a dozen offshore companies hiding money.

Matt chuckles. They've been surveilling all afternoon, taking over for the other team. "Hey, maybe he'll get on a plane to Hawaii," he jokes. "I can work on my tan."

Movies about the FBI depict everything happening quickly, but reality can be a different story. Besides the mountain of paperwork Liam has to contend with, there are all the ins and outs of working with the U.S. Attorney's Office.

"So I hear you impressed Shelby last Saturday," Matt says with a grin, turning toward him. "I take it your date went well."

Liam nods, "It was good."

"Just good?"

He's not sure what else to say. The woman he's been thinking about all week isn't Shelby. "She's great, but I'm not really interested."

Matt's brows rise. "Seriously? After everything Amy's told me about her, I figured you two were a sure thing."

"It's not her. It's me."

His friend's expression turns sympathetic. "You've been through a lot with Rachel. I wouldn't give up on Shelby so easily though. Maybe go out a couple more times."

Liam doesn't reply. Instead, he thinks about how much he's been going on the Happy Pet Nanny website lately. He told himself it was only to check the list of safe foods for Fancy, but every time he goes on there, he can't stop staring at the picture of Tori. There's one of her smiling in a grassy field with her dogs. Seeing her photo lights him up inside. He was tempted to take a screenshot for himself but decided that was crossing a line.

As he's thinking all this, his phone buzzes. He grabs it from the cup holder and reads the message from the ASAC in charge of his squad. "We've got our Rizzo warrants," he tells Matt with a grin. "Arrest along with search and seizure."

"Good news."

Liam nods. It is good news. It also means it's going to be a long night.

After he and Matt switch out surveillance with another team, he goes home for a quick shower and a bite to eat before heading downtown to the bureau's main headquarters in Seattle. There's a meeting with the members of his squad to come up with an arrest plan. They decide on a "knock and announce," which means they'll be knocking on Rizzo's door at six in the morning. They assume he's armed, so the FBI SWAT team will be involved.

Once the meeting's over, Liam's keyed up. It's usually like this before an arrest, and he knows he won't get much sleep. By four in the morning, he's up. By five he's assembling with all the other agents involved at the preplanned location.

They go over a few last-minute details about Rizzo's house with the SWAT team leader. "Our intel shows two exits. We'll station a team in front and back," the team leader says, pointing to a map of the house.

Liam studies it, memorizing the layout.

Everyone is armed and wearing bulletproof vests along with their FBI raid jackets as they drive slowly up the street in three separate vehicles.

"You ready to take this son of a bitch down?" Matt turns to him with a grin.

Liam thinks about all the money Rizzo's stolen. People's retirement savings wiped out after years of hard work. "More than ready." Since it's his case, he's the agent in charge and will lead the group.

It's early morning. A gray sky above them threatens rain. The middle-class neighborhood Rizzo lives in is peaceful. Their team exits each vehicle as quietly as possible, scanning the area as they move forward toward the house, checking the windows for any sign of activity.

Half the team lines up behind Liam on the porch while the other half slips around back.

He grips his weapon, then pounds on the front door, breaking the neighborhood's silence like an explosion. "*FBI! We have an arrest warrant! Open this door!*"

There's silence. Liam strains, listening for movement inside. He senses houses nearby coming to life.

He glances back at Scott, one of the SWAT agents behind him, who's taken lead on the battering ram.

Liam holds his hand up to Scott and then pounds on the door again, repeating what he said moments ago. Dynamic arrests like this are nerve-racking and can be dangerous, but at least there's little time for suspects to destroy evidence or gather weapons.

This time there are sounds inside the house. He tightens the grip on his Glock and glances at Scott. They both hear it.

Adrenaline kicks into overdrive as every detail around him comes into focus. The type of lock on the door. Whether the person who answers it will be armed. He has to be ready for anything.

Someone turns the tumblers, and a tired, irritated woman of about fifty opens up. "What is all this?"

"Ma'am, we have an arrest warrant for Walter Rizzo. Is he on the premises?"

She blinks at them and seems nervous. "No." She licks her lips. "He's not here."

Liam's instincts tell him she's lying. He holds up the legal paperwork. "We also have a warrant for search and seizure. You'll need to step back."

"What? You can't come inside my house!" She seems indignant.

"As I just stated, we have a warrant. If you don't step out of the way, we'll have to arrest you for obstruction."

Her eyes widen. "Arrest me?"

Liam's losing his patience. "Yes, ma'am. Step back immediately."

There's some kind of movement behind her and Liam tenses, but it's only a small dog. It appears at her feet, and she picks it up. He uses the opportunity to push the door open.

She finally moves out of the way to let them enter, and he's relieved. He'd rather not arrest some woman in her nightgown.

The SWAT team behind him swarms into the house, taking it room by room. Liam and two fellow squad members do a systematic search, holding their weapons in front of them. When they discover

Rizzo's office, Liam instructs the other two to confiscate the computers along with any flash drives and papers.

As they get to work, the rest of the agents continue searching for Rizzo. Except there's no sign of him.

"He's not on the premises," Ryan, the leader of the SWAT team, informs him.

While they don't find the subject of their warrant, they do find a cache of pistols and a rifle leaning against the bedroom door.

"Dammit." Liam shakes his head in frustration. "How did this happen? We had him under surveillance."

"We did," Louis, one of his squad members, speaks up. "I don't know how he slipped past us."

Liam sighs. "Let's continue the search and seizure. Hopefully we'll find something that tells us where he's gone."

After an hour, they load most of Rizzo's computers, file cabinets, and office equipment into the van and continue searching through the house. Meanwhile, Rizzo's wife sits on the couch with her dog, glaring at them as she talks on the phone with her lawyer. She still insists she has no idea of her husband's whereabouts.

After the SWAT team leaves and he and his fellow agents are wrapping things up, Liam takes one last look inside the office. He wants to make sure they haven't missed anything.

The space is in disarray. He glances at the closet again. It's not particularly large. He sticks his head in to make sure they've pulled out anything that seemed pertinent.

But then he notices something. One end of the closet appears slightly different from the other. It's subtle, and most people wouldn't notice it, but he's always had a talent for spotting the unusual. On closer inspection, one side is painted wood while the other is drywall.

He knocks on the wood. It's hollow.

"I'll be damned." Feeling around the edges, he tries to open what he now suspects is a false wall.

He crouches, searching along the floor, and discovers one of the corner boards is loose. When he lifts it, there's a small lever inside. He pulls it up and the false wall opens slightly, revealing itself to be a door.

Adrenaline rushes through him as he reaches for his weapon. The space inside the wall is large enough to conceal a man.

He kicks it open with his foot, holding his gun out, except it's empty. There's another laptop on the ground, along with a handgun. He pulls out both and sets them on a chair to add into evidence.

He tries to step inside the small space, but it's a tight fit and impossible with his weapon drawn. He holsters it and slips inside, noticing what appears to be another door. Slowly, he turns the handle and finds it lets out into some foliage on the side of the house. A cleverly disguised exit no one noticed.

Liam steps out and is amazed to see Rizzo himself crouched only a few feet away. He's hiding in a small space between the house and some tall bushes.

The man's mouth drops open as he stares up at Liam with shock. "Pete, is that you?"

Liam pulls out his weapon. "You're under arrest, Walter Rizzo. On your knees with your hands behind your head."

Instead of listening, Rizzo jumps up and appears angry. "I take it you're not Pete Sanchez."

"I'm a special agent with the FBI."

Liam keeps his gun trained on him. He sees no sign that the man is armed, despite all the weapons they found in the house.

"I've done nothing wrong." Rizzo's face is flushed. He's still wearing pajamas. "I don't know why the FBI is harassing me."

"On the ground now." Liam takes a step toward him, reaching for the handcuffs on his belt. Without warning, Rizzo bolts. It happens in a flash. He pushes through the bushes and disappears.

"Dammit, Walter," Liam yells. He pushes through the same bushes. "Stop or I'll shoot!"

Walter glances back at him but keeps running anyway.

Liam is forced to make a split-second decision and goes after him. He'd rather not shoot an unarmed man in the back while he's running away, especially not in a neighborhood with kids going to school. Besides, how fast can Rizzo be?

It turns out, surprisingly fast.

Liam chases him down the sidewalk. Rizzo's running at a sprint, his heavy frame bouncing with each step. Liam is gaining on him quickly. Up ahead, Walter turns right into someone's front yard, then jumps over a short fence.

Liam does the same and follows him around the back corner of the house. Except as Liam rounds the same corner, he nearly runs into a woman who's exiting her back door.

She shrieks and her hands fly in the air. To avoid knocking her over, he's forced to veer out of the way and trips over a pile of gardening supplies.

"Aaargh!" He goes down hard on his left knee. A burst of recognizable pain colors his vision. The same pain he dealt with for years when he played ball.

He groans in agony but forces himself up. Ahead of him, he sees Walter trying to climb the tall wooden fence that borders the property, but he's struggling.

Liam strides over, ignoring his injured knee. He pulls his weapon out and points it directly at Rizzo, who's nearly over the fence, his large stomach hampering him. Ironically, his pajamas are covered with pictures of trout and fishhooks. Very fitting, considering he's been caught.

Liam might have found those pajamas amusing if he weren't so pissed off. "You're under arrest," he yells. "Climb down from that fence with your hands up."

Rizzo glances at him, still trying to gain a foothold.

"So help me, Walter, I will shoot you from where I'm standing!"

Something in Liam's voice must have alerted Walter that he wasn't kidding, because he slides off the fence and does what he's told.

Liam moves closer. He yanks Walter Rizzo's arms down, shoves his wrists together, and finally slaps the handcuffs on him.

CHAPTER TWELVE

"OH MY GOSH, what *happened* to you?" Tori's gaze drops to the brace on Liam's leg as he lets her into his house.

"I was chasing a... squirrel."

"A squirrel? That's weird."

"Weird is certainly a word for it," he mutters.

It explains why he texted her and said he'd be here today. She came in through the garage all last week to dog sit while Liam was at work.

Miss Fancy Pants barks once and wags her tail in greeting. Tori claps her hands in delight when she sees the little dog. "You finally got her coat trimmed!"

"I took her in Friday to that place you recommended."

Tori bends over to pet Miss Fancy Pants, who's a bundle of joyful energy. "You look beautiful," she coos to her. "Just like a puppy again." The little white dog's coat is short all over and really suits her energetic style.

"Your hair's different too," Liam says. "When did you add that?"

Tori touches the blue streak. "Last week."

"For Mable?"

She glances up at him, surprised by his perceptiveness. "Yes, that's right."

After lavishing more compliments on the dog, Tori gets up and follows Liam as he limps into the living room. Miss Fancy Pants, who still has a mild limp of her own, walks behind him.

"You two are a matched set."

He glances at her. "What's that?"

She only shakes her head, though she can't help smiling. There's something cute about them together. "Nothing. Are you okay? That looks painful. Are you able to go into work?"

"It's fine. I'm working from home this week. Can I get you anything to drink? Water or iced tea?"

"No, I'm not thirsty."

He manages to sit on the lumpy couch without bending his leg, then props it up on a pillow.

Tori takes a seat in the nearby chair. She feels the weight of his eyes on her and knows it's because of the kiss. Even though it happened over a week ago, that kiss was still the dancing elephant in the room.

Miss Fancy Pants comes over to be petted some more, but then surprisingly goes over to join Liam on the couch. She sits right next to him, and he scratches her behind the ears.

It does Tori's heart good to see them bonding. "So what really happened to you?" she asks, motioning at his leg.

The television is on some sports station, and he reaches for the remote to mute it. "I have a meniscus tear in my left knee."

She's seen those at the animal hospital. "Those are painful. How bad is it?"

"Not too bad. I've had worse. I just need to rest it for a while."

She notices his open laptop on the coffee table along with an ice pack. There's a bag of tortilla chips, a bowl of grapes, and a glass of iced tea beside it, not to mention a few days of mail piled haphazardly. Looking around, she realizes the place is a mess.

"What do you mean, you've had worse? Is this a common thing for you?"

He shrugs.

She stares at his mouth. The one she kissed, the one she's been trying not to think about ever since.

"I used to play baseball before I was in the FBI." He explains how he was a major league catcher before joining the bureau. "I had to quit because of knee problems."

"Really? I didn't know that."

Her eyes drift lower to his body as he's sprawled on the couch. She's never seen him dressed so casually. He's wearing gray sweatpants and a purple University of Portland T-shirt. His arms are tanned and muscled. His shirt is riding up on one side, and she can tell the rest of his body is tanned and muscled too. She also notices the impressive bulge in his crotch area.

The room seems to be getting warmer. She swallows. An odd daydream comes to her where she goes over to the couch, pushes that shirt up, and runs her hands over his hard chest. "Um... so how long did you play professional baseball?"

"Three years."

She nods, still caught up in her fantasy. "That's... nice."

For some reason he chuckles.

"What's so funny?" Horrified, she wonders if he knows what she's thinking. Quickly she averts her eyes. Was she staring at his crotch? *Oh God.* She can't remember.

"Nothing." He grins. "I like how the things that impress most people don't ever impress you."

"Oh, you mean the baseball stuff? I'm impressed."

"Are you?"

"I guess so." She thinks about it. "It's just that being an FBI agent is so important. You're protecting people. Making a real difference."

He goes quiet at this, studying her. There's an expression on his face that she can't quite place.

"It must be a really hard job though." She glances at his leg. "Is that how you hurt yourself? Catching a criminal?"

He nods but doesn't elaborate.

She wishes that wasn't so hot. A good guy fighting the good fight. Growing up surrounded by her mom's loser boyfriends, she hasn't been around enough men like Liam.

Their eyes meet and catch hold. Butterflies flutter in her stomach.

He doesn't move a muscle, but his voice softens. "I've been thinking about you, Tori."

Uh-oh. Here we go. The dancing elephant in the room.

"I'd like to take you out," he says.

"What do you mean?"

"You know, on a real date. Just the two of us, so we can get to know each other."

She takes a deep breath and leans forward. "We need to have a talk. I can't go on a date with you."

"Why not?"

"You already know why. In fact, I'd like to pretend that kiss between us never happened."

He studies her, clearly not liking this.

"It's for the best. You and I are too different. In the end, it would only lead to misery. Just look at the past."

"Not this again." He rolls his eyes.

"We don't belong together. We have nothing in common."

He doesn't reply, but his gaze goes back to hers. Steady like always. His brown eyes are doing that thing where they look all smoldering and sexy. His mouth is doing it too.

She takes another breath and tries to clear all lustful thoughts. This is ridiculous.

Unfortunately, she can't use that kiss with Dr. Adrian as a distraction because, let's face it, that kiss was weird. It felt like she was making out with a locked door.

The great news is Dr. Adrian asked her out to lunch this week. They're going to that new vegetarian restaurant. She knows he's still hurting over Renée, but she hopes he's ready to put it in the past and give their relationship a chance.

Though obviously they're going to have to work on his kissing skills.

She sits up straight. "Look, you're my client, and I'd like to go back to keeping things strictly professional between us."

Liam's expression turns flat. "Is that so?"

"Yes. I appreciate all your help with Mable, but I need to focus on the new man in my life now."

He snorts. "I take it you mean Dr. Adrian?"

"Yes, I do."

"Tori—" He shakes his head and sighs.

She already knows what he's going to say, so she cuts him off. "You can stop right there. I know why you're doing this, and it's not going to work." She'd told Peyton what Liam said, and her friend didn't believe it either. "My date with Dr. Adrian was great. In fact, he asked me to lunch this Thursday."

There's a grunt from Liam, but no reply.

"You're definitely wrong about him."

He shifts on the couch to get more comfortable. "All right, fine. Let's hear about this wonderful date of yours."

She hesitates. If this relationship is strictly professional, should she be sharing details like that? But then she notices the skeptical look on his face.

She crosses her hands over her knee. "Well, we went to the Arts Festival at Seattle Center."

"Alone?"

"No, his sister was there, but it was nice to meet her. In fact, I have a feeling we'll be good friends in the future." Kind of stretching the truth, but she's sure things will change once Gina learns they're a couple.

"And what did you guys talk about?"

"Lots of things. The art at the festival, of course. We also discussed books, politics, vegan food, calculus, and he's even helping me learn how to play tennis."

"Calculus?"

She nods. "Yes, Dr. Adrian loves math, and so do I."

"I'd never have pegged you for a math nerd."

She shrugs. "I guess I'm full of surprises. Obviously there's a lot about me you don't know."

"What area of calculus?"

"Um, multivariable calculus." She's relieved she remembers the name of it.

Liam seems astonished. "You're interested in multivariable calculus?"

"I am."

He studies her. "So what are your thoughts on Navier-Stokes existence and smoothness?"

"My thoughts?" She shifts uncomfortably in the chair, wishing she hadn't thrown in that bit about calculus. She was on a roll and it sort of came out. "Well, I think it's great." She waves her hand around. "You know, *very* smooth."

"Personally, I find the relationship between kinematic viscosity and external volumetric force interesting."

She stares at him.

He gives her a smug smile. "Did I ever mention I was a math major in college?"

"No, you didn't."

He grins, and it's obvious that he knows she's full of it. "I still enjoy solving a good system of equations problem. How about you?"

"All right, *fine*." She rolls her eyes. "I admit I know nothing about multivariable calculus."

He chuckles.

"But Dr. Adrian and I had a great time. We really did. The sparks between us were flying."

"If you say so."

Clearly he still doesn't believe her. She leans back in her chair and decides to pull out the big guns. "In fact"—her voice turns coy—"Dr. Adrian made his intentions toward me *very* clear, if you know what I mean."

"No, I don't know what you mean."

"He made a move."

A skeptical brow shoots up. "A move?"

"Yes." She presses her lips together and then smiles. "That's right. A romantic move."

Liam seems dubious. "What exactly was this move?"

"Well, if you must know, he put his hand on my knee." She looks at him for his reaction. Unfortunately, he isn't as impressed as she hoped, so she continues. "During one of the exhibits, I sat on a bench to rest and felt something. When I opened my eyes, it turned out it was Dr. Adrian's hand." Now it's her turn to give him a smug smile.

"Opened your eyes?" He looks confused. "You were asleep on your date?"

"No, of course not. I was just... lightly dozing."

"You were lightly dozing on your date?"

"It was nothing. You're missing the point."

He chuckles. "Maybe he put his hand on your knee to wake you up."

"It was only a few minutes," she says crossly. "And as you may recall, I had a long night that Saturday and didn't get much sleep."

He nods, but there's a gleam in his eye. "I do recall."

She knows he's thinking about the dancing elephant again. "My date was plenty exciting, trust me. In fact, it ended with a kiss."

He goes still at this. "Are you saying Dr. Adrian *kissed* you?"

She nods, enjoying his surprise.

Technically, she kissed Dr. Adrian, but does it really matter? All that matters is there was somebody kissing somebody else, and it involved her and Dr. Adrian.

"Where did he kiss you?"

"What do you mean?"

"What part of you? The cheek or forehead? Where?"

She smiles. "The lips."

"That makes no sense."

She sits up straight. "It does make sense. It's like I said before, we're getting involved with each other."

Liam's expression is puzzled.

"In fact, I see this relationship with Dr. Adrian getting serious. *Very* serious."

He considers her words, but then his gaze turns sly. "How was the kiss?"

"What do you mean?"

"Were you moved by it?" His voice drops low. "Did it turn you on?"

Her traitorous body quivers with pleasure at his tone. "That's none of your business. How dare you even ask me that!"

She tries to turn away, but to her chagrin, the memory of Liam kissing her comes back in a full blaze. *God.* It was wicked. A part of her wants to relive it, wants to explore that muscular chest while she's at it.

"You're trying to confuse me again," she says.

"There's nothing confusing here. I like you. And I think you like me too."

She shakes her head. "Just stop it, okay? I've had enough. Stop undressing me with your eyes!"

"What?" He seems taken aback. "I'm not doing that."

Oops. That's right. She's the one doing it to him.

She pushes up from her chair. "I don't want to talk about this anymore. Just let me do my job. I'm your pet nanny, remember? That's all."

"Where are you going?"

"I'm taking Miss Fancy Pants out for a walk."

"Now?"

She snorts. "Isn't that why I'm here? You were begging me to walk her before, and now you don't want me to?"

He frowns and his mouth looks so deliciously sullen that she wants to bite it. Lick it too.

I need to get out of here.

TORI WALKS Miss Fancy Pants around Liam's bizarre neighborhood, where all the houses look identical and the lawns are all the same shade of green. It's as quiet as a cemetery.

She shivers. She can't imagine living here voluntarily.

It's one more example of how they're too different. Totally mismatched. And is she really supposed to forget what he did to her in high school? How even now, he's trying to undermine her feelings for Dr. Adrian?

I don't think so.

Though she has to admit he helped her a lot with Mable and then with Wayne. She can't dismiss that as much as she'd like to.

But why did he have to kiss me?

He's ruining everything. She should be thrilled right now. Jumping for joy. Dr. Adrian was finally making some romantic moves toward her, but all she can think about is this terrible attraction to Liam.

She sighs, and Miss Fancy Pants looks up at her.

"I don't know how my love life got so complicated," she says to the little dog.

Miss Fancy Pants makes a small huffing sound as if to say, *Silly humans.*

As they explore the neighborhood, the dog squats daintily and pees on the corner of one of the perfectly groomed lawns. Tori glances around. She hopes the Stepford police don't jump out and arrest her. Luckily she brought a plastic bag for any poop.

She praises Miss Fancy Pants the whole time they walk, telling her what a great dog she is and how she didn't deserve the way Rachael abandoned her. The little dog sniffs along the sidewalk, then goes over to one of the neighbor's bushes. Tori wonders if any other dogs live here. She suspects Miss Fancy Pants might enjoy a playdate.

By the time they head back to Liam's house, there's a gold SUV parked in his driveway. A dark-haired woman gets out and goes around to the back to open the rear.

Miss Fancy Pants tugs on the leash toward her. When she gets close enough, she barks and puts her paws on the woman's pants. She looks familiar.

"Well, hello there." The woman pets the little white dog. She glances at Tori but doesn't say anything.

And that's when Tori recognizes her. "You're Liam's sister, right?"

Elena turns back to the car. "Yes, I am."

"I don't know if you remember me. We went to high school together."

"I know who you are," she says in a cold voice. "I graduated with your brother."

Tori remembers the way Elena bad-mouthed her to everyone and is guessing she remembers it too.

"Can I give you a hand?" Tori asks as Elena pulls out a couple bags of groceries from the trunk.

"There are just two, so I've got it. The rest are mine." She slams the rear shut.

The three of them walk toward the front door.

"I'm surprised to see you still working for my brother. I thought he fired you."

"What?" Tori glances at her. "Why would he do that?"

Elena sniffs. "Well, I don't think he really needs a pet sitter anymore. Miss Fancy Pants seems to be doing just fine now."

Tori tries not to get annoyed at her dismissive tone.

They enter the front door. Tori crouches to take off the dog's leash as Elena breezes past her. She can hear the television on in the living room.

After hanging up the leash, Tori goes to get her purse and sees Liam and his sister in the kitchen. They're speaking in low hissing tones and appear to be having an argument. As soon as they see her, they abruptly stop.

She goes over to them. "I just wanted to let you know I'm leaving now."

"How did the walk go?" Liam asks. There's an air of frustration around him, and she suspects they were arguing about her.

"It was fine. I still have you scheduled for Friday, right?" He tried to schedule her all week, but Tori's only been able to squeeze him in two days.

"Actually, your services won't be needed anymore," Elena interjects. "I'll be coming over and helping my brother with the dog."

Liam's brows slam together. "Please ignore my sister. I absolutely need your help on Friday."

She glances over at Elena standing next to him. Tori can see the family resemblance. They both have the same hair and eye color, and even the same skin tone. Elena didn't inherit Liam's sensual lips though. Hers are just ordinary.

Tori's glad.

She doesn't deserve lips like that. She's too mean.

"Listen, I was thinking about bringing Miss Fancy Pants over to my house for a playdate next time," Tori tells him.

Elena snorts. "A what?"

Tori ignores her and keeps her eyes on Liam. "A playdate is just what it sounds like. You bring your dogs together to play with each other like kids do."

He glances down at Miss Fancy Pants, who's drinking from her water bowl. "I've never heard of that."

Tori isn't surprised. People new to having a dog usually don't know about them. "I think she'd enjoy it. My boys have done them a lot, so they're very easygoing around other dogs."

Elena is glaring at her like she's just announced plans to kidnap Miss Fancy Pants. "I don't think that's a good idea."

But Liam is obviously of a different mindset. His eyes go back to Tori. "Sure, let's try it. It might be fun for her."

"That's what I was thinking."

They smile at each other, and Tori feels a rush at how handsome he is. His short hair is usually groomed, but today it's kind of rumpled, with some of it falling across his forehead.

"Let me walk you to the door," he says.

She glances down at his leg brace. "You don't have to do that. You should be icing and taking care of that knee."

She senses Elena's disapproving eyes on the two of them.

Despite her protests, he walks her to the door anyway.

"I'm sorry about my sister," he says after they step onto the porch. "I'm not sure what's gotten into her."

Tori shrugs. "Elena doesn't like me. She never has."

"She doesn't know you."

She's tempted to tell him how his sister said terrible things about her in high school but decides not to get into all that. Especially since she's trying to keep this relationship professional.

AS SOON AS Tori's gone, Liam tears into his sister. "Have you lost your mind? I can't believe you treated her like that."

"No, I haven't. But you've lost yours. Are you really starting up something with *her*, of all people?"

"What the hell are you talking about?"

"Please." Elena rolls her eyes. "Do you think I'm blind? It's obvious you still have the hots for her, despite everything that happened."

"Give it a rest. That was a long time ago."

"She made your life hell for a whole year of high school. I was one of the few people who defended you back then, or have you forgotten that too?"

He makes it over to the living room and plops down awkwardly on the couch. Tori was right about his knee. He should be elevating and icing it. The damn thing was aching again. "I haven't forgotten," he mutters. "It's all in the past."

Elena comes around and stands in front of him. "Has she even apologized for any of it?"

He grunts but doesn't reply. Despite what he just said, it does still bother him that Tori thinks he poured a milkshake over her on purpose. Not to mention that business with her brother.

"Her whole family is nothing but lowlifes. How does she even get in here when you're not home? Please tell me she doesn't have a key to your house."

"She comes in through the garage door. I gave her the code." They tried it last week, and it worked great. Tori texted him when she arrived. By remote, he turned off the house alarm for her, then turned it on again after she left.

Elena's mouth drops open. "So she's alone in your house? With free rein to do whatever she pleases? Are you crazy?"

"She's a pet sitter."

His sister crosses her arms. "Well, I don't trust her. And you shouldn't either."

He picks up the bag of ice. "I don't want to listen to this anymore."

"What is it about her? She comes in here with her long blonde hair and flirty blue eyes, and all your common sense goes out the window?"

He settles the ice on his knee and leans back, wondering if he should take the painkillers from his doctor. The problem is he dislikes feeling loopy.

Elena takes the chair Tori was in earlier, and her tone turns earnest. "I know it was hard when Rachel left, but think about what you're doing."

"I'm not involved with Tori, and even if I were, it's my own business."

"I don't want to see you chasing after her and making a fool of yourself. And I don't want to see you getting hurt again either. You don't exactly have the greatest track record with women."

He turns toward the television, trying to tune out this conversation. The last thing he wants is to have a discussion with his sister about his lousy track record with women.

"We all want to see you happy. Look how great you are with my boys. Somewhere out there a good woman is waiting for you."

Maybe I should open up my computer and get some work done. He's been combing through Rizzo's financial records. When he joined White-Collar Crime a few years ago, he discovered an interest in forensic accounting. It's detail-oriented and requires a lot of patience—exactly the kind of thing he enjoys.

"You deserve better than a weirdo like Tori Church."

He clenches his jaw, still staring at the television. Grabbing the remote control, he's tempted to blast the volume and drown her out.

"You need to be thinking about your future. You have nothing in common with someone like that. We're just different kinds of people than they are."

He snorts. Ironically, she's saying the same thing Tori did earlier.

He turns to his sister. "Are you hearing yourself? When did you become such a snob?"

"I'm being realistic." She sighs, studying him. "Did you know Mom and Dad worry about you? We all do."

Liam doesn't like hearing about his parents worrying. He knows they were disappointed when he and Rachel decided to live together. They're old-school Catholic and couldn't understand why he didn't marry her.

"We want you to find someone you can build a life with.

Someone decent. Do you really think Tori Church is that person?"

"Stop it, Elena. You don't know what you're talking about. Tori *is* decent."

"She and her whole hoodlum family. They're nothing but poison."

"I said stop."

His sister scoffs. "You really think she's not like them? That she's so different? I'm sure she'd love to get her trashy hooks into you."

"Dammit, just *shut the hell up!*"

His sister glares at him. "Don't raise your voice at me. What's gotten into you?"

"Do you ever quit?"

"I'm trying to talk some sense into you."

"How about you mind your own business instead?"

"I just brought you groceries, you ungrateful ass!"

"Yes, thank you. I didn't realize the cost of your help was a nasty lecture."

His sister throws her hands in the air. "Excuse me for trying to stop you from making another huge mistake."

In a huff, she goes off to the kitchen.

He stares at the television, trying to calm down. He looks around for Fancy, concerned he might have scared her. Luckily she's outside in the yard.

He rarely loses his temper. And he feels bad for yelling at Elena. He knows life has thrown her some curveballs, and she's only trying to look out for him.

On the other hand, he can only take so much. Bad enough that he has to deal with an injured knee bringing back unpleasant memories. There's no way he wants to listen to Elena talk trash about Tori.

Maybe her family isn't exactly full of upstanding citizens, and maybe he should care more about that, but he doesn't. All he cares about is how he feels when he's around her. Like summer sunlight is shining on him, like a coldness inside of him is warmed for the first time in a long time.

He sees who *she* is, and that's all that matters.

CHAPTER THIRTEEN

"SURPRISE!"

Liam tries to hide his irritation that Shelby has shown up unannounced at his front door in the middle of the day.

"When you didn't text me back, I didn't know what happened. But then Amy told me about the arrest on Monday and how you were injured." She looks down at his knee brace with sympathy. "It must remind you so much of losing your baseball career. Like you're reliving it."

Her comment irritates him further. "No, it's fine." It's more the memory of all the knee problems he had as a catcher he's reliving. He played the same position throughout high school and college without a single hiccup. As soon as he turned pro, his knees started acting up. A lot of catchers have knee issues, but he was young and cocky enough back then to think it wouldn't happen to him.

"Come in," he tells her.

Miss Fancy Pants stands beside him, eyeing Shelby with suspicion.

"I apologize. I know I should have texted or called. At least I brought lunch." She holds up a bag of takeout. "I hope you like Dick's burgers and fries."

"Thanks, I do. That was thoughtful."

They head into the main part of his house. Maybe he can figure out a way to let her down easy.

"Oh, that's funny," Shelby says. "Your dog has a limp too. It's even the same leg."

He glances down at Miss Fancy Pants, who's trotting along next to him. "Yeah, she has a sprain. It's healing though."

"It's sort of cute. You two are like bookends."

They have lunch on the back patio. It's Shelby's idea, and he has to admit it's a good one as they sit outside in the sun.

"I just love your neighborhood," she says, looking around. His yard is fenced though not altogether private. "I know I mentioned it before, but it's perfect. So peaceful and quiet. It reminds me a lot of my neighborhood."

"Really?"

She gives him a coy smile. "Yes, you'll have to come over sometime and see it."

He takes a bite of his burger and tries to figure out how to tell her that's not going to happen.

She's wearing office-type clothes—slacks and a pretty blouse. Her dark hair is pulled back with a clip. She brought burgers, fries, and milkshakes. A woman who knows what guys like to eat.

The milkshake is vanilla, not chocolate, which is a relief, since he hasn't had a chocolate milkshake since high school.

They have an easy conversation, her green eyes lively as they discuss sports and then move on to work. She makes a few more sympathetic comments about his knee.

She has a self-assured way about her, and Liam knows he should be thrilled to have met a woman like this. She comes from a good family. Two brothers. One's a doctor, the other a tax attorney. Shelby studied statistics in college.

"I was a math major myself," he says, dipping his fries in ketchup.

"You're kidding? I didn't know that. I thought all you FBI guys were lawyers."

He chuckles. "Not all of us."

"We have a lot in common."

He has to agree. They both like sports and numbers. Staying in shape. An orderly life. Not to mention Shelby's quite attractive.

He thinks about the argument he had with his sister last night. Elena—hell, his whole family—would approve of Shelby 100 percent.

So why isn't he more excited?

Instead, he feels bored at the thought of a relationship with her.

Fancy, who's been sitting near his feet most of the time, gets up to investigate something on the other side of the yard. She makes a point of ignoring Shelby.

"Have you heard anything from your ex about taking her back?" she asks, gesturing to the dog.

"No, nothing."

"I still can't believe she dumped her on you like that." She takes a pull from her milkshake. "I'm not sure if I'd be as generous as you are about keeping her. I mean, look at what she did to your couch."

He glances over to Fancy, who's sniffing delicately along the edge of the fence. Since he came home with his injured knee, she's been glued to his side, and he gets the impression she's guarding him.

That this twelve-pound dog would appoint herself his protector evokes a feeling in Liam he can't quite put into words.

"You must be counting the days to get rid of her," Shelby continues.

He gazes over at the little dog. "Not at all."

Shelby takes a bite of her burger and chews for a few seconds. "You know, I never thanked you for introducing me to Nelson Coby. That was really great."

"I'm glad you enjoyed it. He's a good guy. I take it everything went okay with him bringing you home?"

She nods. "No problem at all. He was a *perfect* gentleman."

There's an odd note in her voice, one that sounds like regret. It makes Liam glance at her. It's almost as if she wishes Nelson hadn't been such a perfect gentleman.

TORI'S NERVOUS. So nervous she tries on ten different outfits and changes her hair four times.

How exactly do you get ready for the first day of the rest of your life?

Standing in front of the full-length mirror in her bedroom, she takes another selfie, texting the photo to Blair.

What do you think of this one?

I like it. You look pretty. Which earrings are you wearing?

The crystal chandeliers.

I'd switch to the hoops since it's lunch. You don't want to seem like you're trying too hard.

Okay, good idea.

Tori fishes through her jewelry box and pulls out some silver hoops. Her nails are freshly painted a frosty pink. She hopes Dr. Adrian likes pink. She'll have to find out what his favorite colors are, and his other favorites too.

Tori texts Blair again. *I'm so excited this is finally happening!!!*

I know! I'm thrilled for you. I can't wait to meet Dr. Adrian!

You'll love him. He's wonderful!!!

She already told Blair all about their first date and how it ended with a kiss, though Blair assumed Dr. Adrian had kissed her. She'd meant to correct that impression but never got around to it.

Tori's meeting Dr. Adrian at that new vegetarian restaurant. If things go as well as she hopes they do, she'll be able to tell Peyton all about it at work tomorrow. Of course, she'll text Blair right away. Though she might have to text Liam first just to gloat.

When she arrives at the restaurant, Dr. Adrian is already there sitting at a table, studying the menu.

She glances down at herself. She's wearing a flowered skirt and a pink hoodie with a white tank top under it. Casual enough for lunch, but a little dressier than jeans. Her jeweled pink flip-flops round out her outfit.

"Hi!" She grins.

He looks up and smiles. "Hi, Tori."

She takes a seat opposite him at the table. His light blue shirt brings out the blue in his eyes.

She's not going to think about Liam's brown eyes or the richness of them. The way his gaze on her is always steady, and how there's so something hot about that.

"Everything all right?" Dr. Adrian asks. "You're frowning."

"Am I?" She waves her hand in the air. "It's nothing. Just something frustrating with one of my clients, that's all."

"Your clients?"

Tori tells him she has a pet sitting business called Happy Pet Nanny.

Dr. Adrian's seems interested. "I didn't know that. I'll keep you in mind if any of my patients need your service."

"Thanks." She doesn't bother telling him that Peyton and all the girls at the front desk already recommend Tori to people. Dr. Bradley, the other vet at the animal hospital, approved it ages ago.

A waitress comes by to take their order. Tori quickly studies the menu, then orders the soup and bread combo, while Dr. Adrian has a veggie burger.

"So," he says, crossing his hands in front of him, "I'm really glad you could join me for lunch today."

"Me too. And I love trying new restaurants. It makes things so much easier that we're both vegans, doesn't it?"

He nods. "It's nice going someplace where I can order anything I want."

"I know. Such a relief." She beams at him. Tori is filled with happiness. It's only been a few minutes, but so far this lunch is going great.

They discuss the animal hospital and some of their recent patients. Even though she's only a vet assistant, he never talks down to her. It's one of the many things she appreciates about him.

Eventually, she dials things up a notch.

"I hope this isn't too forward of me," she says in a flirty tone, "but I'm glad this is finally happening between us."

"Oh?"

"I know it's been really hard since you and Renée broke up, but I think it's great that you're moving on."

"Yes, about that." He leans back as the waitress brings them their food.

Tori waits until the dishes are placed in front of them before continuing. She lowers her voice. "I hope you didn't think I was being too forward when I kissed you that day."

Dr. Adrian watches her.

She picks up her spoon to eat her soup.

"Tori, I want you to know that was a nice kiss."

"It was? Oh, good." She's relieved. "I worried maybe you thought I was coming on too strong."

"In fact, I think you're a very pretty woman."

"Thank you." She sets her spoon down. She doesn't want to be slurping soup while he's saying romantic things like this.

"You have a kind nature. And in the harsh world we live in, that's no small thing."

She puts her hand over her heart. "What a sweet thing to say. You have a kind nature too."

"It's one of the reasons I hope we can be good friends."

She's still smiling, but her stomach drops. "Good friends?"

"I'm new to the area and haven't made many friends yet. Basically everyone I know is through my sister."

She tries to make sense of this. "I thought, or I hoped, that you and I would be *more* than friends."

Dr. Adrian shifts uncomfortably. "That's not possible."

"It's not?"

"I need to tell you something." He takes a deep breath. Finally, he leans forward and blurts out, "René isn't a she but a *he*."

"What?"

He chuckles, glancing around the restaurant. "This is kind of awkward for me. I haven't had to come out to anyone in a long time."

"Come out to anyone? What are you talking about?"

"Tori, I'm gay."

She blinks at him. For a crazy moment, she wonders if Liam's put him up to this. "I don't know why you're saying that."

"Because it's true. I'm sorry if I've given you the wrong impression, but I thought you knew. I thought everyone at work knew."

She thinks of how the women are all so in love with him at the animal hospital. "No." She swallows and shakes her head. "Nobody knows that."

His eyes are kind. "I've been openly gay my whole adult life. I came out to my family years ago, as a teenager."

She stares at him, but all she can see is the beautiful future she'd built for the two of them exploding into smithereens. There'll be no walks on the beach with their dogs. No picnics in the park. And worst of all, no cozy sweater Christmas cards.

"I'm very lucky," he continues. "I have a great family, and they've always supported me no matter what."

Tori's always supported gay people too, but she doesn't want to support this. She doesn't want him to be gay. "This isn't true. It can't be."

"It is. I'm very comfortable with who I am."

"But what about the look you gave me? What about that?"

He seems confused. "The look?"

"Yes, the *look!*" Hysteria rises within her. "When we first met. You were checking me out!"

"Tori, I don't know what you're talking about."

She tries to stay calm as she explains how when they were first introduced, his eyes were on her face, but then they dropped to her chest. "How else was I supposed to interpret that?"

He nods. "I think I do remember it now."

"And? How do you explain it?"

His tone is gentle—his veterinarian voice. She recognizes it from when he's dealing with a dog or cat in pain. "I was looking at the name embroidered on your smock."

She stares at him. "My *name?*"

"I have a hard time remembering people's names, so I try and use visual cues to help me."

"You weren't checking me out?"

"No, I wasn't." He leans forward, his voice still gentle. "But it doesn't change the fact that I think you're a very pretty wom—"

"Yeah, yeah, I get it." She leans back in her chair. "I can't believe this is happening."

"I hope we can still be friends."

She nods. She's certain Dr. Adrian is a great friend, but it's not exactly what she imagined here. "I feel dumb. I'm so embarrassed."

"Please don't be. Like I said, I'm flattered."

Tori glances around the restaurant. She wanted this perfect guy to be the one. She wanted the fantasy of Dr. Adrian.

Tears well up in her eyes. Why couldn't things have worked out for once?

He looks at her with sympathy.

"You don't know what it's like out there," she says, trying not to cry. "It's really hard. There are a lot of jerks."

"Tell me about it." He sighs. "Believe me, I do know. I've dated my share of them too."

Her brows go up. "You have?"

"Of course."

She takes this in. "I guess you would know, wouldn't you?"

He nods.

She wipes the tear that slips from the corner of her eye. "I'm sorry you've had to deal with jerks." She smiles a little. "That's why I like you so much. I can tell you're not one."

"I appreciate that. It means a lot coming from you. And I can tell you're great as well."

"Thanks," she murmurs and then smiles.

"Let's finish our lunch," he says, still using his veterinarian voice. "Does that sound okay?"

She nods and picks up her soup spoon. She's not hungry anymore, but has to get through this lunch somehow without further embarrassing herself.

WHEN THE LUNCH is over and they're at the cash register, Dr. Adrian insists on paying.

"You don't have to do that. I can pay."

"I want to. Please let me." He puts his hand on her arm. "Let's do this again soon. I meant what I said. I'd like to be friends."

She nods. "That would be nice." What else can she say? He's a great guy, and eventually he'll make some man a wonderful husband.

"Are you working later?" he asks.

She shakes her head. "Not until tomorrow."

"Okay, then I'll see you in the morning." He gives her a brief hug, and she pats his shoulder.

They head out of the restaurant. She's borrowing Blair's Honda again, and when she leaves the parking lot, she winds up right behind Dr. Adrian in his midnight blue Tesla.

A sigh of regret escapes her over that car. She's always imagined herself breezing around in it, Prince Charming at her side.

This sucks.

Tori decides to go home and work on her brother's website, to put all this out of her mind. She's volunteering at the no-kill animal shelter tonight. She also needs to check on her mom, who usually calls ten times a day but only called once earlier asking her to stop by after work.

As usual, her schedule is packed with a million things. She has a hard time saying no to people.

First she goes to Starbucks for a pick-me-up. She doesn't bother with a cinnamon vanilla almond milk latte anymore. No point in that.

Blair texts her while she's waiting in line for her green tea lemonade, but Tori doesn't answer, not ready to share her humiliation with anyone.

And to make this whole thing worse, Liam was right about everything. He knew she and Dr. Adrian were doomed from the start.

It figures.

Taking her drink, she has every intention of driving home but somehow winds up near his neighborhood instead.

There's no way Liam's there.

Not now.

Not in the middle of the day.

But then she remembers his injured knee and how he's been working from home all week.

She doesn't know what's gotten into her, but she grips the steering wheel and turns sharply onto his street, adrenaline spiking through her.

To hell with it.

If it's all going down in flames, then I'm going to burn with it.

She parks across the street from his house. He always has two cars in his driveway, his black truck and a four-door sedan that looks like a government car, and she sees them both.

Her heart pounds as she approaches his front door. *What are you doing?* she asks herself. But she keeps walking until she's standing right on his porch ringing the bell.

She tries to breathe.

Her heart's galloping.

She hears Miss Fancy Pants bark inside the house and bites her lip.

Maybe he isn't home.

Maybe this is a bad idea.

Maybe I've lost my mind.

When the door opens, she nearly moans at the sight of him. His black hair and rich brown eyes. He's wearing navy sweats and a gray T-shirt with the name of some local baseball team on it.

His hair is damp, and it looks like he's just taken a shower. She can even smell the soap.

"Tori?"

"Hi."

"What's wrong?"

"Nothing." She tries to keep her voice steady. "Can you invite me inside for a minute?"

His brows draw together as his gaze flickers over her. "Sure." He opens the door farther.

Miss Fancy Pants is there with her tail wagging, and her paws go up on Tori's shin. She can feel the weight of Liam's curiosity as she bends over to pet the little dog. "Hi, sweetie. It's good to see you too."

Finally she stands and faces him, her pulse still racing.

He scratches his jaw where dark stubble has grown in. It's obvious he's trying to figure out why she's here. "Did I forget you were pet sitting today?"

"No."

"Then why are you—"

She grabs his neck and pulls him down to her, kissing him.

He makes a noise in the back of his throat, but it's nothing like the startled squeak Dr. Adrian made.

It's a growl.

And it sounds approving.

In an instant, his strong arms wrap around her, pulling her tight against him.

All the time she's wasted denying this attraction, this chemistry, how much she wants him.

She's done with that.

"God, Tori," he breathes, coming up for air. "What's happened?"

"Don't talk," she says, pulling him in again. "Not a word."

The two of them go crazy on each other while standing in the foyer, filling it with the hot sounds of them making out.

But then he pulls away. "Come on." He takes her hand in his larger one. He's still limping, she notices. Still wearing the brace on his leg as he leads her over to the lumpy sofa.

"Talk to me," he says, sitting on it.

She admires his body without an ounce of guilt. So freeing. The T-shirt's thin material shows off the muscular outline of his shoulders and chest. The strong line of each bicep in his arms stands out.

Boldly, she sits on his lap, straddling him, and he doesn't stop her. Instead, he exhales sharply when she presses her center right against his hard-on.

She grips the back of his neck to pull him closer. "I don't want to talk."

"I get that," he murmurs.

She tries to kiss him again, but he holds her back. "Tell me what's happened. I want to know."

"Everything is fine. Better than fine."

"Something's obviously changed."

She puts her mouth to his ear and whispers, "Let's talk after." Then she sinks her teeth into his neck.

He gasps. His whole body shudders.

Something breaks loose in him. One hand moves up to grab a

fistful of her hair as his mouth slides over to cover hers. Their tongues move together with heat, just like their bodies. His hands slide under her hoodie, then under her tank top, onto bare skin.

"Do you have any kind of protection?" she asks, figuring there's only one direction this is headed.

He leans his head back on the couch, his breath unsteady, as he considers her. "*God*, look at you." He caresses her neck and collarbone. "So beautiful."

She blinks, stunned at the compliment. It's the last thing she expected from him. She must be more of an emotional wreck than she thought, because her throat closes up and she turns her head away, trying to hide how much she's affected.

"Thank you," she finally manages.

"Are you really okay? Is this about your lunch date?"

It figures he'd remember that. She doesn't want to talk about it, but it spills out anyway. "I feel so stupid."

"You're not stupid." Liam's eyes are steady on hers. "Sometimes we don't want to see the truth."

"I guess I should have listened to you."

"Is that why you came here?"

She leans in close and gives him a teasing smile. "I came here to use you for sex. Can't you tell?"

His gaze flickers over her body. "Mmm... interesting."

"You and I are going to have a hot and dirty fling today."

He slides his hands beneath the material of her skirt, stroking her legs. It's so good that she wants to purr like a cat. "And what happens after that?" he rumbles.

"Nothing." She splays her hands across the hard wall of his chest, delighted that she gets to touch him like this, that for one afternoon she has complete ownership.

His brows furrow. "What do you mean, nothing?"

She shrugs. "I mean we go our separate ways."

The hands stroking her legs stop. There's a frown on that bitable mouth.

"You're serious," he says, staring at her.

"Yes, I'm serious." She gives him a flirty smile, trying to lighten the mood. "Come on, Liam, are you really complaining? I'm offering you no-strings sex."

"And you think I'd be happy with that?"

"Why wouldn't you be?"

He's silent, studying her.

She tries not to roll her eyes. Nothing with him is ever simple. She runs her hands over his shoulders and then down his powerful arms, enjoying the solid feel of him. She can't remember the last time she's been this strongly attracted to anyone. "Do you really have to make this so complicated? Most guys would be thrilled."

He's clearly not thrilled though. "I'm not most guys."

"I just thought we'd have some fun. Forget about the past for a day, forget about everything. Get this out of our systems."

"I can't do that."

"Why?"

He only shakes his head.

She stares at him in amazement. "What are you saying? Are you turning me down?"

He doesn't reply, but he doesn't have to, because it's obvious that's exactly what he's doing. Her face burns. She can't believe this is happening.

"*Fine.*" Angrily, she pushes herself off him, though she still needs his shoulder for balance until she's on her feet. She adjusts her skirt with a clumsy movement.

A wave of humiliation washes over her that's oddly reminiscent of when he poured that milkshake on her years ago.

"Just so you know, I've never thrown myself at a guy like this in my life." She glares at him. "So don't go getting the wrong idea about me."

She closes her eyes and tries to ground herself, but it's hard. It's like she can't get a foothold.

When she opens them, he's still watching her.

"In fact, this was a one-time offer only."

He still doesn't reply, but it doesn't matter. She's mortified at his rejection. This whole day has been nothing but a series of embarrassments. All she wants to do is go home, binge-watch Netflix, and bury herself in a vat of coconut milk ice cream.

She turns to leave, but Liam's hand flies out and grabs hers before she can get away.

"Hey!" she says, jerking back. "What do you think you're doing?"

"Don't go."

"Why?"

He licks his lower lip. "Because I've changed my mind."

CHAPTER FOURTEEN

"SO? I DON'T CARE!" Tori pulls away from him.

"Stay," he says, his voice low and rough to his own ears. "Please."

She glares at him, and he can tell she's ready to leave and never come back. "Maybe that offer isn't on the table anymore."

He stands, though it's with less grace than usual since he's still wearing a knee brace. "You're right," he says. "We want each other. So let's get this out of our systems."

She felt so good in his arms. He must have gone temporarily insane turning her away. Maybe he wants more from Tori than an afternoon, but if an afternoon is all she's offering, then he'll take it.

"I don't know." She seems conflicted.

But then she reaches out and touches his chest. He places his hand over hers, pressing it into himself. It's right over his heart, and he hopes she can feel it pounding.

"I'm having a bad day," she whispers. "Maybe I should quit while I'm ahead."

"I know you are, *rubia*. Let me make it better." He laces his fingers through hers. "I promise I will."

She glances at the fiasco of a sofa in his living room.

"No, not here." He takes her hand and leads her toward his bedroom. He started sleeping in there again recently after throwing all the old bedding away and buying new stuff. There's nothing of Rachel's left at all.

Just before they enter the room, she stops him by tugging his arm. "This is only for today, right? Nothing more."

"I understand."

"We're just two people having down and dirty sex."

He smiles at her wording. Only Tori could make the words "down and dirty sex" sound sweet.

"A... one-afternoon stand. As opposed to a one-night stand," she clarifies. "That's all I'm looking for."

His mouth twitches. "I know."

"Good." She nods firmly. "Then let's get this done."

He chuckles, but as soon as they're in the room together and he sees Tori near his bed, his laughter fades. Disbelief settles over him. What do you do when your fantasy comes true?

Enjoy it, idiot. That's what.

"It's nothing personal," she says, kicking off her flip-flops and scooting farther up the bed. Her feet are pretty with bright pink toenails. "I just can't deal with another dead-end relationship."

He wants to correct her, to tell her he doesn't see it that way, but knows it's futile. She'll leave, and that's the last thing he wants.

"Would you mind closing the blinds?" she asks, her eyes roaming over his bedroom.

He goes over to shut them. It's darker, but it's the middle of the afternoon, so there's plenty of light.

"Is that better?" He moves closer to join her on the bed. She's sitting on what he still considers "his" side.

"Yes, thank you." Her eyes wander to his nightstand, which has a couple of handguns on it. His Glock 22—the one he nearly used on Rizzo—and the smaller 26 he uses for concealed carry.

"I can put them in a drawer."

"No." She turns back to him. "They don't bother me."

"You sure?"

She nods. They gaze at each other in the dim light. Tori's blue eyes seem huge. Freckles run across the bridge of her nose. A peculiar tightness grips his stomach and chest as he gazes at her.

Her blonde hair is pulled back in a ponytail, and he reaches out to touch it. "Will you let your hair down?"

"Okay."

He watches her pull the band out, her blonde hair tumbling over her shoulder.

He can't stop himself from reaching for a handful. "So beautiful," he murmurs.

"You don't have to keep saying stuff like that. It's not necessary."

He smiles. "Why? Because we're getting down and dirty?"

She rolls her eyes, but he can see she's smiling too. "People who are having an afternoon of lust-filled sex don't say things like that to each other."

He moves his hand up to trace along her hairline and then bends in closer to kiss her lips. Soft and lush. "I thought you've never done this sort of thing before," he whispers.

"I haven't," she whispers back.

"Then how would you know?"

She laughs, and he takes advantage of it by kissing her again. This time their tongues mingle, sliding over each other.

When they draw apart, he can't look away. She's both familiar and brand-new.

There's an energy humming through him, his senses heightened. He recognizes it. There've been other times in his life when he's experienced this electricity, always when something important was happening. The first time he crouched behind home plate in the majors. The first time he drew his weapon and stopped a criminal. And right now. Today.

The first time making love with Tori.

She smiles, but then it fades as she stares at his mouth. A needful expression comes over her. "I want to kiss you."

His cock stiffens. "Then do it," he says roughly.

She does, pulling him close. He senses she wants control, so he gives her as much as he's able to, forcing himself to hold back.

The smell of tangerines fills the air along with an underlying sweet musk he knows is simply her.

She pushes his T-shirt up, and he enjoys watching her lusty passion. He helps by pulling it over his head and throwing it aside. His eyes close when she runs her hands over his chest and abdomen.

Before he knows it, she's up on her knees, shoving him onto his back. He goes down, but the angle is awkward with his leg. He lets out an involuntary gasp.

She gasps too. "Oh no! Did I hurt you?"

"I'm fine." He catches his breath. "It's just my knee."

She hovers over him, strands of silky hair brushing his skin. "Are you okay? I didn't mean to be so forceful."

He chuckles. "Don't worry. I like you forceful."

"You do?"

He repositions himself on the bed and sits up. "Let me take this brace off."

She watches as he quickly undoes the straps and places it on the opposite nightstand.

When he turns back, her eyes are roaming his body, but then they go to his face. "I want you to know I think you're beautiful too."

"Thank you." He pauses, taking in her pretty features. He lies on his back with his head on the pillow. "You don't have to say that kind of stuff," he teases. "You've already got me where you want me."

She smiles. "And where's that?"

On my knees.

For you.

But he doesn't say that. "Ready for some down and dirty sex."

She giggles softly, and he reaches for her. She comes readily, lying over him. Her tangerine scent is everywhere, like summer sunshine. He closes his eyes. That feeling of electricity is still there.

It isn't long before their mouths and bodies intertwine, her breasts pressed against him, his hands sliding beneath her skirt.

He discovers Tori makes all sorts of noises when she's turned on. Little sounds of pleasure. He loves each one of them. Loves it when she sighs as his fingers stroke the outside of her panties, loves it when she gasps as they slip beneath the elastic, and loves it most when she moans as he slides them to where she's wet and swollen.

Those little sounds are going to be the death of him.

He wants to continue, but she has something else in mind as she sits up, straddling his thighs. She pulls down the zipper on her hoodie while he watches.

"So pretty," he says encouragingly. "Let me see all of you, rubia."

He's transfixed as the hoodie falls off her shoulders. She's wearing a white tank top beneath it, and that goes next. Finally, all that's left is her lacy bra.

The room is quiet, nothing but the sound of the two of them.

She glances toward the window, toward the closed blinds. He wonders if she's feeling shy.

"It's okay, no one can see us," he whispers. "Show me." He could reach up and help her take it off, but he wants to watch her do it.

Her hands go behind her back, and then the bra slides away.

He tries to breathe. Tori's breasts are full with dusky pink nipples. Pale and milky skin. His own skin looks dark next to hers.

He exhales slowly. The sixteen-year-old kid inside of him is filled with excited disbelief. The thirty-four-year-old guy inside of him is too. *This is Tori Church.* In his bed. In his arms.

He wonders if she has any idea how much she's affecting him.

And then she does something surprising. She reaches up and touches herself, tilting her head as she takes a breast in each hand and plays with her own nipples. She glides her fingers over them, gently tugging, blonde hair spilling over her shoulders. At the same time, she grinds herself against his hard-on with a little smile on her face.

He groans. The pervert in him wants to video this and watch it a thousand times. He'd never tire of it. He could jerk off to this the rest of his life and die happy.

"I think you're trying to end me," he finally manages to say, aching and nearly ready to take himself in hand and finish the job.

"I was hoping it might turn you on." Her voice lowers. "Does it?"

"Yes," he says huskily. "Very much. Does it turn *you* on?"

She seems to reflect on this. "I think so."

"Everything about you turns me on, Tori."

Her breath catches. There's a blush creeping up on her skin that he can just make out in the filtered light. "I'm glad," she whispers. Then she meets his eyes, sincerity in her gaze. "You turn me on too."

He's happy to hear it. He slips his hands under her skirt again, sliding his fingers over her damp panties. "I told you earlier I'd make you feel better."

She doesn't say anything.

"And I live up to my promises."

Her eyes widen as she understands his meaning.

"Scoot up and take the rest of this off," he says softly. "Let me make me you feel good."

TORI'S EYELIDS FALL SHUT. She pictures Liam's sensual mouth and what it's doing to her right now. Tonguing her clit. Licking her.

God.

It's almost enough to make her come.

Almost.

He's good at it too. Patient yet enthusiastic. She's had guys over the years who were terrible. Who didn't know a thing about female anatomy.

Liam isn't one of them.

Later tonight, when she's home alone and finally orgasms, this is what she'll think about. His mouth on her doing these wicked things.

His hands grip her thighs, then stroke her ass. It feels amazing, and at least he's enjoying himself. This afternoon has been a total turn-on. She knew it would be. He's super hot. So hot that a part of her hoped it would be enough.

Why isn't it?

A wave of frustration rises in her, and she could smack the wall in front of her. Every time, she hopes this will be the one, that things will be different, but it never is.

Instead, she'll have the girl equivalent of blue balls.

What's wrong with me?

She sighs to herself. It's not like she hasn't been here before.

She opens her eyes and checks out his room. There are photos on the wall she didn't notice earlier. Black-and-white pictures of the Oregon coast. Haystack Rock. She wonders who took them. Liam never mentioned being into photography.

It occurs to her how little she knows about him.

She glances down at the way he's pleasuring her. What a sight. His eyes are closed, his dark brows furrowed. Even like this, he's so handsome. Especially like this. She takes a mental picture for when she's alone later.

A few more minutes pass. It feels so good. She's tempted to try and come but knows it won't lead anywhere except more frustration.

He's been at it for a while. It's time.

She takes a deep breath, then puts her hands against the wall. Licks her lips. Ready to start the theatrics.

She's seen a number of pornos but doesn't model herself after those anymore. They're too fake. Instead, she models it after her own real orgasms but with a little more fireworks thrown in.

"Oh, yes," she moans loudly. "That's so good." She moves her hips around in circles. It's the same show every time. She throws in one final "Oh, yes" for good measure and figures she's done.

She moves off Liam's face. His mouth is open, his jaw flushed.

"That was wonderful," she says. "Just great."

Most guys are thrilled, cocky even, when she tells them that, but Liam's quiet.

She puts her hand on his chest, then slides it down his abdomen. She doubts he's suspicious. Men never are. Besides, even if he were, she knows the perfect way to throw him off the scent.

She slips her hand inside his sweatpants and boxers and wraps it around his cock.

He exhales with a gasp.

Wow, he's really hard. Like iron. And big too. She's impressed.

She moves closer to him, intrigued. "Do you have any kind of protection?"

He swallows and seems to be getting his bearings. "No, I don't have anything here."

"You don't?" This had never occurred to her. She's surprised at the depth of her disappointment. "Not even in your wallet? I thought all guys carried one in their wallets."

This makes him smile. "Not even in my wallet."

"I wish I'd known. I could have bought some."

He strokes a hand down her back. "Believe me, I wish I'd known too."

Her hand is still on his cock, and she grips him lightly. "Let me take care of you, then. It's not fair if I have all the fun."

The corner of his mouth kicks up. "Trust me, I was having fun. I loved making you feel good."

She nods, except she's getting weirdly choked up inside. The problem is, the more she gets to know Liam, the more she likes him. He's not exactly the jerk she thought he was.

She reminds herself that this is only for one afternoon.

"What are you thinking about?" he asks, watching her.

"Just you." She leans over to kiss him, and he pulls her toward him. She's still gripping his hard-on, and his hand slips over hers, schooling her, showing her exactly how he likes it. "This way?" she asks, following his instructions.

He nods and keeps his mouth close to hers. "That's right."

It doesn't take long before he's breathing hard, his body tense against her. As he gets more excited, she squirms and rubs her thighs together. There's something awfully sexy about straight-arrow Liam on the edge like this. When his breath turns erratic, so does hers.

"God, Tori," he says in a thick voice, his brown eyes half lidded. He exhales on a groan and goes right over the edge.

Afterward, he gazes at her.

"Did you like that?" she whispers.

"Yes," he says, still catching his breath. His voice rumbles. "More than you'll ever know."

She sits up. There's a box of tissue on the nightstand, and she reaches for a few. She's still trying to catch her own breath. In fact, she decides a visit to the bathroom is in order.

"Where are you going?" he asks as she slips out of bed.

"I just have to pee. Where's your restroom?"

He motions to a closed door. "The master bath's right in there."

"Okay, thanks."

She finds her panties and puts them on, then notices the T-shirt he wore earlier on the floor and picks it up. "Mind if I wear this? It's kind of chilly."

"Go right ahead."

Once inside the bathroom, she closes the door, and slips his T-shirt on. It smells so good, like a breezy day. Just like Liam.

Glancing around, she notes the space is bigger than she expected. White and green tile. Double sinks. A big tub. A black bathrobe hangs on the back of the door.

She hasn't had to do this in a guy's bathroom in a long time, but she's so aroused that there's no way she can wait until later.

Pulling his shirt up, she smells it, then leans back against the counter and slips her hand between her legs. Even though she's turned on, it still takes time to make herself climax.

Afterward, she breathes a big sigh of relief. That was necessary. *So* necessary.

Feeling much better, she pees and then washes her hands. There's toothpaste and a toothbrush in a white porcelain cup. A razor and shaving cream. She's tempted to snoop around but doesn't want to invade Liam's privacy like that.

Instead, she studies herself in the mirror. Her hair is a tangled mess. All previous makeup, except mascara, has worn away. Her cheeks are flushed a healthy pink though.

An orgasm will do that for you.

When she leaves the bathroom, Liam is in bed under the covers, obviously naked.

"Everything okay?" he asks. "You were in there a while."

"I'm fine."

He's lying on his side and pulls the duvet back for her. "Come lay in bed with me."

"Sorry, but I can't."

"Why not?"

She thinks of all the things she has to do. "I have a busy day, that's all."

"Just for a little while," he coaxes. "Come on."

The bed does look inviting, especially with his big, warm body in it. His hair is mussed, and he looks boyishly handsome.

Before she knows it, she's walking toward him. "Well, maybe just a few minutes."

"Perfect." He grins. "Take your clothes off, or should I say my clothes."

"I like this shirt." She fingers the hem. "It might have to come home with me."

"I don't think so. That shirt stays here, young lady."

"Geez, you're bossy." But she does what he asks and takes the shirt off. She holds it in front of herself and sees it's for a Little League team. "I take it you're a fan of theirs?"

"I coached them for two years."

"Really?" She tries to imagine him doing that, and it's easy to picture.

"Now bring that gorgeous body over here."

She climbs into bed and finds it's quite comfortable, especially once he's wrapped around her. Safe and secure. Relaxed.

"This is nice."

His throat rumbles in agreement.

They're both quiet, though she hears little dog nails tapping against the wood floor outside the door. "I'm surprised Miss Fancy Pants hasn't tried to join us."

"There's been a squirrel hanging around the backyard all day," he murmurs sleepily. "I think Fancy is guarding the house."

"I'll bet that squirrel is teasing her." She's seen them do it with her own dogs.

"Probably."

She relaxes again but then remembers something. "Why do you keep calling me rubia? What is that?"

His arm shifts around her waist. "It means blondie."

"Blondie?"

"It's a term of affection we use in Spanish."

"You've given me a nickname?"

"I have."

She doesn't know why, but she's secretly pleased.

He yawns behind her. She thinks about what a bizarre day this has been. Whoever thought this was where she'd end up?

In Liam's bed.

It's relaxing here though. She closes her eyes. She can't remember the last time she's felt this snug and cozy and gives herself a few minutes to enjoy it.

Except she doesn't count on falling asleep.

CHAPTER FIFTEEN

TORI'S adrenaline sky rockets when she opens her eyes and discovers the afternoon light doesn't look like afternoon light anymore.

It looks like evening light.

She sits up with a jerk. "Oh my God!"

"What's wrong?" Liam turns to her.

"Where are my clothes? I have to get dressed." She springs out of bed like a wind-up toy and runs around the room naked. "We overslept! I have a million things to do. I'm supposed to deliver Happy Pet

Nanny treats to my clients. I'm volunteering at the no-kill shelter tonight, and I need to update some pages on my brother's website."

Liam sits up in bed too, but instead of moving a muscle, he leans back on his elbows, watching her. He seems to be enjoying himself too. In fact, there's a lazy grin on his face.

"Don't just sit there," she berates him. "Get up and help me!"

He scratches the back of his neck and seems to consider it. Finally, he pushes the covers away and stands with a hop.

She can't resist taking a peek at his bare ass.

Very nice.

He yawns as he puts on boxer briefs that seem to have magically appeared in his hand. It figures he'd find his clothes easily.

"Three of the people buying my dog snacks are new. They're going to think I'm a total flake. Ugh." She gets on her knees to look under the bed. Yes, there are her panties. How did they get there?

"Your brother has a website?" He slips back into his sweatpants with some awkwardness, and she remembers his injured knee.

She nods in affirmation as she finally sees her bra tucked under the duvet. Happily, she finds the rest of her clothes under there too. "It's for his company."

Liam's mouth opens. "His company?"

"Yeah, you know." She puts her clothes on as quickly as possible.

"What kind of company?"

Zipping her hoodie up, she remembers something else. "I'm supposed to stop by my mom's tonight." She slaps her forehead. "She'll go nuts if I don't show up!"

"Damn, Tori. Relax. Is this really how you plan your days?"

Instead of answering him, she struggles into her skirt. At least her flips-flops are where she left them, at the foot of his bed.

She slips them on quickly and smooths her hair. "I'm afraid to ask what time it is, but I don't have my watch on, and I left my phone in the car."

He picks his up off the dresser. "Five thirty."

"No." Her eyes go wide as all the breath leaves her body. "Are you serious? I have to go."

Liam seems nonplussed. "It's rush hour traffic. You might as well wait it out. I'll throw some food together, and we can have dinner."

She stares at him, wondering if he's crazy. "Have you been paying *any* attention to what I just said? Everybody's relying on me!"

He moves toward her, still limping and still shirtless.

Tori glances down at his leg. "You should put your brace back on." She goes to retrieve it from his nightstand. "Here, I can help. Have a seat."

He doesn't argue and sits on the bed, but when she comes over with the knee brace, he takes it from her. "It's faster if I do it."

"You should keep it elevated and iced." Watching him, she has to admit he is fast. It's obvious he's done this a lot.

"When will I see you again?" he asks.

"Tomorrow."

He glances up at her and seems both surprised and pleased. "Good."

"We have a Happy Pet Nanny appointment. I'm bringing Miss Fancy Pants to my house for a playdate."

He's finished with the brace and studies her in that penetrating way. "That's not what I meant."

She sighs and turns her head. "I know what you meant. But this was the deal, remember? One afternoon. In fact—" She licks her lips. "—I'd like to go back to keeping this relationship professional."

He stands and doesn't look pleased anymore. Thunderous would be a better description. "You've got to be kidding me."

"It's for the best."

"The hell it is."

A wave of frantic energy rushes through her. "I'm sorry, but I have to go."

"Hey, slow down." He grabs her hand. "Listen, I'm going into work tomorrow. I'll text you when I'm done."

"No, don't text me." She corrects herself. "Well, only if it's because you're picking up your dog."

"You can't be serious about this one-afternoon stuff."

"I am serious. It was fun, but it's over." He's still holding her hand, and she softens her voice. "I had a really nice time today, but there's no point in seeing each other again. I have to move forward with my life now."

"Then let's move forward together."

She rolls her eyes and laughs. "Seriously?"

"Yes, I'm serious."

"We barely know each other, but don't you think it's enough? We're like total opposites. It would be nothing but a distraction from meeting our true soul mates."

"Like you and Dr. Adrian?"

She pulls her hand from his. "You don't have to rub it in. I feel stupid enough already."

"I'm not rubbing it in. I'm just pointing out how you can't plan everything. Sometimes people surprise you."

"Yes, well." She turns her head. "I was certainly surprised, wasn't I?"

Liam stares at her and seems frustrated. "I don't think we're as different as you say we are. And even if we are, so what? I like you."

"I like you too, but it's not enough. I can't waste any more time. I want to find my special someone."

He opens his mouth to argue, and she puts her fingers to his lips to stop him. "Please, let's just have this nice memory of today and leave it at that."

Except he reaches up and holds her wrist, gently biting her fingers.

Her stomach goes quivery. "Don't."

"I haven't gotten you out of my system. I don't want to."

"Don't say that," she moans. "We both need to stop making bad choices."

He seems taken aback. "I don't make bad choices."

"Oh, really? Was Rachel a good choice, then?"

He lowers her hand and then lets it go. He seems annoyed.

"I don't know the story between you two, but obviously it didn't end well. Obviously she didn't run off to Buenos Aires alone."

"It has nothing to do with you and me. That relationship is over."

She studies him and wonders if he still has feelings for Rachel. "Maybe we are sort of alike," she muses. "We both pick the wrong people."

He shakes his head, then reaches for her hand again. "There's nothing wrong about this."

"I don't have time to argue anymore. I have to leave."

"At least kiss me before you go. Otherwise, I might feel cheap and used by our afternoon of lust."

A burst of laughter escapes her.

"Come here." He grins, pulling her in close.

Before she knows it, she's in his arms, still laughing. Despite the things she said, he's stirring up all sorts of feeling in her. Desire, but a kind of happiness too. Liam feels both wrong and right.

IT'S late by the time she gets to her mom's house. She already texted all her Happy Pet Nanny clients apologizing for not delivering their bag of dog snacks today. She lets them know she'll deliver them tomorrow instead.

One more thing added to another packed day.

At least there's no yellow Charger parked in her mom's driveway, so she won't have to deal with Wayne the pain.

Weeds are sprouting everywhere, and she notes that the grass needs mowing as she crosses the lawn. The house she grew up in is lettuce green on the outside—a color her mom saw in a magazine and thought looked cheerful.

Tori doesn't knock, just walks right in. "Anybody home?" she calls out, closing the door behind her. Familiar smells from her childhood come back—the faint odor of last night's dinner mixed with stale cigarette smoke.

"In here."

Tori follows her mom's voice into the kitchen. She's there in her stocking feet, still wearing her office clothes. She works for the gas utility company and has for many years.

"Hey, baby girl." She glances at Tori. "Did you just get off work?"

Tori doesn't reply, figuring there's no way she can explain her afternoon with Liam. Not to anyone.

"Would you like a drink?" Her mom's nightly routine is to come home from work, make herself a whiskey sour, and then sip it as she prepares dinner.

"No, thanks."

Tori watches her squeeze fresh lemon juice into a short glass before adding a teaspoon of sugar. There's a large bottle of bourbon nearby. As usual, her mom's dark pencil skirt is too short and tight, her blouse cut too low. Even her hair is too blonde. The heels kicked off in the corner are two inches too high for an office job, not that it stops her from wearing them.

When Tori was a kid, she thought her mom was the most beautiful woman in the world. All her friends agreed she had the prettiest mom. Tori was so proud of her. She used to show them pictures of her mom's pageant days, and they'd all ooh and ah.

As a teenager that changed though. She saw her mom with different eyes and realized none of the other moms looked like hers. She didn't want a MILF. She wanted someone normal like Blair's mom, not someone who looked like an aging stripper.

Her mother didn't care and did whatever she pleased.

Now as an adult, Tori neither loves nor hates her mom's clothing choices. She simply accepts them. The four-inch heels and the too-short dresses. The big blonde hair that's too much for a woman her age. Although her age has become a moving target. She's been shaving off so many years lately, pretty soon the two of them will have the same birthdate.

She can't help laughing to herself at this.

"Is there an angel tickling you?" her mom asks glancing over. "Or maybe it's a devil?"

"An angel," Tori says softly. Her mom may have her faults, but she loves her.

"I was hoping it might be a devil." She gives her a wink and sucks on a maraschino cherry. "Maybe a sexy devil, with an even sexier older brother."

Tori laughs out loud. "One for each of us?"

"Exactly, baby girl."

She smiles. This is how she likes her mom best. Playful and funny.

And sober.

Speaking of devils makes her think of Liam again, of the way he tempts her, leading her down the wicked path.

A sexy devil, for sure.

"Let me help you get dinner started," Tori says, going over to the sink to wash her hands. She wants to make sure her mom has an actual meal and not a liquid dinner. She also needs to look through her mom's monthly bills and make sure everything's getting paid.

"Wayne's in Idaho on business, so I was just planning to heat up a Lean Cuisine. Get one for yourself too."

"I can't eat those, remember?" No matter how many times she's told her mom she's a vegan, it never sinks in.

"I don't think they have much meat in them. Some of them are just cheese."

"That's okay. I can't stay long tonight anyway."

"Why not?" Her mom picks up her drink and sips it. "I thought we'd have dinner together."

"Sorry. I just have a lot of things to do." Tori sets the frozen meal in the microwave.

Her mom's tired blue eyes study her. She takes another sip from her glass, and when she speaks, her voice sounds disapproving.

"You're not seeing that FBI agent tonight, are you? I hope you two aren't involved with each other."

Tori glances over. "No, I'm not seeing him."

"Good, because I don't want him in my house again."

"He's just a friend."

Her mother puts her drink down, shaking her head. "I still can't get over you bringing him here. What were you thinking? A fed, of all people."

"I told you he was helping me with Mable. And then I had to come by because Donna called."

"Any more news about Mable?"

"No, but Brody said he'd handle her being towed as soon as the police are done with their investigation." She called her cousin a few days ago, and he said he'd take care of things from here and not to worry anymore. He said he'd help her find a new minivan too.

"Do they have any leads on who stole her?"

"No, I don't think so. Or at least they haven't told me anything yet." She remembers how Liam said he planned to call the detective in charge, but she doesn't mention that.

Her mom sighs. "I'm so sorry about what happened to Mable. You'll let me know if they find out anything new, okay?"

Tori shrugs. "Sure."

Once the microwave meal is finished, Tori grabs a bottle of flavored water from the fridge, which she replenishes regularly, and they both head into the living room.

"I haven't showed you the latest, have I?" her mom says, taking a seat in the recliner. "Look over there and see what Wayne got me."

Tori's mouth drops open when she sees the giant television. "Wayne bought you that?"

"He did." Her mom seems delighted at Tori's shocked response. "You'll have to hear it too. There's a sound system. It's just like being in a movie theater."

"How can he afford that?"

She shrugs, still smiling like the cat that ate the canary. "Guess things are going real good for him."

"What does he do for a living again?"

"He's a tire salesman."

"Last time you told me he worked for a salvage yard."

"He does both. Sells tires and works at the salvage yard." Her mom sets a dishtowel on her lap and then her dinner. "He's a hard worker, that one."

"And he travels out of state for which job?"

"I'm not sure."

Tori sips her strawberry-flavored water. It all sounds fishy, and she knows she's not getting the full story.

"Oh, and I haven't shown you this either." Her mom reaches around her neck for the gold chain tucked inside her blouse. "He gave it to me last week."

It's a ring shaped like a gold flower with a large sapphire in the middle. It's hanging on the chain. Clearly expensive.

"He says it reminded him of me. 'A beautiful flower for a beautiful lady.'" She smiles. "Isn't that sweet? I'm wearing it around my neck, close to my heart, until I get it sized."

Tori stares at the ring and feels uneasy. "Where did he buy it?"

The ring and necklace disappear beneath her mom's blouse. She picks up her fork. "I'm not sure. He didn't say."

"You didn't ask?"

Her mom takes a bite of the hot food and chews slowly. "Why would I ask? It would be like looking a gift horse in the mouth."

Tori doesn't like any of this. God knows where that ring came from. "I just think it might be good to know where he bought it. Maybe the jeweler would resize it for you at no charge."

"Maybe." Her mom takes another bite of food. "I'm not going to worry about it." She reaches for her glass. "Wayne is taking good care of me. The way a man should take care of his woman."

LIAM GETS the call he's been hoping for, the one from Nelson asking if it's okay to invite Shelby to play paintball.

"Sure, that's fine."

"You're cool with it? I thought you guys were involved, but after you called the other day, it didn't sound like it."

"It's no problem at all. Shelby and I are *just* friends." He puts an emphasis on it since he doesn't want any ambiguity. He's relieved things are working out this way. After he saw Shelby the other day and they had lunch on his patio, he called Nelson and dropped some hints that she might be romantically interested in him. The two of them had certainly seemed to hit it off that night.

"I was sorry to hear what happened with Rachel," Nelson says. "You should have called me sooner."

"Thanks. I just wasn't feeling social."

"Hang on a second." There's some background noise on the phone, and it sounds like Nelson is shifting position. Liam knows he pitched last night and figures he's on the table getting his arm and back worked on. "I get that you weren't feeling social, but we go way back. Hell, I talked your damn ear off during my divorce."

Liam chuckles. "True."

"You can rely on me, you know that."

"I know. I appreciate it."

"And you're sure about me hitting up Shelby for some paintball action? We'll probably get a drink afterward. To be honest, I thought she was cute."

"Go for it. Like I said, we're only friends."

"Okay. Let's make some plans soon too. I was thinking the other day that we should do another fishing trip when the season's over. What do you think?"

"Sounds good." A couple years ago, right after Nelson's divorce, the two of them went fishing for four days in Oregon. It turned out to be a nice getaway. A chance to relax with an old friend.

After they hang up, Liam tries to focus on the Rizzo file again. The problem is, he can't stop thinking about Tori. He's been reliving yesterday afternoon constantly. The way she felt in his arms, the way she tasted. It was a fantasy come to life.

He keeps thinking about when he made her come. He loved it. It turned him on so much that he's jerked off to it twice already, replaying it in his mind, examining it.

Except the more he examines it, something about it bothers him. He's nuts for questioning anything, but he can't help himself. It's what he does for a living.

Was it possible that she faked her orgasm?

It's a strange notion, but he keeps coming back to it. He knows all women are different. In his experience though, most women are languid and loose after they come, or sometimes they're even more excited, but there was no change in Tori at all.

He shakes his head with disgust. *What the hell am I doing?*

Ruining one of the greatest afternoons of his life, that's what. Tori was sexy and beautiful, and their chemistry was off the charts. He can't wait to see her later today, even if it's just picking up Fancy from her house.

That's the problem with a job where you're trained to spot a liar, to analyze people and their motives, to be suspicious. Especially when it's a job you're good at.

Sometimes it's hard to turn it off.

CHAPTER SIXTEEN

"I CAN'T BELIEVE IT," Peyton says after Tori tells her about the lunch with Dr. Adrian. "He's so perfect. It just figures he's playing for the other team."

Tori's been working with Dr. Adrian all morning. They've had six patients together, and he's been treating her like she's made of glass.

"It's humiliating," she tells Peyton. "I really thought we had something."

"I know, honey. I thought you did too."

"I had a whole life planned for us." She knows how dumb that sounds and feels even dumber admitting it out loud.

Her friend's expression is sympathetic. "You'll meet someone else. Give it time."

Tori's thoughts immediately go to Liam, who she's been thinking about since yesterday. He made her feel beautiful and desirable, which was exactly what she needed. "I want to meet my special person, that special someone," she says, feeling more desperate than ever. "Why can't I find him? You found yours."

"I got lucky. But like I said before, I had to kiss a lot of toads first."

"But I have kissed a lot of toads! Too many. My lips are chapped from all the horny toads I've kissed."

Peyton laughs. "Girl, you need a break. A step back from all this. Maybe take a vacation."

Tori snorts. "I wish I could. But there's too much to do. You know what my life is like."

"I know, but you need a few days off." Peyton's brown eyes light up. "Hey, I have an idea. Maybe you could stay at my cousin's cabin."

"You mean that place up in Truth Harbor?"

She nods enthusiastically. "It would be perfect. It's small and cute. Very private."

"I don't know. What would I do there?"

"Just relax and regroup." Peyton nods. "I'm going to ask Tara. I'm sure she won't mind. Especially when I tell her about everything that happened recently."

"That I fell for a gay guy?" Tori shakes her head, mortified at the thought of a complete stranger knowing this about her. "Please don't tell her that."

"I'll just tell her you're a good friend who could use some time away. That you've always come through for me, and I want to return the favor."

"But I don't see how I can get away."

"Don't say no yet. Let me ask her first." Peyton puts her hand on Tori's arm. "You're always taking care of everyone else. But you need to take care of yourself for once."

Tori doesn't know what to say. She can't possibly go stay in some cabin, no matter how great it sounds.

During her midmorning break, she delivers dog snacks to all her Happy Pet Nanny clients. Some of them are home, and a few ask about some healthy cat snacks, so that might be her next project.

Flashes of yesterday with Liam keep coming back to her in a rush. Not just the sex stuff, but the way he looked at her with a kind of wonder. Then afterward, lying in bed with him so cozy. She's bummed about Dr. Adrian, but Liam made her feel good about herself.

A small part of her is thinking maybe he's right too. Maybe one afternoon isn't enough to get each other out of their systems. So what if they have a past? Would a little fling be so terrible?

He could be my vacation.

Eventually her morning work is finished, and she swings by his house to pick up Miss Fancy Pants. She texts him when she's parked in his driveway to let him know she's there so he can turn off the alarm, since he's at work today.

On a whim, she decides to be honest in her text. *I'm not sure I've gotten you out of my system either.*

She sees him responding right away. *You don't know how happy I am to hear that.*

What should we do about it?

I have some ideas. :) Can I see you tonight?

She's supposed to have dinner with Blair and Road. Part of her is tempted to cancel. She knows Liam is waiting with bated breath.

I have plans tonight, but tomorrow would be good.

Okay. You've been on my mind so much. I can't stop thinking about you.

Me too. But I have some ground rules.

Whatever you want, rubia.

She can't resist smiling. *I'll see you tomorrow, then.*

She adds three happy face emojis, then sighs and puts her phone away and gets out of the car. After punching in the security code, she waits for his garage door to lift.

She hopes she's not making a mistake with Liam. Her history with men isn't great. While she doesn't pick the kind of assholes her mom does, she's had her fair share of jerks. Her instincts about men aren't always good. I mean, let's face it, even when she did find a nice guy, he turned out to be gay.

She enters the house through the door inside the garage, which leads straight into the laundry room.

Over the years, a lot of clients have trusted her with their homes, and she's always careful with that trust. She never violates it. Being the Happy Pet Nanny is all about helping people and their animals, so it would never occur to her to snoop through their things.

For instance, there's a suitcase in Liam's laundry room. It's the first thing she notices.

Why would he have a suitcase out? He didn't mention going anywhere.

But then that's none of her business, so she doesn't look at it too closely.

As she walks farther into the house, she sees Miss Fancy Pants trotting out from his bedroom.

"Hi, girl. Are you ready for your playdate?" She expects the dog to come to her, but Miss Fancy Pants goes back into the room.

That's weird.

Normally she wouldn't dream of going into a client's bedroom, but since she was in there yesterday, and since they're sort of having a fling, it has to be okay, right?

She walks over to the bedroom's doorway. As soon as she enters it, she shrieks with alarm.

There's a woman standing there, her hair wrapped in a towel.

Startled, the woman shrieks too. "Who the hell are you?"

"I'm the Happy Pet Nanny. Who the hell are *you*?" Tori shouts back at her.

"The what?"

Tori's hand flutters to her chest as she tries to calm herself. This woman's hair is wrapped in a towel, and it's obvious she's just taken a shower. "I'm the pet sitter. Are you a friend of Liam's?" she asks, mystified.

"Wait a minute. I know you, don't I?"

Tori's taken aback. "No, I don't think we've ever met."

"Sure we have. You work at the animal hospital, right?"

"Yes." She glances at Miss Fancy Pants, who's sitting on the bed watching the exchange.

"I'm Liam's girlfriend, Rachel. I recognize you from when I've brought my dog in."

Tori's mouth falls open with shock.

"I didn't know he hired a pet sitter." Rachel walks over to sit on the bed next to the little dog, scratching behind her ears. "I hope you've been taking good care of my baby."

With even more shock, she notices Rachel's wearing Liam's T-shirt. The same T-shirt Tori had on only yesterday afternoon.

It bothers her, but not as much as the way she's petting Miss Fancy Pants and acting like nothing happened, like she didn't abandon her.

"So now Miss Fancy Pants is your baby?"

Rachel glances up. "What?"

"You abandoned this dog, and now you show up and act like nothing happened. Do you have any idea what you put her through?"

Irritation wrinkles her brow. "Um, I don't know you, and I don't owe you an explanation for anything."

"Selfish people always say stuff like that. They do as they please and don't care who they harm in the process."

Rachel scowls. "Where do you get off talking to me like that? You know nothing about me."

"Oh, I know plenty. I know you abandoned Miss Fancy Pants and ran off to Brazil... or Argentina," Tori amends. "I forget which."

She laughs. "Are you for real?"

"Yes, I'm for real."

Miss Fancy Pants huffs, and Rachel glances down at her. "Well, she looks just fine to me."

"Looks can be deceiving. Take you, for instance. You look like a normal person, but you're really a selfish monster."

Her expression hardens. "I don't know who in the hell you think you are, but you need to get out of my house."

"I came here to get Miss Fancy Pants for a playdate."

"She's not going anywhere with you." She pets the little dog and scratches her chin. "Mama's home now. And don't you worry, I'm here to stay."

Tori sucks in her breath.

Rachel's gaze flashes over to her. "I know Liam doesn't like dogs"—her voice is dry—"but he must have been seriously desperate to hire someone as crazy as you."

"I'm not crazy."

"Whatever. Just get the fuck out of my house. I don't want you near me or my dog ever again."

Tori is ready to tell her this isn't her house, it's Liam's, but then she realizes she has no idea who owns this house. The two of them lived here together. They may have bought it together.

As Rachel glares at her, comfortable in her surroundings, the truth drenches Tori like an ice-cold chocolate milkshake.

Liam's done it to her again.

She's humiliated.

It's obvious he and Rachel have unfinished business. They have a history. A life together. And now that she's back, Tori has no business being here in the middle.

What's wrong with me?

Even for a simple fling, she couldn't get it right.

Her eyes sting. She's surprised how upset she is, but there's no way she's crying in front of Rachel. She gazes down at Miss Fancy Pants. The dog's big dark eyes are watching her. "You be a good girl," she says to her softly. "Always remember you deserve the best."

Rachel is staring at her like she's a freak, but Tori doesn't care.

Maybe I am a freak.

She turns and leaves the bedroom, heading toward the front door. She always leaves out of the garage when Liam isn't here, but there's no point in that.

To her surprise, she hears barking and then little nails on the hardwood. When she turns around, Miss Fancy Pants is running toward her.

Her heart squeezes in her chest when she kneels on the floor. "Oh, sweetie. You'll be okay." The words are as much for herself as Miss Fancy Pants. Her little paws are on Tori's chest, hugging her.

By now Rachel has come out of the bedroom. She stands there with her arms crossed.

When Tori gets up, Miss Fancy Pants barks again, her front paws still resting on Tori's legs. "I have to go now."

"Yes, just *leave*." Rachel's hostile tone makes it plain who the interloper is here.

Tori turns toward the door and gets out of there as fast as she can.

SINCE HE'S BEEN out of the office all week, Liam's afternoon is busy. Not just paperwork to contend with but two meetings, one with his ASAC and another with the prosecutor at the U.S. Attorney's Office. Everyone is thrilled with the Rizzo arrest. It isn't until after four that he realizes Tori never texted him back about the alarm. He figures she forgot, so he checks on her.

Everything okay with the playdate? I never heard back about the alarm.

He waits but doesn't see a response. She's probably busy with four dogs at her house. He can only imagine the chaos. He hopes Fancy's enjoying herself and Tori's dogs aren't too much for her.

After another ten minutes pass, he gets a little concerned.

Could you text me? Just want to make sure everything is okay with you and Fancy.

He waits again, but there's still no response. He's ready to call her, but then a message from Tori pops up.

Miss Fancy Pants isn't here. You'll have to ask Rachel how she's doing.

He stares at the text. *What are you talking about?* Except there's a sinking feeling in his gut. He hopes she's not saying what he thinks she is.

I went to your house to get Miss Fancy Pants and Rachel was there.

He curses aloud. This can't be happening. Not now. Not when things in his life were finally improving.

Another text from Tori appears. *Please don't call or text me anymore. You and Rachel should work out your problems.*

He calls her anyway, listens as her voicemail picks up. "Tori, it's me. If Rachel is at my house, I assure you it's not by invitation. I haven't heard a word from her in two months. I want nothing to do with her."

Grabbing his bag, he shoves his laptop into it. On the way out, he sees Matt and lets him know he's headed home.

"Everything okay?" Matt asks. "You seem upset. Is the knee bothering you?"

"No, it isn't that." He explains how it appears Rachel is back.

Matt's brows shoot up. "Damn, seriously? What are you going to do?"

Liam sucks in his breath. "Go home and deal with it."

He heads out to his truck. He drove it to work instead of his bureau car, since it's roomier in the cab and easier to manage with his knee brace. As usual, Seattle traffic is bumper to bumper. He tries calling Tori two more times, but she still won't pick up.

He can't believe this.

Liam calls Rachel too, but to his surprise, the number is disconnected. He had no idea she'd changed it.

By the time he gets home, it's early evening. His neighborhood is quiet as usual.

As soon as he enters the front door, he senses she's there. He smells food cooking in the kitchen. Miss Fancy Pants greets him, and as he heads into the living room, he's disturbed to see Rachel sitting on the chewed-up sofa.

Anger pulses through him, and he tries to tamp it down.

He honestly hoped he'd never see her again. In fact, he assumed he wouldn't, which is why he never bothered changing the locks or the alarm code. A giant mistake in hindsight.

"Hi, Liam." She smiles up at him. There's a glass of iced tea in her hand, and she puts it on the coffee table.

He shakes his head, incredulous. "What the hell do you think you're doing here?"

"I'm making dinner." She glances toward the kitchen. "It's just spaghetti. You need to go grocery shopping. Maybe we can do that this weekend."

He studies her, assessing the situation. She looks the same. Long brown hair with bangs. Big brown eyes.

He used to think she was pretty. Beautiful even.

He used to think he was in love with her.

Hard to believe he'd ever felt that way since she'd destroyed it so thoroughly. Every lie that came from her lips, every time she came home late and took a shower so he couldn't smell another man on her, every transgression a new hammer blow, until finally his love was smashed to dust.

She shifts on the couch nervously. She's trying to act casual, but he knows her body language.

He gazes down at her. "So he didn't want you after all, huh?"

Her eyes flash to him. "I came back for *you*."

"Let's not play this stupid game."

Her lips purse together. She glances at the brace on his leg but doesn't comment. "I was hoping you'd be glad to see me."

"Why would you think that?"

She tries to look contrite. "Because I missed you, that's why."

"I don't care. I want you out of here." He limps farther into the living room.

"Don't be like that. We had some good times. Do you really want to throw it all away?"

He'd laugh if this situation weren't so disgusting. "Rachel, you threw it away yourself months ago."

She turns her head but doesn't say anything.

His eyes roam over her, curious. Searching to see if it really is gone, if he has any feelings left for her at all, and there's nothing. It's true what they say. The opposite of love isn't hate. It's indifference.

"Just let me stay the night," she pleads. "We can talk this over."

"No."

"I know you, Liam. And I know you're not the kind of a man who'd throw a woman out on the street."

"Don't worry." He snorts as he pulls his phone out of his pocket. "I'm not throwing you out on the street. I'm calling you an Uber."

Her expression hardens. "And exactly where am I supposed to go?"

"I don't care. Stay at a hotel. Or go stay with one of your sisters." He glances over at her. "Or have you burned those bridges too?"

She leans back on the couch and crosses her arms. "You've changed. When did you become such an asshole?"

"Call me whatever you want. We both know who the asshole is here."

"It was one time," she says with frustration. "I cheated on you *once*, and now you're holding it against me?"

He stares at her in amazement. "You ran off to Argentina with another man."

"And you never strayed during those trips you took for work? Never got lonely in your hotel room?"

"No. I was always faithful to you."

She sneers. "So I guess that makes you better than me, is that it? You and your moral superiority. You always think you're better than everybody."

"It's not about better or worse," he says heatedly. "It's about right and wrong."

She gets up from the couch and comes toward him, her face earnest. "God, you're such a Boy Scout, but I missed that about you. C'mon, admit it," she says with a sly smile. "You missed me too. Missed my bad influence—even if it's just a little."

She tries to stroke his arm, but he pulls back. "Don't," he says. "There's no point. It's over."

"Even when I was in Buenos Aires, I still thought about you. I couldn't help it."

He rolls his eyes. "Are you hearing yourself?"

"I made a mistake leaving. I know that now. And I swear, I've gotten it out of my system. I'm ready to come home."

There's a pleading look on her face. It's not in his nature to be cruel, but clearly she needs to hear the hard truth. "Rachel, I don't love you anymore. I can't be any plainer than that."

Her expression changes.

"It's over between us. For good."

"You don't mean that."

"I do."

"Fine." She crosses her arms. "Whatever. I'm not going to beg. You want me to leave? I'll leave."

"Great."

"Let me get my dog and I'll be out of your way." She turns and appears to be searching around for Miss Fancy Pants, who's sitting in the corner on the new dog pillow Liam bought her from Amazon last week. He read eight pages of reviews before finally deciding on that one. It sounded the most comfortable.

He goes still. Dangerously still. "What did you just say?"

"I said I'm taking my dog, and then I'm leaving."

"You're not taking that dog anywhere."

She snorts. "Yes, I am. Miss Fancy Pants is mine."

"Not anymore she's not."

Rachel rolls her eyes and looks at him like he's nuts. "What is this? Some kind of payback?"

"You abandoned her."

"Oh my God, you sound just like that crazy bitch you hired as a pet sitter. Yes, this is my dog." She speaks to him like he's an imbecile. "I'm the one who brought her home, remember?"

"I repeat, this dog stays." His jaw clenches. "And that pet sitter is neither crazy nor a bitch."

Rachel blinks at him with astonishment, but then a knowing look comes over her face. She lets out a spiteful laugh. "Oh, I get it now. It's all become crystal clear. You've got the hots for the pet nanny, don't you?"

He doesn't respond because he does have the hots for Tori. The hots and then some.

"She's a total weirdo. I mean, you should have heard the things she said to me."

"I'm sure everything she said to you was true."

"Is that why you want this dog? To impress her so she'll keep coming back?"

Liam pauses at this. Is that why he wants to keep Miss Fancy Pants? It had never occurred to him.

"That has to be it. You don't even *like* dogs."

He glances over at Fancy. She's resting on her side with one of her favorite chew toys between her paws. They play fetch with it in the yard regularly. If she were human, he's convinced she'd be a good ballplayer. He's been eyeing some of the local dog parks and has plans for him and Fancy to check them out soon.

This has nothing to do with Tori.

His voice turns to steel. "You try and take that dog, things are going to get ugly."

Rachel is usually ready to battle, but something in his tone must warn her that he isn't kidding. She seems to back down, but then she smiles at him. "I have an idea. How about we let *her* decide?"

"What do you mean?"

"We'll both call her, and we'll see who she comes to."

Liam takes a deep breath. He doesn't like it. He doesn't want to force Fancy to choose. Plus if he's honest, a part of him is worried she'll pick Rachel.

"Sit in that chair," she instructs him, her tone confident. "I'll take the couch again."

For some reason, he does it. God knows why. There's a knot of dread forming in his gut. He's not sure how it's happened, but he's become attached to that little furball.

"Ready?" She gives him a smug smile. "Let's see who she prefers."

Both he and Rachel begin calling her.

Miss Fancy Pants looks up, startled at her name. She hops up from her dog bed with excitement. But as she trots closer, she slows, and Liam sees the confusion on her expressive face. Her big dark eyes go back and forth between the two people calling her. She seems nervous, maybe even scared, and in that moment he goes silent.

He can't do this. He doesn't want to force her to choose. It seems cruel.

Of course, Rachel doesn't stop. And once he's no longer saying anything, Fancy immediately walks toward her.

His chest goes tight with disappointment.

Rachel is laughing and patting the couch beside her. "That's right, Miss Fancy Pants! Come here! Come to Mama!"

But then something surprising happens. Miss Fancy Pants stops altogether. She sits down. Her little furry head swings between them both. Liam doesn't say a word, only looks at her. The next thing he knows, the dog trots over to him. She puts her paws on his leg, and he reaches down to pet her back.

"Good girl," he says.

"What the hell!" Rachel is fit to be tied. She jumps up from the couch. "No fucking way! What did you do to my dog?"

"Nothing." He's still petting Miss Fancy Pants, who has now hopped up onto his lap. She circles once, then twice, and finally sits facing Rachel.

"You've done something to her. Tricked her somehow," she fumes. "There's no way she prefers you over *me*."

There's a lump in Liam's throat as he strokes Fancy's soft coat. He can't help smiling. To be honest, it surprises him as much as Rachel.

"Looks like she's made her choice," he says. He still has the phone in his other hand. "Now, let me call you that Uber."

CHAPTER SEVENTEEN

TORI'S HOME ALONE, working on her computer and trying not to think about Liam and Rachel.

Ugh. What a mess.

She cringes all over again.

First a gay guy and then a guy with a girlfriend. It's like a bad country song. But then all country songs are bad.

What's wrong with me?

Maybe Peyton is right. Maybe she should take a vacation. Step back from all of this and go hide somewhere.

Except she doesn't have time. She can't leave her mom. There are too many people relying on her.

Peyton texted her last night with excitement. She said her cousin's cabin is booked all summer, but there was a cancellation next weekend. *You should go for it, girl!* Peyton said in her text. But Tori turned it down. *I appreciate it, but no, thanks.*

Her phone buzzes and she picks it up. It's Blair reminding her they're having dinner together tonight. They're picking her up soon. She hasn't told Blair the full story with Dr. Adrian yet and figures she'll get that over with.

Def Leppard's "Foolin'" plays through her speakers, and it's exactly what she feels like. A fool.

At least she finally updated the pages for her brother's site that were supposed to be done yesterday. She opens Photoshop and brings up the new logo she's creating for her Happy Pet Nanny business.

Her boys are all flopped down, napping around her feet. There's a glass of lavender lemonade on the desk next to her. Her house smells like the two loaves of banana bread she just baked—the extra one for her next-door neighbor Mrs. Waligorski.

When there's a knock on her door, she figures it's Blair and Road and they've come early, but is shocked to discover Liam standing there.

"Forget it. There's nothing to talk about." She tries to close the door, but he puts his hand out.

"Let me explain, Tori. It's not what you think."

"I don't want to hear it. Just go away."

But it turns out Miss Fancy Pants is there too and slips past Liam's legs. Tori can't resist bending over to pet her. "You shouldn't have come here. And you shouldn't have brought your dog to try and manipulate me."

"That's not why I brought her. I brought her because Rachel tried to take her when she left."

Tori's eyes go wide. "She did?"

Liam nods, his face stern.

"You stopped her?"

"Hell, yes, I stopped her. Though it turned out Fancy didn't want to go with her anyway." He glances down at the dog and seems pleased, but then his expression turns serious. "You were right in what you said yesterday. I've made some bad choices with women. It's a problem I have."

She pets Miss Fancy Pants, surprised by his admission.

"To be honest, this is the best thing that's happened to me in a long time."

"What is?"

"You."

"Me?" Her eyes flash up to him.

"Yes, *you*, Tori."

A warmth moves through her. She can tell he means it. In fact, she doubts he rarely says anything he doesn't mean. "I'm not sure what to say to that," she says, straightening.

"Say you'll still see me tomorrow night."

Liam looks handsome standing on her front porch. Like a suitor who's come calling. There's something old-fashioned about him that appeals to her.

But then she remembers seeing Rachel in his house earlier. The shock of it. Wearing his T-shirt so comfortably. At home in that bedroom.

"You and Rachel have things to work out. I don't want to get in the middle of that."

"You're not getting in the middle of anything." He seems frustrated. "That's what I'm trying to tell you. There is nothing to work out. Rachel and I are finished."

"I think you still have feelings for her."

"No, I don't. I haven't had feelings for her in a long time. Trust me."

She gives him a skeptical look. "I don't believe that. She only left you a couple months ago. How could you be over it so fast?" There's movement behind her, and Miss Fancy Pants barks. Her boys, who were all napping, have woken up and noticed there's another dog out here. "Go on, get back," she tells them.

Liam pulls on Miss Fancy Pants's leash to bring her away. "Because I knew."

"What do you mean, you knew?" Tori steps onto the porch and closes the door on the chaos inside. "Knew what?"

He glances out at her yard and seems embarrassed. "I knew Rachel was cheating on me for a long time."

Tori's brows go up. "You did?"

"It started last fall before the holidays. Around the same time she brought Fancy home."

"How did you know? Did she tell you?"

"She didn't have to." He snorts. "Rachel's not exactly a criminal mastermind."

"Was it that obvious?"

"Yes, to me, it was."

She studies him, and it occurs to her that he didn't deserve that. She doesn't know him very well, but he doesn't strike her as a cheater. "Why didn't you leave?"

"It's my house."

"Kick her out, then."

He shakes his head. "I couldn't throw her out. I should have. It was a relief when she finally left on her own."

Tori takes this in. She had no idea.

He lowers his voice. "You're the only person I've told this to. No one else knows the truth."

"What about your family?"

"I told them Rachel was having an affair before she moved out, that I had my suspicions, but that's all."

"Were you still in love with her? Is that why you didn't make her leave?"

"Yes, at first." He takes a deep breath. "It's painful to be betrayed like that. I was angry, but then as it went on, I began to see how incompatible we were. We shouldn't have moved in together to begin with."

There's some barking on the other side of the door, but she ignores it. Miss Fancy Pants glances over but then goes back to sniffing around the potted plants.

"She was cheating on another guy when I met her."

"That's never a good sign."

"I know. I didn't find out until much later, until after we were already living together."

Tori nods. "I'm sorry." And she means it. It must have been difficult. And oddly, she understands why he didn't throw Rachel out. It's like he's too much of a gentleman for that. Sad to think someone would use that against him.

"So now that you understand the situation, can I take you out tomorrow?"

She sighs. "I still don't think it's a good idea."

"HOW ABOUT JUST DINNER?" Miss Fancy Pants tugs on the leash, and Liam gives it more slack.

"I doubt it would be just dinner, don't you?"

His eyes flash to Tori's face. She's wearing a little smile. He's not sure what to say. He's so attracted to her that it's hard to even think straight. He keeps trying to analyze the situation, worried he'll say something wrong and screw this whole thing up even more. "If you want to keep it simple, I can do that. I don't want to pressure you."

"Let me think about it, okay? I'll text you if I change my mind."

The scent of tangerines drifts toward him. He wishes he could kiss her but senses that would be a mistake.

As he's trying not to remember what she looks like beneath those jeans and that Mötley Crüe T-shirt, a car pulls into the driveway behind them. He turns. It's a green Mustang from the sixties, beautifully refurbished.

"Oh no." Tori's eyes widen. "I lost track of time."

Liam admires the car as two people step out and walk toward them. An attractive redhead and a tall blond guy.

Unfortunately, Liam recognizes them right away.

Blair and Road.

The pair move closer, and Liam can't take his eyes off the asshole who bullied him in high school.

Road still looks formidable. But as Liam continues his assessment, measuring the man, there's a smug satisfaction in his gut.

I could take him.

A lot of time has passed since then. He's not a skinny kid anymore and hasn't been for a long time. He's put on height and muscle. Not to mention he's well trained on how to subdue someone in a fight.

Granted, Road wouldn't go easy. He'd get in a few good punches. It wouldn't be clean, but Liam has no doubt he could take him down.

"Hi," Blair says. She gives him a once-over and a quick smile before going back to Tori. "Are you ready for dinner?"

"Um, sure." Tori seems uncomfortable. Her blue eyes meet his, and he can see the tension behind them. "I'll text you about pet sitting next week, okay?" She's obviously trying to get rid of him. "See you later."

"Oh, are you one of Tori's clients?" Blair asks, still smiling. Road is there beside her, and Liam grows tense. He can't help it. Though Road only gives him a brief nod, too busy studying his phone.

"Yes, I am," he says.

Blair's auburn brows come together. "You look familiar. Have we met?"

"We went to high school together."

Tori makes a funny squeaking noise and flaps her arms. "Ah, you know, let's not get into all that right now. There's no need."

"We did?" Blair seems taken aback. She's still smiling, but he sees the exact moment she remembers him. *"Liam?"* She looks appalled.

Road jerks his head up, alerted by the tone of his wife's voice. "Something wrong?"

"Yes, something's wrong! It's that loser who poured a milkshake over Tori in high school."

Road's eyes cut to him.

The two men study each other. It's been over a decade. He also knows he's being assessed, measured, the same way he did it to Road only a moment ago.

Meanwhile, Tori and Blair are speaking excitedly to each other.

"He's one of my Happy Pet Nanny clients," Tori explains to Blair. "I told you that! Don't you remember?"

"Yes, I remember, but what's he doing at your house? Did you invite him here?"

"No, not exactly. He just sort of showed up."

Liam glances at Tori. *Really?* While her words are true, he wished she hadn't characterized it like that. It makes him sound like a stalker.

"This guy bothering you?" Road growls. He slips his phone into his front pocket.

"No, he's not bothering me," she says emphatically. "It's fine. Really."

"I'm leaving," Liam says to Road. "You can calm down."

"Good." His eyes remain on Liam. "And I suggest you don't come back unless you're invited."

"This is coming out all wrong," Tori laments, wringing her hands. "It's okay. Honest! I admit I didn't want him here at first. In fact, I told him to go away, but then it was okay!" She's babbling, and Liam wishes she'd stop. It's not making things better.

Finally, he bends down to get Miss Fancy Pants. She must have sensed the tension, because she's standing right next to him. He straightens up, holding her.

Road blinks a few times and seems startled by the fluffy white dog.

"Have a good evening," Liam says to the three of them before he leaves, his voice grim.

"You too!" Tori calls after him.

Blair and Road remain silent.

He heads out to his truck, cursing this whole screwed-up situation.

The Mustang is parked right next to it, and he can't help admiring it again. Shiny and green with a red interior. Road may be an asshole, but Liam can't deny the bastard has great taste in cars.

TORI SPENDS HALF the dinner listening to Blair freak out.

"I know you can't help the way you are, but if you're too nice, some guys get the wrong idea. We've been down that road before."

Unfortunately, she can't deny what Blair's saying. They have been down that road. There have been some guys in the past who took her being nice the wrong way, who thought she was playing hard to get when she ignored their calls and told them she wasn't interested.

"This isn't like that," Tori tries to explain, though it falls on deaf ears.

Blair shakes her head. "You don't want an asshole like Liam getting the wrong idea."

"He's not so bad. I kind of like him."

Tori's tempted to tell her about the afternoon of lust they shared but knows she wouldn't understand.

"Don't forget the bandito test," Blair continues. "There's no way Liam would pass that." The bandito test is this test she and Blair always gave the men they dated. The test is this: If you were captured by a group of banditos, would the guy you were dating rescue you and risk bodily harm, or would he leave you to a terrible fate?

"I don't know about that."

Her best friend picks up her water glass. "We know you always want to see the good in people, but sometimes there isn't any good."

Tori doesn't reply and feels a flicker of annoyance. Whether a guy she's seeing passes the bandito test is *her* decision to make, not Blair's.

When there's finally a break in the conversation, Tori tells them the story of what happened with Dr. Adrian. She's been cryptic about it in her texts.

Road chuckles as he pours salsa over his burrito. "It sounds to me like you were mostly in love with his midnight blue Tesla."

"That's not true! Though I do love that car. It's so cool."

"I'm sorry," Blair says. "He sounded perfect."

"I know." Tori leans back in her chair. "He is perfect. We have so much in common. And you should see how good he is with animals. He's a great guy."

"I thought he kissed you though?"

Her face grows warm. "It was sort of the other way around." She fiddles with her napkin. "I kissed him."

Blair nods. "I see."

"So, anyway." Tori takes a deep breath. "Yeah."

"You'll meet somebody. I know you will. Just give it time."

Such a familiar refrain from all her married friends. "I have given it time. I think I may have to accept the fact that my special someone might not be out there. Maybe we missed each other in this lifetime."

"I don't think that's true."

Tori picks up her water glass, desperate for a change of subject. "So how's it going with you guys? Is anybody pregnant yet?"

Blair sighs. "Not yet."

Her brother grins. "Though not for lack of trying."

"They say it can take months sometimes," Tori offers. "I'm sure it'll happen eventually."

Blair turns to Road. He leans in and kisses her. They smile at each other, tuning Tori out. Usually she doesn't mind how affectionate they are, but today it's getting on her nerves. She doesn't want to sit around with two people who are crazy in love. It's only making her feel worse.

She glances toward the restaurant window and wishes she could escape. Just for a little while. Escape her life.

And that's when she sucks in her breath.

The cabin at the lake!

What was I thinking?

Frantically, she digs through her bag and gets her phone out, searching for the message Peyton sent her last night. She finds it and then types in a new response to her friend.

I've changed my mind!! Is it too late for the cabin?

Blair and Road are being playful with each other. She's feeding him a tortilla chip and pretending to complain about how much Mexican food he eats. Tori's glad for them. She really is. Married life seems to agree with them both, and she's never seen her brother so happy.

A new text pops up from Peyton. *Let me ask Tara.*

Okay, thanks!

As she waits for the answer, worried she's ruined her chance, she considers the logistics of all this.

"Could you guys take care of my boys next weekend?"

Blair tilts her head. "I think so. Why?"

"Could I also borrow your Honda for a little getaway?" She knows she has to replace Mable soon, but hasn't heard from Brody yet.

"Are you going somewhere?"

She explains about Peyton's cousin's cabin.

"You'd stay there alone?" Blair asks. "Is it safe?"

"It's just for the weekend. It sounds like a nice place. Peyton offered, and I said no, but now I've changed my mind."

"Where is it?" Road wants to know.

"Truth Harbor. The cabin is right on Treasure Lake."

He picks up his beer and considers this. "I could get you plane tickets to somewhere more exotic. I didn't realize you were interested in going anywhere."

She smiles. He and Blair are always traveling to the most amazing places. "Thanks, but for now this is good. I just need a little break."

"Yes, of course we'll watch your animals," Blair says. "And you know you can use my car as long as you need it."

"Thanks, I appreciate that."

Her phone buzzes, and Tori grabs it off the table.

She said yes!

Tori grins. *I'm so glad! Thank you!!!*

You're welcome! I'll give her your number, and she can text you with all the details. I'm so happy you're doing this!

Me too!! I'm excited!!!

IT TURNS out the cabin was also available Friday and Monday, so Tori decided to go for it. She figures, why not? The next week becomes a whirlwind as she tries to rearrange her life to be gone four days.

Dr. Adrian said it was no problem taking the time off from the animal hospital, and she's been calling her Happy Pet Nanny regulars to let them know. A couple of them weren't happy, but she offered them a discount on their next bill to make up for the inconvenience. The no-kill shelter she volunteers at was able to find a replacement for her two shifts. It's all coming together with one exception—her mom, who has a complete meltdown.

"You're leaving town?" she wails. "Why would you want to leave town?"

"It's only for a long weekend," Tori says. It's Wednesday evening, and they're sitting in her mom's living room. "I'll be back on Tuesday."

"What am I going to do? What if I need help?"

"Just call Road or Blair. They'll come over."

"Hey, am I chopped liver?" Wayne comes out from the kitchen with a beer in his hand. "I'm here too, woman."

Tori doesn't say anything. She doesn't trust Wayne to be reliable.

"But what if I need my baby girl?" Her mom's bleary eyes stay on Tori. "You can't leave me."

Wayne sits beside her mom on the couch. The *new* couch.

Tori was shocked when she came over tonight and saw all the changes. New living room furniture. New dining room table and chairs. There was even artwork hanging on the walls. For a moment, she thought she'd walked into the wrong house.

"Honeybunch, I'll be here," he says to her mom, rubbing the back of her neck. "If you need something, let your man know. Haven't I done right by you so far?"

Her mom turns and smiles at him. She puts her hand on his leg and purrs, "You sure have. You're my sugar daddy."

Wayne grins. "Damn straight I am." He leans over and kisses her on the mouth.

Tori wants to puke.

"Where did all this new stuff come from?" she asks them.

"Here and there," Wayne says. "I got a special deal on it." He winks at her mom, who's smiling at him like he's the answer to all her prayers.

"I love it so much." Her mom runs her hand over the sofa's green fabric. "Makes me feel like I'm living in a brand-new house."

"What kind of special deal?"

"Oh, you know." Wayne reaches for his cigarettes. "Just a fire sale, that's all. Everything must go." He grins with crooked teeth at her mom, who giggles.

Tori wonders if it all fell off the back of a truck. She's not sure if she wants to know the truth.

Before she leaves, she hides the bourbon under the kitchen sink and switches her mom's whiskey sour to water.

"Please don't let her drink so much," she pleads quietly to Wayne in the kitchen. "That's all I ask."

He's smoking another cigarette. "Don't worry, your mama is in good hands with me. I'll take care of everything."

Tori cringes.

"You go have fun on your trip."

By the time she heads home, Wayne and her mom are curled up on the new sofa, watching Netflix on the new television, and eating a bowl of microwave popcorn.

LATE THAT NIGHT, as Tori's doing laundry and decorating her planner with stickers and washi tape, she knows there's one loose end she hasn't taken care of yet.

Liam.

She's been thinking about him since Saturday, though she tried not to. In fact, she never contacted him about pet sitting Miss Fancy Pants. After that incident on her porch and the dinner with Blair and Road, it seemed like it was best to keep her distance.

Except a strange thing keeps happening.

Every night when she goes to sleep, she imagines him here with her, his arms wrapped around her, like the afternoon they shared. Cozy and safe.

She reaches for her phone and brings up their last text conversation. Her thumbs type in a single word. *Hi.*

There's no reply. It's after eleven though. She types some more. *I hope this doesn't wake you up. I just saw the time.*

Still holding her phone, she stares at the screen, wondering if this is a mistake. Her pulse jumps when she sees him responding.

It's okay. I'm awake.

How's Miss Fancy Pants?

Good. She missed you last week.

Was she okay by herself?

For the most part. I came home for lunch a couple days.

She nods, glad to hear that.

Another text from him appears. *I never heard from you Saturday.*

I know. Sorry.

There's a pause and she's not sure what to say. It's weird. She's not even sure what she wants from Liam, only that she wants *something*.

Tori types some more. *I'm going away this weekend for a little vacation.*

Where to?

She describes the cabin on the lake. Peyton's cousin texted her the link online, and it looked really nice in the pictures. *It's right on the water with an amazing view.*

Sounds great.

Her thumbs hover over the phone. She's nervous, her stomach filled with butterflies, debating what she's about to do. She knows this is crazy, but she types again.

Would you like to come with me?

CHAPTER EIGHTEEN

LIAM'S BREATH STOPS.

He stares at the text from Tori.

Seven little words.

Would you like to come with me?

He responds immediately. *Do you mean that?*

I do.

Instead of texting again, he calls her. She picks up right away.

"I'd love to go away for the weekend with you, rubia."

"Is it crazy that I'm asking you to come?"

"Who cares if it's crazy. Let's do it."

She laughs. "I never knew you had a wild streak."

"You bring it out in me."

He can sense her smiling.

"But can you get the time off work this quickly? There's also Miss Fancy Pants to think about." Tori sounds stressed. "Maybe this is a bad idea."

"Let me handle it."

"Blair and Road will be upset if they find out. My mom too. They all hate you."

Liam has to admit it pains him to hear this. He doesn't want the people in her life to hate him. "Maybe so, but this isn't their vacation. It's yours."

"I know."

She goes silent. He worries she'll change her mind but doesn't add anything more, figuring this has to be her decision.

"You're right," she finally says. "It is my vacation, so I should get to do whoever I want."

He chuckles. "That's one way of putting it."

"I mean whatever! Oh my God, I can't believe I just said that." She laughs. "I hope you're not getting the wrong impression of me."

"Don't worry, it's fine."

"First an afternoon of lust and now I'm inviting you away for the weekend. You must think I have hot pants."

"I'm not sure if I even know what hot pants are. It doesn't matter though, because I like everything about you."

"You do?"

"Absolutely."

She goes quiet, and her voice is soft when she finally speaks again. "You know what? I think we're going to have a nice time."

He closes his eyes. To his surprise, tenderness wells up in him. "So do I."

When they get off the phone, he lies back in a daze. After not hearing from her all week, he figured that was it. She wanted nothing more to do with him, especially after that episode with Blair and Road on her front porch.

He's never been so glad to be wrong.

Fancy, who's at the foot of his bed, comes up to sit beside him. He pets her soft coat. "Except you'll be staying here, furball. I'll have to figure out what to do with you."

The next day at work, he convinces his ASAC to give him the time off. It's last minute, and he didn't exactly follow procedure, but luckily he has some goodwill on his side from the recent Rizzo arrest. It turns out the guy's been running quite a criminal enterprise, way beyond what they initially suspected. It's been making the papers and has been good PR for the bureau.

He texts Tori after his meeting. *I just got the time off.*

Yay! What about Miss Fancy Pants? Should we bring her with us?

I'm going to ask Elena to come over and dog sit for the weekend.

Are you going to tell her you're going away with me?

He's been debating whether he should tell his sister the truth and has come to only one conclusion.

Not if I don't have to.

Because she doesn't like me?

He pauses, not wanting to hurt her feelings.

Tori messages. *It's okay. I already know she doesn't.*

It's complicated. She has the wrong idea about you.

If she says no, we can bring Miss Fancy Pants with us. I don't mind.

It probably sounds selfish, but he does mind. He wants Tori all to himself this weekend and doesn't want to share her, even if it's with a dog.

He thumbs in a reply. *Let's see what Elena says first.*

Luckily his sister has no problem coming over to watch Miss Fancy Pants.

"Sure, the boys and I would love to come over and watch her. It'll be like a mini vacation for us."

"Just make sure they're gentle with her," he says. "She's only a small dog."

"We'll treat her like a queen."

"All right, then. I appreciate it. Thank you."

"Where are you headed, anyway? Or are you allowed to tell me?"

He rubs his jaw. "It's best if I don't." He knows she assumes he's working on a case and sees no point in dissuading her of that notion.

The next morning, he meets Tori at her house. They need a place to park the car she's borrowing from Blair, since they can't leave it at either of their houses. Apparently she asked a friend from work if she could leave it at her house, so he's going to follow her over there.

"I don't think I've ever had to sneak around like this before," Tori says to him. They're both standing in front of the silver Honda.

"Me either." It's not his style, but he doesn't care. He's ready to do whatever it takes to make this weekend happen. A rare excitement's ignited in him since Tori asked him on this little adventure.

"It feels like we're criminals or something."

He chuckles. "Did you pack everything you need?"

"I think so." The scent of tangerines wafts toward him.

Their eyes meet, and he can't resist reaching for her hand to pull her in closer. "I'm going to kiss you now," he says in a low voice. "Because I can't help myself."

"Okay," she whispers.

Her lips are soft and minty. She kisses him back with desire, and he's enjoying it, until there's a coughing noise beside them.

They both turn toward the sound.

"Aren't you two a couple of lovebirds."

"Hi, Mrs. Waligorski," Tori says. "Do you need something?"

Liam waits and watches as Tori's next-door neighbor thanks her for some recent baked goods she brought over. They discuss where he and Tori are going and exactly how long she'll be gone.

He's amazed. He doesn't think he's ever had a conversation this long with any of his neighbors, even if he added them all together.

"You two kids have fun," Mrs. Waligorski says. "And don't worry.

Mum's the word." She puts her fingers to her lips like she's turning a key. "I won't say a thing to anyone."

Apparently Tori explained their need for subterfuge. "Thank you," she says. "I appreciate it."

"It's so romantic. You two are just like Romeo and Juliet!"

TORI CLIMBS into the Honda and makes sure Liam is behind her as she heads over to Peyton's house. Thank goodness Peyton agreed to let her keep the car there. Liam suggested a park and ride, but after having Mable stolen, she's too paranoid to leave the Honda someplace public for the entire weekend.

"Thank you for this, and everything else too," she tells Peyton after pulling the car into her garage. "Also tell Lamont I said thank you."

"Oh, girl, it's fine. Don't worry about it." Her gaze goes out to Liam, who's standing in front of his truck, checking something on his phone. "And I have to say I sure do approve of the company you're keeping these days."

Tori laughs with embarrassment.

"Guess you're getting over Dr. Adrian just fine."

"You could say that."

"Seriously though, I'm excited for you. It's about time you let your hair down and had some fun." Her eyes go back to Liam, watching admiringly as he walks toward them in jeans and a baseball T-shirt. "And you're definitely going to have some fun with *that*."

Tori watches him too. A part of her is in disbelief that this whole weekend is even happening. It seems surreal.

Liam comes over and tells Peyton he appreciates her letting Tori keep the car here and thanks her for setting up the cabin.

"Oh, it's no big thing." She's smiling at him. "Make sure you take good care of my girl here."

He grins. "I promise I'll do my best."

Peyton nods with approval. "I'm glad to hear that." She hugs Tori goodbye. "Have a great time, honey."

Tori hugs her back, thinking it's nice to have at least one person who knows the truth and is happy for her.

When they're finally on the road headed toward Truth Harbor, Tori looks out the front window, giddy with excitement. Nothing can dim the happiness she feels right now. Not even the discovery that Liam listens to country music.

"*This* is what you play in your truck?" She gawks at him as some twangy-sounding song comes on. "It's country and western."

"Yeah, I know. It's what I like."

"But how can that be? You look like a normal person."

He laughs. "I don't know why you're so shocked. This is good music."

"It's... country music."

"What do you listen to?" He glances at her. "Oh wait, all those eighties hair bands, right?"

"Yes, that's right. I believe eighties hair bands are a highly underappreciated art form."

"Let's both keep an open mind. I'll give your hair bands a chance if you do the same for my country music."

Tori listens as some guy with a southern accent sings about heartache and being broke. It could be worse, she decides. It could be soft jazz.

"We'll take turns on the drive there," he says. "You might discover something you didn't know you enjoyed."

"I suppose." She glances over at his handsome profile. She can't imagine enjoying country music, but then she could never have imagined enjoying Liam either.

As they leave Seattle and head north, he tells her he spoke to the detective in charge of Mable's case yesterday.

"I would have told you sooner but wasn't sure when it would be a good time."

Tori studies him. "What did he say?"

"They'll be releasing the van to you next week." He glances at her. "He said a ring of thieves used it. They rob retailers, then use minivans to transport the stolen goods."

Her mouth falls open. "They rob retail stores?"

"You'd be surprised how lucrative that can be. Stealing jewelry, electronics, and even furniture."

Her gut churns as a horrible suspicion dawns on her. "What do they do with the stuff they steal?"

"Sell it to people who'll fence it. If it gets smuggled across state lines or up into Canada, then the bureau gets involved."

Her eyes go out to the highway, to Mount Baker rising in the distance, but she doesn't see it anymore. All she can see is her mom's new sofa and television in the living room. That expensive sapphire ring.

Is it possible Wayne's a thief? That he's the one who stole Mable? But why would he steal a vehicle that could be traced back to his girlfriend's daughter?

And then she has an even worse thought.

What if her mom knows?

That can't be though. Her mom seemed as upset about Mable as she was.

Liam glances at her. "Everything okay?"

She wonders if she should say something. She couldn't care less about Wayne, but she doesn't want her mom to get in trouble. "No, everything's fine. I'm just taking all this in, trying to make sense of it."

"I know it's hard to hear."

"It is." She gulps, feeling nauseous. She prays she's wrong and Wayne really is a tire salesman who works in a salvage yard. One who travels out of state for work.

"What's even crazier is it turns out this whole thing may be linked to one of my cases."

"Really?" Her stomach twists into an even bigger knot. "How so?"

Liam tells her about some guy he arrested recently who they thought was only running a pyramid scheme, but turns out it's part of a much larger criminal network. "He's got ties with crime rings all over the city, including smuggling and retail theft."

"What a weird coincidence."

He shrugs. "Sometimes it happens. You pull one thread and a hundred others unravel."

Tori nods, her heart racing.

She senses Liam glancing at her. "Are you really okay?" he asks with concern.

"I think I need to open the window for some air. I'm getting carsick."

"Of course."

She pushes the button until the glass is all the way down and lets the breeze blow on her face. She closes her eyes. There's some country song on the speakers about letting your troubles go.

That's what I need to do. Let it all go.

Eventually she rolls it up.

"Feeling better?"

"I think so."

By the time they arrive in Truth Harbor and head toward Treasure Lake, she's calmed down. It helps that she's enjoying the battle with Liam over whose playlist to listen to.

The more she thinks about it, she has no evidence against Wayne. Maybe he bought all that stuff from a pawnshop. Maybe it is stolen, and that's how he got a great deal on it. It doesn't mean he's the one who stole it.

And her mom would never let him take Mable. There's no way she'd be okay with that.

"Should we stop and get groceries first or drive to the cabin?" Liam asks her.

"Let's go to the cabin first. I can't wait to see it."

She helps him navigate there using her phone. Soon they're driving down a narrow road with lavish million-dollar homes. They're nice, but not really Tori's taste.

When they finally reach the end of the road, it stops in front of the cutest, coziest little cabin. She saw photos online, but they mostly showed the view.

"This looks great," Liam says, parking the truck.

"Wow, it sure does."

They both get out, and it's like she's stepped into an alternate reality. Here in this beautiful place with an equally beautiful man.

In that moment, she decides to forget all her problems.

They'll still be there next week.

She takes a deep breath. The air feels sultry in her lungs, and she can smell the water. "I already love it here," she declares.

They walk around the outside of the cabin and discover it has its own private sandy beach right on the lake. There's a small firepit with a group of logs around it.

Inside they find the house is equally as cozy and inviting. Downstairs has a kitchen, bathroom, and living room with a wood stove. A black spiral staircase leads to a sleeping loft.

Tori climbs the stairs to peek at the loft. A half-moon window looks out onto the lake from the head of the bed. There's a large skylight window above it. The ceiling is kind of low, but she can still stand. She crawls onto the mattress. "This is so cool. You have to come up here and see this."

Liam climbs the iron staircase but accidentally hits his head on the rafters. "Ow." He crawls onto the bed and flops beside her. "I hope I don't concuss myself in the middle of the night."

"Just remember to duck next time."

They both lie on their stomachs, gazing out at the view. The water shimmers, reflecting the sky in various shades of blue.

She sighs. "I really had no idea it would be this amazing."

"Me either," he admits. They both watch an eagle fly low.

It's not lost on her that they're in bed right next to each other, his warm forearm pressed into hers. When she glances at him, she discovers he isn't gazing at the view anymore but at her.

"What?"

"Nothing." But then he seems to change his mind. "I can't believe I'm here with you."

"What do you mean?"

He seems embarrassed. "Maybe I shouldn't admit this, but I had the biggest crush on you in high school."

"You did?" She's taken aback but can't help feeling pleased. "I never knew that."

"Why do you think I asked you to homecoming?"

Tori tries to remember those days, before the whole milkshake thing happened. "I guess I never thought about it too deeply."

"It took me weeks to get up the nerve to ask you."

"Really? That's so sweet." She considers him. "Is that why you did it?"

"Did what?"

"You know, poured it on me. Was it because I upset you?"

His eyes remain on hers, his gaze unflinching. "Tori, I did *not* pour that milkshake on you."

She studies him, and a part of her wants to believe him.

"It was a freak accident. I just went over to say hello to you. One of my teammates was goofing around and kept trying to grab the cup from me, so I was holding it up. He bumped me, and the next thing I knew, you were drenched."

"But everybody said—"

"I know what everybody said. Everybody was wrong."

She tries to remember the details. "What about all the laughing and pointing?"

"The guys laughed. I never did."

"I want to believe you. I really do."

"You should, because I'm telling the truth."

She doesn't know what to say. It's hard to let go of a memory that's so ingrained.

"Want to hear something else?" He rolls onto his back and gazes up at the skylight. "Even afterward, when you hated me, and your brother was threatening to do me bodily harm, I still liked you. I couldn't stop myself."

She takes this in and feels bad, though she did nothing wrong. "If it's any consolation, I wish I'd said yes when you asked me to the dance."

He turns to look at her. "You do?"

She nods. "Maybe we would have been teenage sweethearts." The words come out before she has time to think about them. It's an odd notion, but not hard to imagine. "I never had a real relationship in high school."

His eyes stay on hers. "Me either. I'd like to think we would have had something special."

They regard each other. The golden afternoon sun shines through the window. A wonderful energy slides through her, moving through her limbs before curling down her spine.

"Let's take our time this weekend, rubia." His voice rumbles between them. "I don't want to rush things. I want to enjoy you."

"Okay," she whispers. She doesn't know what to say. No guy has ever spoken to her like this.

His gaze drops to her mouth.

Her eyelids fall shut when he pulls her in for a kiss. Soft lips. She inhales his scent, his taste. Everything about Liam is delicious.

But then something occurs to her, and she draws back. "Did you listen to country music in high school?"

"Not really. I mostly listened to rock." He strokes her back, then slips his hand beneath her T-shirt to caress bare skin.

"It's too bad we didn't date back then. I could have saved you."

"Saved me?" He chuckles. "You haven't given country music a real chance yet. Trust me, you'll learn to love it as much as I do."

She snorts. "Only if I'm lobotomized first."

"You don't know what you're saying."

"What I'm saying is you have terrible taste in music."

"Oh, really?" There's a mischievous grin on his face. Before she knows it, he flips her onto her back. She lets out a little shriek. "So you think *I'm* the one with bad taste?"

She giggles, bracing her hands on his shoulders. "Yes, it's awful. But don't worry, it's not too late. I can help."

"By forcing me to listen to all those fluffy-haired male singers and their endless screaming?"

"They're not screaming. Well... I guess they sort of are."

"Every song sounds the same."

She turns indignant. "They do not!"

"How can you tell them apart?"

"Because they sound different, that's how!"

His large body rumbles with laughter against hers, and she has to admit, she's enjoying herself. Enjoying the solid weight of him. Enjoying his good humor.

She's glad she invited him.

Even if he does listen to country music.

CHAPTER NINETEEN

> **Tori's Playlist: Daily Song**
> "Rock the Night"
> by Europe
> ♥
> **Liam's Playlist: Daily Song**
> "Give It All We Got Tonight"
> by George Strait

THEY DRIVE out to the nearest grocery store and pick up a few things. "Maybe we should check out the town while we're here," Liam says, reaching for a bag of grapes. "I haven't been there in ages."

Truth Harbor, the nearby town, has a history of pirate lore. "That sounds fun," Tori agrees. "I've never been up here before."

They wind up eating sandwiches with chips on the cabin's back deck. Liam says he doesn't mind eating the veggie bologna she bought, which is a nice surprise. She's dated too many guys who freaked out when she told them she didn't eat meat.

It's a warm summer evening, and she can hear frogs down by the water. Grasshoppers too. A symphony of buzzes and croaks.

She picks up her glass. "Most guys buy beer, but you bought a six-pack of iced tea."

"I know. I drink it all the time. My whole family does, actually."

She imagines his nice, normal family. All of them sitting around drinking tea and being civilized. Nobody's drunk. You don't have to hide liquor bottles or fight anybody for their car keys.

It sounds like heaven.

Unfortunately, this makes her think of her mom and Wayne again. She can't seem to get them out of her mind.

And to make matters worse, she's spending the weekend with a lawman.

Talk about irony.

She knows she told herself to forget her problems, but they don't seem to be listening.

"Do you want to make a fire down on the beach?" he asks as they're finishing up dinner. "I thought that might be fun."

"Um... sure." She's nervous about something else too, about what exactly happens later tonight. It's the new dancing elephant in the room, and this time it's X-rated.

She follows him into the kitchen, admiring his muscular shoulders beneath the soft cotton T-shirt. Her eyes drop lower to the way his jeans fit both loose and snug.

When he turns to take her plate, she quickly looks up at his face again.

The corner of his mouth twitches. "Were you just checking my ass out?"

"Yes. No! Maybe." She panics. "What's the right answer?"

He seems to find this amusing. "The truth is usually the right answer."

"That makes sense. Okay, I admit it. I was checking you out."

"Is everything all right, rubia? You've been jumpy all afternoon."

She licks her lips. "I know I asked you away for the weekend, but I'm just wondering about your, um… you know… expectations?"

He shrugs. "That depends. What are yours?"

"I asked you first."

He puts the plates in the sink and turns back to her. "It's like I said earlier. We don't have to rush into anything. Let's take our time."

"But we'll be sleeping in the same bed. Are we going to have intimacies?" Even she can tell how dumb that sounds. He's gazing at her with affection though and not like she's a weirdo.

"Only if you want to."

"Obviously we had our afternoon of lust, and that was very nice. This is way more than an afternoon though."

"Is this why you've been acting so nervous?" He reaches for her hand. "Let's just see how it goes. We don't have to have sex."

"Okay." She nods but then rethinks it. "What if I want to?"

Drawing her near, his voice rumbles low. "Then I'm happy to oblige."

Her breath catches at his tone. Tendrils of desire shimmer through her body. "I think my knees just went weak."

He chuckles softly. "You're something else."

Bending down, he kisses her. Tastes her. Gentle and perfect. Not a horny toad kiss but the kind you give someone you care about.

The kiss deepens, and she slides her arms around his neck. A part of her still can't believe Liam's here with her, that she's getting to know him like this. He seems to be a genuinely good person. Look at how he's helped her, how he called that detective about Mable.

Unfortunately, the thought is a douse of cold water. Mable being stolen brings back the worry about her mom and Wayne again.

"What is it?" he murmurs when she draws back. "I promise I won't jump you." He gives her a sly grin. "Unless you want me to."

"No, it's not that."

"Then what?"

"I just…." She considers how to phrase this. "I have a weird question to ask. What happens if someone knows about a crime but doesn't report it?"

His brows shoot up and his demeanor shifts. "That depends on the crime."

"It does?"

"Sure." His gaze turns to one of concern. "You're not in any kind of trouble, are you?"

"Me? No, not all."

He seems relieved. "Like I said, it depends on the crime. Anything violent involving a minor needs to be reported right away."

"Oh, I don't mean something like that. I was wondering if one person knows about another person doing something illegal. Can the person who knows about it get in trouble?"

He shakes his head. "Not usually. Not reporting a crime isn't typically an offense."

"It's not?" Relief washes through her, since she's mostly worried about her mom. If Wayne's robbing stores and smuggling stolen goods, she doesn't want her mom to get in trouble if she knows about it.

"Active concealment is though."

"What's that?"

"Actively or intentionally trying to conceal a crime you know about. In other words, taking steps to make sure it stays hidden."

"Oh." Her relief evaporates. If her mom knows about Wayne, she's most likely helping him hide it.

Liam's watching her carefully. "What's this about?"

"Nothing. I was asking out of curiosity."

"Curiosity?"

She tries to come up with an explanation. "I was thinking about Mable, you know? Wondering if anybody saw something, then why didn't they report it?"

"Ah, I see." He seems to accept this. "Oftentimes people are too scared to get involved."

"Maybe that's it." She thinks of her mom again. She doesn't seem afraid of Wayne. Just the opposite.

His expression softens. "I know this has been hard for you. Many people feel violated after they've been robbed."

She nods. "It has been like that."

"I'm really sorry." He strokes her back. "Have you thought about getting another vehicle yet? Like I said before, I'm happy to help you look."

"You are?"

"Sure."

"That's nice of you. My cousin Brody's going to help though. He's a mechanic and owns a garage. It's how I found Mable."

"Okay, but let me know if you change your mind."

It's nearly dark outside by the time they head down to the little private beach. Tori brings the bag of vegan marshmallows she brought for the trip and relaxes on a nearby log while Liam puts the fire together.

Water laps against the shore as she breathes in the summer air. It reminds her of when she was a kid, back when life was full of possibilities. The future an open book.

She's melancholy thinking about her own book, how it's already written and not that interesting.

But then she perks up watching Liam.

There's something about him. Something that excites her, makes her think maybe life is still full of possibilities.

"You're putting that fire together like an expert," she says, taking out a soft marshmallow to eat. She enjoys watching him. He's a treat for the eyes. "Let me guess. You were a Boy Scout, right?"

He glances over at her from the stack of wood he's built and grins. "Guilty as charged."

She's not surprised. There's such a wholesomeness about him. It makes him even sexier.

It doesn't take long before he's got a nice little fire started. He comes over to her with two sticks and sits beside her on the log.

"I figured we'd use these to roast marshmallows," he says.

Instead of handing her one, he takes out a Swiss Army knife from his pocket and starts whittling.

She watches his capable hands. "How's your knee? You're not limping or wearing the brace anymore."

"Yeah, it's good." He runs a finger over the edge of the stick. "It's mostly healed now."

Once he's done whittling, he gives her the first stick. She waits for him to finish the second one before pushing marshmallows on each end. They scoot closer and hold them in the flames.

"Do you always know the best way to do everything?"

He turns his marshmallow to brown evenly. "What do you mean?"

"It seems like you always know how to do everything, handle every situation."

"I suppose." He shrugs. "My dad's kind of like that. He was always teaching me stuff, so I learned a lot from him."

"You're lucky. I grew up without a dad. He left when I was three and then later we found out he died in a car accident."

He turns to her. "I'm sorry to hear that."

"I wish I remembered him. Road says he does, but only vaguely." She turns her marshmallow to change the angle.

"That must have been tough, growing up without a father."

"At least we had our uncle Lance—my mom's brother. He passed away, but he was a father figure to me and Road."

"What was he like?"

Tori thinks about how to answer that question. "He always looked out for us. Made sure we were okay."

Liam nods with approval. "He sounds like a good man."

She smiles to herself, wondering what the two of them would have thought of each other. "In a lot of ways, he was great." She hesitates, wonders if she should tell him the rest. "Except he was a criminal. An outlaw."

She feels him shift beside her, giving her his full attention. "Your uncle Lance was a criminal?"

"He tried to keep that part of his life hidden from me and Road, but we knew. A lot of people were afraid of him." She reflects back to when she was a kid. Despite all her mom's loser boyfriends, no one ever laid a hand on her, her mom, or Road, and it's because they were too scared of Lance.

"But he was good to you and your brother?"

"He was. I miss him." She looks at Liam. "Sometimes people aren't just black and white but shades of gray, you know?"

"I suppose." He shrugs. "Not sure if I believe that."

"Maybe I shouldn't have told you about my uncle." She studies him with worry. "Your family is so different from mine. Are you shocked?"

"No. I'm glad you told me. It doesn't change how I feel about you."

"It doesn't?"

"I can tell what kind of person you are, Tori. That's all that matters to me."

She nods with relief.

He pulls his marshmallows out from the fire. She does the same, and they blow to cool them down, except she can't resist pulling some of hers off to eat.

"Ow, that's hot."

"We should have picked up the ingredients for s'mores when we were at the grocery store," he muses. "I didn't even think of it."

She pulls off another hot piece while Liam waits patiently for his to cool.

"So, what happened with Elena?" she asks, taking a bite. "I guess she agreed to watch Miss Fancy Pants?"

He tests his marshmallow. She watches his mouth as he licks his thumb, that handsome face lit by firelight. Her eyes drop lower to his shoulders and then his neck—which is impossibly sexy.

"It wasn't a problem. Luckily, she was happy to do it."

"Did you tell her about me?"

His dark eyes flicker over to her. "No."

Tori nods. She understands why he didn't, but a part of her feels bad that they have to sneak around.

"I plan to though," he says. "I don't want to lie to anybody, and I definitely want to keep seeing you."

"You do?"

His voice softens. "You know I do."

She takes a breath. "Let's see how this weekend goes first, okay?"

"Sure." He grins, eating his marshmallow. "Are you taking me out for a test drive? Kicking my tires and revving my engine?"

"Maybe," she teases. "How do I know what I'm buying here?"

He leans closer. "Don't worry. You can drive me as long as you like."

Desire flames up in her as all sorts of images dance through her mind.

Liam seems to notice it too. He leans in and kisses her. She licks the sugar from his mouth, and a small rumble of approval emanates from his throat.

It sends even more flames through her. Soon she'll be just like that fire.

"You taste so sweet," he murmurs. "You always do."

The two of them gaze at each other.

A fun notion comes to her mind, something she hasn't done in a long time. "I have an idea. Let's dance."

"Dance?"

Taking his marshmallow stick, she puts it down next to hers.

"But there's no music." He seems confused. "What are we going to dance to?"

"It doesn't matter. We don't need music."

"We don't?"

She stands. "No, silly. We have the crickets and frogs. The crackling fire."

He still seems confused but joins her anyway. Tori takes his hand and moves her hips to a silent beat. She hasn't danced without music in years, but used to do it all the time when she was a kid. Dancing everywhere she went, listening to the music that played inside her.

Liam lifts her hand and twirls her in a circle.

She giggles with delight. "See, you're getting the hang of it."

The two of them continue to dance near the fire, then move down to the beach for more space. They're holding hands, twirling each other.

"This is weird, but kind of fun," he says with a grin.

She puts her hand up and spins him around. He's so tall he has to duck beneath her arm. They take turns until they're both dizzy and finally collapse next to each other on the beach.

"Wow." She tries to catch her breath. "I haven't done that in ages, not since I was a little girl."

He grins. "I'll bet you were a sprite, weren't you? Blonde and delicate."

"Except I'm not as delicate as I look." People always think she's a pushover, that she's too nice, but she's had to be plenty tough in her life.

His eyes find hers in the dark. "I know you're not."

"You do?"

"I saw how you handled your mom and her boyfriend. That whole situation can't be easy."

She grows quiet.

"Can I ask you something? How long has that been going on?"

She already knows the "that" he's referring to. Her mouth opens, ready to spin a lie, since that's what she always does. But then she thinks of how he didn't seem shocked over Lance, and how he's already seen her mom drunk. "My whole life."

He nods solemnly. "I had a feeling. Is there any way to get her some help?"

"No. She doesn't want any help. It's why I never go anywhere. I had to fight to come here to this cabin."

Liam's expression fills with compassion. "It's not right what she's doing to you. What about your brother? Can he help?"

She runs her fingers over the sand. "I don't want to bother him and Blair. They're so happy. It would only bring them down."

"It shouldn't be all on your shoulders though. Is there anyone else who could help?"

"My sister, Kiki, but she wants nothing to do with my mom."

"You have a sister?"

"Half-sister. She's eight years younger than me. Married and lives in Idaho."

"I never knew that."

Tori draws circles in the sand. "She's closer to her dad. It's why she moved there."

"It's not fair that it's all on you."

Tori shrugs. "I'm used to it."

"There must be some way to get your mom into rehab."

She knows he wants to be helpful, but he hasn't lived it. He doesn't know what it's like dealing with someone who has problems like her mom does. "Let's talk about something else, okay?" She wipes away the circles. "I don't want to think about this anymore."

"Okay, sure."

She leans back and looks over at him from the corner of her eye. "Let's discuss you for a change. If I'm taking you out for a test drive this weekend, I have some questions."

"What do you want to know?"

"I've been thinking about something you told me recently. Why do you pick the wrong women?"

He smirks. "So you're going for the meaty stuff, huh? I thought you were a vegan."

"Hey, it's like you said. I'm kicking the tires and revving the engine." She reaches for his hand again and tugs on it. "Come on, I'm genuinely curious. If it helps, I've made some bad choices in my love life too."

He shakes his head. "I don't know why I make so many bad choices with women."

"You must have a theory."

He gazes at the lake and seems embarrassed. "I'm not sure if I want to say it out loud. You might agree with it."

"What do you mean?"

He glances down to where they're still holding hands and then looks at her. "I'm kind of a boring person."

Tori's taken aback. "You're not boring. You're an FBI agent, and before that you were a professional baseball player. There's nothing boring about that."

"But those are just things on the outside. I'm talking about me as an individual." He sighs. "The truth is I'm basically a fuddy-duddy."

She laughs. "That's silly."

"It's true. I'm too old-fashioned. Too rigid. I always feel like I'm a step behind the times."

"But why would that make you go for the wrong women?"

"Because I'm attracted to women who aren't like me. Who are unusual. Who don't seem boring."

She goes silent, reflecting on this. She knows she's sort of an oddball. "Women like me?"

"Yes." His voice softens. "Just like you."

"So, I'm your type?"

He nods. "You are. Except you're not crazy. And believe me, I've dealt with some real crazies."

She doesn't say anything. She thinks about some of her issues: how she recently fell for a gay guy, how she's been faking orgasms for years. And now this new possible mess with her mom and Wayne. "How do you know I'm not one of the crazy ones?"

"Because I can tell you're not selfish. I guess that's what I'm really talking about."

She moves closer. "I don't think you're boring. You are kind of old-fashioned, but I like it."

His eyes stay on her face.

"I think it's sexy."

A smile plays around the edges of his mouth. He lowers his voice. "You know it's a crime to lie to a federal agent."

"I'm not lying."

He reaches out and drags her onto his lap. "Damn, you turn me on," he murmurs, nuzzling her neck. "I can barely think straight around you."

"I must be a real weirdo, then."

His lips touch her ear when he whispers, "The best kind."

CHAPTER TWENTY

> **Tori's Playlist: Daily Song**
> *"Born to Be My Baby"*
> by Bon Jovi
> ♥
> **Liam's Playlist: Daily Song**
> *"In Case You Didn't Know"*
> by Brett Young

LIAM LETS Tori take the lead. He wants her to feel comfortable. More than anything, he doesn't want to mess this up.

They hold hands as they walk back up to the lake house. Once inside, she puts the bag of marshmallows on the kitchen counter, then gazes back at him as they climb the spiral staircase to the loft. It's dark inside, though moonlight shines through all the windows.

"Watch your head," she warns when they get to the top, crawling onto the bed.

He ducks just in time.

There's an excitement building in him. He's nervous. Turned on.

Bedazzled. Not even sure which emotion to pick. He's never felt like this. He thinks about the things Tori told him about herself and her family, how it should matter but doesn't.

Liam wants her. Deep down, a part of him knows this is important with her.

He joins her on the bed. They kiss and make out for a while, using their hands and mouths to get each other worked up. Both of them grow sweaty in the warm loft. The heavy bed cover gets in the way, so he pushes it aside.

"What's it like when you work undercover?" she asks, helping him pull his T-shirt off. "Do you like it?"

He smiles at the way her mind works. "I do."

She leans down and kisses his chest. He tries to breathe as her mouth trails lower.

"I can't imagine how you do it." Her fingers glide over the hard-on straining against his zipper.

A short groan escapes him, and he takes a moment for himself. "It's kind of like being an actor."

"Has anybody ever recognized you from playing baseball?"

"No." It's something he used to worry about before joining the bureau, that his short-lived baseball career would draw attention, but it hasn't been an issue. "Once when I was undercover, someone commented that I looked like a particular baseball player."

"Oh my God. What did you say?"

"I was a little nervous." He chuckles. "Turns out they weren't even talking about me."

"Really?"

"The player they thought I looked like wasn't even Latino."

"You're kidding." Tori laughs. "Has anybody ever figured out you were in the FBI while you were undercover?"

He quiets. "Once."

"Was it bad? What happened?"

"No. It turned out fine. The person became an asset of mine."

"Oh... that's good."

He reaches over for her. "Take your T-shirt off," he whispers.

Tori helps him remove her shirt and bra. He can't take his eyes off her. He can just make out her breasts in the dark. Silky and pale. Beaded nipples.

When she lies back down with him, they're skin to skin. The smell of tangerines falls all around him, luscious and ripe. He wonders how far she wants to go. He's happy to taste her again, use his mouth, if that's all she wants.

For a while they simply lose themselves. Bodies and mouths tangle together. That electric feeling is back, humming all through him. "You're amazing," he says, their faces close. "So beautiful and amazing."

He sees her surprise, and it makes him wonder if anyone has ever told her that.

"I'm nothing special," she whispers.

"That's not true."

She pulls him closer, kissing him passionately while straddling his thigh. Their heavy breath fills the small space of the loft as they move against each other.

He slips his hand over her shorts. "Let's take these off too." He hears the urgency in his voice. He's trying to tamp down his arousal, but it's more difficult than he thought it would be.

She rolls on her side and shimmies out of them, and then she's naked. Her ivory skin is illuminated under the moon shining through the skylight.

Desire hits him hard, followed by lust. He's trying to reel it back, but it's taking over, rocking his senses. Sweating, his whole body goes tense. Finally, he turns his head away.

She moves closer, hovering over him. Strands of soft hair tickle his chest. "Are you okay?"

He searches for some kind of humor, something to lighten this moment, but there isn't anything. "No."

She strokes his face. "I think you're amazing too."

He closes his eyes. Warm fingers lightly caress his jaw.

"You're always kind to me," she whispers. "I can tell it's who you really are."

He likes hearing that, wants to be someone she can rely on.

Tori inhales sharply.

"What?" he asks, looking at her with concern.

"I *believe* you."

His brow wrinkles. "What do you mean?"

"I know you didn't pour that milkshake on purpose." Her eyes light up. "It isn't even like you to do that, is it?"

"No, it's not."

He watches her expression change from amazement to regret. She lays her hand on his chest. "I feel terrible. I should have believed you this whole time."

"It's all right." He puts his hand over hers. He's glad though. Glad to be seen for who he is, especially by Tori. Her opinion was the only one that ever really mattered.

She shakes her head. "I'm sorry I had it so wrong."

"It's okay. It was ages ago. And for what it's worth, I'm sorry I ruined that night for you, that I drenched you with an ice-cold milkshake."

She smiles. "It was pretty awful."

"Maybe I'll let you dump one on me, and we'll call it even."

She giggles. "I might take you up on that."

He watches her face as she laughs. So beautiful.

She leans closer, her breasts pressed into his chest. There's an expression on her face he can't quite place, like she's deliberating something.

"What are you thinking about?" He strokes his hand down her body, her skin soft as satin.

"Do you want to know why I invited you on this trip? The real reason."

"Why?"

"Because I wanted *you* to be my vacation."

His eyes don't leave her face. "I hope I live up to it."

"You already have."

They gaze at each other. That electric sensation hums through him, lighting him up brighter than ever.

He pulls her close and kisses her with everything he's got, then pushes her onto her back. Her hands grip his neck as she softly moans. All those pretty sounds inflame him.

"Tell me what you want." His breath shakes. "I'll do anything."

"You," she whispers, her mouth close to his. "All I want is *you*."

He strips his jeans off and gets the condoms from his travel bag. Lying over her again, he takes it gentle, slow, enjoying each other. But it isn't long before she doesn't seem to want it gentle, before she's pulling him, grabbing and scratching. She wraps her legs around him, digging her heels into his ass as he takes her. He's half out of his mind.

When Tori moans and bites his shoulder, his body decides it's had enough. Ecstasy comes out of nowhere, white hot, blinding him as he gives in to it with a loud groan.

"Damn," he breathes afterward. His surroundings finally drift into focus again. "That was intense."

Her hands are gripping his back. She's still moving her hips, and he moves his too. He lifts up to see her face, barely making out her features in the dark room.

She's breathing hard, and it occurs to him that maybe she didn't finish. He thought she had, but he must be wrong. "Did you come? Do you want me to go down on you or use my fingers?"

"Oh, no, I came," she says, still trying to catch her breath. "It was wonderful."

"Okay." He nods. He wouldn't want to leave her unsatisfied.

He kisses her lips, then her neck. Finally, he lifts up and takes care of the condom before lying next to her on his back.

She scoots in and puts her head on his shoulder. It feels like sandbags are weighing his eyes down. Tori still seems restless.

"I need to go to the bathroom," she announces, sliding out of bed. She slips on his T-shirt from earlier. His eyelids fall shut as he listens to her bare feet pad down the iron staircase.

He dozes lightly, but pressure from his bladder wakes him up. The bed's still empty beside him.

He doesn't bother with clothes. Standing up, he cracks his head on the ceiling. "Ow, dammit." That's the second time now. He knew those rafters would be a problem. Reaching for the rail, he maneuvers his large frame down the tiny spiral staircase.

There's light coming from around the bathroom door. He knocks lightly. "Everything all right in there?"

The bathroom fan is on, and she replies with what sounds like "Fine."

"Are you almost done?"

"Almost."

He waits for a few more seconds. "Can I come in?"

"No!"

He's surprised by her tone. He's not sure how long he was dozing upstairs, but he knows she's been in there for a while. As he's about to ask again if she's okay, the door swings open.

Under the bathroom's stark light, her color is high, her eyes glossy.

She meets his gaze but then quickly looks away. "You can come in now." She goes over to wash her hands in the sink.

"What were you doing in here?" His eyes roam over her. She's still wearing his T-shirt.

"Nothing. Just peeing."

Liam continues to watch her in the mirror as she blasts the water and then vigorously pumps the soap dispenser, two dots of pink on her cheeks.

He wants to say more, but it's obvious from her body language that she doesn't want to talk. Instead, she washes her hands in record time and runs out of there.

After finishing, he heads back upstairs. At the top of the loft, he forgets to duck and smacks his head a third time.

"Ow, *shit*! This is ridiculous."

Tori's in bed, under the covers, but she shifts a little. "Are you all right?"

He climbs onto the bed beside her. "I keep hitting my head on the damn ceiling." He rubs around, feeling for a lump, and grumbles. "I'll probably have brain damage by the time we leave here."

She rolls toward him, laughing lightly. "You have to duck."

"No kidding. Someone should put up a warning light."

"I'll recommend it to Tara, Peyton's cousin."

He slips under the sheet and rolls toward her.

Neither of them speak. Moonlight shines through the skylight, though not as bright as earlier.

He's still thinking about what she was doing in that bathroom so long. Her flushed cheeks and bright eyes.

"Listen, Tori, if you need something more from me in bed, you can tell me. You know that, right?"

He hears her intake of breath. "I don't know what you're talking about."

"I'm happy to get you off any way you want." He softens his voice. "A lot of women don't orgasm from just having intercourse."

"I don't want to discuss this."

"There's no reason to be embarrassed. Believe me, making you come is a turn-on for me no matter how it happens."

She rolls away from him and lies on her back. "Are you deaf? I said I *don't* want to talk about it."

Liam studies her profile in the dark. He's not sure what else to say. He doesn't want to make her feel bad. Finally, he rolls over and lies on his back too.

The house creaks as it settles around them.

He studies the shadows on the rafters, wishing Tori would open up to him, would trust him. Then he thinks about the way she was raised. She probably doesn't trust easily.

He turns his head toward her. "Will you come lie next to me?"

She doesn't respond at first. Remains still. But then she turns and scoots toward him. He lifts his arm so she can lay her head on his shoulder.

Tangerines mixed with her own sweet musk envelopes him. He's happy to have her close, at least.

They both lie silently. He shuts his eyes and starts to drift, but then Tori whispers, "Is it dangerous?"

"What?"

"You know." Her fingers trace along his jaw where stubble is growing in. "Going undercover for your work. Is it dangerous?"

He's not sure why she's asking. "Yes," he admits. He thinks about some of the arrests he's made. Usually it goes smoothly, but there have been armed suspects who were definitely dangerous. "Sometimes."

She continues to caress him lightly, then stops and lifts her head to face him. "Please be careful."

His chest tightens. There's an intimacy like this in the dark together. Even though he's always careful at his job, he's moved by her concern.

His voice is rough when he speaks. "I promise I will be."

THE NEXT MORNING, Liam opens his eyes to the sound of a woodpecker against a nearby tree. *Tat-a-tat, tat-a-tat... Tat-a-tat, tat-a-tat.* He listens to the way it goes in bursts, stopping and starting.

Not a sound he usually wakes up to.

He rolls onto his stomach and checks outside through the half-moon window. He studies the quiet of the lake and the cloudless blue sky. Everything is peaceful. It makes him wish he'd brought his camera.

When he gazes at Tori, she looks peaceful too. Pretty as always and sleeping soundly.

He's not surprised he woke up first. He's a morning person and usually can't sleep in even if he tries.

He thinks about how good it feels being with Tori. Not just sexually but in every way. She's still kooky and offbeat. It makes her fun to be around. Whoever heard of dancing without music?

She's unique. Just like she was in high school.

And he still likes it. He still has the same crush on her that he had back then. In a way, nothing's changed.

She shifts beside him in her sleep, and his mind goes back to last night. To everything she told him about her childhood. He's glad she opened up. Although he's still not sure what to make of that situation in the bathroom.

He watches her a little more. As usual, he has morning wood, but ignores it. He wants her to know he's willing to give her whatever she needs.

Smiling to himself, he decides Tori's getting his A game this morning.

He plans to blow her mind.

Slipping under the sheets, he moves lower on the bed. Happily, she sleeps in the nude.

Caressing her legs, he moves up and positions himself between her thighs. He begins there, kissing her soft flesh before lightly running his thumb over her center.

She stirs.

He continues playing with her, enjoying himself. His cock's enjoying it too.

She shifts again, and he tongues her gently. Over the years, he's learned most women like it soft at first, working up to more pressure, so he keeps it light.

Somewhere in there, he senses she's awake. She pushes the sheet away and stares down at him.

"What are you doing?" she asks, her voice husky.

Glancing up, he smiles. "I think it's obvious what I'm doing, isn't it?"

"I guess so." She blinks sleepily. "I didn't expect this."

"Sometimes I like to bring on the unexpected."

She nods and seems to study him.

His slides his left hand up her body, caressing her. "Just relax and enjoy yourself, rubia. Let me do the driving."

She's still studying him, and there's something intense in her gaze, but then she puts her head back on the pillow. "Okay," she whispers. "I'll try."

He gets back to it, using his fingers and mouth to make her feel good. Judging by how wet and swollen she's getting, and by how her hips are moving against him, she seems to be enjoying herself.

The whole thing is turning him on so much that he's tempted to jerk off, but he doesn't. Remaining solely focused on Tori, he wants to bring her to a shattering climax.

He applies every trick he knows. Licking and blowing on her, tonguing her all over, using his fingers and mouth in every way possible.

More than a few times, she gasps with pleasure, moaning, her hands in his hair, though she doesn't come.

He continues, his cock so hard that a cool breeze would push him over the edge.

She squirms and moves against him, her breath thready. He senses she's reaching for it and loves seeing her like this, loves the taste of her, the way she's right on the edge. It's taking a while, but he doesn't mind. He could do this all day.

It seems like she's been close for a long time. He tries to concentrate on what she seems to enjoy the most.

"Aaargh!" Out of the blue, she pushes him away. "This isn't going to work."

"What's wrong?"

She shakes her head with obvious frustration and closes her thighs, a sad smile on her face. "I'm really sorry, but it's not going to happen."

"I can keep going." He puts his hand up to massage his jaw a little. "I don't mind."

"That's okay."

"Am I doing it right? Just tell me. You seemed like you were into it."

"It's not you." She takes a shaky breath, her cheeks pink. "You're doing it right. It's perfect."

He studies her. "Is there something else going on here?"

She turns wary. "What do you mean?"

"I don't know. You tell me."

"It's fine. Everything's *just* peachy." Her voice trembles, and she looks away. "Except I need to use the bathroom."

She slips out of bed, searching around until she finds his T-shirt and her pink lace panties.

He sits up with his back against the pillows. "Come on, Tori. Talk to me. Don't go downstairs." He watches her throw the T-shirt on and then wiggle into the panties, enjoying the sight of her plump ass.

"There's nothing to talk about. Please just drop it, okay?"

She disappears down the spiral staircase, and he hears the bathroom door shut below.

He thinks back to that afternoon they shared. He's certain now she was faking it in bed with him. Not to mention last night when they had sex. She's not being honest, though he has no idea why.

This would bother any guy, but he's mostly saddened by it. Saddened that she'd feel the need to pretend with him about an intimacy he wants to share.

He's pretty sure he knows what's going on downstairs in that bathroom too. But why wouldn't she let him make her come?

Sighing with frustration, he lifts the sheet and stares down at his large erection. Tori's tangy-sweet scent still lingers, only making it worse.

Leaning his head back, he closes his eyes and takes himself in hand. He thinks about the way she was squirming against his mouth only moments ago, how hot that was, and then he thinks about what she's doing downstairs. He wonders what she looks like when she isn't faking it, when she climaxes for real.

Damn, I'd love to see that.

TORI CATCHES a glimpse of herself in the mirror. Hair a tangled mess. Face flushed.

She tried. She honestly tried.

I should have known.

She was so hopeful though, and everything Liam did felt so good. He was so patient too. More patient than any guy she's ever been with. It was obvious he would have kept going for hours if she wanted him to.

There's no point in that though.

She stays in the bathroom for a long while. Masturbates, pees, and then stares at herself in the mirror again.

What's wrong with me?

He's just not my special person. That's all. If he were, then it would all work like it's supposed to.

It's what she's been telling herself for years. For a long time, she accepted it, but deep down, she knows it's a lie.

I'm the one with the problem.

Finally, she leaves the bathroom. To her surprise, Liam is downstairs. The smell of brewed coffee fills the air.

She should go upstairs and get dressed but wanders into the kitchen instead. He's wearing the same jeans from yesterday but has on a different T-shirt, a blue one advertising a sporting goods store.

He's loading the dishwasher and glances over at her. "Hey, I made coffee."

"That was nice of you, thanks."

She pours herself a cup, then gets her almond milk from the fridge to whiten it.

"How did you sleep?" he asks, dumping in detergent.

She sits at the small table with her mug. "Okay, I guess." She appreciates the way he's making normal conversation and not acting weird about what just happened upstairs. "It's so quiet here. I'm not used to that."

"Me either. I still slept all right though. Did you hear the woodpecker this morning?"

She perks up. "No, but I wish I had."

"He might come back tomorrow."

"I hope so."

Picking up his mug of coffee, he comes over and sits across the table from her.

"So you drink coffee in the mornings?" She motions at his mug. "Not iced tea?"

"I switch to iced tea at noon."

"That's very civilized of you."

He leans forward in his chair. "Listen, I was thinking we'd go into Truth Harbor today. Check out the town. Maybe have breakfast there. What do you think?"

"That's a great idea."

"I found some menus in one of the kitchen drawers too. A pizza place and a diner nearby that delivers. We could try that later, if you want."

"Just like a hotel. Not that I've ever ordered room service from a hotel before."

"You haven't?"

She shakes her head. "I've never had the opportunity."

"Guess I'll have to take you to a nice hotel sometime and let you order room service."

He's grinning at her, and as she takes in his handsome face, his good-natured way, something inside of her relaxes. She's grateful he's not going to ruin the first vacation she's had in years. Grateful he's not letting the new elephant in the room stand in the way of them having fun.

She takes a sip from her bitter coffee. "I might hold you to that."

"I hope you do."

Grimacing, she takes another sip and puts her cup down. "This coffee is gross."

"I know. I can barely drink it either."

"It's disgusting."

"Unfortunately, the beans might be past their prime."

"Let's go into town and get lattes." She gets up and goes over to the sink, dumping the rest of her coffee down the drain. She rinses out the mug and puts it in the dishwasher. When she turns around, Liam's eyes are on her legs.

Instead of embarrassment at being caught, he grins and puts his hand out. "Come here, rubia."

She goes over to him, and he pulls her onto his lap. Her breath catches when he kisses the sensitive skin on her neck.

He draws back and they consider each other, both of them quiet. It's a relaxed quiet though, not an uncomfortable one.

"Thank you." She strokes his bristly jaw where a black beard's growing in.

He watches her mouth. "For what?"

"For making me the worst cup of coffee I've ever had in my life."

His arms tighten around her waist. "You're welcome."

CHAPTER TWENTY-ONE

> **Tori's Playlist: Daily Song**
> *"Pour Some Sugar on Me"*
> by Def Leppard
> ♥
> **Liam's Playlist: Daily Song**
> *"I'm Gonna Getcha Good!"*
> by Shania Twain

"WOW, LOOK AT THIS PLACE," Tori says as they drive around downtown Truth Harbor, searching for a parking spot. "I love it here. I feel like I've stepped back in time."

He grins. "I had a feeling it would appeal to you."

They have breakfast at a crowded café, sitting outside and enjoying the sunshine. Liam asks her all sorts of questions about herself.

"Hmm." She takes a bite of toast with jam, secretly pleased by his attention, though she'd never admit it. "Am I being interrogated again? Is this your special agent thing?"

"I just want to get to know you better."

"I thought I was the one kicking the tires and revving the engine."

He laughs. "You are."

"I don't think any guy has ever found me this fascinating."

He sprinkles hot sauce on his eggs. "Well, I hope by now it's obvious I'm not just any guy."

She picks up her coffee and eyes him over the rim of her mug. His hair is casual, the way she likes it, a lock of it falling onto his forehead. "I'm starting to think that's true," she murmurs mostly to herself.

He asks more questions and especially wants to know about all her jobs. "Why so many?" he asks. "You always seem stressed."

She explains how it happened without her planning it. She started by creating the website for Happy Pet Nanny. Then Blair wanted one for her bakery, and when Road heard about it, he hired her to work on his blog.

"His blog? You mentioned that before." Liam looks confused. "What does your brother do for a living?"

"He's a travel blogger."

"What's that?"

Tori explains how her brother travels and writes for his blog, Edge of Zen, selling travel merchandise. "He's an author too. I haven't mentioned that part. He has two bestselling books."

Liam appears stunned. "You're kidding me."

Tori laughs and pours more maple syrup on her oatmeal. "What did you think, that he did something illegal?"

"I don't know. Maybe. That guy was a real dick to me in high school."

She goes quiet. It pains her to hear this. "I really didn't know he was threatening you. I would have told him to stop if I had."

He shrugs. "Sure. It's no big deal now."

"You believe me, don't you?"

He smiles at her from across the table. "Of course I do."

They go back to the previous subject, and Liam wonders if maybe her life would be easier if she focused on one job instead of four.

She plays with her napkin. "My friend, Fiona—she's a marketing expert—thinks I should focus on Happy Pet Nanny, that there's a lot I could do with it. I sell those snacks, but she wants me to branch out and create a whole line of products. She even thinks I could find an investor."

"That's an interesting idea."

"Yeah." Tori sighs and then laughs. "I guess I need enough nerve, you know? I've never done anything that bold."

"I think you'd be great at whatever you put your mind to."

"You do?"

"Absolutely. And I think your friend is right about Happy Pet Nanny. You have a real talent with animals."

She studies him as he goes back to focusing on his plate of food. A warmth blooms inside her. She can tell he means it.

Usually the guys she dates tear down her ideas. They're always finding reasons why she'd fail, then claim they're helping her by being "honest."

After breakfast they stroll around town together, holding hands and wandering through all the little shops. To her amazement, they come across one that sells nothing but thick, cozy sweaters. The exact kind she always imagined for those Christmas cards with Dr. Adrian.

Dr. Adrian! Tori wonders if she should feel bad that she hasn't thought of him in days.

She glances at Liam's handsome profile. *Let's face it. Dr. Adrian has turned into a fuzzy memory.*

"I have to buy one of these sweaters," Tori announces. "I *have* to."

Liam raises a brow. "It's eighty degrees outside. Are you sure you want to buy a winter sweater?"

"I don't care." She thinks about how much she wants that Christmas card, how she's been knitting all those sweaters for her dogs. She doesn't need a man. This year that card is happening no matter what.

They look through the store, and Tori finally settles on one that's white cable-knit cotton. It's thick and perfect. She imagines herself sitting by a fire with all her dogs, wearing this sweater as she reads them *The Night Before Christmas.*

Liam's been browsing through the men's selections. He comes over holding up a sweater similar to hers, except it's brown. "What do you think?"

"Um... it's nice."

"I'm going to get it."

"You *are?*" Tori's eyes bug out. She can't hide her shock. "Really? Why would you do that?"

"I don't know. I've never owned a sweater like this." He tilts his head, admiring it. "I think it's kind of great."

She tries not to gawk at him.

They get in line to pay for their purchases. He wants to buy hers too, but she won't let him. "You paid for breakfast."

"Come on, Tori. Let me get it for you. I want you to have something to remember this trip by."

She stares at his brown sweater, still reeling from the fact that he's buying it at all. "Why is that?"

"Because"—his gaze softens as he leans toward her—"you're *my* vacation too."

TORI CAN'T STOP RUMINATING over Liam's words as they explore the town.

"You're my vacation too."

She's never been anyone's vacation before.

Obviously he's hers, but that's different. She never goes anywhere or does anything. Despite his insistence that he's boring, Liam leads an interesting life.

"Do you have any hobbies?" she asks, taking a lick from her strawberry sorbet as they window-shop. "Besides baseball, I mean. Or do you even consider that a hobby?"

"Baseball will always be a part of my life, but it's strictly a hobby now. I also like to take photographs."

She nods, remembering the ones she saw during their afternoon of lust. "Did you take the ones of the Oregon coast in your bedroom?"

He glances at her with surprise. "You noticed those?"

"I did. I liked them."

He seems slightly embarrassed. "They're okay. I wish I'd brought my camera with me on this trip."

"You should have. Can't you just use your phone?"

"I can. You have better control with a camera though."

"Do you usually do nature shots?"

"Usually, or sometimes people. I took some of Fancy when we were at the dog park recently."

"Oh, how fun! You'll have to show them to me."

He nods and takes a bite of his maple pecan ice cream.

She's been taking photos since they arrived in town and has been sneakily putting Liam in most of them. "You know, we haven't done a selfie yet. Should we take one?"

He chuckles. "Sure, let's do it."

Tori holds her phone out, and he moves closer. She snaps a few photos of them smiling, but then to her surprise, he turns and kisses her cheek for one of them. It's so romantic, and she secretly lingers over it afterward.

"I'm going to take some too," he says, pulling his phone out from his jeans pocket. He puts their bag with the sweaters on a nearby bench. "Let's get some with our ice cream cones."

The two of them stand on the sidewalk together, taking silly photos of each other. At one point, Tori pretends to lick her cone provocatively while Liam crosses his eyes and tries to eat from the side of his mouth.

"You look so funny," she says, laughing afterward when they flip through the pictures. "There's ice cream on your face."

"I was being goofy." He grins, still looking through the photos. "But check out the ones of you." He waggles his brows, referring to the pictures of her licking the cone like a porn star. "I might have to save some of these for private use later."

"Very funny." She slaps his arm. "There's no way you're doing that."

He chuckles. "I'm not promising anything."

"I guess I'll know when you lock yourself in the bathroom with your phone, won't I?" As soon as the words leave her mouth, she wants to take them back. She nearly slaps her palm over her mouth. Heat spreads across her cheeks.

Her eyes flash to his face, but he doesn't seem to notice her embarrassment and is still looking at the pictures.

Thank God.

They continue wandering around town, and when they come across a pirate museum, they decide to take the tour. It shows them about the town's infamous history. As they're leaving the gift shop, Tori sees a small pirate doll holding a camera and gets it for him.

"You don't have to buy me anything."

"Well, maybe I want you to have something to remember this trip by too. Have you ever thought of that? I wouldn't want you to forget me."

His eyes hold that steady gaze on her where they look all sexy. "Tori, I'll never forget you. I couldn't even when I tried."

She's taken aback. "You tried to forget me?"

"Sure." He shrugs as the cashier wraps the pirate doll in paper before putting it in a bag. "I tried to forget the whole mess that happened in high school."

"I can't believe you tried to forget me," she says in mock indignation. "And here I am buying you a gift. I must need my head examined."

He slips his arm around her waist and pulls her close. "I'd like to examine a few other parts of you too," he whispers.

Her breath catches, and when she turns to face him, he kisses her. Kisses her right there in front of all the pirate dolls and summer tourists.

By the time they head back in his truck, she's glowing inside. Lit up like a star. The window's rolled down and her hair's blowing in the breeze. It isn't until she catches a glimpse of herself in the truck's side mirror that she finally understands it.

For the first time in a long time, she feels young, beautiful, and alive.

Meanwhile, she and Liam are in the middle of another dispute over whose playlist to put on first.

"Damn, I'm a pushover with you," he grumbles, giving in and letting her play her music. "It's pathetic. Better not let anyone on my squad see me like this."

"Oh, stop complaining," she says with glee, hooking up the USB for her phone. "I think you secretly want to hear my music because deep down, you know this country music thing of yours isn't healthy."

He rolls his eyes. "Give me a break."

"All those songs about being drunk and broke? Please. That can't be good for your psyche."

"That's ridiculous. Most country songs are love songs."

"You could have fooled me."

He starts naming every country love song he knows. It appears to be an endless list.

"Just stop." She waves her hand. "That doesn't prove anything. All it proves is they sing about love while they're drunk and broke."

"For someone who dislikes country music so much, you sure think you're an expert on the subject."

"I don't have to be an expert to have good taste."

Liam chuckles, and they continue to banter. When "You Give Love a Bad Name" comes through the truck speakers, he objects.

"Not Bon Jovi," he says. "I've been tortured enough."

"*What?*" She stares at him in astonishment. "Are you saying you don't like Bon Jovi?"

"No, I don't."

She scoffs. "I don't believe you. In fact, I don't believe *anyone* who says they don't like Bon Jovi."

He laughs. "That's nuts."

"No, it's not."

"Their songs have been played to death. I've heard this a million times."

"Well, duh. That's because they're like the greatest band ever." As they drive to the cabin, she plays a few of their less well-know songs for him. "Come on, they even sound kind of country sometimes."

"I guess that 'Wanted Dead or Alive' song isn't half bad," he admits grudgingly as they pull into the driveway of the house. "But next time we go somewhere, we're listening to *my* playlist."

Once they're in the cabin again, Tori puts her cozy sweater away. After going to the bathroom and pulling her hair up in a messy bun, she changes into a white bikini with pink daisies on it. She finds Liam standing on the front porch, drinking a glass of iced tea while he gazes out at the view.

"I was thinking of going for a swim. Do you want to join me?" she asks.

He glances over, then does a double take when he sees what she's wearing. His eyes roam over her approvingly. "Damn, you look good enough to eat."

"Thanks." She smiles, pleased at the compliment. She doesn't have the most perfect body in the world, but thanks to a beauty queen mother, knows how to carry herself.

He puts his glass down and gives her a wolfish grin. "Why don't you come on over here?"

"Actually, that iced tea looks refreshing. Is there any left?

"There are a few bottles in the fridge. Help yourself."

Tori goes back inside. She gets a tall glass from the cabinet, fills it with ice, and then pours in the tea. When she heads back out to the back deck, she sees him through the screen door. He's leaning against the post in the same position as earlier, admiring the view.

She's admiring the view too. The rear view. The expression "a tall drink of water" was invented for men like Liam.

She opens the door to go outside.

That's when the oddest idea comes to her. She's not sure what possesses her to do it, but it's like she can't stop herself. She walks right up to him and, without a second thought, dumps her entire glass of iced tea over his head.

"Hey!" he shouts, jumping back from the porch rail. "What the hell!"

Her eyes grow wide at his strong reaction. "Wow." She takes in his drenched appearance. His flattened hair. Ice cubes still falling off him. She wonders if this is what she looked like right after he dumped that milkshake on her.

He wipes his face. "What is this?" He's licking the corner of his mouth. "Iced tea?"

She's still watching him with wide eyes. "It is."

"Did you really just pour that on me?" He seems astonished, gesturing to the empty glass in her hand.

She nods, trying not to smile.

"Why would you do that?"

"Because you said I could."

He's incredulous. "When did I say that?"

"You said I could pour a milkshake on you sometime so we'd be even."

He snorts and wipes tea off his face. His shirt is wet too. In fact, it looks kind of hot the way it's clinging to him. "I said maybe I'd *let* you pour a milkshake on me. This isn't a milkshake, and this is hardly me *letting* you."

She shrugs, unable to hide her grin. "Well, obviously I took matters into my own hands."

His gaze narrows, and for a moment, she sees the lawman behind those brown eyes, the one bad guys must see right before he slaps on the handcuffs.

It thrills her.

He takes in her smile and his mouth twitches. "You're quite pleased with yourself, aren't you?"

"I am." She beams at him.

He brushes off a few stray ice cubes still sticking to his shirt. "Well, you've forgotten one thing."

"I have?"

He nods slowly. "Payback."

"What do you mean?"

"When I dumped that milkshake on you, it was an accident. But you did this on purpose."

"Payback?" She's not sure if she likes the sound of that, or the way he's looking at her either.

"Yes." His eyes flicker down her body. "You've been a bad girl. I'll have to punish you."

"Punish me?"

He gives her a wicked grin.

Uh-oh. He's right. She didn't consider payback. Not sure what to do, she does the only sensible thing that comes to mind.

She runs.

Straight down the steps from the back deck and onto the sandy area below. Unfortunately, Liam is right behind her. She could run faster if she wasn't barefoot or laughing so hard.

It only takes him a minute to catch up with her. The next thing she knows, she's plucked right off the ground and swooped into his arms.

"Hey, put me down!"

"Forget it. I've got plans for you."

"Plans? What kind of plans?" She hugs his neck as he carries her back up the porch steps. "Where are you taking me?"

"Bad girls aren't allowed to ask questions."

He pushes the screen door open with his foot and maneuvers her inside the house. She can't remember the last time a guy carried her anywhere, and she has to admit it's fun.

The bathroom door is open, and he walks toward the shower. "I don't want to get wet!" she complains.

"Stop griping. You're already wearing a bathing suit. I'm the one soaked in iced tea over here."

She giggles. "I guess I should apologize, but I'm not going to."

He gives her a stern look. "Still a bad girl, then."

"I guess so. What are you going to do about it?"

He doesn't reply, only pushes the shower curtain aside and steps into the tub with her. He lets her slide down his chest, one arm still around her waist. The other reaches behind her, and the next thing she knows, they're sprayed with cold water.

"Aaaah!" she squeals. "That's freezing!"

"It'll warm up," Liam says with a grin. He reaches behind his back and pulls his tea-soaked T-shirt off.

"I can't believe this!" She dances around as cold water streams down her neck and back.

He chuckles and unzips his jeans. Soon he's standing before her completely naked.

"Is this the payback you had in mind?" she asks, her eyes roaming lower. She can't help herself. He has a great body.

He pulls her close. "Don't worry," he murmurs. "I'm just getting started." And then his mouth comes down hard on hers.

She moans with pleasure. Wraps her arms around his neck and sucks his tongue, which tastes slippery and wet mixed with the cool shower water.

He unhooks the back of her bikini top and it falls away. Liam bends lower, licking and sucking her nipples, sending streams of pleasure through her.

She grabs his dark hair, holding him close, encouraging him. He draws back and then moves his hands to her hips. He hooks his thumbs into her bottoms, dragging them down her legs. She uses his shoulder for balance as she steps out of them.

Then he's back up and the two of them are kissing again. Deep tongue kisses. Kissing with lips and teeth. Everything mixes with the flowing water. His hard-on presses into her stomach.

"We don't have to keep using condoms," she says breathlessly, coming up for air. "I have an IUD."

"You do?"

She nods. "I'm always safe too. Are you?"

"I am."

The two of them study each other.

Drops of shower water cling to his skin. She holds his jaw still and kisses his beard stubble, his cheek next, licking it. "I think the tea is mostly gone," she murmurs. She slides her hand lower and wraps it around his thick cock.

Tori hears his sharp intake of breath.

"The water's finally warm," she whispers.

"Yeah" is all he says as she continues to stroke him. He has his hand against the wall for balance. She does it for a while, watching his face, his eyes hooded with lust.

Eventually he draws back and pulls her hand away. Reaching down, he cups her ass with both hands and lifts her. "I need to be inside you." His voice is rough.

She wraps her legs around him, her arms on his shoulders, and gasps when he slides home. Her eyes fall shut. It's all so good, saturating her senses. In the back of her mind, she knows she'll have to start pretending soon, but for now she wants to enjoy it.

He takes it slow and steady. She moans every time he pushes up to the hilt.

"Open your eyes," he breathes. "Look at me, rubia. I want to see you."

She does, and the two of them gaze at each other, bodies coming together. Warm water flows around them.

"Don't fake it," he says. "Not this time."

Adrenaline shoots through her. She stares at him in shock. "I... I don't know what you mean."

"Yes, you do. Let's be honest with each other."

Her breath shakes.

"I want to know you, Tori. The *real* you."

For a moment she's lost in his brown eyes. The way they're aroused but filled with kindness too.

She plays with the back of his neck nervously, finger-brushing his short hair.

He kisses her gently. "Please let me in."

He's already inside her, but she knows what he means. Not her body, but her mind and heart.

He's still moving his hips, sliding up all the way, and it's incredible. He's touching places inside her, deep ones, exciting her. Despite her inability to orgasm like this, she enjoys sex. Enjoys the closeness, but also how great it feels with the right guy.

There haven't been a lot of guys who were right though.

It occurs to her that not having to fake it is a relief. She can relax, get into the experience without having to give a performance. And then there's the other part.

The intimacy.

She wants that. Hungers for it. Though she's scared too.

"Okay," she says nervously. "I'll be honest."

Something flames behind his eyes. "Good."

They continue to move together, and it's amazing. His body against hers, so much bigger and stronger than she is. She grips his muscular arms as waves of pleasure ripple through her.

At one point, Liam slips his hand between her legs and plays with her, but she pushes it away.

He eyes her questioningly.

"It won't work," she says. "I can't come like that."

He nods, his breath shaking. "Okay."

After a while, his pace quickens. He's getting close. "God, you feel good," he says. "So damn good."

"So do you." She gasps, clutching his shoulders, letting herself enjoy every moment.

He grips her ass, kneading her, the intensity building until finally he groans. Tori watches his face. His mouth is open, jaw flushed. It's so hot seeing Liam like this. She's awash in the pleasure of it, all her nerve endings lit up.

Afterward, he kisses her lips, then her cheeks before raining soft kisses all over her.

She sighs. "You can punish me like that anytime you want."

His large body rumbles against hers with his amusement.

Eventually she slides her legs down so she's standing in the tub with him. He strokes her face. "Thank you for being your honest self."

A strong emotion wells up in her, but she doesn't want to name it. Her eyes sting. She's not ready for this conversation. "I think the hot water is running out," she says instead.

"You're right," he agrees.

Despite the now tepid water, they take a shower together, scrubbing each other back and front, though Liam spends an inordinate time on her breasts and ass.

She bats his hand away, giggling. "Trust me, they're clean."

"I know." He tilts his head admiringly. "I just like seeing you all slippery with soap."

After they get out of the shower, Tori wraps a towel around herself, then gathers all the wet clothes. She puts Liam's in the small washing machine and then goes outside with her bikini.

It's late afternoon, and the lake dazzles against a blue sky. The summer air's as warm as bathwater, luxurious on her skin. She hangs her wet bikini on the deck rail, then gazes out at the view filled with happiness.

That glow inside her is still there.

Liam joins her after a few minutes with a white towel wrapped around his waist. He's carrying a couple of glasses while also juggling a box of crackers, a knife, and the jar of peanut butter they picked up at the grocery store yesterday. He puts everything on the small table and takes a seat in one of the patio loungers.

"I brought you another iced tea," he says, "seeing as you had an unfortunate mishap with your previous one."

She glances over her shoulder and smiles. "That was nice of you."

He opens the box of crackers and covers one with peanut butter. "Damn, I can't believe how hungry I am."

"Really? We ate not that long ago."

"I know." He pops the cracker in his mouth. "I guess punishing a bad girl uses a lot of energy."

She laughs and then comes over to join him, adjusting her towel before taking a seat on the opposite lounger and putting her feet up. He hands her the next cracker.

"Thanks." She takes a bite, her eyes wandering over him with admiration. Healthy and muscular. Liam is straight-up beautiful. "Your skin is naturally a tan color, isn't it?"

He nods, spreading more peanut butter on a cracker. "Yeah, I have a perma-tan. Elena and I both take after my dad."

"Lucky you. I think your skin looks amazing."

He glances over at her and seems pleased. "Thank you." He gives her a sly grin. "I like yours too."

"Really? I'm so pale." She holds up her arm and studies it. "The opposite of you. I can't tan to save my life, though I wish I could."

"My mom's coloring is more like yours." He gives her another cracker. "She always complains about it too."

Tori thinks back to high school, to that meeting they had with all their parents and the principal. "I remember your parents. Doesn't your mom have red hair?"

"She colors it red. I think it's light brown naturally."

"And you look more like your dad. I remember him too. He seemed kind of serious." She remembers his dad as being tall, dark, and intimidating.

Liam chuckles. "He's a good guy. That was the first time he'd ever been called to the principal's office, I can tell you that."

"Did your parents believe you when you told them what happened?" she asks, curious.

"Of course."

"Really? No questions asked?"

He picks up his iced tea. "None. They believed me."

"Wow. You guys are really close, huh?"

He takes a long drink from his tea and puts it back on the table.

"We are." His eyes rest on her, and she knows they're both thinking about the unpleasant history between them.

"If we keep seeing each other after this weekend, how's that going to work? Your sister hates me, and I imagine your parents won't be too crazy about me either."

His expression turns considering. "Let me worry about that. They just have to get to know you."

"They're going to think I'm one of your weirdo girlfriends, except we have a history that makes it even worse."

He spreads peanut butter on another cracker. "Like I said, once they get to know you, that'll all change."

She falls silent as she accepts the cracker from him. It's nice that he's optimistic, but it's already obvious how much his sister dislikes her. She highly doubts anything will change. And it isn't just his family they have to worry about.

It's hers too.

CHAPTER TWENTY-TWO

> **Tori's Playlist: Daily Song**
> "Holiday"
> by Scorpions
> ♥
> **Liam's Playlist: Daily Song**
> "Die a Happy Man"
> by Thomas Rhett

"WHAT SHOULD WE DO NOW?" Liam asks, closing up the box of crackers. He's still hungry, but the snack helped take the edge off. "Do you still want to go swimming?"

Tori shakes her head. "Maybe tomorrow. I mean, we just took a shower." She gazes out at the lake. The sun's getting low in the sky. "How about we relax and watch a movie upstairs? I saw a bunch of DVDs in the living room bookcase."

"Sounds good."

Tori goes to pick out a movie. He puts the snack away and cleans some grapes.

They head up the spiral staircase, both of them still wearing towels.

"Watch your head."

He ducks just in time.

It's hot in the loft, but he opens the skylight window, which brings in a nice breeze. Tori picks a movie called *My Big Fat Greek Wedding*. She seems surprised when he admits he's never seen it.

"Oh, you're so lucky," she says, stripping her towel away and settling under the sheets naked. "This movie is the best."

He gets in beside her and takes his towel off too, both of them propped up against some pillows. They could put clothes on, but since she's not suggesting it, he's certainly not going to.

"You eat kind of healthy for a guy, don't you?" She pulls off some grapes. "I hardly ever see you eating junk food."

"I suppose." He pops a grape in his mouth. "It comes from being an athlete all those years. Occasionally I indulge, but I never really developed a taste for it."

"My being vegan doesn't seem to bother you either."

He shrugs. "Why would it?"

"I don't know. I've dated guys who were definitely bothered by it."

"Really? That's weird. Come here." He pulls her closer so they're cozied up together. He kisses her hair, inhaling her clean scent. "By now it should be obvious that I like everything about you." But then he reconsiders. "Everything except your taste in music, of course."

She lightly smacks his leg, and he laughs.

They settle in to watch the film. He's enjoying it, though his mind keeps wandering back to the way Tori looked after she poured that iced tea on him. Her mischievous grin. She does something to him, moves him in ways he can't even explain. It was incredible between them in the shower too. He's glad she stopped putting on an act.

But then he reflects over the conversation they had about his family. Despite what he said, he knows she's concerned. Not to mention there's her family to contend with.

The movie is still playing, and Tori laughs at something on-screen. Ironically, the plot has some similarities to their own situation.

Reaching for her hand, he laces their fingers together. "Hey."

She turns and looks at him. Her cheeks are pink, slightly sunburned from today. She's so pretty. He can't resist leaning in to kiss her.

"I really want this," he whispers. "You and me."

Her blue eyes soften, and she reaches up to stroke his jaw. "I know you do."

"Do you want it too? Be honest. I can take it."

She grabs the remote control to pause the film and then smiles at him. "So far my weekend test drive has been amazing."

"Yeah?"

"The best ever. In fact, I've decided I'd like to buy this car."

He chuckles with happy relief. "I'm glad to hear that. You'll be pleased to learn it comes with a special offer."

"It does?"

"We want your satisfaction, so we're offering a money-back guarantee."

She giggles, scoots closer, and slides her leg over his. "I like the sound of that. Where do I sign?"

He points at his lips. "Right here."

She kisses him, and then her voice turns husky. "Is there anyplace else that needs my signature?"

His eyes drop to her mouth and his pulse quickens. Her lips are small and have a pretty shape to them. He tries not to get excited, but blood is already rushing between his thighs. "There might be. That depends on you."

She slides her hands across his shoulders and then bends over to kiss his chest. She continues kissing him, leaving a trail of electricity across his skin as she works her way down.

Pushing the sheet back, she takes in the sight of his hard-on. "This is an impressive cock."

"Thank you."

She glances up. "I guess I'd better sign on the dotted line now, huh?"

He's enjoying her playfulness, but his grin fades as soon as she takes him in her mouth. "Damn," he murmurs. He slips his hand into her soft hair. The sensation is off the charts, way off. He watches her work him over. Reaching out to stroke her body, he caresses her silky skin, enjoying the sight and feel of her.

Eventually his breathing turns rough and uneven. "I'm so close, rubia. Maybe you should pull back." But she doesn't and instead keeps going until he has no other choice but to give in to ecstasy with a long groan.

Afterward, she sits up and smiles at him. Sweet and sexy. He reaches over and hands her his towel from earlier.

"You're amazing." He pulls her close. "Let me go down on you too. I want to make you feel this good."

"Oh, that's okay. But I have to use the bathroom."

She starts to get up, but he puts his hand on her arm. "Wait, don't go." He tries to get a handle on the situation. "I just want to be clear—are you masturbating in the bathroom downstairs?"

"Oh my God." She freezes. Her sunburned cheeks turn an even brighter shade of pink. "I can't believe you just asked me that."

"Please be honest with me. I swear, I'm not trying to embarrass you."

She closes her eyes and lets her breath out. "Okay, I admit it. You caught me."

"Why not let me make you come? I'm more than happy to do whatever you want."

"I know."

"Talk to me, then. Tell me the truth." He lowers his voice. "Is it me? Am I doing something wrong?"

Her eyes grow wide with concern. "Oh, that's not it at all! Please don't think that. It's not you. I'm the one with the problem."

"What do you mean?"

She leans back on the pillow, groaning. "All right, fine. I'll tell you." She stares up at the ceiling, her cheeks blazing pink. "I can't come unless I'm alone."

He takes in her words. He's not sure if he's understanding her. "So you've never had an orgasm during sex?"

"Never. I can't, no matter how much I want to."

"Well, maybe no one's doing it right. Just tell me what you need."

She shakes her head. "No, you're not getting it. Everything you're doing feels great, but I just can't... I can't let go with someone else." She turns to him. "Do you see now? That's why I keep going in the bathroom."

He nods. "Okay, I think I do get it. But maybe I can still help."

"How?"

He thinks it over. "What if instead of going into the bathroom, you stay here in bed and do it?"

Her mouth drops open. "With you *watching* me? Are you crazy? I could never do that!"

"Just pretend I'm not here."

"But you *are* here."

"I'll turn my head the other way."

She's still looking at him like he's nuts.

"I'll turn my whole body. We could put the movie back on too. There'd be no pressure."

Tori glances up at the television and seems to consider his idea. "I don't know."

"I'll blast the television. And I promise I won't look at you at all."

She bites her lip. "I suppose we could try that. Maybe if the television is loud enough, I could pretend you're not here."

"It would be a start."

"You wouldn't mind doing all that?"

"Of course not. Let's give it a shot."

They switch sides on the bed so he's better angled to face the television. Tori slips under the sheets. When he glances over, she's completely covered.

"Can you breathe all right under there?"

"You're not supposed to be looking at me!"

"I'm not." He chuckles. "My eyes accidentally strayed in your direction."

There's movement beneath the sheets and then her voice again. "Well, don't let them stray anymore."

He starts the film and turns the volume up loud, tries to concentrate on watching it. Although he just came, the idea that Tori's masturbating beside him is kind of turning him on.

After a few minutes, he senses her pull the sheet off. She takes some pillows and stacks a row between them.

"Everything all right?" he asks.

"I think so."

"Do you want me to go down on you? Get you worked up?"

"That's nice of you to offer, but I'm good."

She disappears under the sheets, and he goes back to watching the movie. Not that he can concentrate worth a damn. All he can think about is Tori next to him playing with herself.

What a situation. If he had to analyze it, he's guessing it's a trust thing. She's probably never been with anyone she's trusted enough to let go.

Another ten minutes pass, and she emerges from beneath the sheet. Her hair's mussed and her skin glows with sweat. Her cheeks still pink.

"How did it go?" he asks, stirred up at the sight of her.

She sighs. "I couldn't do it."

"That's too bad. Are you sure you don't want me to help?"

"I came close a couple times, but I just couldn't." She turns to him, her blue eyes shining bright. "I'm sorry, but I'm going to have to go downstairs."

"Don't be sorry. We'll figure this out. It'll probably take some time."

She sits up and puts her hand out to touch his face, kisses him. "Thank you for being so nice and not treating me like a freak."

"I would never do that."

"Just look at all this." She laughs, gesturing to the loud television, the pillows stacked between them, and the sheet she was hiding under. "And you thought I wasn't one of the crazy ones."

TORI FINISHES up in the bathroom and then tries to detangle her hair with her fingers. She still can't believe she told Liam about her issue.

At the beginning of this weekend, she already knew he wanted a relationship with her, but she was still unsure. Not anymore. Now there's no doubt.

She studies herself in the mirror and smiles.

That car passed its test drive with flying colors.

She heads back upstairs and slips beneath the covers, letting her eyes adjust to the dark. She notices he put the blanket back on the bed, since the skylight window is open and it's cooling things down.

"I was getting a chubby thinking about you in that bathroom downstairs," he tells her with a grin as she scoots closer.

"A chubby?" She laughs.

He waggles his brows. "I'm thinking next time you're in there playing with yourself, I could do the same thing up here. It's sort of like we're doing it together, then."

"Together, but separate?"

"Yeah, whatever works."

She rolls all the way toward him and caresses his face. He slips his arm around her. "You keep telling me I'm amazing," she whispers. "But you're the amazing one. I honestly couldn't have imagined sharing this with anyone before tonight."

His fingers lightly caress her back. "I'm glad you did."

"I am too. You're so accepting of me."

"It's because I like you, Tori. A lot."

"I like you too."

They contemplate each other. Moonlight shines through the skylight, illuminating the loft. The lake outside is peaceful and quiet.

But there's something changing inside her. Like plate tectonics. Whole continents are slowly shifting and dividing, creating brand new landscapes.

"I can't remember the last time I've felt this way with anyone," he says, still contemplating her. "I don't know if I ever have."

"Me either."

"Let's not let anything get in our way. After this weekend, let's tell everyone we're together. I don't want to keep it a secret anymore."

"Okay." She licks her lips. "We're going to get a lot of grief from people though."

"I know, but eventually they'll come around. And even if they don't, we have to live our best lives."

She nods. "You're right." She doesn't even want to think how much her mom is going to freak out. Not to mention Blair and Road. But then she thinks about how they dislike Liam over a misunderstanding.

Sitting up partway, she looks out the window toward the lake. "Do you want to do something crazy?"

"What do you have in mind?"

She turns back to him. "Let's go skinny-dipping."

He chuckles. "There's my wild girl."

She laughs. "I've never done anything like that before, have you?"

"Nope. Never."

They make their way down the spiral staircase. Tori's excited, still feeling that glow.

"Wait, should we grab some towels?" she asks when they get to the back deck. "Maybe we should cover up walking outside."

Liam disappears into the house, and when he comes back, he's carrying the blanket from the couch. "Here, let's use this."

He throws it around both of them, and they head down the steps and onto the sandy beach. The night air has cooled from earlier but is still warm.

"I'm glad it's so private," Tori says. "Do you think anyone can see us out here?"

He looks around toward the other homes. "I doubt it."

Once they're closer to the water, they drop the blanket on the sand and head into the lake together.

"That's cold," she squeals, splashing in with her feet. "It's colder than I thought it would be."

"It'll feel warmer once we get used to it."

They go in until they're both up to their waists. She glances over at him and discovers he's already looking at her. "I feel like Adam and Eve."

"So do I." He grins. "It's like we're in the Garden of Eden."

"All right, I'm going to take the plunge," she announces.

He tugs her hand. "Wait, we'll do it together. Let's go out a little farther though."

She follows his lead, and soon they're out in the deeper part of the lake. They take a breath, then dip under all the way. A cold plunge.

"Oh, wow," she says, coming up sputtering and slicking her hair back. "That's refreshing."

"Yeah, it is." He wipes water from his face.

They both look around. It's dark out, but with the moonlight they can still see part of the landscape. The lake is inky black though and smells mossy. Since Liam's still able to touch bottom, she wraps an arm over his shoulder and treads water in front of him.

"I can't believe I'm doing this," she says, breathless. "Have you really never gone skinny-dipping before? It's okay to admit it if you have."

"I really haven't."

"What about when you were a big baseball player? You must have done it then."

He gives her a funny look. "I'm confused. How does playing baseball equate with skinny-dipping?"

"Oh, you know. All the orgies and stuff. Everybody running around naked."

"Orgies?" He nearly chokes with laughter. "What are you talking about? There are no orgies in baseball."

She rolls her eyes. "I'm talking about sports groupies. You didn't go skinny-dipping with any of them?"

"No," he says decisively, looking out at the landscape. "Definitely not."

"Did you sleep with any of them?"

Liam gives her a wry look. "Are you still kicking the tires? I thought you bought this car."

She shrugs and smiles. "I'm just getting the feel of it. I want to know what kind of history it's had."

"Ah, I see."

"So, tell me. Did you ever sleep with any of the groupies?"

He sighs. "All right, occasionally when we were on the road, I may have slept with a groupie or two."

She doesn't like the idea of him sleeping with sports groupies, then realizes she doesn't like the idea of him sleeping with anyone.

"You realize that was a decade ago, right? I was much younger." He eyes her curiously. "How do you know about any of this? I thought you weren't into sports."

"I looked up stuff online last week. I'm not in the dark about baseball anymore. I did some reading."

"Is that so?" He skims his hand down over her ass. His voice softens as he pulls her in close and nuzzles her neck. "All right, then, tell me what you learned."

"Lots of things." She remembers some of the articles she came across. "I learned sometimes catchers wear nail polish. Is that true?"

"Yes, it is," he murmurs. "I used to wear it during games."

She slips one of her legs around his hip as they drift farther out into the water. "Really? What color?"

"White or yellow. It made it easier for pitchers to see my hand signals." He chuckles then. "Is that what you got out of all your reading? Sports groupies and fingernail polish?"

"That's what caught my attention."

He shakes his head with a grin.

She props her forearms on his shoulders, still treading water. "I learned other things too. I learned catchers don't squat, they crouch. I also learned they control the rhythm and direction of the game. That they're the most important position on the team but get none of the glory."

His brows go up. "Well, I take it back. You did do your homework."

"See? I told you."

She quiets as she gazes out at the sprinkling of house lights across the lake. There were other articles she read too. Ones specifically about Liam. By all accounts, he was forced to give up a very promising career.

"Do you miss it at all?"

"Sometimes," he acknowledges. "But I have no regrets. I wouldn't change anything."

"Because you love what you do now?"

"Yes." His eyes linger on hers. "That, and because I wouldn't be here skinny-dipping with you."

She smiles and moves closer, pressing her breasts right against his chest so their faces are only inches apart. "We're a couple of skinny-dipping virgins."

"That we are." And then he kisses her. His mouth tastes hot in contrast to the cool water. His arms pull her in tight.

Eventually they draw back, gazing at each other. The sound of the lake gently laps around them. The sky filled with stars shines above.

"I think this is the best weekend I've ever had," she whispers. "I wish it would never end."

His eyes soften, inky deep like the water. "Me too. Let's stay here forever."

CHAPTER TWENTY-THREE

THEY SPEND the last day of their trip getting to know each other better. Hanging out on the back deck, Tori has on her bikini while Liam wears swim trunks as they talk. He tells her about some of the cases he's had in the past, and she's fascinated.

"Are you glad you left Violent Crime and moved to White-Collar?" She eats an apple slice drizzled with honey and cinnamon.

He nods. "I needed the change, and it's a better fit for me. There's been more undercover work too."

"I can't imagine doing that. Do you ever get scared when you're undercover?"

"No." He reaches for a piece of apple. "Sometimes I'm on edge before a big arrest, especially if we know the suspect is armed, but my squad works hard to try and anticipate every scenario."

She listens with interest as he describes more of his life with the FBI. Unfortunately, all this talk about arresting people has her worrying about her mom and Wayne again.

When they're not hanging out on the back deck talking, they're up in the loft having the best sex of her life. She's never been so honest with a guy or given so much of her real self.

Liam doesn't mind at all when she goes down to the bathroom. He waits for her patiently, stroking his hard-on, so when she comes upstairs, he's ready for her.

They do it with her on top. Him on top. Back, front, and sideways. Tori wants to try every position like she's tasting a box of naughty chocolates.

"Damn, you're on fire," he says after another round of wild lovemaking. He turns toward her with a purely male grin. "I think they may need to carry me out of here on a stretcher—not that I'm complaining."

She laughs and arches her back, loose-limbed. "I've never felt so free in my entire life."

He doubles the pillow under his head and studies her. "Is this really the first time you've had sex without faking orgasms?"

"Basically."

"I can't believe you've been doing it all these years. That must have been frustrating as hell."

Her throat tightens. She hadn't realized how much she hated giving a performance until now. "It was."

"Why didn't you stop?"

She shrugs. "I know it sounds weird, but I felt like that's what guys expected. I didn't want to disappoint anyone."

"It sounds like they're the ones disappointing *you*."

"It was my problem, not theirs."

"And nobody was ever suspicious until me?"

"No." She smiles at him. "But then you're my first lawman."

He chuckles. "I guess it helps that I'm a trained expert at spotting a liar."

"You are?" She rolls toward him, curious. "Really? Trained how?"

"At Quantico, but I've taken classes since then. It was part of my job when I was a catcher too, analyzing body language."

"No, I mean, like how can you tell if someone's lying?"

"A number of ways." He shifts position, propping his head up on his hand. "It's easiest if you can get a baseline on the person so you know when they're telling the truth. Then you slip in something that not's true and watch them."

"What will they do?"

"It depends, but once you understand what's normal, it's easier to spot a change. Another technique is to ask them the same question in different ways."

She nods. "Looking for inconsistencies."

"Actually, you're looking for similarities. Often liars will use the same words and phrases in a rehearsed way."

"That's interesting." She thinks back to all the orgasms she's been faking over the years. There *was* a rehearsed quality to it, since she basically did it the same every time. "So is it like in the movies where you sit someone in a chair with a bright light overhead and interrogate them?"

"No." He chuckles. "Typically, we get better results by chatting with a suspect in a more relaxed way."

She tries to imagine Liam doing that and then thinks of her mom and Wayne, especially Wayne. "What other ways do people give themselves away if they're lying?"

He slides his hand down to her hip. "Are you planning to interrogate someone soon? For the record, I think you've already dug up all of my secrets."

She tucks her arm under the pillow. "I just find it interesting. I once read that people look up to the left or right when they're lying. Is that true?"

"No." He shakes head. "That's been debunked."

"It has?"

"Trust me, I've questioned plenty of people, and their eyes go all over the place. They will sometimes touch their face. Cover their mouth or eyes. They'll use their hands too, but usually after they lie."

"Wow, you really do know a lot about this."

He shrugs. "It's my job."

Her eyes stay on him, and a thrill rushes through her. It's sexy how he catches bad guys. "Gosh, there's nothing boring about you in the least bit, Agent Castillo."

He grins. "Thanks. I'm glad you think that."

The bedsheets and covers tangle around them. She can see a hickey on his neck from earlier. There are scratch marks on his back. She's in similar shape. Her thighs ache, and the last time she checked the bathroom mirror, her cheeks and neck have beard burn.

She sighs to herself with happiness.

Tori scoots closer and puts her leg over his hip, then trails her fingers lightly across his muscular chest, plucking at one of his nipples. "Maybe you could read *my* body language right now. What am I thinking?"

His eyes turn a darker shade of brown. "You're thinking it's time for the next inning."

LIAM WAKES up with Tori's warm body pressed into his, her head on the pillow beside him. His phone buzzes, and he reaches for it quietly.

"What time is it?" she murmurs.

"Sorry, I didn't mean to wake you."

"That's okay." She yawns and stretches. "How long have we been napping?"

"A few hours. It's almost seven in the evening."

"Wow, really? I guess that explains why I'm starving."

"Me too." He thumbs through his messages. A couple from Elena telling him her weekend with Fancy is going fine. The boys have been playing with her in the backyard. One from Matt telling him about another case they're working on together.

"Let's order from those menus we saw downstairs." She rolls toward him. "What do you say?"

"Great idea."

Tori grabs his T-shirt and shimmies into some panties while he puts his swim trunks back on.

They head downstairs. He digs out the menus and leans against the counter looking them over.

She slides up beside him and wraps her arms around his waist. "What should we get? Pizza or diner food?"

"I don't care." He sticks his nose in her hair, inhaling her scent, enjoying how easy they've become with each other. "I could eat the ass end of a bear right now."

She wrinkles her nose. "That is the weirdest expression."

They decide on pizza, but when he calls the pizza place, it turns out they're not delivering.

"I suppose we could drive over and get it," he says.

"No, I don't want to leave our cabin again. Let's try the diner and see if they'll deliver."

He calls them next, and it turns out they're happy to deliver, so he gives them both of their orders. "Is there anything else?" he asks Tori. "Should we get dessert?"

"Barbecue sauce. I love french fries with barbecue sauce."

He tells the woman on the phone and also asks her to bring two slices of apple pie after being assured they're vegan.

They go onto the back deck together, waiting for their food to arrive. Treasure Lake gleams only a stone's throw away while the sky swirls in shades of orange and blue. The whole effect reminds him of a watercolor painting. Instead of sitting in her own lounger, Tori comes over and joins him on his.

"Hmm, this is nice." He rests his chin on her head.

"It's so pretty here, isn't it?" She gazes out at the view. "I wish we didn't have to go back tomorrow."

"Same here."

"I'm so glad I invited you. This weekend has been a big deal for me."

He considers her words. "I'm curious. What made you invite me in the first place? When I didn't hear back from you, I figured you didn't want to see me."

She looks up at him, and her smile turns naughty. "I guess I had a tingly feeling about you."

He laughs. "A tingly feeling?"

"Yes. *Very* tingly."

He tightens his arms around her and lowers his voice. "I have some tingly feelings about you too."

When the food arrives, they put it on the table between the loungers and Tori moves to sit across from him.

"I've been thinking about something," she says, dipping a french fry into barbecue sauce. "A couple Saturdays from now, I'm having a party at my house. My brother and Blair will be there, along with some other friends. Do you want to come?"

He swallows a bite of food and reaches for his iced tea. "Of course I do. Are you sure you're ready for that?"

She nods. "I think you're right about telling everyone. Let's rip the bandage off. I'll tell them in advance that you're going to be there so it can be our first outing as a couple."

"Okay. I'll tell Elena and my parents too. They'll probably want to meet you sometime."

She puts ketchup on her veggie burger. "I wonder how your sister's going to react."

He already knows how his sister's going to react, but he doesn't care. Tori is too important for him to worry about his sister's grudge. "She'll either come around or she won't."

"Did she like Rachel?"

"For the most part, until everything blew up."

Tori goes quiet at this, then looks out at the lake.

"What is it?"

She hesitates. "Elena was really mean in high school. She spread a lot of ugly rumors about me that weren't true."

He puts his burger down with concern. "I've never heard this before."

"I wasn't sure if I should tell you. I didn't think you knew about it."

"You're damn right I didn't know. I would never have allowed something like that. What kind of rumors?"

"That I was a slut and that I'd been with a lot of guys at school—which I hadn't."

"How do you know it was Elena making up stories about you?"

She picks up a french fry but then puts it down. "Because I was friends with one of the cheerleaders, and she told me. Other people confirmed it too."

He shakes his head. "I'm sorry. I had no idea." He leans back in his chair. "How did one accident with a milkshake grow so large? It's crazy."

"I know. It snowballed."

They study each other.

"It happened a long time ago," he says. "If we can move on, then surely everyone else can too."

"I hope so."

They continue to eat. "So, why are you having a party?" he asks. "Is there a special occasion?"

Tori swallows a bite of her burger. "Yes, sort of. My friend Lindsay will be on TV for the World Series of Poker. We're going to watch it and cheer her on."

"That's interesting. So you have a friend who plays poker?"

"I do. She's flying to Las Vegas next week and is scheduled for a tournament that Saturday. We're hoping we'll catch a glimpse of her on TV."

He wipes his mouth with a paper napkin. "Sounds exciting."

"It should be."

After they finish their meal, they go for a walk by the water. Tori seems subdued.

"Everything okay?" He picks out a flat stone from the sand and throws it sidearm across the surface of the lake, skipping it a few times.

"I'm fine."

He glances over at her. She's sitting on a log, leaning back, staring out at the view.

"Come on, talk to me. Obviously you're not fine."

"I guess I'm just sad our long weekend is over. The only good thing about going home is I miss my animals."

"When's the last time you got away like this?"

She shrugs. "I don't know. I can't remember. How pathetic is that?"

"I agree that it's not good." He finds another flat stone.

"It's what I'm used to though. I never go anywhere." She looks around. "Being here has made me realize what I'm missing."

He throws the stone, and it skips three times.

Her eyes follow it with interest. "How did you do that?"

"It's easy. Come here, I'll show you." She gets up and comes over to him. When he finds a good flat rock, he hands it to her. "Now keep your hand low. Then snap your wrist when you throw it."

She tries, but her stone sinks right into the lake. "That's hard."

"Try it again. You'll get the hang of it."

She attempts it a few more times, but every one of her stones sinks. She groans. "This is ridiculous."

They search around for more rocks. He takes one and skips it four times. "I'm going to make sure we have plenty of long weekends, rubia."

She turns toward him. "You are?" Her blonde hair is pulled back and appears golden in the evening light.

"You're always taking care of everyone else, except no one's taking care of you." He reaches for her hand. "But I'm going to."

Her eyes widen. "Can I bring my dogs on these long weekends?"

He grins. "Whatever you want." Then he hands her another stone. "Put a good spin on it this time. That's the trick."

"Okay." She sighs. "I'll give it another try."

He watches as Tori positions herself closer to the water and concentrates. She keeps it low and throws the rock with a good wrist flick. It bounces twice before sinking.

"I did it!" She turns to him. "Did you see that?"

"Yeah, I did. You totally got it."

She walks back over to him, a spring in her step that makes his chest ache with happiness. He wants to give her everything. The whole world. And when she hugs him, that electric feeling is back.

She puts her face up to his, and he kisses her smile, running his fingers along her hairline. "I want you to know, that this weekend has been a big deal for me too."

"I MISSED YOU, MY BABIES!" Tori reaches for her dogs when she gets home. Blair is there, and she gives her a quick hug too. "Thank you so much for taking care of them."

"Nathan and I were happy to watch them. How was your weekend getaway?"

"Wonderful." The dogs are all swarming around her, tails wagging. She laughs as she tries to hug three squirming, excited dogs at the same time.

After a good ten minutes of hugs, kisses, and praising them, Tori gets up from the floor.

Blair comes out from the bedroom with an overnight bag.

"Did you guys sleep here?" Tori asks, looking at the bag.

"Yeah, we stayed the weekend. It was kind of fun being back here together." She laughs. "Sort of like old times."

Tori remembers all the trials and tribulations Blair and her brother went through when they were dating. She's so glad it worked out and Blair became her sister-in-law. "Listen, there's something I need to talk to you about."

"Oh, that reminds me. I have to take the Honda today. You can still borrow it, but Nathan wants to give it an oil change."

"Sure." Tori nods.

Blair studies her phone. "Sorry, I have a meeting with a bride in a little while. I don't usually do them on my day off, but this woman begged and pleaded."

"Oh, if you have to go, that's fine. We can talk later."

"Are you sure?" Blair's eyes roam over her. She tilts her head. "You look really pretty. It's like you're glowing from the inside."

"Thanks." Tori can't help her grin.

"Getting away agreed with you. You should do it more often."

She takes a deep breath. "Hopefully I will."

"Nathan and I were talking about how we could help, like give you some of our travel points. There's something else too." Blair quiets for a second but then seems to reconsider. "But let's meet up soon, okay?"

They hug goodbye, and Tori thanks her again for everything. When the door closes behind her, she sighs with relief.

Obviously, she has to tell Blair and her brother about Liam, and she *will*, but she's glad it wasn't right now. She's still reveling in her happiness.

Her dogs stay close to her as she unpacks her stuff, putting her new cozy sweater away in a drawer. "I missed you guys," she says, petting them and telling them all about her weekend while she putters around the house. "Though I can't tell you everything. Some things are too personal even for dog ears."

She starts a load of laundry and tries not to check her phone.

"We said we'd cool it a little," she explains to them. "We discussed it on the way home. I mean, we were together every single second for three days, so I figured it was best to give ourselves some breathing room."

Eddie, her golden retriever, studies her with his dark eyes as he sits outside the door of the laundry room. Tommy Lee, her Chihuahua, tilts his head. Duff, her pug mix, watches with his tongue lolling.

"What?" She looks at the three of them. "You don't agree?"

Tommy Lee's ears quiver. He's a little high-strung, and the ear quiver usually means he's excited, probably because she's home.

"You think I should call him? Am I being dumb?"

She goes out in the backyard and plays with them for a while. Her cats, Lita and Joan, finally emerge and come over when she takes a break on the back patio. She made herself a glass of iced tea and is sipping it as she looks through her schedule for the coming week.

"So I guess you two aren't mad at me anymore, huh?" She pets them. "I was only gone a few days."

Joan jumps up on her lap while Lita lays her body across the table, covering most of Tori's planner pages.

Surprisingly, her mom hasn't called yet, though Tori knows she needs to call her soon. She figured there'd be a lot of messages, but maybe Wayne took care of things.

By the time she gets ready to go to sleep, she still can't stop thinking about Liam. Lying in bed, surrounded by her dogs, she picks up her phone from the nightstand.

Her pulse jumps when she sees there's a text from him.

I know we're supposed to take a breather, but I can't stop thinking about you. I miss you.

There's a big smile on her face as she reads the message four times.

"Oh, this *is* dumb," she mutters.

Her dogs all look up at the sound of her voice.

Instead of texting him back, she calls Liam's number. He answers on the first ring.

"Hey, rubia."

She smiles, hearing her nickname. "I just saw your text."

"I couldn't help myself. I miss you already."

"Me too."

"So how was everything when you got home today?"

Her dogs are still watching her. "It was great to see everyone. How is Miss Fancy Pants?"

"She's fine. Sitting right here in bed with me."

"I'm sure she missed you."

"I told Elena about us, that I went away with you for the weekend."

"You did?" Tori sits up. "What did she say?"

He snorts. "Nothing I want to repeat."

"That sucks. I'm sorry."

She hears him take a deep breath. "Don't worry about it. I knew she'd overreact."

"I haven't told anyone yet, but I will soon."

"Okay."

They both grow silent.

"I've gotten so used to sleeping with you next to me," he says. "It's going to be tough tonight."

"I know." She considers her options. "I'd invite you over, but my dogs would never tolerate that. Miss Fancy Pants would probably feel threatened too since she hasn't seen you for a few days and wants you to herself."

He chuckles. "I never thought my life would be run by dogs."

"Do you want to meet tomorrow after work?"

"Yes." His voice softens. "I can't wait."

The next morning, Tori takes an Uber to her job at the animal hospital. She knows she needs to get a new van soon and texts her cousin Brody to see how the search is going.

When she gets to work, Peyton is wearing a huge grin.

"I want to hear *all* about your weekend." They're both in the back office. "Lamont said you and that special agent had satisfied smiles on your faces when you came by to pick up your car yesterday."

Tori laughs at the description. Apparently Peyton's husband is very observant. "What can I say? It was the best weekend ever."

"Oooh!" She claps her hands. "I *knew* it."

"Life changing even."

Her friend grins. "So you and the G-man are a thing now, huh? I can't wait to tell Tara. She's going to be thrilled."

"You guys are so nice. In fact, I got her a thank-you card and a small gift. Do you think you could give it to her for me?" She knows Tara lives up near Bellingham, but Peyton sees her regularly.

"Of course I will." She sighs. "I'm so happy for you. My instincts were right about that man from the first moment I saw him."

Later that day, Tori's with Dr. Adrian in the lunchroom. She wonders if she should feel bad she's gotten over him so quickly. It was the idea of him that attracted her more than anything else.

"That's great," he says after she tells him about her long weekend. "Truth Harbor is a beautiful area."

"It really is. I hope everything is going well with you too."

He stirs his coconut yogurt. "Actually, things are going very well." He pauses and grins at her. "René and I have been talking."

Tori's brows go up. "You're kidding. That's a good thing, right?"

He nods. "We're having dinner on Friday. He says he misses me."

"Well, he should. You're a catch. And I should know!"

Dr. Adrian laughs. "Thanks, I appreciate that."

That evening she meets Liam and Miss Fancy Pants at a dog park near her house. Her boys are with her. She decided it would be best to introduce them in neutral territory for now.

"I've never seen so much butt sniffing in my entire life," Liam says, watching the dogs. "Is this normal?"

Tori laughs at the disturbed expression on his face. "Very normal. Dogs have a natural hierarchy. All the butt sniffing is how they get acquainted with each other."

Happily, the dogs seem to get along fine. She worried a little about Tommy Lee, since despite his small size, he's quite an alpha. There are a few growls, but for the most part he seems okay. In fact, Miss Fancy Pants seems to be the new leader. Tori's not surprised, since she's very assertive.

After a short while, the dogs are all running around playing. She and Liam have been holding hands and sneaking kisses.

"It was torture without you last night," he whispers, squeezing her hand. "How much longer will I be tortured?"

She strokes his clean-shaven face. "I miss the beard. Though I like you like this too."

"Don't worry, I'm sure I'll be growing another one for undercover work soon."

"Tonight is probably too soon for everyone, but do you and Miss Fancy Pants want to come over tomorrow?"

He agrees, and they stay at the park a while longer. Later that night, he calls her while she's in bed. They talk so long she has to plug her phone into its charger. Her dogs are all asleep and snoring. Joan and Lita are curled up near her pillow.

When he comes over with Miss Fancy Pants the next evening, it all goes fairly smoothly, though Liam is amazed when he comes to bed and discovers how crowded it is.

"You let all these dogs sleep with you every night?"

"They have their doggie beds, but I let them sleep here too."

He laughs. "I didn't realize I would have so much competition for your affections."

Even though the plan was to give them each breathing space after their passionate weekend, that plan has gone out the window. It's like they can't resist each other. During the day they're texting constantly, and during the night they're in each other's arms—though at Liam's insistence, her boys and Miss Fancy Pants have been relegated to their dog beds.

They spend all their free time together. He's over almost every night. They watch movies or hang out and talk. They take their dogs to the park. She's even been letting him play country music in her house. And when they have sex, he never seems the least bit bothered about her alone time in the bathroom.

Tori feels like she's walking on a cloud. Like she's finally having the kind of relationship she's been yearning for.

"I called my parents yesterday," he says. They're lounging on the couch having breakfast. It's been over a week since their cabin trip. "They've invited us to come visit when we have a chance."

"Really?" She pours almond milk over her cereal, then puts the carton back on the coffee table. "Do they remember who I am?"

"Yeah, they do. And they're fine. They both understand it was a long time ago."

She stirs her cereal, then stretches her legs out, resting them on his. "Road and Blair are coming over today to talk about something, and I'm going to tell them about us."

"Good. I'm glad to hear that."

"I'll finally see my mom tonight too. I didn't want to tell her anything over the phone." She already knows her mother is going to have a conniption. It's bad enough she hasn't seen her since she got back from her trip.

"Do you want me to come with you? I can be very charming when I need to be."

"That's okay."

He looks around her living room. "I should go home and pick up some more clean clothes, but I was thinking, what do you say we spend the night at my house for a change? You can bring your dogs."

She takes a bite of cereal. "I'd rather not."

"Do you think your dogs would mind that much?"

"I'm sure they'd be fine. It's not that."

He studies her. "Is it because of that whole thing with Rachel? Trust me, she's not coming back. And I lived there long before I met her."

"No, it's not that either. It has nothing to do with Rachel."

"Then what?"

"I don't like your neighborhood."

His brows go up. "You don't?"

"It's spooky."

"Spooky?" He laughs out loud. "My neighborhood isn't spooky."

She nods. "It is."

"What are you talking about?" He puts his mug down. "I live in a great neighborhood. Do you know how much the houses there cost?"

"Who cares? It's too quiet. And all the houses look the same."

"Quiet is good. Sameness is good too."

"No, it's not. Have you ever seen a single neighbor? It's like a ghost town. Nobody wants to be there." She motions at him. "Even *you're* not there."

"That's because I'm here with you. My neighbors are all at work. They're professionals."

"Do you ever talk to any of them? How come there are no kids playing outside or old people? Where is everybody?"

He stares at her.

"It's unnatural." She eats a spoonful of cereal. "Like I said, spooky."

"All right, fine." He rolls his eyes and seems bemused. "You won't have to go to my spooky neighborhood."

CHAPTER TWENTY-FOUR

"WHERE DID YOU GO?" Road asks, his arms crossed. "Because it sure as hell wasn't Truth Harbor."

"What do you mean?" Tori's eyes travel back and forth between her brother and Blair, who both study her with concern.

The three of them are sitting on her back deck after she poured them each a glass of iced tea with blackberries and sage. She's discovered she could add flavors from her herb garden to iced tea the same way she does lemonade.

"Please, just tell us the truth." Blair leans forward. "We're worried, that's all. It isn't like you to lie. Is everything okay?"

"I'm not lying," she says, mystified. "I *did* go to Truth Harbor."

Road watches her. "How did you get there? There's no way you drove the Honda."

Tori opens her mouth but then closes it. She planned to tell them about Liam today, but she didn't imagine it happening like this.

"I changed the oil in that car, and the mileage had barely moved since the weekend," he says. "You think I don't keep track of that?"

Tori's brows go up with surprise. It had never occurred to her that he'd notice the car's mileage.

They're both studying her again. Her brother's green eyes flicker with anger. He doesn't like being lied to. Of course, who does?

She takes a deep breath. "I did go to Truth Harbor, except I didn't drive there in the Honda."

"How did you get there?" Blair asks.

Tori licks her lips. "I went with Liam in his truck."

There. Whew. The cat's out of the bag.

Blair is staring at her like she's a crazy person while Road appears mostly confused.

"You spent the weekend with *that* guy?" Blair gawks. "Are you kidding me?"

"No, I'm not. In fact, we're dating now."

Blair shakes her head. "Oh, Tori. You're doing it again. Can't you see? Falling for the wrong person."

"Jesus," her brother says. "I wish you'd told us the truth. Couldn't figure out what the hell was going on."

"He's really great. I want you two to give him a chance."

"Why lie, then?" Blair asks. "If he's so great."

Her brother's arms are still crossed. "People usually lie about things they're ashamed of or want to hide."

"Look at you two." Tori leans back in her chair. "It's because I knew I'd get a reaction like this. That's why I didn't tell you."

"People don't change that much," Blair says. "I know it was a long time ago, but I remember how he treated you in high school."

Tori shakes her head. "It was an accident. That whole thing with the milkshake. He poured it on me accidentally."

Blair rolls her eyes. "Come on, everybody *saw* him do it. I saw it too."

"No, everybody misinterpreted what they saw, including you."

Blair and Road both eye her with skepticism.

"It's the truth," Tori says. "I've gotten to know him, and there's no way he did that on purpose."

"Listen to you." Blair lets out a humorless laugh. "You're deluded."

Her brother shakes his head. "We know you like to see the best in people, but this guy is bad news."

"No, he's not." She huffs in frustration. "Look, he'll be here at my party on Saturday, so please be nice. I want you to give him a chance. Do you hear me?"

The two of them glance at each other.

"We'll try," Blair says. "That's all I can promise."

Tori picks up her iced tea and takes a sip. She's tempted to continue arguing and making a case for Liam but realizes it's pointless. They'll have to get to know him the same way she did.

"There's something else we wanted to talk to you about." Road leans forward. Tori hoped they might tell her they're pregnant today, but judging by the grim expression on his face, that's not it. "What the hell is going on with Mom?"

"What do you mean?"

"She called me five times while you were gone. And then some neighbor of hers named Donna called me threatening to bring in the cops."

Tori's brows go up. She has no clue how Donna got Road's number.

"We went over there," Blair says. "And your mom and that Wayne guy were in the front yard yelling at each other."

"Mom was shit-faced." Her brother shakes his head. "Hell, she sounded drunk off her ass every time I talked to her."

Tori nods. "It's been a problem lately."

"Lately?" her brother asks. "And how long has that asshole Wayne been in the picture?"

"A few months."

He shakes his head. "Jesus, I wish you'd let me know this was happening. I had no idea she'd gotten so bad."

"I didn't want to bother you guys or bring you down."

"You're not bothering us," Blair says. "We want to help."

Tori sighs. "I don't know what's going on. Wayne seems to bring out the worst in her." She wonders if she should tell them her worries about him being a thief and a smuggler, but she has no evidence and doesn't want to get them worrying too.

"Maybe I need to talk to this Wayne guy some more," Road says. "Tried when we were there, but the dude was hammered."

"I've already tried. He keeps saying everything's fine and that he's taking care of her."

Road snorts. "Yeah, right."

"We were amazed at all the new stuff," Blair says. "Do you know where it came from?"

Tori explains how Wayne said he got it on sale somewhere, and they both appear skeptical.

They talk for a little longer, but Tori has to go pet sit a German shepherd for one of her Happy Pet Nanny clients. Thankfully, Blair and Road leave her the Honda.

As she's playing catch with King, the German shepherd, she gets a call from her cousin Brody to tell her he may have found her a new minivan.

"It's a used Town & Country in great condition. About six-years-old. I'll check it out thoroughly, but the price seems reasonable." He tells her how much the owner wants.

"Oh, really? That does sound reasonable."

"I could probably talk him down a little more even. I'll text you a photo, and you can tell me what you think."

"You know I trust your judgment. Are you coming over on Saturday?"

"Yeah... I think so." There's a subdued note in his voice.

"Is everything okay?"

"I might bring someone. Is that all right?"

"Of course it's fine."

They hang up, and she's glad to hear Brody's dating again. He and his longtime girlfriend Kiera split up a while ago, and he's been kind of down ever since.

When the photo arrives, Tori studies it. The minivan is white and a different style than Mable. A little more modern, but classy too.

She texts him back. *I love it!*

Okay, good. I'll let the guy know.

She has a couple more pet sitting appointments that afternoon and then heads straight over to her mom's house.

Wayne's yellow Charger is parked in the driveway, and for once Tori is glad to see it. She wants to question him using some of the interrogation tricks Liam told her about.

"Baby girl!" her mom exclaims. She gets up from the sofa and totters over in her sky-high heels to give Tori a hug. "It's so good to see you."

Wayne gets up. "Did you have yourself a nice trip?" he asks. She's worried he's going to try and hug her too, but thankfully he's just going into the kitchen.

"It was great," Tori says.

"Are you hungry?" her mom asks. "We ordered pizza. It should be here soon."

"I'm okay."

"How about a drink?" Wayne calls out to her. "I made a pitcher of margaritas."

"No, thanks. I'll just have one of my flavored waters."

Eventually he comes out with a bottle of water for her and the three of them have a seat in the living room. Tori glances around nervously, hoping she doesn't find more new stuff, but doesn't see anything.

"I saw Road and Blair earlier today," she tells them.

"Is that right?" Her mom takes the margarita glass from Wayne's hand. "How are they doing?"

"They said they came over during the weekend when I was gone. You don't remember?"

"I remember." Her mom smacks her lips and puts her drink on the end table. "That's really good," she tells Wayne, who grins with crooked teeth.

Tori tries to relax and pretends to glance around the room admiringly. "All this new stuff looks amazing. How did you find such a great deal on everything, Wayne?"

"Oh, you know." He scratches the back of his head. "It was just one of those things. A real good sale."

She studies the head scratching. *Is that a sign he's lying?*

He reaches for his cigarettes and lights one. "Let's hear about your special weekend. Where did you go again?"

"Truth Harbor."

"Pretty area up there. You go alone?"

Tori takes a sip from her bottle. "I went with a friend." Her eyes go to her mom, who's sipping her margarita.

He nods. "Friends are good to have."

Tori leans forward. "You know, I've been looking for a new TV. Do you think I could get the name of the place where you guys found yours?"

Her mom doesn't say anything. Instead, her eyes go to the television, where the evening news is on.

"What kind of TV are you looking for?" Wayne asks.

"Something like the one you got my mom." Tori stops talking as a terrible thought enters her mind. What if he steals a television for *her*? "I was thinking I'd like to shop around first though," she says quickly. "You know, see what's out there."

"Sure."

"So what's the name of the place?"

Wayne tells her the name of some outlet store in south Seattle.

"Thanks, I'll have a look."

He blows out a stream of smoke and rubs his jaw. "You may not get as lucky as we did. They were having quite a fire sale. One of those 'everything must go' type deals."

Tori thinks back and is certain this is the same way he described it last time she was here. *Does that mean something? Is it a lie?*

"Doubt it's still happening."

Her mom has grown quiet and is studying her. "What friend did you go away with? You've never mentioned any friend to me."

Tori has been debating how to handle this and decides the best thing is to tell it like it is. "I went with Liam."

"Liam?" Her mom blinks at her.

Wayne sits up straight and appears to have gone on high alert. Tori watches him and can tell he remembers exactly who Liam is.

"You guys both met him that one time."

"Holy shit!" Her mom's eyes go wide. "Are you talking about that fed you brought here?"

"Yes, he's a federal agent."

"Baby girl," she wails. "What are you doing? This isn't right!" Her mom turns to Wayne. "Talk some sense into her!"

Tori takes a drink of her strawberry-flavored water. She knew her mom would freak out, and she also knew there was nothing to be done about it.

"I'm sure your daughter has a mind of her own," Wayne says carefully as he watches Tori. There's something almost menacing in his gaze. "It's her decision the type of person she chooses to get friendly with."

"Are you nuts?" Her mom is practically shouting. "I'm not going through this a second time. Are you hearing me? I've been through enough."

"What are you talking about?" Tori asks bewildered.

"Don't you dare bring him here," her mom says. "I never want to see the law in my house ever again!"

She tries to ask more questions, but it's obvious her mom is drunk and ranting.

Eventually Tori leaves, though she's none the wiser about Wayne, who seems to have dropped his harmless loser act and is making her nervous. She still can't tell for sure if he's involved with any criminal activity.

When she gets home, the first thing she does after hugging her animals and giving everyone dinner is call Liam.

"How did it go?" he asks.

She loves the sound of his voice. Right away she relaxes. "Please come over. Can you come over tonight?"

"Sure. Let me get Fancy and we'll be right there. Are you okay?"

"No, it's been a rotten day."

By the time Liam arrives, she's changed into a sundress and is warming up leftover Indian food she made yesterday.

They have dinner on the couch together while she pours out the details of everything that happened today.

He nods. "So Road figured out you didn't drive the Honda because of the mileage."

"You almost sound approving." She eats the last of her garlic naan and puts her empty plate on the table.

"I guess I am. It's the kind of detail I'd normally have caught myself."

She rolls her eyes. "I can't believe my brother keeps track of the mileage on his cars. Who does that?"

He shrugs. "I do."

"Really?"

"I usually know the mileage for both my truck and my bureau car."

She takes a sip of water and shakes her head. "Guys are weird." Miss Fancy Pants comes over to join them, and Tori pets her. "If you're the same way, then why didn't you think of the mileage thing?"

He smirks and puts his plate next to hers. "Because I was too distracted by a pretty girl."

She grins. "So I distract you, huh?"

He reaches over to join her in petting the dog. "Actually, I was referring to Fancy here."

"Ha ha." She kicks his ankle with her bare foot, and he laughs.

The two of them study each other, smiling. Tori's noticed they smile a lot when they're together.

"So how did it go with your mom and Wayne?" he asks, leaning back.

She shakes her head. "About as bad as you'd expect. My mom ranted and raved. Demanded I stop seeing you. At one point, she even called me Victoria."

His brows draw together with interest. "Is that your name?"

"Yes, but nobody uses it."

"I didn't know that."

Tori thinks back to the episode at her mom's house. "She was saying all this weird stuff. It didn't make any sense."

"What do you mean?"

"She was going on about how she's been through enough, how she never wants the law in her house again."

"Really? I wasn't at her house very long."

Tori pets her dogs, who all came over when they noticed the attention Miss Fancy Pants was getting. "That's what's weird. I don't think she was talking about you."

"Has Donna ever called the police? Maybe she's talking about that."

"Maybe."

She wishes she could tell him how she tried to question Wayne and about all her suspicions. It would be a relief to tell him. She's too worried about what will happen though.

"Oh, I almost forgot. I want to show you something." She gets up and goes into the kitchen. When she comes back, her cat Lita is draped across Liam's lap. "One good thing did happen today."

"What's that?"

She scrolls through the texts on her phone and brings up the one from Brody. "Meet Samantha," she says with a grin, handing it to him.

He stares down. "Who?"

She sits beside him, and they both look at the screen. "That's my new minivan. Brody found her for me. What do you think? Isn't she gorgeous?"

"I'm surprised you've already named it."

"It came to me as soon as I saw her. She looks just like a Samantha, doesn't she?"

He hands the phone back. "I can't believe I'm saying this, but she does."

They talk some more about the minivan, and he agrees it sounds like a good price. Eventually they push the cat off and relax on the couch together. Liam lies on his back while she drapes herself over him like Lita did a few moments ago.

"Thanks for coming over tonight."

"Are you feeling better now?"

She nods. "Everything's better when you're here."

"I'm glad you think so."

"I do." He strokes her hair, plays with it, and she closes her eyes. "That feels nice."

They lie together for a while, just relaxing.

The steady beat of his heart soothes her. If only they could stay like this forever.

He takes a deep breath and exhales. "Tangerines."

"What's that?"

"You always smell like tangerines."

She lifts her head to look at him. "No, I don't."

"Sure you do. It's your perfume or something."

"It's grapefruit."

"Really?"

She laughs. "Yes."

"Well." He shrugs. "It smells like tangerines to me."

"Do you like it?"

"Yeah, definitely." His eyes drop to her mouth. "It turns me on."

"So tangerines turn you on?"

"Apparently, though I think it has more to do with the woman than the scent."

She leans in and kisses him, then bites his lower lip. He rumbles with approval as he slides his hands down to her ass, pulling her in tight. Small wildfires are already starting in her. They continue kissing, and it isn't long before he has her flipped under him on the couch, his solid weight pressing into her.

She strokes his muscular back, then up to his shoulders.

"Why do I feel like I'm being watched?" he says in a dry voice.

"What?" She turns her head, and all the dogs are sitting right there. She lets out a laugh.

He stands and offers her his hand, and the two of them make their way into her bedroom, where he shuts the door.

Her eyes go to her nightstand, to where his FBI badge, gun, and holster are resting. Whoever thought this would happen? That she'd be here with Liam, that he'd be the one making her feel like this?

Like anything is possible.

"I want to try something tonight," she says.

"What's that?" he murmurs, pulling her in close. He's sitting on the edge of the bed while she stands in front of him. He slides his hands up her legs under her sundress. "I like this dress. I'm going to like the ease of removing it the most."

She runs her hands through his short dark hair. "I want to try to come with you."

He looks up at her, his gaze thoughtful.

"Maybe I can do it or maybe not, but I want to try."

He nods. "Let's try, then."

She closes her eyes as he continues to caress her. Everything he does always feels so good. She's not sure if she's ever felt so easily turned on.

After a little while, he stands and unzips her dress down the back. It falls straight to the floor.

"Now that's what I'm talking about," he says.

She smiles as he brings his warm body in close behind her, his chest hard against her. Fingers slide down her arms, creating sparks on her skin.

He pushes her hair aside, her breath trembling when he kisses her softly on the back of her neck.

"I can't believe how much I want you," he murmurs. "It's never been like this with anyone."

"Me either," she whispers.

Warm hands slide to her breasts, fondling them, his nails lightly grazing her nipples. Sucking in her breath, she turns around to face him. She wants to taste him, touch him, devour him whole.

That wildfire burns all through her.

He moans into her mouth, and then they're consuming each other. It's like a thirst that can't be quenched.

She's not even sure how they wind up on the bed, but when he slips her panties off and moves his face between her thighs, she knows this is it. It's finally going to happen for her. And she's ready—oh so ready.

She lies back and gets comfortable.

It goes on for a long time, Liam so patient, so willing in his passion.

Tori squeezes her eyes shut.

Time seems suspended. She's so close. Hovering. Dancing around that star. She wants it to burn her, wants it so bad.

"I can't," she finally moans, staring up at the ceiling with frustration. "It's not going to happen."

He doesn't stop, so she pushes him away.

His eyes are dark, nearly black. His mouth is open. "Are you sure? I'll keep going."

"Yes, I'm sure."

He nods, and she can see the state he's in. Hot with need. When he moves over her, there's no preamble. He takes her with a groan. It's intense. She wants it though, wants his desire. His excitement. If she can't have one, she'll take the other.

Afterward, she cries. She doesn't mean to, but she can't stop her tears.

Liam hugs her as they lie side by side, their faces close.

"This is a dumb thing to cry about," she whispers. "When there's so much suffering in the world, and I'm so lucky."

"It's not dumb, rubia."

"But I have so much good in my life. This should be nothing."

He kisses her cheeks, softly brushing her tears away. "Just give it time. It'll all work out."

"I don't know what's wrong with me."

"There's nothing wrong with you. You're perfect."

She wants to believe him. Wishes she could.

"Do you want to go in the bathroom?" he asks softly.

"No, forget it."

He strokes her hair. "I don't want you to feel bad about yourself. I like you just the way you are."

"You're so patient. So accepting."

"I'd do anything for you." He kisses her gently. "You must know that by now."

CHAPTER TWENTY-FIVE

> **Tori's Playlist: Daily Song**
> *"Bad Reputation"*
> by Joan Jett
>
> ♥
>
> **Liam's Playlist: Daily Song**
> *"Kick It in the Sticks"*
> by Brantley Gilbert

"OH, MY FUCKING *GOD!*"

The woman standing in front of Liam has straight black hair, pale skin, and brilliant blue eyes. She looks like Snow White, or maybe the evil queen. He hasn't decided which.

Tori introduces her as Fiona. She's the first person to arrive for the party today.

"So you're the new boyfriend!" Fiona eyes him with excitement. "The one everybody hates?"

His brows go up.

"Where did you hear that?" Tori accepts the bottle of wine she brought. "Not from my brother, I hope."

"Who else?" Fiona smirks. "As soon as I mentioned this party, it was obvious something was wrong. Like he could keep a secret from *me*." She laughs with satisfaction. "He cracked open just like a walnut."

Tori seems worried. "Did he really say that?"

"Don't worry about it." Fiona's tone becomes sympathetic. "He thinks he's being the protective older brother. He'll calm down."

"I hope so."

Fiona turns her blue high beams on him again. "Just so you know, *I* don't hate you. At least not *yet*."

He's not sure how to respond. Fiona has a beautiful appearance, but there's something wrong with her personality.

"I know I'm early," she says, turning back to Tori. "But I thought I'd come and help."

"Where's Sachi? She's coming too, I hope."

Fiona nods. "My better half. She'll be here later. Also, I haven't told you the latest with Lindsay." She explains how their friend Lindsay's been getting a lot of attention from the media at the World Series of Poker. "Apparently *someone* told them her father used to be a famous poker player, and now the press is swarming around her. Not to mention she's winning all her tournaments. Isn't it wonderful?"

"That is great," Tori says. "I'm glad she's winning. I hope we'll catch her on TV today."

The dogs come over as the three of them stand in the kitchen. They all seem to know Fiona, and after sniffing her, and some awkward petting on Fiona's part, they go back to their usual routine.

"Most everything is ready," Tori tells her sweetly. "There really isn't much else to do. Why don't you and Liam sit out back and get better acquainted?"

Liam nearly protests. He doesn't want to get better acquainted with this strange woman.

"I'd *love* to!" Fiona claps her hands.

As a result, he's stuck outside with her alone.

He hasn't been looking forward to dealing with Tori's family today—especially Blair and Road—but after five minutes of Fiona's unblinking stare, he decides Road's threats are going be a welcome relief.

"So what do you do?" He takes a sip from his iced tea, trying to be polite. Tori's added blackberries and sage to the tea, and he has to admit it's delicious.

"I'm a media and marketing specialist."

He tries to think of something else to say, then notices she's still staring at him intensely. "Is there something wrong?"

"You're handsome," she declares. "Nobody told me how *handsome* you are."

"Um... thanks."

He looks out at the yard, wondering where all the dogs have gone, wishing they'd come to his rescue. They're probably in the kitchen with Tori.

There's a gasp from Fiona, and when he turns back to her, she's studying him with an even keener interest.

"What?"

"Your profile! My *God*. You have an incredible profile!"

Before he knows what's happening, she's whipped her phone out and is taking pictures of him.

His mouth falls open. "What the hell are you doing?" He nearly grabs the phone from her hands. "You can't take pictures of me!"

In that moment, Tori slides the screen door open and comes onto the back patio. "Everything okay out here?" she asks in a helpful voice. "Would anyone like more to drink?"

Meanwhile, Fiona is still snapping away. "Yes, that's perfect! Hold that expression!"

His brows slam together as he glowers. "Give me that phone," he demands with his hand out. "This instant."

"Could you grow your hair out longer in back?" Fiona asks excitedly. "And lose ten pounds? You're a little bulky." She reconsiders, studying his shoulders. "Maybe just five."

Liam turns to Tori incredulous. "Who the hell *is* this woman?"

"What are you doing?" Tori asks her with curiosity.

Fiona tells them about one of her clients, a photographer who's putting together a book of photos featuring everyday life in America. "He'd be perfect for the cover!"

"Are you nuts? I'm a federal agent."

"I know!" she shrieks. "I love it! It's so real life. You're just like a real person."

"I *am* a real person."

"Liam can't have a picture of himself on a book," Tori explains to her patiently. "He works undercover."

"That's right. A picture of me on some book is the last thing I need."

"Don't be silly," Fiona says. "No one will recognize you. It's just your profile."

"You think people won't recognize my profile?"

She rolls her eyes. "Trust me, people are idiots."

AFTER A LOT of fuss and more eye rolling from Fiona, Liam finally gets her to delete all the photos of him off her phone. He's still amazed she took them without his permission in the first place.

As more people arrive, he's introduced to a lot of Tori's family and friends. The family is mostly cousins as far as he can tell. Plenty of tattoos and long hair. A few of them arrive on motorcycles. Tori invited her mom and Wayne, though they both declined to come.

He pastes a polite smile on his face. No one seems to know or remember their unpleasant history from high school, which is something of a relief. He's drinking iced tea and considers switching to beer, then figures it's best to keep a clear head. The television is on in the living room, showing live coverage of the World Series of Poker.

"It's too bad you won't be able to meet Natalie and Anthony," Tori says, coming up to where he's watching the TV screen. "Natalie is Lindsay's sister. They flew to Las Vegas a few days ago to cheer her on in person."

He glances around the room at the new faces he's already met. "This is plenty for now."

She slips her arm around his. "How are you doing? Are you overwhelmed?"

He gives her a wry grin. "Don't worry about me. I'm good."

"Okay." She puts her hand up and strokes his jaw. "Kiss me."

He does and is instantly surrounded by sunshine. Tori warms him like a summer day. They smile at each other. And in that moment he knows he'd meet a thousand of her cousins, deal with a million of her biker relatives, as long as he gets to be with her.

"Sorry we're late!"

They both look up. Blair, with her auburn hair and hazel eyes, rushes up to them, holding a large cake platter filled with cupcakes. She glances at him but mostly focuses on Tori.

Unfortunately, Road comes up right behind her, carrying another platter of pastries.

"Thank you so much for bringing those," Tori says, obviously thrilled. "Let's put them in the kitchen."

"I can take that from you," he says to Blair, trying to be helpful.

"That's okay." She sniffs in a haughty way. "I've got it."

Road walks past him, and the two of them give each other a level stare.

Once he's alone again, he blows his breath out.

This is going to be a long party.

For the next couple hours, he mingles, drinking endless glasses of iced tea as he makes small talk. A lot of eyebrows go up when people find out he's with the FBI. Some are curious and ask questions, though others prefer to keep their distance.

Happily, Peyton and her husband arrive, and he enjoys talking to them.

"Brody's here," Tori announces to everyone excitedly. "He drove my new minivan, Samantha!"

They all go out to inspect the vehicle. It's white and shiny, and by all appearance seems to be a step up from the previous one.

Liam's introduced to a middle-aged blonde woman named Lisa, who's Brody's mom.

"Nice to meet you," he says, shaking her hand.

She smiles and eyes him with interest. "You too." Lisa looks like a toned-down version of Tori's mother, and he figures the women must be sisters. She gives Tori a quick hug. "Congratulations on your new van, honey."

"Thanks, Aunt Lisa."

Tori walks around the outside of it as everyone watches. People are commenting on how it's a good-looking vehicle.

"What do you think?" Brody asks her.

"Just perfect." She hugs her cousin. "I love her. She's beautiful."

"Glad you approve." He grins and hands her the keys. "I had the guys at the shop detail her for you, so she's looking real sharp."

"Thank you."

A few people come over and speak to Tori. After a short while, most of them head back into the house.

"Is my sister here?" Lisa asks her.

"No, she and Wayne didn't want to come."

Lisa rolls her eyes. "It figures." She glances at him. "Don't you two worry about her. Just enjoy each other."

Aunt Lisa leaves to join everyone inside the house. Liam stays with Tori to watch as Brody shows her how everything works with her new van.

Unfortunately, Blair and Road also stay. The air between the three of them is thick with tension.

After her cousin's done going over the specifics with her, she comes over to stand beside Liam. Brody describes to all of them how the transaction happened and how much he was able to bring the seller down from his initial asking price.

Liam senses something's off with Tori. She's grown quiet, fingering the blue streak in her hair. He reaches for her hand. "You okay?" he whispers.

She nods, though her gaze is conflicted. "I'm sad about Mable. Is it wrong for me to feel like that when I have Samantha now?"

He squeezes her fingers. He considers pointing out to her that these are just cars. Cars don't have feelings. But he already knows that's not how she sees it. Her attachment and loyalty seem to extend beyond most people's. She's unique. And it's her uniqueness that he's grown to love so much. In some ways there's a childlike quality to Tori, and he suspects it's something she uses as counterpoint to the heaviness she grew up with. She needs that lightness in her life. He needs it too. He's never seen magic in the world like she does, but Tori keeps showing him it exists.

"It's not wrong to miss what you had," he says. "But I think Samantha seems great."

She smiles. "She does, doesn't she?"

They tune back into the conversation. He notices Blair's eyes flicker down to the way he and Tori are holding hands. Road's watching them too, though glaring would be a better description.

Liam ignores them both.

"I better go check on the party inside," Tori tells everyone. "Make sure people have what they need."

"I'll join you," Blair says.

Unfortunately, this leaves him alone with Brody and Road.

An AC/DC song drifts out from the house. He's tempted to go back inside too but stays. He figures it's time to have a conversation with Road, clear the air. If it has to happen with his cousin here, then so be it.

"Do I know you?" Brody asks, stroking his black goatee, studying him. "You look familiar."

"I don't think we've met." He takes Brody's measure. He's big like Road, though he appears to be a few years younger. They don't look much like cousins. Where Road is blond like Tori, Brody has dark hair and eyes.

"Really? What's your name again?"

"Liam."

He continues assessing him like he's trying to figure something out. "And your last name?"

"Castillo."

Meanwhile, Road's hostility hasn't changed. "You better be careful with my sister, and I'm not fucking kidding."

"Tori means the world to me." Liam looks him directly in the eyes. "I'd *never* hurt her."

"Better pray you don't."

"Holy shit." Brody's face lights up.

"Don't know what you think you're doing here," Road goes on. "But if I hear one bad word from her, there'll be hell to pay."

"Dude." Brody turns to his cousin with confusion. "What the fuck is wrong with you? You know who this is, don't you?"

"'Course I know who this is." Road's expression turns menacing. "I know *exactly* who this is."

"He played for San Diego ten years ago. He was their catcher."

Liam's eyes widen and flash to Brody. This is the last thing he expected.

Road is still glaring at him, but glances sideways at his cousin. "What?"

"Damn," Brody says to Liam with a grin. "You were one hell of a ballplayer. Three hundred batting average. A hundred RBIs and fifty home runs."

"Actually, it was .330 with 103 RBIs and 67 home runs." He can't help smiling.

"All right, man. Nice!" Brody high fives him, and they slap palms. "Real tough break about your knees."

Road is staring at Liam with his mouth open. He appears shocked. "Jesus Christ, you're *that* Liam Castillo?" He puts his hand on his forehead like he's going to faint. "Can't believe I never put that together."

Brody's gone back to stroking his goatee. "You were in the minors too, weren't you? Let me think about that. Was it Chicago? No." He holds his finger up. "Texas, am I right?"

"You're right," Liam says, impressed with his baseball knowledge. "I played for a year with the minors in Houston before I was picked up by San Diego."

"I knew it. So what are you up to these days?" Brody asks. "Anything with baseball?"

"He's an FBI agent," Road says.

Brody's brows shoot up to his hairline. "Damn, no shit. Is that true?"

"Yes, it's true," Liam acknowledges. "I'm a special agent with the FBI."

Brody nods slowly. "So now you're catching criminals instead of baseballs." He chuckles and puts his hand out to shake. "Well, damn, it sure is a pleasure to meet you."

Liam grips it. "You too."

"And you're Tori's boyfriend. Can't believe she never mentioned any of this to me."

"Me either," Road mutters. "A heads-up would have been nice."

"I don't think she's into baseball," Liam says.

"No, definitely not." Brody chuckles some more, and even Road cracks a smile. "So, what's it like playing pro ball? That must have been a hell of a ride."

"Yeah." Liam grins. "It was."

Brody peppers him with more questions, wanting to know about some of the other guys he played with. Road is still standoffish but seems unsure how to act toward him now.

"So, are you playing any kind of ball these days?" Brody asks.

Liam shrugs. "Occasionally the local law enforcement gets together and we play each other."

"I'll bet you're in high demand there."

"You could say my dance card fills quickly."

"The belle of the party."

"Something like that." They both laugh.

"I wonder if you'd be interested in playing on a team I put together every year."

"Oh, what's that?"

Brody leans against the minivan. "Well, I own a garage, and at the end of every summer, a bunch of us local business owners play each other. Softball. Just for fun. All the money raised goes to charity."

"And you want *me* to play?"

"I don't know if you'd consider it. We've lost three years in a row now, and I'm sick of losing."

"It would finally even things out," Roads says to his cousin.

Brody nods. "It sure would." He turns back to Liam. "Bill, the owner of Double A's Auto Supply, keeps bringing his brother-in-law over from Spokane. The guy played some minor league ball back in the day and is good."

"It's been giving them an unfair advantage every year," Road tells Liam.

"Send me the dates, and I'll check my schedule," he says to both men. "No promises, but if I can do it, I will."

"Damn, really?" Brody's grin grows wide. "That would be awesome."

BLAIR HAS Tori cornered in the kitchen and is asking all sorts of questions about Liam. She has to admit her best friend's interrogation skills are way better than hers were with Wayne the other day.

So far, Blair's gotten all the details of the cabin trip out of her and has moved on to how much time she and Liam have been spending together since then.

"You've still got that pretty glow about you," Blair says. "At first I thought it was the vacation."

"Trust me, it's Liam." Tori smiles. "I've honestly never been this happy."

Blair's expression softens. "Road and I want that for you. You know that, right?"

"Then stop being so rude to him."

"We're not rude."

Tori rolls her eyes. "Please. You two have been scowling at him since you got here."

"We're just concerned, that's all. I'm worried you're making another mistake with the wrong guy."

"I'm not, okay? And if you'd give him half a chance, you'd see that."

Blair doesn't seem convinced. "What about the bandito test? Does he pass that?"

"Yes, he passes the test. Heck, he'd rescue me, and then he'd go back and arrest all those banditos. Throw every one of them in jail."

Blair smiles. "That's one way to end it."

"Seriously, give him a chance."

They head back out into the living room, and Blair helps her refresh everybody's drinks. Fiona's girlfriend, Sachi, has arrived, and Tori goes over to give her a hug.

"I'm so glad you made it."

"Me too. I saw your new ride." Her trio of small gold earrings catches the light when she nods. "She's a beauty."

"Thank you. I named her Samantha."

"Love it. It's perfect."

Fiona is talking to someone on her phone, giving instructions on how to answer questions from the press. "Always keep it positive and high level. *Don't* say anything negative. *Ever.*"

"Who's she talking to?" Tori asks Sachi.

"I think it's Lindsay."

"Really?"

After Fiona gets off the phone, she tells everyone that ESPN will be interviewing Lindsay in a half hour.

There are some cheers and a few "fuck yeahs" from people. Tori looks around the room, searching for Liam. She wants to make sure he doesn't miss this. Blair sees her and comes over filled with excitement.

"I've got better news than that interview," she says. "Natalie just texted me from Las Vegas. Apparently Lindsay and Giovanni found out this morning that their adoption is being approved."

Tori's eyes widen. "That's wonderful!" She knows Lindsay and her surgeon husband have been trying to adopt a baby girl for the past six months. "They must be thrilled."

"They are. Lindsay's so happy, she's worried she might not be able to play poker tonight."

Tori laughs. "That would be a funny reason not to play."

"It would be." Blair's expression changes, darkens.

"What is it?"

She shakes her head. "I guess I'm just worried. I don't know why I haven't gotten pregnant yet."

"Oh, sweetie. It hasn't been that long."

"I know." Blair seems worried. "Except as you might remember, it happened really quick last time." She's referring to the miscarriage she had years ago.

"It'll happen soon. I have a good feeling about it."

"You do?"

Tori nods. "I really do. I predict I'll be an auntie before we know it."

"I hope so." They hug each other. "I'm sorry about the way I've been acting toward Liam too. I can tell you guys are happy together." Blair smiles. "I promise I'll stop scowling at him."

"I'd appreciate that." They hug again. Tori's glad they're making up. It's been terrible not being able to share her happiness with her best friend. "I hope my brother comes around."

"I'll talk to him." Something catches her attention. "Although this doesn't look so bad."

Tori turns and sees Liam, Brody, and Road all coming through the front door together. They seem to be having a pleasant conversation.

Liam sees her and puts his hand up. He says something to Brody and then heads her way.

"Everything okay?" Tori asks him.

"It's fine."

Blair gives him a big smile.

He seems surprised by it. "Did I miss something?"

"We had a talk," Tori says.

"Yes, I've decided to stop being a bitch to you," Blair tells him.

His brows go up. "Okay.... Well, I'm glad to hear that."

"I just want to let you know that what happened in the past stays in the past." She puts her hand on Tori's arm. "I'm going to go find my husband, but I'll talk to you both later."

After she's gone, he turns to Tori. "That was interesting."

"What can I say? She's finally coming around." She takes his hand. "Come on, I want you to meet Sachi."

Tori pulls him across the room. Fiona's eyes light up as soon as she sees Liam again.

"Oh my *God*, have you changed your mind about the book?"

His expression grows stern. "No, I haven't."

Fiona lifts her phone and does something to the screen with her thumb.

"Don't even think about it," he says. "You take another picture of me and that phone's getting run over by my truck."

"Aren't *you* a lively one." Fiona smirks. "But don't worry, I have my ways. I'll get you in the end."

"Listen to you two." Tori laughs. "You guys are silly."

"Yeah, ha ha," Liam mutters.

She introduces him to Sachi, and the four of them talk for a while. Sachi's a software programmer, and it turns out Liam has some interest in the subject.

The whole party is going really well. When Lindsay shows up on

TV, it's almost surreal. Everyone's watching her give the interview to ESPN.

"Look at her." Fiona studies the screen with a satisfied nod. "She's *perfect.*"

Tori has to agree Lindsay is great on screen. She's articulate and beautiful. Afterward, they continue to show clips of her playing poker.

Eventually the party winds down, and a few of her cousins come over to give her a hug goodbye. They're all polite to Liam. Some are friendlier than others, but Tori knew that would be the case.

Bringing a lawman into her family was like bringing a fox into the henhouse.

"ARE you sure I can't get you to spend the night at my place?" Liam asks Monday morning.

He's getting ready for work while Tori watches him from bed. She enjoys how he puts on a nice suit every day. She's never dated anyone who dressed like that unless they were going to a wedding or a funeral.

It's oddly arousing when he slips that gun into his shoulder holster.

"Do I have to?"

He leans closer to the mirror, inspecting his jaw where he shaved this morning. "No, of course not."

"Are you staying there tonight?"

He comes over to the bed, where she's still wearing nothing but panties and a pink tank top, and sits next to her. "Fancy and I have to sleep there sometimes. It *is* my house."

She sighs. "I suppose so."

"You should come over. Bring your dogs. They might enjoy a change of pace."

"They might." She considers his words, then thinks about

spending the night apart and how much she'll miss him. "All right, fine. We'll come over."

"Great. I'll meet you there tonight."

He starts to get up, but Tori reaches for his hand. "Do you have to go in right away?" There's a husky note in her voice.

His eyes flicker down to her little tank top and panties. "Not necessarily."

"Good." She pulls him closer, surrounded by his freshly showered scent. Wrapping her arms around his neck, she kisses him.

He rumbles with approval. The kiss deepens before he draws back, reaching around to pull his gun off.

"No, leave it," she murmurs. "Don't take it off."

His hand stills, and he looks at her with a questioning gaze. His mouth kicks up in the corner. "All right, if that's what you want."

She swallows and nods, amazed at how erotic she finds this. "Yes, that's what I want."

The gun stays in place as he moves his hands to caress her hips before sliding up to pull her tank top off.

Within seconds, she's naked, while Liam's still fully dressed.

That's what she wants too.

They kiss some more, and soon he's on his back. She straddles him, his breathing uneven as he fondles her breasts, plays with her nipples. She unzips him and then positions herself over his hard-on.

"I didn't know this turned you on," he says. "I might have to arrest you next time."

She laughs and then gasps when he pushes up at the same time she slides down. Pleasure floods her veins like warm water. The feel of him deep inside is so good. They move with each other.

Crazily, her eyes keep going to that gun in its leather holster. And then there's that crisp white shirt beneath her fingers. His whole FBI vibe.

The truth is Liam is a man to be reckoned with. He catches bad guys and puts them behind bars.

It shouldn't arouse her so much, but it does.

After a short while, his expression grows hot. His brown eyes turn nearly black. Strong hands grab her hips as he takes control.

He's not gentle anymore, but she doesn't want it gentle. He's getting close to his breaking point. She knows him so well. Heat radiates out from where they're joined.

When he groans and pulls her in tight, her eyes fall shut. Passion washes through her. Desire. Filling her limbs and womb with a kind of bliss.

Afterward, she lies over him, both of them catching their breath.

"Are you going to play with yourself after I leave?" Liam asks, stroking down her back. "Make yourself come?"

Tori's lying naked on top of his fully clothed body. The various fabric textures press into her skin. "Yes." She lifts her head to look at him. "I am."

He smiles softly. "I'll be thinking about you, then."

She caresses his jaw, filled with tenderness. No one's ever accepted her like this. "It's amazing how you make everything in my life okay."

AFTER HE LEAVES, she stays in bed for a little while and takes care of herself like she told him. Then she gets up, takes a quick shower, and sits at the table with her planner, going over today's schedule. She has work to do for her brother's website, three pet sitting appointments, and Happy Pet Nanny snack deliveries.

Instead of being stressed though, there's an easy smile on her face. Thinking about Liam makes her feel warm and happy inside.

She remembers last night in bed together, talking quietly until late. Moonlight filtered through the blinds.

"I'm your man," he whispered, stroking her hair while they lay face-to-face. "You know that, right?"

"I know," she whispered back.

All those continents shifting inside her had produced this whole new landscape, a place she'd never been before, one that was blooming in a rainbow of beautiful colors.

When evening rolls around, she packs a small bag for herself, then loads all of her dogs' stuff into Samantha, and they drive over to Liam's house.

She parks her minivan right behind his black truck. Glancing around, she notes that his soulless neighborhood is exactly the same. Not one blade of grass out of place. She feels sorry for him living here.

"Your dogs don't exactly travel light, do they?" he says when he sees how much she had to bring.

"It's sort of how I imagine it is traveling with children."

He grins. "I guess you'll be ready if we ever have any, huh?" He scoops up all three doggie beds and carries them up to his front door.

She watches him for a long moment, enjoying the view and thinking about his words. It was only a joke, but it occurs to her if there were ever a guy she'd want to have kids with, it would be Liam. Without a doubt she knows he'd be a great dad.

Not that she has any experience in that area, having grown up without one, but she was around Blair's dad enough to have a good idea.

Once everything's unloaded, Tori sets up the doggie beds. Miss Fancy Pants is keeping a stern eye on her visitors. There are a few territorial growls, but Tori's dogs catch on pretty quick as to what's off-limits.

It isn't long before they're all playing in the backyard. Liam decides it'd be fun to have a barbecue and is cleaning the grill.

"Your brother texted me today," he says, scrubbing burnt food away with a metal brush. "He invited me out for a beer later this week."

"Really?"

"I agreed to go."

Tori considers this. "No one's mentioned it to me. I wonder what he wants."

Liam shrugs. "I guess we'll find out."

"How did he get your number? I didn't give it to him."

"From Brody. I told him it was okay." He explains how he's going to play on the softball team for her cousin's garage in September.

She tears a paper towel off and hands it to him. "That's nice of you."

"I figured, why not? It sounds like they could use my help."

"Every year, he and my brother take that softball tournament so seriously you wouldn't believe it." She rolls her eyes. "They strategize like two generals planning a war campaign."

Once the grill is clean, he puts it all back together. They check what groceries he has at home. He's been staying at her place so much, his cupboards are bare.

"Normally I'm happy to go shopping, but it might be best if I stay with the dogs," Tori says. "Since this is a new place for them and all."

"Sure, that's fine. I'll be quick."

They make a list and he heads out, except she parked her minivan right behind his truck. "Here, take my keys and drive Samantha." She digs them out of her purse. She's been enjoying her new ride lately, though she still misses Mable.

Liam leaves for the store, and she feeds all the dogs their dinner.

Right after she puts their bowls out, the front doorbell rings.

Thinking it might be Liam with his hands full, she swings it open eagerly, but unfortunately it's not him.

It's his sister, Elena.

CHAPTER TWENTY-SIX

> **Tori's Playlist: Daily Song**
> *"Shout at the Devil"*
> *by Mötley Crüe*
>
> ♥
>
> **Liam's Playlist: Daily Song**
> *"Always Been Crazy"*
> *by Waylon Jennings*

ELENA'S EYES roam over Tori with obvious disdain. "It's *you*."

"Yes, it's me."

"Where's my brother?"

"He went to the grocery store."

Elena motions toward the driveway. "His truck's here."

"I know. He took my minivan."

They stare at each other. Elena's dark hair is pulled back in a ponytail. She's wearing a sweatshirt and jeans, sunglasses on top of her head. Very little makeup.

"Would you like to come inside and wait for him?" Tori asks politely.

"Yes, I will." She barges in and marches right past her.

Tori follows her into the living room. At the sound of a new person's voice, there's barking, and all four dogs come scrambling out from the kitchen.

Oh no.

Tori tries to wrangle them, telling them to sit, but they're only half listening. And Miss Fancy Pants isn't listening at all.

"What is all this?" Elena asks with obvious disgust. "Whose dogs are these? Get them away from me."

"They're mine." She pulls Duff and Eddie away by their collars. At least Tommy Lee's hanging back. "Sorry. They're very friendly and get excited meeting new people."

"It figures you'd have a pack of wild dogs."

Tori bites her tongue. She walks them to the backyard and then closes the dog door. They'll be safe out there from any more mean comments.

Elena is bent down, petting Miss Fancy Pants.

"Can I get you a glass of iced tea while you're waiting?" Tori asks, knowing Liam's whole family drinks the stuff like water.

"Wow." She stands and looks her over. "You're offering *me* iced tea in my own brother's house."

Tori's temper frays. "Does that mean you'd like some or not?"

"You've got quite the nice setup, don't you? I'll bet you'd just love to move in."

"Move in *here*?" Tori's disturbed at even the thought of it. "I would never want to live here."

"We both know that's a lie. I'll bet you've got my brother running around in circles for you."

"I don't know what you mean."

Elena snorts. "Oh, I think you know *exactly* what I mean."

"No, I don't."

"It means your sweet and innocent act doesn't fool me. It didn't in high school, and it doesn't now."

"I'm not acting like anything."

Elena's brown eyes, which are unfortunately the same rich shade as Liam's, glare at her. "You're just another one of his mistakes. Don't forget that." She sneers. "At least you'll be gone soon enough."

This is Liam's sister, she reminds herself, gritting her teeth. Liam told her how his sister was widowed three years ago, leaving her with two small children, and despite everything, Tori felt sad hearing that. She also reminds herself that he spent hours on Saturday meeting and dealing with her family. The least she can do is be nice to this one relative.

"Whatever you might think of me, I care about your brother very much."

"Please." She rolls her eyes. "You're obviously using him."

"Using him for what?"

"Who knows? But I don't trust you. And my brother deserves a whole lot better than a weirdo."

There's a sound as the front door opens, and a few seconds later, Liam walks into the living room carrying two bags of groceries.

"Elena? I saw your car out front. I didn't know you were stopping by."

She adjusts the sunglasses on her head. "I was in the area and thought I'd take a chance that you were home. I haven't seen you in weeks. We all miss you, especially the kids."

Liam's expression turns stricken. "I miss those monkeys too. I wish you'd brought them with you."

Elena's expression hardens as she glares at Tori. "It's just as well I didn't."

He doesn't seem to hear her comment as he heads into the kitchen to put the groceries away. The two women follow him.

"We're going to grill tonight," he says, emptying one of the bags while Tori stands beside him and empties the other. "Would you like to stay for dinner?" He looks over his shoulder at his sister.

Tori hopes she says no.

"I'd love to."

Great.

"Great." He turns to Tori. "I got those ice cream bars you like so much." He grins, holding up a box of her favorite coconut cream treats.

"Thanks, that was sweet of you."

To her surprise, he leans down and kisses her. "To be honest, you've got me hooked on them too."

She senses Elena's disapproval pouring out like smoke from a fire.

As they get everything ready for dinner, both women are in the kitchen. Tori makes the salad and gets out the package of her favorite veggie burgers. Elena does something with the chicken. He gives each of them a glass of iced tea.

"Sometime you'll have to try the blackberry sage tea Tori makes," he says to Elena. "It's incredible. I would never have thought those flavors go together, but they do."

"Is that right?" his sister says.

"She makes another one with lemongrass and ginger that's also delicious."

"Sounds... unusual."

Weird is what she means. Tori can tell by the tone of her voice.

By the time they have everything set up and have moved outside, the two women haven't spoken one word to each other. Liam is carrying the entire conversation.

Tori knows him well enough that she can tell he's really trying hard with his sister.

"So you don't eat meat?" Elena asks her. "None at all?"

"No, I'm a vegan."

Elena rolls her eyes.

Smoky barbecue smells drift out from the grill. Liam cooks the food while he talks to his sister, catching up on the latest news about various family members.

Tori sips her tea, listening politely.

"You should come over for dinner soon," Elena says to him. "The boys would love to see you. How about next week?"

He uses tongs to turn the chicken on the grill and seems cheerful. "That sounds great. We'll be there."

"Actually, I just meant *you*," she says to him, then turns to Tori. "No offense."

"None taken."

But Liam does seem offended. He turns around, still holding the tongs. "What do you mean, just me? Tori's not invited?"

"No, she's not."

He puts the utensil down and turns the grill off. "I thought you came here to make peace. That you finally came to your senses about all this."

"What gave you that idea?"

"Because you're *here*, having dinner with us."

Elena shakes her head. "I'm here because you're my brother, and we miss you. Apparently your priorities have changed though."

"My priorities haven't changed. They've expanded to include someone new, that's all."

"My God." Elena leans back in her chair. "How can you be so smart and so dumb at the same time?"

Liam goes still. "I'd tread carefully here if I were you."

"Oh, so now I can't speak my mind? It's like high school all over again. And you know what? Just like high school, *this*"—she points to Liam and Tori—"isn't going to end well."

"You have no idea what you're talking about. I've never been this happy in my entire life." He looks over at Tori and grins.

She smiles too, though her stomach's tied in knots, sick at the way Liam and his sister are arguing.

Elena seems frustrated. "She's just another one of your crazies, and you refuse to see it."

His expression hardens. "Stop it."

"Except she's worse than all of them put together. She's only going to drag you down."

Liam straightens his shoulders, his voice stern. "That's enough. I'm not listening to you disparage Tori."

"I know the truth is hard to hear, but I can't stand by silently as you make another mistake."

"I don't believe this." He throws his hands up. "I honestly thought you came here because you realized how ridiculous you were acting."

"I'm not the one who's *acting*." Elena turns to Tori. "I can see you've got your hooks deep into him. You must be quite pleased with yourself."

Tori doesn't even know what to say to this strange assertion. "Hooks? I don't have any hooks."

Liam's expression is grim. "Just leave, Elena. Before you embarrass yourself any more than you already have."

"So you're kicking me out of your house? That's nice. Your own sister."

"Please go."

She pushes her chair back and stands up. "Don't say I didn't warn you." After having the last word, she leaves, slamming the screen door behind her. A few seconds later, the front door slams.

Tori gets up and immediately goes to Liam, putting her arms around him. "I'm so sorry."

"Are you kidding? I'm the one who needs to apologize to you. My sister has lost her mind."

"She thinks she's protecting you from me."

He laughs. "That's the dumbest thing I've ever heard."

"Maybe I *am* one of your crazies."

His arms tighten around her as they both hug each other. "Rubia." He sighs. "What you are is the best thing that's ever happened to me. With you, I finally hit a home run."

THEY WRAP up the leftover barbecue and take the dogs out for a walk. There's a trail near his house that goes through a wooded area.

It's still early evening, so there are plenty of people out, some with dogs or kids, others on bikes.

He takes Tori's hand. The woods smell mossy and green, sunlight shining golden through the trees.

They don't talk about Elena. Instead, Tori tells him about her day, about the work she did for her brother, then about the various animals she was pet sitting. She's lively and animated. He laughs when she describes how one dog gets frantic if she comes inside the house before he finds his rubber duck, how he likes to greet her at the door with it. It reminds him of Fancy's antics.

Whoever thought he'd enjoy hearing dog stories? But so much has changed in his life since Tori came into it.

He's never felt so at ease with a woman before. And every time he sees her, or knows he's about to see her, he can't stop grinning.

"I'm glad I'm staying over tonight," she says later when they're back at his house and getting ready for bed.

"Are you? Despite what happened with my sister?"

She nods and climbs in beside him. Flashes of her feet and hands show she's wearing her usual pink glitter nail polish. "I hate to think of you all alone here in this neighborhood. It's so sad."

"So it's gone from spooky to sad?"

"The more I think about it, this neighborhood isn't *you*."

He studies her pretty face, the light sprinkling of freckles across her nose, and realizes she possibly understands him better than he does himself. "I used to think it fit me perfectly, but you're right. I'd rather have what you described. A place where I know my neighbors."

In some ways, this neighborhood is a metaphor for everything that's been wrong with his life.

She slides under the cool sheets next to him and they make love in a slow, unhurried way. He enjoys taking his time like this, savoring her. She's tried to come with him a few more times since that first attempt, and he knows it's still bothering her.

"I want it because I want the intimacy with you," she tells him after another bathroom visit.

"We *are* intimate." He runs his fingers along her hairline. "This is intimacy, rubia. Right now."

Her eyes drift shut as he plays with her hair. "I want it all though. Every level."

"I know."

She gazes at him. "Does that make me greedy? I already have so much."

"No, of course not. I just don't want you to feel pressured."

Her eyes are still on his face, studying him. "You should accept your sister's invitation for dinner next week. After what she's been through, it can't be easy for her."

He strokes her hair, kneading her scalp with his fingertips. "It has been a while since I've seen my nephews."

"Elena's probably threatened by me. Especially with how much time we spend together."

"There's no reason to be. I have room in my life for all of you." Though he sees Tori's point. They've been so wrapped up in each other, he's seen little of Elena and the boys lately.

"I don't want to come between you and your family. Just go. Please. I'd feel so much better."

"Okay, I will." His mouth turns up at the corner. "You're amazing. I always knew I was right about you."

"You'd do the same for me."

"Hopefully my sister let's go of this grudge soon. She doesn't like to admit when she's wrong about anything. I'd love for you to meet my nephews. They're great kids."

"I'd like that too."

WHEN WEDNESDAY ARRIVES, Liam's supposed to meet Road at a Mexican restaurant after work. Tori's been texting him about it all day.

Please don't kill each other tonight!!!

Don't worry, I'll only arrest him.

Very funny.

Did you ask him why he wanted to meet with me?

I texted him, but he hasn't responded. I asked Blair, and she has no idea either!!!

Her brother is already there when he arrives at the restaurant, studying his phone. Liam slides into the booth across from him.

Road glances up. "Thanks for meeting me. Do you mind if I order dinner while we talk?"

"Knock yourself out." The waiter brings Liam a menu, but he only glances at it. He doubts he'll stay long enough for a meal. Meanwhile, Road is eating chips and salsa.

"Bet you're wondering why I asked you here," Road says, taking a sip from his beer.

"I have to admit, I'm curious."

"There are a couple reasons." He puts the bottle down. "First off, thank you for agreeing to play on Brody's softball team. That's seriously cool of you."

"Sure. Like I said, so far my schedule looks fine, but unfortunately, that could change."

He nods. "I still appreciate you not holding anything that happened between the two of us against my cousin."

Liam doesn't reply, wondering where this conversation is headed.

"And then there's a second reason I invited you here." Road takes a deep breath and seems uncomfortable. "I want to apologize for the shit that happened between us in high school."

This surprises him, though he's careful not to show it.

"Been thinking about it since the weekend, and I know I was a real dick to you."

"That's true. You were." The waiter brings him his iced tea. "*Gracias.*"

"You have to understand the situation back then. My little sister was crying her eyes out. She told me some dude asked her to homecoming, and because she said no, he poured a milkshake over her head."

Liam drinks from his glass and puts it down.

"It was fucked up," Road says. "I was pissed as hell at you after I heard that story."

"When you tell it like that, it sounds bad. That's not the actual story though."

He leans back against his seat. "Yeah, I know. Tori gave me a new history lesson. Turns out I was wrong about everything. I'm sorry, man. I acted like a real asshole."

Liam can't help grinning a little.

Road grins too. "Bet you're enjoying this, aren't you?"

"I admit, I am."

"That's understandable." Road nods and then meets his eyes. "So, are we square?"

Liam considers him for a long moment. He didn't see this coming. It occurs to him Road isn't quite what he thought. "Yeah, we're square."

Road lets his breath out. "Good."

The waiter comes back and asks them if they'd like to order. Liam consults the menu. He didn't think he'd be staying for dinner, but he's changing his mind.

Meanwhile Road orders, asking a few questions about the food. To Liam's surprise, the whole exchange happens in Spanish. Once the waiter's gone, he leans forward.

"*Hablas español?*"

"*Sí,*" Road says. "*Viví en España durante un año.*"

"*Mis abuelos son de Mexico,*" he says, telling him how his grandparents are from Mexico. "*Crecí hablando español e inglés.*" As a result he spoke both Spanish and English growing up.

They talk more, and by the time the waiter brings Road's meal, Liam decides to order dinner. He points at Road's beer and says he'll take one of those too.

They spend the rest of the evening getting to know each other, speaking Spanish the whole time. Liam learns about Road's travel blog and the books he's written. It's an enlightening conversation.

When he goes to Tori's place afterward, it's obvious she's been on pins and needles waiting for him.

"How was it? You're still in one piece obviously, and I assume he's not in jail. I hope he wasn't rude. I told my brother I'd stop speaking to him if he doesn't stop acting like a jerk."

Liam tells her how Road apologized for everything that happened between them.

"He did? That's great news!"

"Yeah, we talked for a while. You never told me he speaks Spanish."

"Oh, yeah." She goes into the kitchen and fiddles with the oven. From what he can see, she's making a fresh batch of the dog snacks she sells. "He lived in Spain for a while. Is his Spanish any good?"

"Surprisingly good."

"I have to say, when my brother realizes he's wrong about something, at least he's quick to admit it."

Liam nods and can't help thinking of Elena. She's convinced Tori and her family are nothing but lowlifes, but who's the one acting poorly?

"He invited me to a ball game next week with him and Brody."

She pulls out a pan of dog snacks and sets it on a cooling rack. "Are you going to go?"

"I think so." He pauses. "Listen, there's something else I wanted to talk to you about."

She adjusts the temperature knob then closes the oven door. "What's that?"

"My parents want us to come down and visit them in Portland this weekend."

Her eyes flash over to his. "They do?"

"Yeah, my mom called me today." She called while he was at work and wanted to know if he really threw his sister out of the house. He tried to explain how it wasn't as dramatic as that.

"I suppose we could go down there." Tori seems worried. "They won't be rude to me, will they?"

"No, they'd never behave like that." When she comes closer, he reaches for her hand. "I'd really like you to meet them."

She goes quiet at this.

"It's important to me."

"Okay." She takes a deep breath. "Then I'll meet them."

TORI'S NERVOUS. She's worried Liam's parents will think the same thing Elena does.

That she's another one of his crazy girlfriends.

"You can play country music if you want," she tells him once they're in his truck, heading south on the interstate. "I don't mind."

"Really?" He glances over at her with concern. "Are you feeling okay, rubia?"

She laughs lightly. "I'm just nervous."

"There's no reason to be nervous." He reaches over and takes her hand. "They're going to love you."

Tori sighs. "I hope you're right."

She looks down at the way they're holding hands, then back up at Liam's handsome profile as he drives.

Love.

They've been throwing that word around a lot lately. Neither of them has said "I love you," but they've been saying things that are awfully close. "I love how you make me feel" and "I love everything about you."

And it's all true. She's never felt so connected or intimate with anyone.

Along with faking orgasms in the past, she also used to tell guys she loved them. But only if they said it first, and only because she didn't want to hurt their feelings or disappoint them.

More and more though, she's been thinking about what Liam said—that maybe those guys were disappointing *her*. No one ever looked too closely or tried to understand her. He's the only one. And that's when a strange thought occurs to her.

What if he's my special someone?

What if they were supposed to be one of those high school sweetheart couples? The ones who got married and stayed in love the rest of their lives, and all these years apart were just a big mistake. Maybe that's why the universe brought them together again.

The thought takes her breath away.

By the time they arrive at his parents' house, it's late Friday afternoon. It was raining off and on as they drove down but has since cleared up. They live in an upper-middle-class neighborhood where all the houses are well spaced apart. She sees kids on bikes and people out working in their yards.

A petite woman wearing a floppy yellow hat is out front adding flowers to a clay pot.

"There's my mom," he says, pulling into the driveway.

They climb out of the truck, and his mom takes off her gardening gloves and walks toward them. She gives Liam a big hug. "It's about time you came down. We haven't seen you in almost two months."

"Things have been nuts at work."

His mom nods. "I know, I heard. The Rizzo arrest has been making it into all the papers here."

"It's starting to get national attention."

Adrenaline spikes through Tori at the mere mention of his big case. All her worries about Wayne and her mom come rushing back.

When they're done hugging, his mother's light blue eyes turn to her. "And you must be Tori."

"Yes, it's very nice to meet you."

To her surprise, his mom gives her a big hug too.

"I'm Moira. Liam's told us a lot about you."

"He has?"

"Come on inside. Are you hungry? I made some vegetarian chili for a late lunch. I understand you don't eat meat."

"Yes, that's right," Tori murmurs. "But don't go out of your way cooking for me. I can always find something to eat."

"It's no bother," Moira says cheerfully.

Once inside, she sees the house is decorated nicely. Comfortable and not ostentatious. Moira is talking a mile a minute, asking her son questions interspersed with lots of lively laughter. She's not at all what Tori thought she would be. Despite what Liam said, she was still picturing someone more severe like Elena.

Moira pulls her floppy hat off, and Tori sees her short hair is colored bright red. Even though it's not natural, it suits her.

"Where's Dad?"

"Upstairs. He should be down soon."

They sit at the kitchen table, where Moira pours everyone iced tea with lemon. Liam tells her about Tori's tea flavors and how creative she is, and Tori feels embarrassed. Though she has to admit, it's the first time she's been with a guy who bragged to his parents like this.

"Now, let me have a real look at you." Moira turns toward her and reaches out to take her hand. Her eyes roam over Tori's face. "Well, you're just lovely, aren't you?"

"Thank you." She's not sure what to make of all this. The hand holding and the scrutiny. It doesn't seem ill-intentioned though.

"Liam's told me you have a kind nature, and I see it now too. Tell me a little about yourself."

"Well, I have a pet sitting business called Happy Pet Nanny. I bake dog snacks and sell them. I also work on websites and create graphics for them."

"You're quite industrious."

Tori's brows go up, and she laughs. "I never really think of myself that way, but I suppose I am."

Moira nods approvingly and smiles at Liam. "I do like her."

He grins. "I told you you would."

Tori studies Moira. "Thank you." Despite all this scrutiny, there's something warm and welcoming about her. "I like you too."

She beams. "Then we're off to a good start. Would you two like a bowl of chili?"

They both say yes, and Moira goes to get it for them. Tori offers to help, but Moira tells her to sit back down. A minute later she comes over with two bowls. As they begin to eat, a man who's obviously Liam's father comes into the kitchen.

"Sorry I missed your arrival." He puts his hand on Liam's shoulder. "I was cleaning out the garage all morning and needed a quick shower."

"Mom told me you were doing that today, but I didn't believe her."

His father chuckles. "It reached critical mass." His intense gaze shifts to her. "And you must be Tori." He puts his hand out. "I'm Ray."

She shakes it. "It's nice to meet you." It's clear Liam takes after his dad. They have a similar height and build. Neither of his parents has Liam's sensual mouth though.

Ray sits at the table and asks how the drive down went. Tori remembers him from that meeting in the principal's office years ago. How he seemed so serious and intimidating.

He still seems that way.

Moira, who's like the opposite of her husband, comes over with two more bowls of chili. She sets one in front of him and then takes a seat with the second one.

"So what can you tell us about Rizzo?" Ray asks, drizzling honey over his cornbread. "That case of yours has been creating a lot of good press for the bureau."

Liam nods. "It's really blown up. The U.S. Attorney's Office is still adding to the list of charges, and we've arrested a number of his associates. A lot of separate investigations are happening."

Ray listens while eating his chili.

"That's about all I can say for now. Ironically, there's even a connection with Tori and how we first met again."

"Really? Is that so?" Both his parents look at her.

Liam relays the story about Mable and how the ring of thieves is likely part of Rizzo's crime network. "It turns out they're using these minivans to smuggle stolen goods across state lines."

She tries to smile and not look nervous during his retelling. Except it isn't easy. There are two FBI agents staring at her. She feels like a lamb sitting in the lion's den.

It must show too, because Liam reaches over and squeezes her hand. She knows he thinks she's nervous meeting his parents, and she is, but talking about all this is making her queasy.

More than anything, she wishes she could tell him everything. All her suspicions about Wayne. It would be such a relief. What's the worst that could happen?

They could arrest my mom.

After they eat, Moira shows her the guest room where she'll be sleeping. Apparently Liam will be on the pullout bed downstairs in the family room. He'd already warned her that his parents are Catholic and would put them in separate bedrooms.

"You should sneak down to me tonight," he whispers when they're alone in the guest room. His mom left to go grab her a towel and washcloth.

"*Me* sneak down?" She imagines herself navigating these unfamiliar halls alone at night. With her luck, she'd knock over a vase and wake up the whole house. "Why don't you sneak up?"

"Because my parents' bedroom is right across the hall."

"What if we get caught?"

"We won't get caught. The family room is on the first floor and has a door."

She chews her bottom lip. "I don't know. Your dad's an FBI agent."

He chuckles. "So am I, remember?"

"I know, but he probably has the place booby-trapped with alarms and motion detectors and Lord knows what else."

For some reason he finds this amusing. "They're all on the outside of the house. Or most of them anyway."

"Gee, that's reassuring."

"Don't worry." He leans closer. "I'll draw you a map with coordinates that show all the blind spots for the interior cameras."

She stares at him with wide eyes.

"Just in case though, wear a black leotard and a mask."

"What?"

His mouth twitches.

"Oh, *you!*" She smacks his arm, and he cracks up. "You think you're so funny, don't you? A real comedian."

CHAPTER TWENTY-SEVEN

Tori's Playlist: Daily Song
"When It's Love"
by Van Halen
♥
Liam's Playlist: Daily Song
"Love Your Love the Most"
by Eric Church

LIAM CAN TELL Tori's nervous meeting his parents. She's been jumpy since they arrived. All he can do is reassure her that everything is okay.

After dinner they decide to play a board game, then settle on cards instead. One of his family's favorites called Bullshit.

"Can I say bullshit in front of your parents?" she asks when the two of them are alone in the kitchen. "What will they think of me?"

"They won't think anything. My family loves that game."

The evening's warmed up, so they sit on the back patio. After

Tori's initial discomfort passes, she seems to be having a blast as they all try to fool each other.

"It's particularly satisfying pulling the wool over someone's eyes who's *trained* to spot deception," his mom says to Tori. "Ray and Liam always assume they have the edge, but trust me, they don't."

As if proving his mom's point, Tori winds up calling bullshit on his dad twice and is right both times.

"We'll have to keep an eye on this one," his dad says, giving Tori a wink.

Liam grins and is glad to see her laugh with delight.

They play cards until the late hours. Finally, his mom announces it's time for her beauty sleep. Not long after, Tori says she's turning in too. The porch light catches the blue streak in her hair. He watches her go inside the house, enjoying the sway of those hips. Unfortunately, he doubts she's sneaking down to him tonight.

This leaves him and his father alone on the patio. He glances up at the sky. Despite the rain earlier on the drive from Seattle, it's a clear night. The scent of a neighbor's fresh-cut grass lingers in the air.

"I like her," his dad says. "I'm glad you brought her with you. She's not what I expected."

"What did you expect?"

He shrugs. "More drama, I guess. Someone high-strung. She's not like your other girlfriends."

Liam goes quiet, embarrassed that his parents know his dating history so well, and that it's filled with head cases. "No, she isn't. Ironically, she worried you guys wouldn't like her, especially after what happened with Elena."

"What did happen there?" His dad's expression turns concerned. "The way she described it, you threw her out of your house."

Liam shakes his head. He relays the situation that led up to him asking his sister to leave. "She left me no choice."

"How do you plan to make it right?"

He leans back in his chair. "I'll call her next week and accept her dinner invitation. It'll be great to see the boys."

"Good. I'm glad to hear that. We both know your sister has had it tough these past few years."

Liam goes quiet. "I know."

"She can be stubborn sometimes, but it won't last forever."

"If so, it's her loss, because I have to tell you, this is it for me." He looks at his dad. "Tori's the one. I've never felt like this about anybody."

His father nods. "I'm happy for you. She seems like a fine person."

TORI'S up early the next morning. After a quick shower, she heads downstairs to find Moira and Ray at the table, drinking coffee and eating breakfast. Unfortunately, Liam is nowhere in sight.

"Good morning," she says.

Moira glances up from her iPad. "Good morning. There's oatmeal on the stove, or cold cereal if you prefer. There's coffee too."

"Thank you." She helps herself to a bowl of oatmeal with blueberries, grabs a mug of coffee, and then brings everything to the table.

"Did you sleep well?" Moira asks with a smile.

Tori takes a sip of her coffee. "I did. Thank you." She puts the cup down. His parents are super nice, but this is still awkward. One thought keeps going through her head.

I'm sleeping with their son. We have s-e-x.

Ray is reading something on his phone but puts it down. His intense gaze shifts to her, and she realizes it's sort of like Liam's, but on steroids. "I understand you own your own business. More than one even."

Tori swallows a spoonful of oatmeal. "I do." She describes more of what she does, trying not to sound like a scatterbrain, which is probably exactly what she sounds like.

As they're talking, there are noises from another part of the house, and she realizes it must be Liam waking up.

Thank God.

"He'll be coming upstairs any minute now," Moira says to her husband.

Ray nods. "We better act fast."

They both stare at her.

Tori stops chewing her oatmeal. "What?"

"How would you like to have some fun with Liam this morning?" Ray says with a grin.

"Fun?"

Moira reaches for her hand. "Come on, we don't have much time." She pulls Tori up from her seat and guides her over to the kitchen's island. "Crouch down here, and when I give you the signal, you'll jump out in front of him, okay?"

"Um... okay."

"What about hiding her in the pantry?" Ray says. "We could put the cereal back in there."

"But what if he goes for the oatmeal?"

"True." He strokes his chin. "Let's only give him the option of oatmeal. That way we control the situation."

Tori watches with amazement as the two of them stand there planning the best way to scare the bejesus out of their son.

Finally, she's crouched behind the kitchen island, and his parents are back at the table, sipping coffee and staring at their phone and iPad like everything's normal.

It doesn't take long before she hears Liam come into the kitchen. She holds her breath. Despite how weird all this is, she has to admit, it's fun. Kind of exciting.

Liam says good morning to everyone. "Has Tori been down?"

"She already ate," his mom says. "She went back upstairs to take a shower." She glances up at him. "There's oatmeal on the stove and fresh fruit for breakfast."

"Sounds good."

Tori hears him go over to the stove as she waits with anticipation. She looks over at his parents. The three of them can see each other clearly. They're acting perfectly normal—you'd never guess what they were up to. His mom gives her a quick grin when their eyes meet.

"Could you come here for a second?" Ray says to his son. "You need to see this."

"What is it?" she hears Liam ask.

"It's a message I just got about Rizzo."

"What?" Liam's voice sounds concerned. "Why would you be getting messages about that?"

"You need to see it." He motions him over. "Leave the oatmeal."

The anticipation builds.

Tori watches Moira closely, waiting for her cue. When Liam rounds the corner, his mom flashes her a smile and nods.

"Surprise!" Tori leaps out from her hiding spot with her hands in the air.

"Aaaah!" Liam jumps back with alarm. His eyes wide. "What the hell!"

She bursts out laughing. The startled expression on his face is priceless. His parents are both howling with laughter too.

"Damn, you guys really got me," he says, grinning and trying to catch his breath. He puts his hand on the counter. "You scared the shit out of me."

"I'm sorry," Tori says, though she can barely speak, she's laughing so hard. "Your parents put me up to it."

"Oh, I'm sure they did."

"Your face," his mom says, wiping her eyes. "You had no idea!"

His father chuckles. "Just trying to keep you on your toes."

"Yeah," Liam says, still grinning as he eyes Tori. "And *you*, I may have to get you back for that one."

"That's okay," she says with a big smile. "It was worth it."

ODDLY, Tori feels more relaxed around Liam's parents after jumping out and scaring him half to death. It's like a bonding experience between them. They seem more comfortable with her too.

The four of them head into Portland to do some sightseeing, showing her around the city. She's never seen so many bicycles. They take a picturesque walk along the Willamette River.

The whole time, Liam is affectionate with her, holding hands.

"I'm crazy about you," he whispers in her ear. "You're all I can think about."

She strokes his neck when he bends down to give her a quick kiss. "I'm crazy about you too."

Eventually they wind up at a restaurant in Chinatown for dinner. The food is delicious, and after walking all day, it feels good to sit. The conversation is light and easy. By the time they wind up back at the house, it's almost nine. Both Ray and Moira decide to turn in for the night. Liam and Tori wind up on the couch in the family room watching a movie.

"You didn't sneak down to me last night," he says when the film is over. "What the heck happened?"

"I didn't bring my ninja suit."

He smirks. "I told you I'd draw you a map." But then his voice turns low. "What about tonight?"

She laughs. "You can't go for two nights without sex?"

"It's not the sex." He moves the bowl of popcorn they've been sharing onto the coffee table. "It's *you* I can't go without."

"Is that so?" She can't help smiling at this.

They're sitting next to each other on the couch, where she's had one leg thrown over his thigh during the whole film. He reaches down and scoops her up, bringing her onto his lap.

She slips her arms around his neck, inhaling his breezy scent.

"My parents really like you," he murmurs.

"I like them too," Tori admits. She likes how they seem normal, but when you scratch the surface, they're a little kooky. *Sort of like me.*

"Is everything okay? You still seem on edge, rubia."

"I'm fine." She knows she can't tell him about the worries plaguing her since she got here.

"You sure?"

They gaze at each other. His brown eyes are so rich and toasty. She wants to fall into them and stay there forever. "I'm good."

"Okay, just checking." He threads his fingers through hers. "You're so important to me."

She plays with the back of his neck. Her throat goes tight.

"Hey, what's wrong?"

But she only shakes her head.

"You know you can talk to me about anything, right?"

"I know."

"Look at me. I want to tell you something." When she faces him, his gaze is steady. Clear and true. "I love you, Tori."

Her heart pounds. "You do?"

"I think you already know I do."

Time seems suspended. Even the Earth spinning on its axis has slowed.

Here I am.

Everything she's ever wanted.

Her eyes roam his face. Liam's so handsome, but it's gone far beyond handsome for her. "I love you too."

"Yeah?" He smiles.

She strokes his cheek, rough with stubble, and takes a deep breath. "I think you're my one special someone."

He nods. "I already know you're mine. It feels like I've been waiting for you a long time."

"Same here." Her voice trembles. "I was worried you'd never show up."

"I know, but I'm here, and I'm not going anywhere."

"Do you promise?"

"Always." He hugs her tight, and joy rushes through her as she holds him close. Her heart is so full, brimming over.

It's finally happening.

She lays her head against his shoulder, and they stay that way for a while. It's so good to be held. They're both quiet, and it's a comfortable quiet.

She sighs. "I guess I should head upstairs to bed."

"Are you going to sneak down later?"

"No." She rolls her eyes. "Of course not."

"Are you sure?" He grins. "I promise I'll make it worth your while."

"I can't. What would your parents think of me?"

"They're not going to find out."

"Listen to you. I thought you were such a straight arrow. A fuddy-duddy."

He chuckles. "I *am*. See, what you do to me? I can't resist you." He wraps his arms around her again. "You're like an addiction."

She kisses him, then pats his cheek. "Sorry, but you'll have to go cold turkey tonight."

"Cold turkey?" He groans. "You're cruel."

Laughing lightly, she stands up. "It's only one more night. You'll survive."

TORI HEADS UPSTAIRS and notices Liam's parents' bedroom door is partially open. There's light coming from the room, and when she walks past, they're both still awake reading in bed.

It's midnight, and she wonders if they've been waiting for her to come upstairs.

"Good night," she calls out to them, and they both respond in kind.

She closes the guest bedroom door.

After changing into her short nightgown, she gets into bed, hugging herself with excitement. She's found her special someone. At long last, he's arrived.

She's so excited, she's having trouble sleeping. There are

plumbing sounds as someone in the house uses the water, but then eventually everything goes quiet.

The bedroom window is open, and she can see the partial moon shining up in the sky. She studies it as she lies there. The way it reminds her of their time at the lake. How much fun they had. How Liam always makes her feel loved and cared for.

And then she thinks of him downstairs sleeping on the couch's pullout wearing nothing but a pair of boxer briefs. She loves the way he looks when he sleeps on his stomach. The muscular dips and curves of his back. The way his skin feels smooth against her hand. His delicious smell.

Finally, she kicks the covers off and stares at the ceiling, debating with herself.

He wants you to go down to him, the devil on her shoulder says. *So you should go.*

What if his parents catch you? the angel replies. *You don't want to risk that.*

They won't catch you, the devil says. *Everyone's asleep.*

And then the devil shows her Liam's neck. Why she finds his neck so erotic, she'll never know, but she does. It's perfect. Masculine, but not brutish. And it connects to his incredible shoulders and then down to that hard chest.

She swallows as desire moves through her limbs.

The devil appears to be winning.

It's okay to want to go to him, because he's the man you love.

And that appears to be the clincher, the thing that gets her out of bed and walking quietly to her door.

Slowly, she opens it, trying not to make any noise. His parents' bedroom door is shut. Thank goodness. Stepping out into the hall, she turns and quietly closes the door behind her.

For a long moment, she remains still. Waiting. Her pulse pounding in her ears.

She bites her lip and then creeps slowly along. It's dark and unfamiliar. Moving at a snail's pace, she tries not to make a sound.

There's a loud creak when she reaches the top stair. An explosion in the silence, startling her. She stops and holds her breath.

Maybe she shouldn't have listened to that devil.

But there are no other sounds or movement in the house, so she continues to inch her way down the steps one at a time.

She prays there are no security cameras watching her, that Liam was only making that up. The thought of his father's stern expression studying her on some surveillance tape as she sneaks around almost makes her hightail it back up to the guest bedroom.

Eventually she walks through the kitchen and then down the second set of stairs, toward the closed family room door.

She opens it into a dark room. There's an outline of the couch that's been turned into a bed. Liam's on it. He's sitting up.

"You came," he whispers, sounding pleased.

"I guess I'm just crazy enough," she whispers back.

She senses his smile. "My wild girl."

Moving closer, she climbs onto the springy mattress, which creaks and dips beneath her. Liam reaches out to help her.

"I'm going to die of embarrassment if your parents catch us together."

"Don't worry, they won't."

"That's what all guys say."

He laughs softly as he strokes her leg. "I wish I could see you better. Do you mind if I turn the lamp on?"

"Are you crazy? Don't you dare."

"All right, fine. I'll use my imagination."

She sighs and lies next to him. He pulls her into his arms, and the desire moving through her is as thick and sweet as honey.

"I'm happy you came to me," he says, but it's the last thing he says before his mouth comes down hot and hungry on hers.

She kisses him back with the same heat, pulling him close. Her need for him has eclipsed everything, even her common sense. Passion moves through her, unleashing itself, touching every part of her body and mind.

Liam groans when he slides his fingers between her thighs and discovers how wet she is, how turned on.

"Don't make noise," she whispers, admonishing him.

He swallows. "I'm trying."

Despite her worries about getting caught, Tori's glad she snuck down. Very glad. When Liam tells her to scoot up and sit on his face, she does it without hesitation.

Right away her eyes fall shut. As soon as his mouth is on her, she sighs. She knows she won't come, but she doesn't care.

She wants it anyway.

He strokes her body all over, dirty and sweet at the same time. She lets herself enjoy how patient he is, how giving.

She's never felt so cherished or loved before. Not with anyone.

And that's when the strangest thing happens. All those good feelings seem to mingle together. The love and the sex. A swirl of kaleidoscopic colors.

She's been dancing on the edge for so long. Forever. She's used to it, but this time, there's something new. This time, for the first time, she's falling... down... down.... She gasps as it all rushes through her.

Oh my God, I'm coming!

With Liam!

She cries out with pleasure and disbelief.

Below her, he's groaning and gripping her hips with both hands, fully aware of what's happening as it goes on and on.

She's shaking as she comes off that high.

When she's done, he moves away briefly and switches on the lamp beside them, filling the room with a golden light.

"I did it!" She laughs. Tears stream down her face. "Can you believe it? I finally did it!"

He sweeps her into his arms. "I love you," he says fiercely, hugging her tight.

"I love you too." Pure joy floods her veins.

They pull apart, and she's still crying and laughing at the same time.

"You should see yourself right now," he says with wonder. "So beautiful."

"That was amazing. I've never felt so close to anyone. Not like this."

He strokes her hair. "Me either."

She meets his gaze. Tenderness wells up inside her as more tears flow. "Liam Castillo, I want you to know, you're the best thing that's ever happened to me."

His face changes. The emotion there is stark and raw, beyond words. And then he kisses her with passion, trembling, holding her still with his hands.

Breaking away, he scoots back and shoves pillows behind him before reaching for her. "Come here, rubia," he breathes. "I want to be even closer to you."

She does as he asks, straddling him. He holds her hips, thrusting up at the same time she sinks down. They both moan as erotic shock waves spiral through them.

"That's it," he says roughly as they move together. "*God*, just like that."

It's so perfect. They're so right together. She never wants it to end and hopes it goes on forever.

But then somewhere in the middle of all this perfection, there's a noise.

"Wait, stop." She turns her head.

"What?" Liam's mouth's open, panting.

But then he must hear it too because he does stop. They both listen as someone walks around upstairs in the kitchen.

"Do you think they heard us?" she whispers.

He's still listening. "No." He swallows, then tries to catch his breath. "They didn't hear us."

Whoever's upstairs appears to be getting themselves a midnight snack.

Tori's arms are on Liam's shoulders, and she caresses him. Down his back. His muscles tense all over, covered in a sheen of sweat. Even his hair's damp.

"What should we do?" she whispers. "Should we stop?"

His hands tighten on her hips. Their eyes meet. His are so dark, they're black. And in that moment, he's very male. It seems difficult for him to speak. "I don't...." He licks his lips. "I don't want to stop."

She strokes his jaw, and his eyes close. She senses the way he's struggling with himself for control. "We have to be quiet, then."

He nods. "We will be."

Tori doesn't reply, but she knows he's waiting for her. "Okay."

His breath shakes on an exhale, and then he's pulling her tight onto him, onto where he's still hard inside her. She nearly moans out loud anyway. It's so good. He grips her hips and thrusts up, the two of them moving together like before.

They keep at it, quietly sharing this sensual experience. Liam slips his arms around her, one hand on her ass. She hugs him close. His scent all over her like an erotic musk.

"God, Tori...." His breath is hot against her neck. "You feel amazing."

They continue this way, lost in the bliss of each other. Their hearts pounding. Until finally his breath hitches.

His arms tighten around her as he increases the pace. There's an excitement building in her too. He must sense it, because he reaches down and slips his fingers between her thighs, touching her.

She nearly groans, nearly comes out of her skin, but he covers her mouth with his own. Her climax overtakes her like a storm. Their mouths stay glued together, and he moves faster, thrusting hard. So close. He gasps, and then she feels him deep inside her, filling her, his body taut with ecstasy.

Afterward, neither of them moves or speaks. They stay wrapped in each other's arms, his heart still hammering against hers.

"I'm so happy," she says, filled with joy and disbelief. "You make me so happy."

He whispers in her ear, "You make me happy too."

CHAPTER TWENTY-EIGHT

A SEA OF BLISS. That's what Tori's life has become. Every day she's floating in warm turquoise waters.

"And I thought we were spending a lot of time together before," she says, stretching out next to Liam as they both relax in her bed.

It's been a week since they visited his parents in Portland. Currently, it's a normal Thursday night, which means they're naked and sweaty after another round of the best sex ever. Faking orgasms seems like a lifetime ago, because now it's all so easy. A living dream. She's never loved anyone like this, never felt so loved and cherished in return.

"We were amateurs back then," he explains, drawing her close. Their bodies tangled up in each other's. "We've turned pro."

She laughs. "This feels like an addiction. I can't get enough of you." He starts singing the song "Addicted to Love," and she rolls her eyes. "Wow, you're so corny."

"Hey, you're the eighties aficionado."

"Hello? Is that a hair band? I don't think so."

"I see. So you have your limits."

Stroking his cheek, she smiles. "Don't worry, I love you even though you're a cornball."

"And I love you even though you listen to Poison."

"My music's not poison."

"I'm talking about the band."

She giggles, and they gaze at each other. This is what they do. Tease and play around, have endless sky-rocket sex, and tell each other "I love you" at least fifty times a day.

"Our brains are swimming in a brew of dopamine and oxytocin," she informs him. "I happened to read about it in a magazine recently."

"So we're high on love drugs, huh?" He trails his fingertips down her arm, a thoughtful expression on his face.

"Even Blair said we were annoying to be around." They had dinner with Blair and Road last night. The tables have turned, since usually Tori was the one getting annoyed with them.

"All we did was hold hands," Liam says. "And I guess I kissed you a few times."

"And then I fed you some of my enchiladas, and you fed me some of your burrito." She pauses and laughs. "Gee, that sounds dirty."

He grins. "For the record, I'm always happy to taste your enchilada."

"Oh, *you*." She pushes his shoulder and pretends to act coy, and then they go back to gazing at each other.

That's the other thing they do. His brown eyes have become her happy place. So rich and warm. Every time she looks into them, she knows she's finally found him. Her special person. The one.

"I hit a home run with you," he whispers.

"You keep saying that."

"Because it's true. You mean the world to me. Everything."

She caresses his jaw. "You're my everything too."

Tori knows it's all over the top and doesn't care. She's never experienced anything even close to this. The new landscape of her life is filled with blue skies.

The only cloud is the one that's always been there, and unfortunately, it's getting darker.

Her mom's been calling her every other night, drunk and speaking gibberish. She wants to know if Tori's still involved with that "fucking fed," and when Tori says she is, her mom goes off on a crazy nonsensical rant.

She's managed to keep the whole thing hidden from Liam. Doesn't want it to spoil what they have.

Just business as usual.

Hiding the truth about her mom has been a way of life so long, it's all she's ever known.

Tori went over there twice last week, right after they got back from Portland, trying to convince her mom to stop seeing Wayne. Unfortunately, she was too drunk to listen to reason.

She's trying again tomorrow, planning to be there when her mom comes home from work while she's still sober.

"Hey, what is it?" Liam asks, tracing her hairline in that way he does. "You've got that look again."

It's not easy keeping a secret from someone she's this intimate with, not to mention someone who's a trained professional at catching a lie.

She shakes her head. "It's nothing. I'm fine."

"Are you sure?"

"Yes." She scoots closer and grins. "But if you don't mind, I'd like to taste a very particular Mexican dish."

He grins and opens his arms. "My burrito is all yours."

LIAM WISHES Tori would tell him what's bothering her. He's certain it has something to do with her mom. Probably her drinking. She wears the same expression every time her mom comes up in conversation, so he recognizes it.

He doesn't push though. He figures she'll tell him eventually.

The two of them are in sync in every other way. All the women he's been with in the past seem inconsequential now. In some ways it's like he was a different person back then, living another life.

Their relationship has grown even deeper since visiting his parents. It's richer. Telling her he loves her was a relief, and finding out she felt the same way was a gift. He never minded those bathroom visits, but they were obviously a big deal to her.

He has to admit, it's sexy as hell watching her climax.

At long last, his life is coming together. Not just his personal life but work too. Everything feels right, and he knows it's because of Tori. He's never been this energized, this clear-headed and in control.

Combing through Rizzo's books and meeting with witnesses, he's in the zone, connecting dots, putting pieces of this giant jigsaw puzzle together. A map of Rizzo's criminal activity has emerged, and so far this is proving to be the biggest arrest of his career. Liam's whole squad is getting accolades.

Matt and Amy invited them over for dinner and took to Tori right away, just like his parents. So far everybody likes her, except one person.

Elena.

He finally goes to his sister's house Friday after work. It's great to see Marcus and Sam. They have dinner, and then he plays catch in the backyard with the kids.

"Good try," he calls out to Sam. "But don't forget to keep your eye on the ball."

"Okay, Uncle Liam."

He throws the next one to Marcus, who catches it easily. He's older and has more practice than his brother. "Great. Now widen your stance a little before you throw it back."

They continue to play, and Liam reminds himself not to give too many instructions since he doesn't want to kill the fun.

His sister sits silently in her lawn chair on the sidelines. "You look healthy and happy," she says, watching him. "I'm guessing that Rizzo case will open up new doors for you at the bureau."

He shrugs. "Maybe. We'll see."

"I know the boys sure miss having you around."

"I've missed them too. They're welcome to come over anytime, you know that."

She remains silent, and he glances at her. There's a stubborn look on her face. His sister's a fierce advocate for those she loves, but has difficulty forgiving anyone who crosses her family.

Under normal circumstances he understands it, but this is not a normal circumstance. "How's work going?" he asks, searching for a neutral topic.

"Fine." She tells him about her new manager and how she's picked up a few more projects.

"Sounds great." He catches a ball from Marcus. "Nice throw."

"So I heard you took Tori down to meet Mom and Dad."

He nods. "That's right. I did."

"Apparently they like her."

"They do."

"Unbelievable." She snorts. "She's fooled everyone."

"Let's not go there again," he says. "Seriously. I'd like to have a pleasant evening."

She seems to wrestle with something. "Look, whatever you do, just don't marry her, okay?"

He doesn't reply, only retrieves the ball Sam threw.

Elena stares at him with wide eyes. "Oh my God, please don't tell me you're thinking about marriage."

"I'll tell you the same thing I told Dad." He meets her angry expression. "This is it for me. Tori's the one."

"BABY GIRL," her mom says with surprise when she comes home to see Tori waiting on the front steps for her. "What are you doing here?"

"I came to have dinner with you." She picks up the bag of groceries she got for her mom on the way over.

"That's so sweet. Come on inside."

The bag's filled with the kind of TV dinners her mom likes. She also bought her fruit, salad mix, and a variety of smoothies. "Is Wayne coming over?"

"No, he's out of town on business." Her mom unlocks the door and they both enter.

Tori's relieved he won't be here. She follows her mom into the kitchen, noticing how all the new furniture and stuff has brought its own scent. The house smells like cigarettes, but something foreign too.

As usual, her mom is dressed like she's filming an office porno. Tight pencil skirt and a low-cut top. Four-inch platform pumps. Her blonde hair's teased up high at the crown. It doesn't usually bother Tori, but today it makes her sad. It's like her mom's always trying so hard, always wants to maintain this image of glamour.

But for what? Guys like Wayne?

"I wanted to talk to you about something," Tori says, unloading the groceries.

"Please tell me you're dumping that FBI boyfriend." She reaches for the bottle of whiskey and pours a good amount into a glass.

"No, I'm not."

"You're making a mistake." Tasting her drink, she puts it down and adds sugar and a squeeze of lemon. "I wish you'd listen to me. You can't trust a person like that."

"You need to stop seeing Wayne."

Her mom laughs. "Why would I do that?"

"You *know* why."

"I have no idea what you're talking about."

Tori sighs and glances around the kitchen. She spots a new blender in the corner. A fancy one there's no way her mother could afford.

"He's a thief, isn't he? A smuggler too."

Her mom stops what she's doing and turns toward her. "Where did you hear that?"

Tori doesn't answer. Instead, she studies her mom, disturbed by what she finds. Her eyes are bloodshot with deep lines around them. Her skin color is uneven and sallow. The woman she grew up with, who was once so beautiful, looks old and wrung out.

"Who told you that?" she demands to know. "Did that fed say something to you?" Her words slur slightly, and Tori blinks at her with surprise. She sounds like she's been drinking, but she's only had a sip of that whiskey sour.

With worry, her eyes flash to her mom's purse. For all her problems with alcohol, the one rule her mom seemed to stick with was staying sober at her job. "Were you drinking at work today?"

"What? Don't be ridiculous."

Tori reaches for the purse sitting on the counter.

"What are you doing?"

"Is there a bottle in here?"

"Of course not. Get your hands off that." Her mom tries to grab it, but she isn't fast enough. "You have no right to go through my things!"

Tori ignores her and reaches inside the bag while her mom rants hysterically.

"It's that fucking boyfriend of yours, isn't it? This is what happens when you let someone like that into your life. No respect for your family!"

Right away, Tori feels the small bottle and pulls it out. It's vodka.

Her mom shakes her head. "It's just temporary. You don't know what I've been going through lately. The kind of stress I'm under."

"This is crazy. Your drinking is out of control." She goes over to the sink with the bottle. "We need to get you some help, but first you have to stop seeing Wayne. He's nothing but trouble."

To her surprise, her mom bursts out crying. "*Oh my God.* If I'd known, I would have stopped him."

"What are you talking about?" She dumps the vodka down the drain.

"That's why I've been so stressed. It's the guilt. You have to believe me when I tell you I'm so sorry, baby girl."

"Sorry about what?"

"You haven't figured it out?" She takes a shaky breath. "Mable."

"What about her?"

"Wayne's the one who took her."

Tori freezes. It's one thing to suspect something, but another to have it confirmed. "He told you that?"

"He found the keys. But he only said he would borrow her. If I'd known what he was going to do, I'd never have let him!"

Her head swims. Ironically, Mable being stolen was the one thing that made her doubt Wayne was a thief. I mean, why steal from his girlfriend's daughter and create a trail back to himself? "What keys?" Tori asks. "I never gave you keys to Mable."

Her mom nods and appears nervous. "You did. Right after you got her."

Tori leans back against the counter, feeling queasy. She'd forgotten her mom had a set of keys. "How could you let him take her? You put Wayne before *me*?"

"No, baby girl. I would never."

"But you *did*."

"He was only borrowing her, that's all."

"He lit her on fire." Tori's face grows hot. "Did you know that? Did you know her interior was a burned-out shell?"

"I'm so sorry." Her mom cries. "I never wanted to hurt you."

"Why didn't you break up with him?"

Her mom tears off a paper towel and dabs her face. "He said it was an accident. That one of his guys did it before he could stop him."

"And you believed that?"

"It was just a big misunderstanding. The insurance paid you, right? He told me they would." Wiping her eyes, there's a hopeful note in her voice as she moves closer. "And now you have Samantha." She tries to stroke her daughter's ponytail, but Tori jerks away.

"Don't touch me." She pushes back from the counter. It feels like her head is going to explode. Her chest is tight and painful. "I have to get out of here. I can't breathe."

Her mom follows her to the door. "You can't tell anyone about this, you understand? Especially not that boyfriend of yours. Wayne could get in a lot of trouble."

"I don't give a shit about Wayne."

Her mom's hand flies out and grabs Tori's arm, her fingers tight. "This is serious. Promise me you won't say anything. I could get in trouble too."

"Let go of me."

"Promise first."

Tori studies her mom's tired and worn-out face. She knows it wasn't easy for her raising three kids as a single mother. Times were tough, and money was tight. And then there was the endless succession of men. Nobody wanted to stick around.

"Promise me." Her mom's voice rises with panic. "You have to promise!"

Deep down, Tori's always been scared she'd wind up exactly like her.

"Please, baby girl."

She tries to take a breath, but it hurts. *"Fine.* I promise."

TORI TRIES to stay calm as she heads home in Samantha, tries to catch her breath though she's shaking all over. There's a text from Liam reminding her he's going to a baseball game tonight with Road and Brody.

She pulls over to finish reading it.

It'll run late. Do you still want me to come over afterward?

She hesitates. It's Friday, and normally she'd say yes, but she doesn't want him to see her like this. *I'm going to turn in early tonight. I'll just see you tomorrow.*

Everything okay?

I'm fine. Have fun tonight. I love you.

I love you more.

Her gaze lingers over his words.

By the time she arrives home, she's full-on crying and can barely see the road. She's furious at Wayne for stealing Mable. Furious at her mom's part in this whole mess.

After feeding her animals their dinner, Tori takes a long, hot bath. She tries to work on her knitting but then watches TV instead. Wrapped in her bathrobe, surrounded by her dogs, she tries to figure out what to do.

She's gone through plenty of hard times with her mom. Times where her drinking got worse. Times with asshole men. Somehow they've gotten through them all, and they'll get through this too.

A little after eleven, there's a knock on her front door. She's startled by it. *Who could that be?*

A freaky thought comes to her. *What if it's Wayne?* What if her mom said something to him, and now he wants to make sure she keeps quiet?

Holding her breath, she slowly pushes a corner of the living room curtain aside.

The first thing she sees is Liam's black truck parked behind her minivan.

Thank God.

She goes over to open the door. Even though she told him not to come over, she's glad he did anyway.

"You're here," she says, nearly crying at the sight of him.

"Is this all right? I wanted to make sure you're okay. I'll go if you want me to—" He stops talking as he takes in her expression. "What is it?"

She only shakes her head.

He steps inside and closes the door behind him, and the next thing she knows, she's wrapped in his arms. Surrounded by the smell of popcorn and mustard from the ballpark, she starts crying again.

They wind up on the couch. She tries to stop, but it's all bubbling to the surface, ready to spill over.

"What's wrong?" he asks. He kisses her cheek and then her lips. "Tell me. You can tell me anything."

Her mouth opens. The words are right there on the tip of her tongue. All of them.

"Is it your mom?"

She nods. A hiccup escapes her.

"Her drinking?"

"Yes." Her breath trembles as she tries to speak. "It's bad. She's been drinking at work." She hiccups again.

"You have to get her into rehab, Tori. She needs help."

The dogs have gathered around, and she puts her hand out and pets each of them. She suddenly remembers Mable and how she brought all her dogs home for the first time in that shiny blue minivan.

Liam's watching her closely. "Is there something else?"

"No." She swallows and shakes her head. No matter what's happened, she can't rat out her own mother.

He strokes her back over the robe. "I know you said she doesn't want help, but maybe I could go over and talk to her."

This almost makes Tori smile. She reaches for a tissue from the box on her coffee table. "That's sweet of you to offer, but I think you're the last person she'd listen to."

"Are you sure? I can be very convincing."

She takes a breath and wipes her nose. "Not in this situation. Let me work on her, or maybe I can ask Road to help." She glances over at him, hoping to change the subject. "How was the baseball game tonight? Did you guys have fun?"

"Yeah, we had a good time." He tells her more about the game.

Tori's glad he's getting along with her brother and Brody. It sounds like they're becoming friends.

Later, when they're in bed together, he brings her a spoonful of peanut butter to help with the hiccups. "Thanks." She smiles at him. "I love you."

"I love you too."

She licks the spoon. "Why did you come over tonight? How did you know I was upset?"

He lies down, propping his head up on his hand. "It was your text. There were no emojis or exclamation marks."

"What do you mean?"

"You always text me with lots of hearts and kissy faces. When you sent me that plain text, I realized something wasn't right."

This had never occurred to her. She takes in Liam's handsome features as she finishes the last of her peanut butter. The sharp intelligence behind those brown eyes. A sense of unease settles over her. "You don't miss much, do you?"

"No, I don't."

TORI HAS A FITFUL NIGHT. Strange dreams. Dreams about Mable and Wayne, and a blowtorch. Even after Liam makes love to her, the dreams are still there.

Sometime during the early morning hours, she finally falls into a deep sleep. When she wakes up, Liam is in bed beside her, barechested and reading his Kindle.

"Hey, sleepyhead." He smiles over at her. "I'm glad you finally got some rest."

She scoots closer to him, and he lifts his arm so she can wrap herself around his warm body. "What time is it?" she murmurs, snuggling against him.

"Almost noon."

"*What?*" She lifts her head in alarm. "I have to feed everyone!

They must be starving." Surprisingly, the only dogs on the bed are Miss Fancy Pants and Tommy Lee, both of them snoozing contentedly.

"Don't worry, I gave them all breakfast." He thumbs his Kindle to turn the page.

"You did?"

"Sure. I've seen you do it enough times."

"What about Lita and Joan?"

"Them too."

"Really?"

He chuckles. "I'm not completely useless."

"I guess not," she teases, then hugs him tight. "Wow, I can't believe I slept so late."

"I'm not surprised. It seemed like you were tossing and turning all night."

She thinks back to her terrible dreams, but she doesn't want to talk about those.

They both go quiet after that, and she lets her eyes drift shut. Liam strokes her hair absentmindedly while he continues to read.

Tori listens to the steady beat of his heart. It soothes her soul, relaxing her.

It's a lazy Saturday, and the summer sun shines clean and bright. Someone's mowing their lawn in the distance. Her bedroom window's open, and she imagines all her problems floating away on a breeze.

This moment.

If she could capture it in a bottle, she would. And whenever she's lost or sad, she could open it and remember how peaceful and loved she once felt.

"Uh-oh. I just realized something."

"What's that?" he murmurs, still playing with her hair.

She turns her face toward his. "I've been awake fifteen minutes, and we haven't said 'I love you' yet."

He gazes down at her with mock concern. "Damn, you're right.

We're slipping." His dark eyes stay on hers. "I love you, rubia," he whispers.

"I love you too."

She sighs and hugs him close again. Miss Fancy Pants picks up on the good vibes and comes over so Tori can pet her.

"What are you reading?" she asks, glancing up at his Kindle.

"*Edge of Zen.*"

"My brother's book?"

"It was a best seller. I have to admit, it's good."

Tori stares at him with amazement. "What's happening here? Are you and Road becoming BFFs?"

He laughs. "I don't know about that. It turns out he's an interesting guy though."

"I suppose I should be glad you're getting along."

"You should. That reminds me, I'm going to a batting cage to hit some balls with him and Brody soon."

"Wow, I think Hell just froze over."

They lounge around for a while longer, but Tori gets restless. She goes to check on her animals, who are all out in the backyard enjoying the sun. Since it's so nice out, she works in the yard for a while, weeding around her garden, trimming all the various herbs she grows.

Liam joins her outside, mowing her front and backyard. She makes a big pitcher of iced tea and brings him a glass, figuring he could use one.

"Thanks," he says. She watches his throat work as he drinks half of it down.

"Why did you put your shirt back on? It was a treat watching you get all sweaty."

"Because I seem to have acquired an audience." He motions over her shoulder.

"You have?" Tori turns and sees her neighbor Mrs. Waligorski having drinks on the back deck with three of her lady friends.

They've positioned their chairs with a clear view of Liam. "Hello," she calls over.

Mrs. Waligorski grins, and all the ladies wave.

"It's their monthly book club meeting. They've invited me to a few of them." What she doesn't tell him is they read some pretty racy books in that club.

When the evening rolls around, they take a shower together and then go out for dinner and a movie like a normal dating couple.

"Look at you, so pretty," he says to her from across the table at the Italian restaurant. "I can't take my eyes off you."

"Just sexily slurping my spaghetti noodles." She bats her lashes at him.

"I love you when you eat pasta," he purrs.

"And I love you when you drink iced tea," she coos.

He picks up his glass. "I drink a lot of iced tea."

"Which means I love you all the time."

He chuckles. "Damn, we're disgusting. If I wasn't so crazy in love with you, I think I'd throw up."

"I know." She laughs. "It's revolting. You couldn't pay me to have dinner with us."

The movie is a sexy romantic comedy. They eat popcorn, laughing at all the jokes and having a great time.

"Gosh, Agent Castillo, it turns out you're the perfect date," she says as they walk to his truck afterward holding hands. It's a warm night, the sky dark and cloudless above them.

"And you're just plain perfect." He leans in and kisses her.

A glow of happiness surrounds her like the summer night.

He squeezes her hand. "What do you say we go park somewhere and make out like teenagers?"

"Sounds great."

They get back in his truck and are driving toward Seattle when her phone rings. Bon Jovi's "Living on a Prayer."

She glances at the time on his dashboard. It's almost eleven.

All her happiness drains away. A dark cloud moves in, sucking the air out of the truck's cab.

"You going to answer that?"

"Yeah." She sighs.

She's not surprised to see it's Donna. Not surprised to be told her mom and Wayne are out in the front yard screaming at each other.

"What's going on?" Liam glances over at her.

She listens as Donna tells her Wayne is throwing beer bottles at the house. "Please don't call the cops. I'll be there shortly."

"Just let her call the police," he insists. "They can handle it."

"No." Tori puts her phone back in her purse. "I don't want the police involved. Could you take me home, and I'll go deal with this?"

"I'll take you there."

"That's not necessary."

Liam pulls his truck over into a strip mall parking area and turns to face her. "Look, there's no way in hell I'm letting you go there alone."

Tori tries to take a deep breath, but her chest feels tight. "Please, just take me home. I prefer to handle it on my own."

"Why?" He studies her. "Why would you argue about this? It makes no sense."

"I just think my mom will be easier to deal with if I'm alone. She'll freak out if she sees you."

"And what about Wayne?"

She shifts uncomfortably. "He's mostly harmless."

"Mostly?" Liam puts the truck in gear. "Forget it, I'm coming." He drives toward her mom's. She's tempted to keep arguing but knows it will seem weird.

As he pulls into her mom's neighborhood, a dark blue minivan speeds past them.

Tori's mouth drops open. She catches a glimpse of the driver and is certain it was Wayne.

She flashes over to Liam and sees how he's watching the van in his rearview mirror.

When they pull up to her mom's house, things are surprisingly quiet. Her mom's sitting outside on her front steps, barefoot and dressed in what looks like a slip. She has her face in her hands.

They both get out of the truck and walk toward her.

"Mom, are you okay?"

She lifts her head, bleary-eyed, crying, and definitely wasted. "Baby gurrl. You came back."

Guilt eats through Tori for the way she ran out of here yesterday. She knows she had every right to be upset, but this is still her mom, and she doesn't want her to be sad. "Come on, I'll help you up."

"He left me," her mom says, fumbling as Tori tries to help her stand. "Wayne's gone. Says he doesn't want me anymore."

"Everything's going to be okay."

"That thieving bastard!" she yells, lashing out at the night. "You think I want all your stolen shit in my house? Take it back. I don't care!"

"Let's get you inside," Tori says quickly, trying to cover up her mom's words. She doesn't dare look at Liam. "You're just angry and talking nonsense."

Her mom sees him behind her and glares. "What are *you* looking at?"

"I'm here for Tori," he says quietly.

"You're the damn problem," she says, her speech slurring. "My daughter needs to stay away from men like *you*."

Tori gets her mom inside the house and guides her toward the bedroom. When she glances back at Liam, he's following her. "I've got this," Tori tells him. "I'm just going to put her to bed."

He nods, looking around the house.

It takes a lot of coaxing and a few lies, but Tori finally manages to get her mom to lie down. As usual, she rolls her on her side and tucks pillows and blankets behind her in case she throws up.

After washing her hands, Tori goes back out to the living room to find Liam sitting on the couch.

"I'm going to have to stay over," she tells him. "I can't leave her alone when she's this bad."

He doesn't say anything.

"You can go home. I'll call you tomorrow."

A strange vibe's coming off him. When he meets her eyes, there's a hardness she doesn't recognize.

"What is it?" she asks.

His voice is quiet when he speaks, though his words are louder than a gunshot. "How long have you known this was going on?"

CHAPTER TWENTY-NINE

"WHAT DO YOU MEAN?" Tori asks, panic shooting through her as she feigns innocence.

"Don't." Liam shakes his head. His dark eyes are serious on hers. "Don't do that."

The room is dim, but he doesn't turn on the lamp.

Dread fills her like black poison. She takes a seat on the couch. Normally she'd sit right next to him, but this time she sits on the opposite end.

"One day," she finally says. "That's how long I've known. That's why I was crying last night."

He's quiet, considering this. "Why didn't you tell me?"

"Because I was scared." She's shaking inside, but sits up straight. "I still am. I don't want anything bad to happen to my mom."

"When did all this new stuff show up here?"

"A while ago."

"How long is a while?"

Tori hesitates, then tells him, "Last month. Right before our trip to the lake."

He nods, his expression grim. "All those questions about a person not reporting a crime. That's why you were asking?"

"Yes." Despite the dread, a part of her is relieved that she doesn't have to keep this secret anymore. "I suspected something was going on, but I didn't know for sure."

"And why is it you know for sure now?"

Tori shifts uncomfortably. "Do I need a lawyer?"

He stares at her. "No, you don't. Just tell me the truth."

"Wayne is the one who stole Mable. I found out yesterday."

"How?"

She goes quiet. "My mom told me."

"Jesus." Liam rubs his forehead. "You should have said something to me. The minute you suspected him, you should have said something."

"What are you going to do?"

"What I have to. I'm going to arrest Wayne."

"No!" She moves closer on the couch. "You can't. My mom will get in trouble. She could go to jail."

"She should have thought of that before she got involved with a criminal."

Adrenaline rockets through her. "This is why I didn't tell you! I didn't want anything bad to happen to her."

"I can't believe you've kept this secret the whole time. I sensed there was something, but I thought it was your mom's drinking."

"She's my family. I have to protect her."

"You're enabling her, Tori."

"Don't say that. I hate that word!" She smacks the couch cushion. "Is it enabling to help someone when they need it? To take care of them when they're sick?"

"Yes, sometimes it is. Your mom's never gotten help for her problem because she doesn't have to face the consequences. She has you to fix everything."

"I'm all she's got."

"It's a burden she never should have placed on you."

"Please don't do this," she begs. "Can't you just pretend you never heard or saw anything?"

His grim expression turns even more bleak. "How can you ask me that?" Those brown eyes that have become her happy place are troubled. "You know I can't do that."

"Why? It doesn't hurt anyone."

"Crime always hurts someone. I have to do what's right. This is my job."

"What if it were me? What if I were the one in trouble? Would you still turn me in?"

"Don't make me answer that." He shakes his head and lets his breath out. "God knows what the hell I would do if it were you, but it's *not* you."

And then in a blind panic, Tori says something she knows is wrong even as the words leave her mouth. "If you loved me, you wouldn't do this."

She sees the wounded look on his face, the hurt her words are causing him. "*If* I loved you? You think I don't love you?"

The black poison is still there, except now it's taken over her mind, consumed her thoughts, so there's nothing left but fear. "I don't know. Do you?"

"I've never loved anyone like this."

"Then prove it."

They stare at each other.

She takes a shaky breath, hysteria rising within her. "You said you'd do anything for me, remember?"

He seems dazed. "I don't even know who you are right now." His expression turns desolate. "I can't believe you'd ask this of me. That you'd ask me to be the kind of man I'm not."

TORI LOADS the washing machine and then continues cleaning her mom's house. It's two in the morning, but she has to keep busy so she doesn't freak out.

Liam left over an hour ago.

Things were bad between them.

Worse than bad.

That black poison has polluted her whole world. It's all she sees now.

She knows she shouldn't have said what she did, but she was desperate and panicked. If Wayne goes down, her mom goes with him. Like rats on a sinking ship.

"What if it were *your* mom? Would you turn her in?" she asked him before he left. "I'll bet you wouldn't."

"These questions are nonsense. My mother doesn't have a drinking problem, and she'd never associate with known criminals."

"Please don't do it. She made a mistake with Wayne, that's all. Are you really so coldhearted?"

"Listen to me." His voice deepened, cutting through the room. His FBI voice. "After Wayne's arrested, she'll need a lawyer. You should get her one now."

"She can't afford a lawyer!"

His expression turned even more grim.

"I can't believe this is happening! You're making me choose between my mom and *you*?"

"No, I'm not. You're the one turning it into that. Like always, you're only believing what you want to believe."

"But how can we be together if you do this? I can't betray her!"

"It's my job, Tori. If you can't handle that, then maybe we shouldn't be together."

They were both silent.

It wasn't long before he left.

She goes to check on her mom. There's vomit on the side of the bed. Tori cleans it up as best as she can and then places a clean towel over it. She'll wash the sheets tomorrow.

"Baby gurrl." Her mom's words slur. "Where's the... fuzz?"

Thinking she's referring to Liam, Tori tells her he's gone.

"Good. Can't trust them," she mumbles. "Look at... Lance. My own brother." She mumbles something more, but Tori can't make out her words. She has no idea how this has anything to do with Lance, who's been gone for years.

When she was a kid, she used to sleep in her mom's bed sometimes. She'd sit there awake all night, watching her mom, terrified she was going to stop breathing.

While she doesn't do that anymore, she still checks on her regularly.

After cleaning the kitchen, she's tempted to vacuum but knows that's too loud, so she scrubs the bathroom instead. She replays the conversation with Liam in her head. The stony expression on his face when he left.

It was awful.

Like they were strangers.

Her hands shake when she scrubs the sink and bathtub. Her vision blurry with tears. She thinks about her dogs and hopes they're okay all night. In the past, she's called Blair to help, but it's too late for that.

Eventually Tori collapses onto the living room couch. Surrounded by the smell of stale cigarettes and stolen furniture, she falls into a restless sleep, waking up every hour confused and crying.

The next morning, as usual, she helps her mom deal with her hangover. Gives her a smoothie and then sadly watches as she sneaks into the kitchen to add vodka to it. Her mom seems to have little memory of last night's events. Tori decides not to tell her about the conversation with Liam. There's no reason to upset her now.

When she finally makes it home and takes a shower, Tori lies on her bed. There's a hollow feeling inside her. Empty and dark. At least her dogs seem fine and are gathered around her, including Miss Fancy Pants, who's still here since she stays over with Liam so much.

She already misses him.

But I can't think like that.

Instead she calls Road, figuring he needs to know there's a storm brewing. To her surprise, he already knows.

"You do?"

"Liam called this morning and explained what's happening."

"Did he tell you they're probably going to arrest Mom?"

Her brother sighs. "Yeah, he told me it was a possibility. That we need to get her a lawyer."

"What did you say?"

"Said I appreciated the heads-up, and that I'd find someone."

"Are you kidding me? You were grateful to him?" Tori is furious. How dare Liam act like he's being helpful. "He's the reason all this is happening! He's not on our side."

"I don't think it's a matter of taking sides."

"Of course it is. I can't believe you don't see that." The tears come back, and all she can think about is how she's spent a lifetime trying to help her mom, to protect her, and now this happens.

After she hangs up, she notices a text from Liam, and her pulse jumps.

I'm going into work today. Do you mind if I stop by afterward and pick up Fancy?

I heard you called Road.

I thought he should know.

Tori's breath shakes as her thumbs fly over the keyboard. *Are you really doing this?? Really???*

There's a long pause.

This isn't about you and me, though I know you see it that way. But I don't have a choice.

You always have a choice.

He's probably already put the wheels in motion for Wayne's arrest. He obviously doesn't care about her mom at all.

Tori types some more. *I'll just bring Miss Fancy Pants to your house today like when I dog sat.*

There's no way she wants to see him face-to-face. It'll only upset her.

There's another long pause from him, and she nearly puts her phone down, but then he answers.

If that's the way you want it.

THE NEXT COUPLE weeks are like something from a nightmare. Wayne's arrested by the feds for transporting stolen goods across state lines. There's a separate police investigation for the retail theft, so five days later, the cops arrest her mom. They confiscate all the stolen goods in the house and charge her as an accessory. She's forced to spend the night in jail. Luckily, Road already found her a lawyer, so at least she posted bond quickly.

Tori's whole life is turned upside down. Her mom's a nervous wreck, terrified she's going to prison. As a result, her drinking is even more out of control. Tori has to call her mom's work and lie, tell them she's sick with the flu so she doesn't get fired.

"It's just like old times, baby girl. You and me against the world."

She used to say that a lot when Tori was a kid, when the two of them would hang out after one of her mom's bad breakups. She'd stay home from school, and they'd eat ice cream and watch soap operas together.

"A couple of bastards did us both wrong," her mom says. "To hell with men. Who needs them, right?"

All Tori's worst fears are coming true. She brought her dogs over and has been staying at the house she grew up in, sleeping on the old couch they pulled back out from the garage, buying all the groceries and paying bills as she tries to take care of everything.

It's exhausting.

In the morning she gets up and goes through the motions of her day. And at night she cries.

And to make it all even worse, she misses Liam.

She knows she shouldn't and chastises herself, tries to focus on her anger instead. Tries to tell herself she's over him. Obviously he wasn't her special person despite all the intimacy they shared. If he were, he would never have made her choose.

When the weekend arrives, she packs up her clothes and dogs in Samantha to head home for a couple nights. It's a Saturday afternoon, and her mom has friends over, all of them sitting around the living room, drinking margaritas as they loudly discuss the situation.

"You should be glad that asshole fed is out of your life," Lenora, one of her mom's best friends, says to Tori as she's leaving. "See what happens when you associate with someone like that?"

All the other women shake their heads, staring at her like she should have been bright enough to know better.

"My baby girl's been helping me a lot," her mom says, coming to her defense. "It's that rat bastard Wayne who's the problem." Apparently Wayne ratted her mom out, or at least that's the conclusion everyone's come to.

This sends them all on another tirade, and Tori's relieved to get out of there.

She spends the rest of the afternoon baking Happy Pet Nanny dog snacks and then weeding her garden, trying to find peace within herself but failing. At least her dogs seem thrilled to be home. After running around the house and the backyard, they're piled up together in the living room asleep.

Tori's glad to be home too, though it reminds her too much of Liam. She thought she took all his stuff back along with Miss Fancy Pants, but she finds one of his T-shirts in her laundry hamper.

I shouldn't.

She stares at it in her hands, then holds it straight to her nose.

It smells just like him. That breezy scent.

So good.

Pain cuts through her heart.

She should throw it away. Burn it. Instead, like a criminal, she tucks it under her pillow.

The next day, Blair, Road, and Brody all come over. Tori hugs them as they enter the house.

"What's that sound?" Blair asks, holding still for a moment, listening. "Holy shit, are you listening to country music?"

"It's just a playlist I had. It's not so bad." She forgot she was going to change it before they arrived.

"Not so bad?" Blair's eyes pop out of her head. "Have you had a psychotic break?"

"Some of the songs are okay."

"I'm sure they are, but I can't picture *you* listening to them."

"I'm expanding my horizons," she says defensively. "That's all."

But then Blair's expression changes as she studies Tori with sympathy.

"There's some decent country music," Brody says, bending to pet the dogs. "Johnny Cash and Waylon Jennings are both badass."

Road shrugs. "It's not my taste, but to each his own."

The four of them wind up on the back patio. Brody informs them he has to leave in an hour.

"Are you seeing someone?" Tori asks, bringing out a pitcher of iced tea and setting it beside a plate of oatmeal cookies. She's been experimenting with the tea and came up with a new basil and raspberry flavor.

"Yeah, I guess you could say that."

"I was surprised when you brought your mom to my party last month. I thought you were bringing a date."

He leans back in his chair. "It's all kind of new, so we're still figuring things out."

"When did you get so into iced tea?" Blair asks. "Every time I come over you're drinking it."

"I don't know. I just like it, I guess." They each take a glass, except Blair, who requested ice water. Tori waits for her brother and cousin to comment on the flavor, but nobody says anything. "What do you guys think? I mixed basil and raspberries."

They say it's good, but she feels oddly disappointed and can't help thinking of Liam and how pleased he'd be. He loved all her unusual tea flavors.

After Blair's comments and her sympathetic expression, Tori switched the music back to her usual standards. Cinderella's "Gypsy Road" drifts out from the house.

The four of them eat oatmeal cookies. Road and Blair keep glancing at each other.

"What's going on?" Tori asks them.

"Yeah," Brody says. "You two are acting squirrelly."

Blair smiles and takes a deep breath. "I'm pregnant."

"Oh my God!" Tori yells and claps her hands. She jumps up and hugs them both. "Congratulations! I finally get to be an auntie."

"Thanks." Blair beams. "It's exciting." She turns and looks at Road, who's wearing a huge grin.

"Damn, you guys. That's fantastic news." Brody gets up and hugs them.

They discuss the pregnancy. It turns out Blair is still in the first trimester and nervous, though her doctor says everything looks great.

Tori is beyond thrilled. "Have you told Mom yet? It's nice to have some good news in the middle of all this bad stuff happening."

"We haven't told her yet," Road says. "Probably tell her in a few days, since it looks like there might be more good news."

"What do you mean?"

Road tells her he saw Liam recently and how he spoke to the prosecutor on their mom's case. "He thinks they're willing to lower the charges to accessory after the fact."

"You saw Liam?" Tori is stunned.

"Yeah. Since it's only a first offense, he said the prosecutor is willing to go a little easier."

"Does that mean she won't go to jail?"

"Most likely not. Sounds like she'll get probation instead. He told me to tell her lawyer to push for court-ordered rehab as part of the deal."

"Rehab? I doubt she'll go for that."

Her brother snorts. "She won't have much choice if she wants to avoid jail."

Tori fiddles with her straw. "Where did you see Liam?" She wants to ask how he looked but forces herself not to.

Road feeds a piece of oatmeal cookie to Eddie. "Brody and I hung out with him at one of the batting cages a few days ago. Grabbed a beer afterward."

"What?" She stops fiddling. "Are you kidding me? Liam arrested our mom, and you two are *socializing* with him?"

"We were practicing for the tournament," Brody tells her. "It's only three weeks away." He turns to Road. "I think we're going to nail it too. That dude's still amazing."

"Yeah, no shit," her brother agrees.

"I can't believe my own ears," Tori rants. "Where's your sense of loyalty? All you care about is Liam playing in your stupid softball game."

"Fuck yeah, I care about him playing," Brody says. "I want that gold trophy back in my garage where it belongs."

Her brother frowns. "Liam did *not* arrest Mom. The cops did."

"Close enough," she retorts. "He's the one who put the wheels in motion."

"Yes, about *Wayne*."

"I can't believe you're defending him. You used to hate him."

Brody shrugs. "Well, I sure as hell never hated him."

"I don't hate Liam for doing his job." Road looks at her, his green eyes serious. "Tori, you need to hear some hard truth. Mom got herself into this mess. Maybe you've forgotten, but she had a house full of stolen goods."

Having also been one of Wayne's victims, Tori feels bad for all the stores that were robbed. And obviously her mother never should have accepted any of that stuff, even though she claims she didn't know it was stolen at the time.

"I hear you've been staying with her," Road says. "But she's a grown woman who shouldn't need a babysitter."

"I want to help her."

"I know, but you're blaming the wrong person for all this."

"What do you mean?"

Road shakes his head. "You already know what I mean."

Tori grows quiet.

After Brody leaves, and while Road is playing fetch with her dogs in the yard, Blair scoots her chair closer and eyes Tori with sympathy. "You look tired," she says. "Are you taking care of yourself? How about I go hang out with your mom?"

"No, I can handle it. And you shouldn't be around all that cigarette smoke while you're pregnant."

"Have you thought about calling Liam? Maybe you guys could talk things out some more."

Tori watches her brother throw a rope toy she created for Happy Pet Nanny across the yard. The dogs all love it. "Why would I do that?"

"Because you told me you were in love with him."

She shrugs. "I guess I was wrong."

"I don't think you were."

"I can't believe all you guys are on his side. The irony is incredible."

Blair leans closer. "I'm on *your* side. You know that. But I never saw you so happy as when you two were together."

"I don't want to talk about this." It hurts to even think about Liam. Not that it stops her from thinking about him all the time. "You were right from the start. Once again I picked the wrong guy."

LIAM TAKES a couple of aspirin for his headache. He gets them when he doesn't sleep enough, and he hasn't slept in days. Instead, he's been throwing himself into work.

Thank God he has the Rizzo case. They've been unraveling the guy's books, and he's grateful for how complicated and arcane they are, because it helps take his mind off the giant hole in his life.

Tori.

My rubia.

By day he manages to keep busy enough, but the nights are a misery. That's when everything he misses about her comes back in a flood. That sprightly energy. Those sparkly pink nails. How she finds magic everywhere—a minivan, an herb garden, or skinny-dipping at midnight. She excites him, and yet he's never felt so peaceful. And then there's every curve on her body. Those freckles. That sexy hip sway when she walks.

He bought a bag of tangerines the other day just so he could smell them.

You can't get more pathetic than that.

He hasn't told his parents what happened yet. Doesn't want to say it aloud because then it's too real. He'd have to admit that he made a colossal mistake. That he fell in love with a woman who asked him to betray himself, to throw out his own moral compass.

On the weekends, he works from home because he feels guilty leaving Fancy alone too much. She seldom leaves his side when he's home, and he suspects she misses Tori and her crazy gang of dogs just like he does.

When Elena texts him Saturday afternoon and asks if he'd be willing to come over and watch the kids while she goes out for dinner with some friends, he readily agrees.

Except as soon as he walks in the house, his sister's expression turns concerned. "You look terrible," she says. "What's going on?"

Liam doesn't reply as he takes Fancy's leash off. The little dog looks around apprehensively. "It's okay," he murmurs to her. "We're only babysitting."

As usual, Fancy stays by his side.

"Seriously," Elena says. "Is the bureau overworking you?"

"I'm fine," he tells her. "I haven't been sleeping well."

"Why is that?"

He hesitates, wonders if he should tell Elena about Tori, knowing the news might get back to his parents. "Tori and I split up."

Elena's eyes widen.

"Go ahead," he says. "Get it over with. Tell me 'I told you so.'"

"Why did you two break up?"

"It's a long story."

"Give me the short version."

He looks around the house. "Aren't you going out for dinner?"

"We're not meeting until seven." She studies him. "Come on, I want to know what happened. I thought it was true love."

He doesn't reply.

She reaches down to pet the dog. "The boys are watching a movie, so we can talk if you want."

They wind up sitting in the living room. Fancy's beside him. Elena gave her some fresh water and dog snacks, but she doesn't seem as interested in them as she was in Tori's snacks.

He tells his sister what happened, asking that she not tell his parents. He prefers to tell them himself.

"I can't believe she asked you to ignore a crime," Elena says, appalled. "Especially one that's linked to your own case."

"I agree. It wasn't her finest moment."

"Why does it sound like you're still defending her, then? I hate to say it, but I was right about her all along."

He glances down and pets Fancy, who's resting her chin on his leg. "Because I know she did it out of loyalty to her mom."

"That doesn't excuse it."

"No, it doesn't. But it explains it." He describes how Tori was raised by a single mom who drank too much, how she feels an obligation to take care of her.

His sister puts her glass down. "I'm sorry to hear her mother's an alcoholic, but what she did was wrong. It's a betrayal of everything you stand for."

"I know."

"This makes me like her even less."

"You don't have to like her." He leans his head back on the couch and shuts his eyes. His headache is still there.

He senses his sister watching him.

"My God," she whispers. "Even after all that, you're still in love with her, aren't you?"

He doesn't answer right away. Instead, he thinks about what Tori said when she described her outlaw uncle, how people aren't black and white but shades of gray. He's always preferred to see the world as black and white. It's simpler. Cleaner. But Tori has shown him there's more.

"I've never felt like this," he says. "I can't explain it, but loving her has strengthened me. Broadened my view. I'm always my best self when I'm with her." He looks at his sister. "Have you ever had that with anyone?"

She studies him, absorbing his words. "Yes."

"Gabe?"

She nods.

"Then you're lucky to have experienced it, because I never have before. It's changed me."

Elena's expression grows thoughtful. There's a sadness there too. "You're right. That kind of love changes you forever."

CHAPTER THIRTY

TORI'S DAYS MERGE TOGETHER. Between her jobs, taking care of her mom, and the volunteer hours she puts in at the animal shelter, it's become one big blur.

She decides it's okay because it helps keep her mind off Liam. Off the way he once made her feel young, beautiful, and alive. Because now she feels old, tired, and half dead.

Nobody knows she sleeps with his T-shirt under her pillow and sniffs it every night. Or that she listens to country music and secretly enjoys it. Or that she drinks iced tea all day because it reminds her of him.

If anyone asks her how she's doing, she tells them, *"Just* peachy."

On Wednesday, while she's eating lunch at the animal hospital, she nearly chokes on her salad when she gets a text from him.

I have something I need to talk to you about. Could we meet?

She drops her fork on the floor, fumbling with her phone while her heart pounds. *What is it?*

It's better if we discuss it in person.

They agree to meet at a Starbucks near her house the next day.

First thing she does is text Blair and ask her if she's heard anything. She knows Road and Brody still see him. Their softball tournament starts in a couple of weeks.

Tori's phone buzzes in response. *No, I haven't heard anything. Maybe he wants to get back together!*

Too much has happened.

Don't say that. Look at the way he's helped with the prosecutor and the charges.

Despite her secret obsession, Tori knows it wouldn't work. It's true Liam had a hand in getting the prosecutor to lower the charges. And yes, she's glad Wayne will go to jail, but that's all. It doesn't change anything.

Liam made me choose, and I chose my mom.

The next day, she parks Samantha in front of Starbucks. She glances at her reflection in the window as she walks up to the door. It took an hour to decide what to wear this morning. In the end she wore a simple sundress with a short jean jacket and pink flip-flops. Her hair is long and wavy because she knows he likes it that way.

Starbucks is crowded as usual. Her palms sweat. She's so nervous, it's like she's having an out-of-body experience. Any second she's going to float up to the ceiling.

Looking around, she doesn't see Liam anywhere.

"Tori."

Her breath catches. He's standing in front of her in living color.

Oh my God.

Her heart nearly stops.

Those brown eyes and that sensual mouth. He's taller and hotter than she remembers, though that seems impossible.

Neither of them speaks.

Finally, he smiles. *He's beautiful.*

"I'm fine," she says.

"What?"

Her cheeks burn. *Why did I just say that? I'm already being a freak.* "I thought you said 'How are you?'"

His expression turns quizzical. "No, I didn't say that."

"Oh."

"You look pretty," he murmurs. "But you always do. Do you want to grab something to eat or drink?"

"Um, okay."

They both get in line.

He's standing behind her, and she's extremely aware of him. His wholesome Liam vibe. She turns around, and her eyes linger on his neck. On his smooth perma-tan skin. A terrible yearning burns through her.

"Tori," he says, gazing down.

"Yes," she whispers.

"It's your turn." He motions toward the register.

"Huh? Oh, right!" She moves up to the front and orders something. She's so flustered, she doesn't even know what it is. Some frothy drink that's advertised. Thankfully, she at least remembers to say almond milk.

When they finally take a seat, she's pulled herself together a little more. "So, what is this about?" she asks, trying to sound cool and collected.

He takes a sip from his hot coffee and puts it down.

"You're not drinking iced tea?" she asks.

"No."

"But I thought you switched at noon."

He smiles at that. "Not lately. I've been drinking more coffee."

And that's when she finally looks at him for real and sees what she missed before. The lines on his face are harsh. He looks tired. "Is everything okay?" But then she regrets her question, because it doesn't sound cool and collected.

"Just working a lot of late nights."

Tori remembers all the late nights they used to share, but she tries not to think about those. "How's Miss Fancy Pants?"

"She's all right." His eyes linger, roaming over her face. He doesn't seem to want to look away.

She wonders if he's going to tell her he wants to try again, that he still loves her. Despite what she told Blair, deep down she hopes he does.

"I came across something recently," he says. "And I knew I needed to talk to you."

"Oh?" She smiles a little, waiting for him to tell her he misses her, that he'd do anything to get her back. Maybe she's reading into things, but she senses regret from him. Deciding to help out, she leans forward. "I miss you too," she admits.

His eyes widen, and he seems surprised. "You miss me?"

"Yes...." She glances around. "Isn't that why you asked me here today. To try and win me back?"

He seems stunned but then regroups. "No, not exactly." He takes a deep breath. "The reason I asked you here has to do with your father."

"What?" She's taken aback.

"There's something I think you and Road should know, but I wanted to tell you first. I thought you should hear it in person."

She's starting to feel foolish. This wasn't at all what she expected. "I don't understand."

"I came across it accidentally when I was looking at your mom's arrest record. Then I looked at your uncle's record."

"What are you talking about?" There's a sinking feeling in the pit of her stomach. Obviously Liam's not trying to win her back.

His gaze is steady on hers. She remembers those brown eyes and how they used to be her happy place. How they were once so warm and cozy.

"Tori, your father was a cop."

Even though he's speaking English, it sounds like an alien language. "What?"

"His name's Daniel Church. He was a detective with the Seattle Police Department."

"That's not true." She tries to laugh. "You're mistaken. I don't know where you heard that, but you must have mixed something up."

"I didn't. And there's more. It turns out he's the one who put your uncle in prison."

She stares at him. "That's absurd."

"He was the arresting officer. The one who built the case against Lance."

Her head swims. She looks around the crowded coffee shop, trying to make sense of what he's telling her. "I don't believe you." But then she thinks about all the strange things her mom's been saying the past couple months.

"I take it your mom never told you any of this."

"No." She swallows. And then she thinks about her mom's intense hatred of cops. The way Uncle Lance always looked out for them. Why would he do that if her dad was the one who put him in jail? "That can't be true. You're confused. My dad wasn't a cop. He left when I was three and then died in a car accident."

"That's the other part." He's studying her with sympathy. "Tori, he's not dead. He lives in upstate New York."

"What?" She stares at him in shock.

"It's the truth."

"That can't be," she whispers. It would mean her mother's been lying to her all these years. "Why are you doing this? Telling me these things? Are you trying to turn me against my mom?"

"I'm not. I thought you and your brother should know."

"You're making this up." Her voice trembles. She tries to take a breath but can't. "You're lying. I don't believe you. I have to go!"

Blindly, she gets up and runs toward the door, pushing her way through the line near the front. Once outside, she stops and tries to catch her breath.

Liam is there beside her, his face stamped with worry. "Listen to me, Tori. I'm not telling you these things to hurt you. I would *never* hurt you."

"Get away from me." She nearly chokes on her sob. "Don't come near me ever again!"

SHE DOESN'T EVEN REMEMBER DRIVING to her mom's house. The shocked look on her mother's face when she confronts her.

"Is it true?"

"It's true he arrested Lance," her mom says. She's standing barefoot in the kitchen, already drinking even though it's barely past noon. "Put him in prison for years. That's the kind of man your asshole daddy was."

"You told us he died in a car accident!"

"He was dead to *me*."

Tori tries to calm down. "I had a right to know my own father."

"No, you didn't. He was a liar who betrayed me, betrayed my whole family. I know what's best for you, baby girl."

"Did he ever try to see us? Me and Road?"

She snorts. "I wouldn't let him see you. I made it difficult as hell for him, and eventually he stopped trying."

Tori's sick to her stomach. "You had no right to do that."

"I had every right. I'm your mother."

"What about us? I don't believe this. You said he was *dead*."

Her mom puts both hands on the counter and glares at her. "Who told you all this? Where did you hear it?"

"What does it matter?"

"Was it my sister?" Then her expression grows thunderous. "It's that fucking fed, isn't it? You're seeing him again, aren't you?"

"No, I'm not."

"Poisoning you against me. That's what he's doing."

"He told me the truth."

At this, her mom becomes unhinged, starts screaming. "How *dare* he? *That fucker doesn't know anything!*" Tori tries to leave, to get away, but she isn't fast enough. Her mom grabs a handful of hair and yanks her back.

"Ow!"

Before Tori knows what's happening, there are fists pummeling her, smacking and hitting her. "You don't know what I went through!" her mom continues to scream. "*My husband* arresting my own *brother!* Putting him in *prison!*"

Tori's shocked. For all her mom's faults, she's never been violent. She tries to defend herself and then finally pushes her mom away as hard as she can.

Her mom stumbles back into the refrigerator.

"All these years I've taken care of you, defended you!" Tori yells. "And all these years you've been lying to us!"

"JESUS CHRIST," Road says when Tori tells him everything she found out. He seems as shocked as she did earlier. "This is fucking nuts."

She's over at their condo in Eastlake. Apparently they got an offer on it and will be moving soon.

"So, your dad's been alive this whole time and lives in upstate New York?" Blair confirms with astonishment. She came home from work because of morning sickness and is lying on the couch. "That's crazy."

"I know," Tori says. She's still shaking from her mom's violent outburst. She hasn't told Road and Blair about it though. She doesn't want to make this whole thing worse.

"Can't believe he was a cop," Road says, still in a daze. "And that he arrested Uncle Lance."

"I know. Uncle Lance was always so good to us. I'm surprised he didn't hate us."

"No reason for him to hate us. We were just kids."

"I don't know what to think of all this." Tori shakes her head. "Finding out we have a father. What should we do?"

"Not doing anything." Her brother's expression turns hard. "This is bullshit. Where's he been all these years? He couldn't contact us?"

Tori nods. It was the same thought she had. "Maybe he is an asshole. Maybe Mom was right about that."

Her brother snorts. "There's no maybe about it."

They talk for a while, but in the end there isn't much to say. Road doesn't want to find him, says it's pointless.

Tori agrees, but deep down she isn't so sure. I mean, this is their dad. She always tried to imagine what he was like, and now to find out she could meet him and see for herself?

She leaves their place and goes to work at the animal hospital. Afterward, she heads back to her mom's. When she arrives, there are cars parked all along the street, the house full of people. Her mom's going into rehab tomorrow and has apparently decided to throw one last party.

The music's too loud for a weeknight, and Tori's already worrying about Donna. She doesn't know half the people. *To heck with this.* She gathers her overnight bag to escape and go home.

"Baby girl, stay," her mom says, acting like nothing's happened. Like she didn't attack her earlier, like a nuclear bomb didn't go off.

Tori leaves without a word.

Early the next morning, Road picks her up and they drive over to their mom's together. Of course, she's still asleep. The place is a mess. While Road rouses her from bed and tries to get some coffee into her,

Tori packs a suitcase. They'd already gotten a list of what was okay and not okay to bring.

Unsurprisingly, their mom complains the whole way there and then doesn't want to go inside. "I don't need rehab. I can stop drinking anytime I want. It's just all the stress lately."

"You don't have a choice," her brother says. "It's rehab or jail."

"This *is* jail," she grumbles, but gets out of the car.

Eventually they get her admitted and a counselor speaks to them both, tells them they won't be allowed to visit for two weeks. She also tells them about group meetings and other support that's available for family members. Road doesn't pay much attention, but Tori listens.

That night, as she's sitting in bed with all her animals curled up around her, a text pops up. It's Liam.

Are you okay?

She studies his message. She was so furious at him yesterday.

Another message from him appears. *I know I'm the last person you want to hear from, but I've been worried about you.*

She responds. *I'm all right.* She tells him how her mom went into rehab this morning. How she's still trying to wrap her head around all this stuff with her dad. *It's been a lot to process.*

I didn't mean to upset you, but I thought you'd want to know.

I'm glad you told me. I'm sorry for the way I acted.

They text a little longer. She's exhausted though and finally says she's going to sleep.

Good night, rubia.

Her eyes sting when she sees her nickname. A wave of longing washes through her.

Over the next couple of weeks, while her mom is in rehab getting the help she needs, something shifts inside Tori. She makes changes too. She slows down. Signs up for fewer volunteer hours, fewer work hours, and tries to give herself some breathing room.

For the first time in her life, she doesn't have to take care of her mom, and it's freeing in a way she never would have thought.

She starts going to meetings for people who have family and

friends who are alcoholics. She begins to see how she's not alone, and how so many things she's always thought were normal aren't.

Her whole world view is changing. Everything's always fallen on her shoulders, but she's learning that it doesn't have to be that way.

As she's working in her garden early one evening, her dogs start barking at the front door. Tori goes to answer it and is astonished to find Elena there.

"Can I help you?" Tori asks, flabbergasted. Her dogs want to sniff at her, but she pulls them back.

"I know this is a surprise, but could I speak to you?"

"How did you know where I live?"

Liam's sister seems embarrassed. "I found your address on the internet."

"What do you want?"

Elena's wearing cropped jeans, and a short-sleeved shirt. She pushes her sunglasses to the top of her head. "This won't take long. Can I come inside?"

"I don't know. Did you come here to gloat? To tell me how you were right all along?"

"No, I need to speak to you about my brother."

"Why?" Panic shoots through Tori. "Is Liam okay?"

"He's fine. It's nothing like that. I just want to talk."

She hesitates but lets her in. "I'm working in my garden, so you'll have to talk to me out back."

Elena follows her through the house and into the backyard. Tori nearly offers her iced tea but then changes her mind. She's tired of being nice to people who are rude.

She puts her gardening gloves on and gets back to weeding her herb garden, sensing Elena taking in her surroundings.

"I didn't know you were into gardening," she says.

"Why would you? You know nothing about me."

Elena nods. "You're right, I don't." She glances around some more. "I have a garden too."

"How about you get to the point of why you're here."

"I guess I deserve this hostility."

Tori flashes her a look. She knows Elena's been through a lot, and it must have been terrible losing her husband, but it doesn't give her the right to be mean.

Elena takes her sunglasses off her head, then folds them, and sticks them inside her purse. "Did you know my brother had the biggest crush on you in high school?"

"He mentioned it to me once." She's on her knees, pulling some weeds out around her basil plants.

"It took him ages to get up the nerve to ask you to homecoming." Elena smiles. "At the time I thought it was cute. My baby brother and his puppy love."

There's a funny feeling inside Tori. Even though she's heard this from Liam, it's different hearing it through someone else's eyes.

"Personally, I never understood what he saw in you," Elena continues. "I always thought you were odd."

"Do you have a point with all this?"

"I do." She sits on the grass not far away. "Do you want to know why I never liked you?"

"No, but I guess you're going to tell me."

"Because I knew you were trouble. Liam didn't think so, but I was right."

Tori throws some dandelions onto a weed pile but doesn't bother commenting.

"I thought my brother deserved better. He's a good man."

She pauses with weeding, and her voice softens. "I know he is."

"He's always been one. He'd never harm someone intentionally. And yet, for a full year of high school, you and your family made his life a misery."

Tori's stomach twists with guilt. When she glances over, those brown eyes—such a familiar shade—stare at her.

"That's why I said all those things about you back then," Elena admits. "Why I made up lies. It's because I wanted you to suffer, even if it was just a little."

"That doesn't make it right."

She shrugs. "It was messed up, but that's how my teenage mind worked. The irony is the minute I saw you at his house walking that dog, I knew you'd make him miserable again." Elena snorts. "And look what happened."

Tori sits up, angry. "So this *is* why you came here. I'm done talking. I'd like you to leave now."

"It was wrong of you to ask him to ignore a crime your mother was involved in."

Tori sucks in her breath and goes still.

The two women study each other.

Tori turns away but senses Elena watching her. She looks up at the sky, and instead of thinking about that awful night and the terrible things she said to Liam, she remembers their wonderful trip to the lake. Her heart aches at the memory.

"How could you do that to him?" Elena wants to know.

"I was in a dark place," Tori admits. "I knew it was wrong, but I was desperate to protect my mom."

Elena appears to think this over. "And what about now? Are you still justifying it to yourself?"

"No. It was a terrible mistake. I deeply regret it. I've learned how you can take things too far protecting your family."

They're both quiet.

Elena glances around the yard some more, and then her gaze falls back on Tori. "Are you still in love with my brother?"

"Why are you asking me that?"

"Because if you are, I don't think you should give up on him."

Tori's eyes widen. "You don't?"

"No. Keep trying."

"I never thought I'd hear that coming from *you*, of all people."

Elena shrugs, but then her expression turns thoughtful. "I guess it's time I learn from the mistakes I've made too."

CHAPTER THIRTY-ONE

ELENA'S WORDS stay with Tori. And even though she's nervous, she contacts Liam. It's been well over over a month since they split up.

They text a few times. Light and friendly. She tells him how she's made her life less frantic, how she's slowed down.

One evening, she describes the meetings she's been going to and what she's learned. *You were right all along. I've been enabling my mom for years. I just didn't know it.*

It's not your fault. You were raised that way.

I'm sorry for what I said to you. I know I asked things of you I shouldn't have.

There's a pause, and then he types some more. *I appreciate the apology.*

I'd like to apologize in person. Could we meet?

There's another pause, this one longer.

I'm on assignment. Let's talk later.

Since honesty has become her new policy, she lays it all on the line. *Is it too late for us? Because I miss you every single day. Sometimes I can't breathe from missing you so much.*

She stares at her phone. Her hands tremble while she waits for his reply.

This is it, she tells herself. *My life. Will he ever be in it again?*

Except this time the pause goes on much longer.

Seconds slip past. And as each one goes into the next, her heart sinks further into her chest.

She thinks of all the hard truths she's had to learn lately. And there's one that's the hardest of them all. *I'm worse than all his crazy girlfriends put together because I asked him to betray himself.*

There's nothing from him. No more texts.

Not that day or the next.

It's not easy, but she knows she needs to accept what his silence means.

Brody's softball tournament starts. Tori doesn't go to any of the games because she doesn't want to see Liam. It's too sad and humiliating.

Later she finds out from Blair that he hasn't played yet, that he's had to work all week, but plans to be there for the final game on Saturday. Ironically, it's the one game she feels obliged to attend herself since it's so important to Brody.

Friday night, she's stunned when she gets a text from Liam asking if she's going to the game.

Yes, probably, she tells him.

Good. Because I have an answer to your question.

She stares at her phone, then grips it tighter. *What question?*

If it's too late for us.

Is it too late?

Just be there tomorrow.

It's difficult to sleep that night, and even though the game isn't until noon, she's up early. She nearly tells Blair about Liam's text, but then decides to keep it to herself until she finds out more.

It's a warm September day, so she wears jean shorts and a pink tank top with sparkly butterflies and hearts. She's nervous to see Liam and checks herself twice in the mirror before heading to the park where they're having the game.

Blair is already there sitting next to Natalie. She sees Lindsay, Fiona, and Sachi too, along with a few other familiar faces.

"Hey, what are you guys all doing here?" Tori asks with amazement.

"Brody works on my car," Natalie says.

"Mine too," Lindsay chimes in.

"Oh my *God*, he's the best mechanic in the city!" Fiona tells her.

She didn't realize they all took their cars to Seattle Motor Works, Brody's shop.

"Brody invited his whole client list to the game and offered them a discount on oil changes," Blair tells her in a dry voice. "He wants his cheering section bigger than Double A's Auto Supply. I think my parents are even coming."

Tori laughs and shakes her head. Her cousin's demeanor is laid back, but he has a surprisingly strong competitive streak.

Everyone scoots down on the bleachers, and Tori takes a seat next to Blair. She notices someone out there sweeping home plate with a broom.

The two teams gather on opposite sides of the field.

Tori watches Brody's team, searching for Liam. "You'd think this was the World Series, the way they carry on."

"I know," Blair says. "Nathan and Brody were on the phone last night until midnight. They're really excited for Liam to play today."

She nods, still searching. *Where is he?*

"Apparently the brother-in-law from Double A's Auto Supply has been killing it all week."

Brody's team separates, and Tori sucks in her breath when she finally sees Liam. He's wearing the same black T-shirt as all the guys on the team with the familiar SMW lettering on the front and Seattle Motor Works on the back. Some of them are wearing sweats or those cropped baseball shorts. Liam's wearing black track pants with white stripes running down each leg.

The guy who's acting as umpire flips a coin, and Double A's goes to bat first while SMW takes the field. Liam has a glove with him and heads over to first base.

The game begins. Tori doesn't know much about softball and spends most of the time ogling Liam, though she tries not to make it obvious. He seems relaxed, catching balls and throwing them back to the pitcher with easy grace. He looks out at the crowd too, his eyes scanning. Her heart aches at how much she misses him.

When Brody's team is on offense, Blair tells her how Road has a spreadsheet on his computer. "They spent days agonizing over the batting order."

Tori watches as her cousin goes up to bat first.

He hits the ball into the outfield and runs fast enough to make it to first base. Road goes up next and hits a ground ball that gets Brody to second while her brother makes it to first. One of the mechanics from SMW hits another grounder.

By the time it's Liam's turn, the bases are loaded. Her stomach clenches for him. Even though it's supposed to be a friendly game, it looks nerve-racking.

He seems calm walking up to the plate. When he gets there, he stops, but instead of lifting his bat, he turns toward the crowd. He appears to be searching for someone.

Her breath catches when his gaze stops on her.

People are watching him, and some turn her way, trying to see who he's looking at.

"It's *you!*" Blair whispers beside her.

Liam grins and then nods once in her direction before finally getting into position to bat.

The pitcher throws the ball toward him. It's underhand like all softball pitches, and there's a solid sound as his bat hits it.

Crack!

The ball flies high and far, way past the back fence, and out of the park.

Everybody around her starts clapping and cheering as each one of the players makes it to home plate. She watches Liam jog to each base, and when he gets back, the guys are all slapping his palm.

Tori is reeling with excitement, trying to understand why he was looking at her before he hit that ball.

The game continues.

Liam isn't up to bat during the next inning, though SMW's team scores a point. Unfortunately, Double A's team scores two. When it's finally his turn again, the bases aren't loaded, but there are still two people on them.

He strolls up to home plate, and the crowd goes quiet. Once again he stops and turns toward the stands, though he narrows in on her right away.

Like last time, he grins and nods at her before taking his position.

Crack!

"Oh my God! It's another home run!" Blair squeals.

People are clapping and whistling.

It keeps happening each time Liam goes up to bat, he stops and grins at her, then hits the ball straight out of the park.

All around her, people are talking excitedly, laughing, and patting her on the shoulder. Even people she doesn't know are smiling at her. Everyone telling her how awesome this is.

Tori's reeling with joy because she finally understands what it means. It's what he used to say.

"I hit a home run with you."

When they get to the seventh and final inning, people hoot and holler as soon as he walks up to the plate. With the bases loaded and the score tied, there's a lot riding on this.

She chews her bottom lip. She doesn't know how he can stand the pressure.

"This is the most romantic thing I've ever seen in my life," Blair says in awe. "I can't believe he's hit a homer every single time."

Liam turns toward Tori and grins. She grins back. Her stomach's filled with butterflies, nervous for him as he takes his position. Can he possibly do it one last time? The pitcher throws it.

Crack!

Unbelievable.

People in the stands jump to their feet, screaming and shouting their heads off.

The guys on the bases all run toward home. They swoop in and pick up Liam, who's laughing and seems surprised as they carry him around.

"You have to go down to him!" everybody tells her. "Do it now!"

The opposing team comes in from the field, and they take turns shaking hands. Brody's whole team looks ecstatic, like they've died and gone to heaven.

There's a sense of unreality as Tori makes her way down the bleachers trying to find Liam. When she gets down on the field, she senses a lot of attention on her from the stands. The crowd quiets as people watch her walk toward where the guys are grouped.

Brody sees her first and then says something to Liam. He turns. Their eyes meet, and a thrill rushes through her.

People whistle and holler when they come together, when she throws her arms around his neck and he lifts her off the ground.

"Rubia," he whispers in her ear. "Finally."

She hugs him close, surrounded by his familiar scent, her heart so full it's ready to burst. "I've missed you so much."

He kisses her, and everyone in the stands goes berserk, clapping and cheering. The whole experience is surreal.

"I can't believe you did that," she says trying to catch her breath when they draw apart. "Hitting all those home runs. That was the craziest thing I've ever seen!"

He strokes her cheek, his gaze tender. "The only home run I care about is the one I hit with you."

"SO YOU'VE BEEN LISTENING to country music?" Liam asks with amazement, stroking Tori's soft hair.

They're lying in her bed together. After the game they went to celebrate with everyone at a local pub. Brody and Road were both laughing and calling him a show-off. "You can show off like that anytime you want, as long as you're playing for *my* team," Brody said with a grin.

Liam stayed and shared a beer with everyone, but to be honest, he couldn't wait to leave and be alone with Tori.

That electric feeling is back, humming all through him. He knows he'll remember this day for a long time.

"I have one of your playlists on my phone," she admits grudgingly.

He eyes her with satisfaction. "I finally turned you into a country music fan. I told you it would happen."

"I suppose you're going to gloat now."

"Maybe a little."

"I only listened to it because I missed you so much."

He trails his fingers down her skin. "That's sweet."

"Yeah, I guess so."

He chuckles. "You just don't want to admit how much you like it."

"All right, fine." She rolls her eyes. "I like it."

"I knew it."

She looks up at him. "What about you? Did you listen to any hair bands while we were apart?"

"No. I didn't miss you *that* much." She kicks him under the covers, and he laughs. "Okay, don't get violent. I may have listened to a Bon Jovi song or two."

"See." She smiles. "They're the best, aren't they?"

"I have to agree they're good."

"Look at us making musical peace over here. There's hope for the world." She slides her hand across his chest, and he captures it with his own.

"I may have also bought a large bag of tangerines," he admits. "More than I could ever possibly eat."

"Really? You were smelling them?"

He nods, his face warms with embarrassment. "They reminded me of you."

"Well, I slept with your T-shirt under my pillow every night."

"You did?" He likes hearing that. "I guess I don't feel so pathetic after all."

"It sounds like we were both pathetic."

He squeezes her hand. "That's okay. I love you even when you're pathetic."

"And I love you even when you're sniffing tangerines."

They regard each other in the quiet bedroom. Afternoon sunlight filters through the blinds. He pulls her close, kissing her soft lips. She feels so right in his arms. It's like he doesn't even remember his life before he met Tori. She's changed everything.

After a couple hours in bed, they get up and make dinner, then sit out on her back patio to eat, enjoying the warm evening.

He watches Fancy run around and play with the other dogs, glad to see her so happy. She obviously missed them too.

He never dreamed when Rachel left that this is what his life would look like. Her abandoning him and Fancy turned out to be the best thing for both of them.

He picks up his glass of iced tea and takes a sip. "Is this a new flavor?"

"It is." She seems pleased. "Basil and raspberry. What do you think?"

"Mmm, I like it."

"Do you? I know it's kind of unusual. A bit odd."

He smiles, considering her. "I like things that are unusual and a bit odd."

They gaze at each other, and there's no denying it. He's so damn in love. She's the one. She's always been the one.

After dinner, he reaches for her hand and pulls her up from the chair. "Let's dance."

Tori glances toward the house. "Should I put some music on?"

He draws her close, her soft body pressed into his. "Since when do we need music?" he says in a low voice.

She laughs as he holds her close. Barefoot, the two of them slow dance on the grass to the sounds of a summer night.

He lowers his head to kiss her and sees a worried expression on her face.

"What is it, rubia?"

"I have to say this." She takes a deep breath. "I'm so sorry for everything that happened between us."

"It's okay." He strokes her back. "I know how difficult it was with your mom."

"It was wrong what I did. Is that why you waited to contact me? Were you angry?"

He shakes his head. "I couldn't call because I was on assignment, and this was too important for a text." He grins. "And then I decided I'd just show you how I felt at the game."

"That was amazing." She caresses his jaw but still seems worried. "Can you really forgive me?"

"I already have. You're everything. I want to spend my life with you."

"You do?" Her expression turns thoughtful and then coy. "Agent Castillo, that almost sounds like a proposal."

"It's a promise," he says, knowing he does plan to propose.

She sighs with happiness. "You really are the one. If only I'd known it all those years ago."

"That reminds me. I have a food request for our future wedding reception."

"A food request?" She gives him a curious look. "What would that be?"

He grins. "I want to serve chocolate milkshakes."

EPILOGUE

"WAIT, HOLD STILL," Tori calls out, trying to wrangle four dogs and two cats. Unfortunately, the cats have now vanished into the deep recesses of her yard, or more likely one of her neighbor's yards.

She blows her breath out in frustration and looks over at Liam, her handsome new husband. "I was hoping the cats would cooperate."

He's setting up the tripod for the camera. It's almost December, and she's finally getting her cozy sweater Christmas card.

"I don't know," he says, playing with the camera adjustments. "Something tells me those cats will never stay still for a photo."

"I figure I'd hold Joan and you could hold Lita."

He chuckles. "I suppose it's worth a try."

Her eyes roam over him with pleasure. They've only been married a month, and it's been the best month of her life. He proposed to her on a warm September day. It was on the beach at the cabin by Treasure Lake. She loves telling the story of how he got down on one knee and asked for her hand in marriage.

It was old-fashioned and sweet. Just like Liam.

Of course, afterward they went skinny-dipping in the lake.

They got married at a small mansion up in Truth Harbor and kept it simple, inviting only close family and friends.

And yes, they served chocolate milkshakes at the reception. Both dairy and vegan ones. Liam was happy everyone got the joke.

They went to Hawaii for their honeymoon. Her husband's skin turned a beautiful nut brown under the sun while hers turned ever so slightly darker—you could see it under certain light. Her hair turned pale gold. He seemed pleased with it, judging by how much time they spent alone in their hotel room. Before the honeymoon, Tori also had her IUD removed. The two of them decided to let things happen as they may.

Liam put his spooky house on the market before the wedding, and it sold quickly. He says he doesn't miss it.

Tori's developed Happy Pet Nanny treats for cats and has been working with Fiona on broadening her business.

Her mom, Lori, got out of rehab and is still maintaining her sobriety. One day at a time. She's on probation and is grateful to be getting a second chance. Tori's proud of her and how far she's come.

Blair and Road found out they're having a baby girl. Everything looks perfect with the pregnancy. The whole family is excited and can't wait for the new addition.

Lindsay and Giovanni named their adopted daughter Isabella. They're thrilled to be parents and have said they plan to adopt more children. Lindsay's also made a splash in the world of poker. She won a bracelet at the World Series Ladies No-Limit Hold 'em event and has done well playing in more tournaments since then.

Dr. Adrian married René. Tori and Liam went to their wedding. Liam had fun discussing multivariable calculus with Dr. Adrian and his sister during the reception. A conversation Tori was happy to sit out.

To everyone's surprise, Fiona and Sachi announced their engagement recently. Fiona's already planning the "event of the century." Sachi has been good-humored about it so far.

Fiona also got her way in the end with Liam. He posed for the cover of her client's photography book. It turns out the pictures were done in a way so stylized that he isn't recognizable. The project was fun and has inspired him to do more with his own photography hobby.

His friends Nelson and Shelby are still dating each other. No wedding bells, but they seem happy together.

Everyone at Brody's garage is still gloating about the softball game and how Liam hit those home runs. They're ecstatic to have that gold trophy back, and Liam's already agreed to play in next year's tournament.

After careful thought, Tori decided to contact her father, Daniel Church. She found him on Facebook and sent him a message. It turns out he remarried years ago and has three other children. It's a slow process, but Tori is thinking she might like to meet him and his family someday.

Her aunt Lisa told her more about what happened in the past, how Uncle Lance and her dad were good friends before the arrest.

"It's why your mom took it so hard," Aunt Lisa explained. "She divorced your daddy and then kept you and Road from him as punishment. I never agreed with her, but she's my sister and Lance was my brother, so what could I do?"

Tori wanted to know why Lance was so good to them.

"He loved you both, and your sister too," Aunt Lisa said. "But I think he felt guilty about you and Road. The way Lori cut Danny out of your lives. He blamed himself and always looked out for you."

Lori isn't pleased with any of this. Despite her sobriety, she maintains that Danny betrayed her and her brother, and still believes she made the right decision keeping him away.

Tori and Road disagree with her. However, Road still wants nothing to do with their dad. In fact, he was against Tori contacting him.

The situation remains complicated in the way that things with families often are.

"Are you almost ready?" Liam asks, making some final adjustments to his camera's tripod. "I figure we'd take the photo from a few different angles."

Tori's wearing the cozy white sweater she got in Truth Harbor. She finishes wrangling her dogs into the ones she knitted. They each get a different color. Eddie's is forest green, Duff's is gold, and Tommy Lee's is bright red. And for Miss Fancy Pants, she did something extra special—she knit her a blue sweater that says "FBI" in yellow letters.

"Almost," she says, smoothing each dog's ears and telling them how cute they look. "Do you think you could find Joan and Lita?"

"I'll try," Liam says. He's wearing the cozy brown sweater that matches hers.

She hums "Jingle Bells" and grooms each dog some more using a soft brush.

Eventually he reappears carrying two cats, a blonde tabby who's clinging to him and a black one who looks like she's ready to escape.

Tori reaches for Joan.

Liam pauses and sets the timer for the photo.

"Everyone, *sit*," Tori says to the dogs.

Her husband comes over, still holding Lita, and kneels beside her.

They grin at the camera as it captures the moment. Both of them happily surrounded by four dogs, two cats, and the tiny baby boy growing inside Tori's womb who she isn't even aware of yet.

The End

AUTHOR'S NOTE

Thank you so much for reading Tori and Liam's story. I loved those two and enjoyed writing about them. I hope you enjoyed it as well.

This is the fourth book in the Sweet Life in Seattle series. The next book will be *Too Much Like Love*. It's Brody's story.

I love hearing from my readers. If you'd like to contact me, you can find me at my website andreasimonne.com or drop me an email at authorsimonne@gmail.com.

If you enjoyed this book, please consider telling a friend about it or leaving a review. I'd very much appreciate it.

With so many book choices out there, thank you for choosing one of mine.

xo,
Andrea

p.s. If you'd like a copy of Tori's playlist, you can find a few Spotify versions of it on my website at: https://www.andreasimonne.com/playlists-for-object-of-my-addiction/

NEWSLETTER SIGN UP

If you'd like to hear about new book releases and other authorly musings, please join my mailing list. To sign up go to my website at andreasimonne.com.

ALSO BY ANDREA SIMONNE

Sweet Life in Seattle series

Year of Living Blonde

Return of the Jerk

Some Like It Hotter

Object of My Addiction

Too Much Like Love (Coming Soon...)

About Love series

Truth About Men & Dogs

Other

Fire Down Below

ACKNOWLEDGMENTS

People always say it takes a village, and in this case, that's true. So many people have helped me on the journey to bring this book into your hands. As always, my first reader Erika gave it to me straight. All the parts that needed work (and all the parts she liked too!) Thank you so much, Erika. I don't know what I'd do without you. I also want to thank Annette, Peg, Jody, and Susan for their valuable insights, beta reading, and amazing proofreading skills. You helped make this story the best it could be. This is the third book my editor at Hot Tree, Kristin Scearce, has edited for me, and she did an incredible job. Thank you, Kristin. My writing group, the Plot Princesses, helped me get the baseball information correct. Thank you, ladies for all your combined sports knowledge. If there are any mistakes, they are definitely on my end. My son, Max, helped me write the discussion about multivariable calculus. (Like Tori, I thought it all sounded like gibberish!) Thank you so much, Max. I also want to thank my husband, John, who always supports me, and is my biggest fan. He read the early drafts for this book and offered many wild suggestions. He also offered some that were invaluable. John, you are the best.

I also want to thank *you*, my readers, for sticking with me and for all the kind words and messages about my books. I appreciate it more than you'll ever know. <3

ABOUT THE AUTHOR

Andrea Simonne grew up as an army brat and discovered she had a talent for creating personas at each new school. The most memorable was a surfer chick named "Ace" who never touched a surfboard in her life but had an impressive collection of puka shell necklaces. Andrea still enjoys creating personas though now they occupy her books. She's an Amazon best seller in romantic comedy and author of the series Sweet Life in Seattle and About Love. She currently makes her home in the Pacific Northwest with her husband and two sons.

    She loves hearing from her readers. You can find her on the web at www.andreasimonne.com.

    Email: authorsimonne@gmail.com.

Made in the USA
Middletown, DE
10 August 2021